Gail
Black
Kopf

Rubicon

Rubicon

Gail Black Kopf

A
JANET
THOMA
BOOK

THOMAS NELSON PUBLISHERS
NASHVILLE

Published in Nashville, Tennessee, by Janet Thoma Books, a division of Thomas Nelson, Inc., Publishers, and distributed in Canada by Word Communications, Ltd., Richmond, British Columbia, and in the United Kingdom by Word (UK), Ltd., Milton Keynes, England.

Unless otherwise noted, the Bible version used in this publication is THE NEW KING JAMES VERSION OF THE BIBLE. Copyright © 1979, 1980. 1982, Thomas Nelson, Inc., Publishers.

Scripture marked NIV is from The Holy Bible: NEW INTERNATIONAL VERSION. Copyright © 1978 by the New York International Bible Society. Used by permission of Zondervan Bible Publishers.

Library of Congress Cataloging-in-Publication Data

Kopf, Gail.
    Rubicon / Gail Kopf.
      p.   cm.
    ISBN 0-8407-7800-7
    I. Title.
PS3561.O643R8   1993
813'.54—dc20   93–7431
                                                  CIP

Printed in the United States of America
97 96 95 94 93   5 4 3 2 1

To Mike, my husband and friend.
You gave me the freedom to pursue my dreams,
and the courage to attain them.
Thank You.

Gail
Black
Kopf

Rubicon

"And everyone who calls on the
name of the LORD will be saved;
for on Mount Zion and in Jerusalem
there will be deliverance,
as the Lord has said,
among the survivors whom the LORD calls."
                        Joel 2:32 (NIV)

Ruth Morgan, clutching the New Testament the evange-
list had given her, found her daughter outside the entrance to the revival tent.

"Oh Faith," she said clasping her hand, "I feel so wonderful,
but I don't think I can explain what happened. Not yet."

"Good, because we don't have time."

Her mother looked as if she'd been slapped.

Faith's voice softened. "I mean . . . if this helps you, Mom,
I'm glad." She quickly changed the subject, avoiding her mother's
glistening eyes which seemed to rebuke her.

"We have to hurry or we won't be able to see Hope." Faith dug
the keys out of her purse, and her mother followed her to the
beige compact car sitting alone in the dirt parking lot. Faith
started the electric engine, silently hoping that her mother would
have the good sense not to tell anyone about her conversion; in
the year 2010 that was even more dangerous than coming to the
tent meeting.

Faith Morgan put the car in reverse and looked at her mother's
silhouette in the shadowy light. Maybe it was just a phase her
mother was going through, an escape mechanism to help her
come to terms with what had happened to Faith's twin sister.

She pulled out of the parking area, the tires squealing angrily
as they met the pavement. She had enough problems to handle
without the added burden of an eager, new religious convert,
even if it was her own mother.

Ambassador Logan Washburn had met the president countless times before, but on this languid September morning he still felt edgy as he waited outside the Oval Office. He'd just returned from The People's Republic of China where, under his guidance, they'd adopted a new policy: two children per family without fear of reprisal. His suggestion—that rather than deprive the workers of children, it was better for the Chinese to rid themselves of the unfit, incompetent, and politically undesirable—had done the trick. For each birth, a person in one of the "nonessential" categories would be eliminated. After his success with the Chinese, he'd been booted up to the major leagues. If he could stay there, he'd have a good shot at the presidency in 2012.

He looked down at his copy of the *Washington Post,* flipped to his horoscope, and looked under *Virgo:* "Any efforts you make today are pivotal to your success. It's time to start a major career-related project that will take you to the top." He felt himself relax. It just confirmed what his personal astrologer had predicted that morning when he'd called her for his daily reading before he left his condominium in Chevy Chase, Maryland.

The well dressed, older secretary smiled at the President, as most women did, as she motioned him to enter the office. He rose, left his paper on the chair, breezed by the prominent "THIS IS A NO SMOKING ZONE" sign, and opened the door.

"Logan, come in. It's good to see you again," President Blanco said as he came around his desk and shook Logan's hand. His dark, expressive eyes never left Logan's face.

"So, we're on a first name basis now, Mr. President. That means you want something from me. What is it?"

The president flashed a smile which brightened his Hispanic features. "Cut to the chase, eh Logan? I like your tactics. You don't waste time on small talk. You're right, your country and I both need you."

He opened the box on his desk, unwrapped a Cuban cigar and lit it. "My wife wants me to give these up, but I think every man needs some vices. Of course, I can't smoke them in public. That would be like stabbing the surgeon general in the back, wouldn't it?"

Logan refused to take the bait. He waited patiently as the president inhaled and blew smoke rings into the overhead.

"Leaders from Israel and the Arab countries have agreed to use you as a mediator in their peace talks. You'll leave tomorrow."

"And if I don't agree?"

The president laughed, then choked on the smoke he had inhaled. It took a few minutes for him to regain his composure.

"Let's not play games, Logan. You want this so badly, you can taste it. What you accomplished in China was extraordinary, but if you can pull this off . . .

"The Middle East is the only conflict left that must be resolved before this notion of peace on earth can become a reality. The other nations are fed up with these flies in the . . . oil barrel." The president chuckled at his own joke. "Their constant bickering, the roller coaster price of oil, and the funds it takes to support the United Nations peace keeping forces stationed there have become intolerable."

"I thought nuclear energy would take the sting out of the oil cartels." Logan said as his eyes flitted around the office. When it was his office, he'd replace the desk.

President Blanco seemed to read his thoughts. He glared at him. "Eventually. Until then . . ." He pointed his cigar at Logan. "We could use any one of a dozen diplomats for this."

"Really? If I remember correctly, Israel's premier said I possessed a dash of Solomon's wisdom, and most of the Palestinians voiced the opinion that they thought I would be impartial and objective in this matter."

The president laughed. "Now you're beginning to believe your own press releases. Policies are made in Washington and carried out in the field by couriers like you," he said gruffly.

Logan bristled. "I'm no errand boy. You're sending me because I know which buttons to push to get results."

"You're here because we need your diplomatic skills to mobilize the collaborative efforts of both sides. You get that peace pact signed, and in two years you'll be sitting in this chair. The Independent Party is willing to finance you all the way to the White House."

Logan leaned forward. Their faces were only inches apart.

"Thank you, Mr. President. I appreciate this opportunity to serve my country."

"Serve your country! You're serving your own interests, and

we both know it. Don't try to fool someone who's been that route. Just remember, Logan, everything has a price tag."

Ambassador Logan Washburn turned and left the room. His astrologer was right; he was on his way to the top.

While the newly installed Medicine Management robots, nicknamed Theo-Dur I, II, and III by the nurses, moved smoothly from room to room dispensing medications, the evening shift at Quantico Memorial Hospital went through its paces. The nurses recorded fluid inputs and outputs and tucked their patients in for the night, but they had neither the time nor the energy for social pleasantries or sympathetic gestures.

As he waited for the elevator, Dr. Stephen Bradley watched the nurses try to catch up on their computer charting between the new admissions and their routine duties. The hospital was chronically understaffed. Many nurses had threatened to walk off the job because of the overwhelming work load. Spurred on by their complaints, eager union organizers held meetings in one of the abandoned churches only a few blocks away.

A shortage of doctors added to this crunch situation. That was why, although he'd chosen pediatrics as his specialty, Stephen Bradley had been assigned to the Hope Morgan case. The entire staff was at the breaking point. Absentmindedly, Stephen ran his thumb across the scar under his chin, a trophy from his hockey playing days. With this constant shifting of medical personnel from one crisis to the next, he was *still* playing in the defensive zone.

Stephen knew the health care system was decaying. Unless the government woke up and began to subsidize the system, there would be less qualified personnel and more hospital closures.

He shook his head as a sense of frustration overcame him. The year 2000 had been the target date to bring subsidized health care to a nationwide vote, but because of extensive lobbying by CEO's in both the health care industry and the pharmaceutical corporations, ten years had elapsed and the issue never found a place on the ballot. Apparently profits were more important than equal access to health care. He'd just seen the latest figures: high premiums prevented more than forty million Americans from obtaining health insurance. Many of them were children like Jimmy Minder.

Jimmy Minder . . . In spite of his weariness, a smile flickered across Dr. Stephen Bradley's face. That kid had made an amazing recovery. Nine months ago, he'd seen the eight-year-old boy for the first time. He vividly remembered that night. It was two weeks before the legalization of drugs.

The police brought Jimmy to the emergency room after they'd raided his home. They had found him huddled in the closet where his crack-crazed parents had thrown him to keep him quiet—after they'd fractured both his legs.

Stephen could still see the terrified look in Jimmy's eyes as he gently probed and located seven other broken bones and large circular welts on the boy's buttocks. It had taken months of treatment and a loving foster home, but now Jimmy was more likely to give him a tentative smile than a grimace.

Impatiently, Stephen pushed the elevator button again. He still wasn't sure if he agreed with the legalization of drugs, but at least the emergency room wasn't swamped with injuries from drug-related crimes anymore. The government taxed drugs as they did cigarettes and liquor, using the revenue for drug rehabilitation, medical research, and education.

The elevator doors finally opened. It was past visiting hours, and he blinked twice when he saw Ruth Morgan, the mother of the comatose patient he was going to check next, standing in front of him with a bunch of black-eyed Susans. Faith, who was by her side, gave him her usual "keep your distance" glance. Her ash-blond hair was pulled back into a fashionable chignon, and with her high cheekbones, long lashes, and exquisite figure, she could have been a cover girl on one of the fashion magazines his younger sister, Jamie, was always reading.

"I was just going to see Hope," Stephen explained as he stepped inside. He was surprised when Ruth gave him a wide smile, quite a change from the brittle looks she'd given him when they first met.

"I know we're late," she said, "but after Faith finished working at the bank, she had to register for her fall classes. We just couldn't get here any sooner."

They stepped out of the elevator together. "You two go ahead," said Ruth. "I want to get a vase at the nurses' station."

"I don't know why she bothers," said Faith flatly as she and the doctor walked down the hall. "Hope doesn't even know we're here."

"Maybe she does. Case studies indicate that some coma patients are able to hear everything that goes on around them, they just can't respond."

"But if there's no brain—"

The lights in the hall suddenly dimmed. A blinding light streamed through the windows at each end of the hall and flooded the corridor. Faith put up her hands to shield her eyes, but not before she saw a massive pillar of clouds through the end window. As quickly as the light had appeared, it disappeared. The sky was dark again.

"What was that?" Faith exclaimed.

"Did you hear . . . music?" Stephen said incredulously.

"Music? I'm not sure. But that light—"

"The Lorton Correctional Facility is practically next door," said Stephen as they walked towards Hope's room. "It was probably a helicopter's search light. We're usually the first ones to know when an inmate escapes."

"You're not making me feel any better," said Faith, laughing nervously as she pushed open the door to Hope's room.

The bed was empty.

"Where is she?" asked Faith. They could still see the indentation of Hope's body on the rumpled sheets.

"I don't know." Stephen felt a strange prickling sensation come over him. "I should have been notified before they moved her. I'll check with the charge nurse."

"Dr. Bradley!" A young nurse with a coil of thick black hair pushed under her cap ran towards them as they left Hope's room—a stunned expression on her face.

"I was checking Mrs. Harmon's vital signs and suddenly she was gone!" she said in a heavily accented voice.

"You means she left the room?"

"No sir, she just vanished."

Stephen looked at her name tag: Nina Sanchez. She was a Peruvian nurse they'd recruited with the promise of American citizenship in three years.

"She was supposed to be in restraints, Ms. Sanchez," he said tersely. "Check the other rooms."

Stephen pushed his glasses up on his nose and made a mental note to call the personnel office and request to see the Sanchez file. Preliminary screening of hospital personnel always included a drug check, but mistakes had been made before in attempts to expedite the hiring process. Maybe Nina Sanchez was having flashbacks.

The perplexed nurse began checking the other rooms while Faith and Stephen walked to the nurses' station.

"Mrs. Locke, why wasn't I notified before you moved Hope Morgan?" Stephen asked.

The charge nurse, who was in her mid-fifties, brushed her hand through her short salt and pepper hair. She liked Dr. Bradley, but she was in no mood for his accusations. She should have been on her way home by now, but the powers that be in the Nursing Office fouled up the scheduling and she was looking at another eight-hour shift. And that flash of light outside had spooked everyone. Almost all the patients' call buttons were lit up.

"You weren't notified, Dr. Bradley, because I wasn't." She checked her floor chart. "I have Hope Morgan listed in room 630B. She's been in that room since the first day she arrived on this floor."

"Her bed is empty."

"Well, that's news to me."

"Dr. Bradley, is it possible Hope . . . came out of the coma?" Faith asked.

"Anything is possible, Faith, but under the circumstances, it's highly unlikely."

"But that would explain it, wouldn't it? Have you seen my mother?" said Faith turning to Mrs. Locke. "Hope is probably with her."

"This isn't the lost and found department," said Mrs. Locke. Dr. Bradley gave her a sharp look, but she ignored him and took a sip of cold coffee before she said, "Mrs. Morgan went into the bathroom a few minutes ago."

Faith hurried to the bathroom. "Mom!" she hollered as she pushed the door open. When there was no response, she stepped inside.

Amid a broken vase and puddles of water, black-eyed Susans were scattered in the middle of the floor. Her fear grew as she checked the empty stalls. Maybe her mother had gone to get someone to clean up the mess.

She ran into the hall, then stopped suddenly and leaned against the wall. Something was horribly wrong! Faith could see it in the eyes of the nurses as they scurried down the hallways. She spotted Dr. Bradley on the phone at the nurses' station. His face was ashen as he slowly replaced the receiver.

"I need everyone's attention," he shouted. "We're implementing our emergency disaster plan. All staff members will remain at the hospital until further notice."

Someone turned on the television in the visitors' lounge. With the others, Faith clustered around it, waiting for an explanation from the anchorwoman on the screen.

"The wire services have been flooded with reports of unexplained crashes, fires, and disappearances throughout the world. Some nations suspect chemical warfare, but at this time we have nothing to confirm these allegations until satellite dispatches are examined. The federal and state governments request that you stay in your homes unless you are considered essential disaster personnel. Until further notice, only emergency and military vehicles should be on the streets. We will report any new developments—" The screen went blank.

Faith rushed to the pay phone to call her father. Where was her phone card? She gave up trying to find it and fumbled in her purse for some coins. She dialed the number. The phone rang several times before the scratchy recording of an operator's voice came on the line. "All lines are in service at this time. Please try again."

She repeated the process, but the same recording accosted her. A line of anxious employees began to form behind her. Reluctantly, she put the phone receiver down and moved aside. She returned to the lounge where the nurses were grouping some of the patients together to make space for the new arrivals. In all the excitement, had Hope been moved to another floor?

Faith hurried to the elevator and punched the down button. The elevator wheezed and came to a stop on the sixth floor, but before she could step inside, the lights went out.

Now what was she supposed to do? She felt herself drowning in a sea of uncertainty as she stood there in the blackness. With a click, the emergency lighting came on. She raced to the fire exit and threw open the door. Dr. Bradley pounded down the cement stairs ahead of her. Faith caught up with him as he pushed open the fire door which led to the emergency room.

Both of them stopped in their tracks and stared open-mouthed at the disastrous scene. Screams of pain filled the air, but it was the look of helplessness, not only on the faces of the injured, but on the faces of those trying to help, that sent a surge of fear through Faith.

Emergency personnel were bringing in victims on blankets and stretchers, but there was nowhere to put them. As she watched, an old man with an injured leg hobbled in. He tried, without success, to weave his way around a wheelchair to join the group that overflowed the triage area. Exhausted, he slumped down on the cold tile floor and lay back against the apricot-colored walls which were now smeared with blood.

The street outside was clogged with automobiles and emergency vehicles. In the blackness their red, blue, and yellow lights bounced wildly off the building and in through the windows, adding an eerie quality to the already frenzied atmosphere.

"Oh, God," said Faith as the grotesque shadows leaped across the walls and ceiling. "What's happening?"

2

The shrill sound of the pager pierced Randy Morgan's groggy dreams, and he awoke with a start. A red light meant he should call in; a blue light was an emergency. He propped himself up on his right elbow and peered through one bleary eye at the pager—the light was blue. He had to be at work in an hour.

His elbow collapsed, and he found himself staring at the ceiling where the clock threw an illuminated time display: 12:31 A.M. A low moan escaped his lips.

He could either stay perfectly still or throw up. He clung to the sides of the mattress while he ran his tongue—which was the size of a slobbering Saint Bernard's—around his dry, sour mouth. With a great deal of effort he rolled over and put his hand out to awaken Ruth. When his probing fingers couldn't find her, he sat up.

"Ohhhhhh!" His head throbbed and bursts of white hot pain ripped through his eyelids as he tried to focus on the rim of light underneath the bathroom door. He staggered towards it like a runner with his shoelaces tied together and wished he'd stuck to beer instead of switching to whiskey.

"Ruth?" There was no answer. He pushed open the door and barely made it to the toilet before he vomited. He stood up and his bloodshot eyes stared back at him from the mirror on the door of the medicine cabinet as he rinsed out his mouth. He dropped his head to his chest and looked past the spare tire he'd gained in the last three months to his swollen ankles. He'd become a bum. He grabbed the bottle of aspirins and took four, grinding them up with his teeth and washing down the bitter pieces with a gulp of water.

He'd better get cleaned up, he thought. He didn't want Ruth to see him like this. She was probably in the den. He'd found her there before, reading her Bible at odd hours of the night. It seemed to give her solace, something he still didn't have, no matter how much alcohol he consumed.

To shave or not to shave. Randy Morgan ran his fingers over the stubble on his chin and reached for his electric razor.

He might as well take the MGA instead of using the twenty-four hour mass transit system. Driving his own vehicle was one privilege Randy didn't want to relinquish, even though it made him ineligible for a hefty government tax rebate. As Ruth had reminded him on more than one occasion, he was a clone of his late stubborn father.

The familiar hum of the shaver soothed his jagged nerves as he wondered what earthshaking event transpired to cause the troops to assemble at the Orange County Underground Communications and Intelligence Center (UCIC).

Ruth and the girls, who fondly called him a "computer jock," weren't aware of what he really did at the industrial park location. They thought he collected information for direct marketers who in turn used the massive mailing lists he compiled to target products and services to specific groups. He even came home with samples of new products and questionnaires, supposedly from some manufacturer who was trying to pinpoint a market trend before he'd invest the really big bucks which a new product required. If they only knew . . .

Randy didn't have time for a shower so he splashed on one of the samples of after-shave lotion which the CIA furnished. He dressed, then admonished himself to get a haircut as he brushed his thinning, dark hair, already threaded with silver. At least he still had all his own teeth. He smiled at himself in the mirror to bolster his sagging ego, but it didn't work.

He wandered to the den and turned on the light, but only the cat blinked at him from it's spot on the couch. Where was Ruth?

He went to the girls' room. Faith's bed hadn't been slept in.

Ruth and Faith—they'd never returned from the hospital. Something must have happened to Hope!

Quickly, he picked up the phone and punched in the hospital's number. The harsh whine of a busy signal greeted him. He hit the redial button. Nothing! He checked the printout by the phone; no incoming calls were recorded.

"Take it easy," he said aloud as he tried to calm himself. "If anything is the matter, they'll call. They probably just stopped to have a pizza."

He stuck a mug of water in the microwave oven to make instant coffee while a barrage of chastising thoughts thrashed through his aching head. Earlier that evening, he'd drunk himself into oblivion by ten o'clock. It was a miracle the beeper had roused him. He couldn't keep this up; it was only a matter of time before his work was affected. His guilt tightened like a screw until he thought his head would explode.

Randy inhaled the aroma of his coffee, but he drank it too quickly and the scalding liquid burned the roof of his mouth and dripped from his mouth. "Great!" he sputtered and grabbed a paper towel, dabbing at his mouth like an angry hornet bent on revenge.

He looked at the kitchen clock. It's hands were just a blur as they spun wildly in a circle. What the—? He unplugged it. Maybe it was time to get one of those new solar clocks. He'd check into it later; he had to get going. If he didn't show up at the UCIC within an hour, it would mean instant dismissal and the end of his insurance benefits. He scribbled a note for Ruth and Faith, posting it on the front of the refrigerator before he went to the garage.

Randy slid the window of his classic 1958 MGA forward and took a deep breath of the September night as he backed out of the driveway. He loved northern Virginia; that was one reason he'd accepted this assignment. The sweet scent from the thick masses of honeysuckle which entwined the white fence surrounding the five-acre estate drifted through the window. It made him feel almost human again, despite the dull ache behind his eyes.

He looked with pride at his brick, colonial-style house as one would look at a cherished antique or at the last of a species—

because it was. His father, Jason Morgan, had seen it coming twenty years ago. In a lifetime of widespread social changes, Jason Morgan had fought the enactment of laws that made abortion legal, euthanasia an option, and ownership of a gun unlawful.

His father predicted the inflation and increased taxes which caused land and building costs to spiral and the harvest of disappointment experienced by a generation of adults who could barely afford to rent an apartment or house, let alone own one. Responding to the cries of outrage, the government had enacted laws which made it illegal for Americans to possess more than five acres of land and one residence. Foreign investors weren't bound by those restrictions—not yet anyway—and more than one person had a Japanese, European, or Arab landlord.

If rental rates and sale prices weren't based on a sliding scale determined by the individual states, they would all have been homeless by now.

Yep, old dad had seen it coming.

Randy Morgan smiled at the well-kept lawn as he pulled out of the driveway. Just before Hope's accident, he splurged and re-seeded the lawn with the latest horticultural breakthrough: velvet green grass that grew three inches and stopped. He hadn't used his riding lawn mower in over six months.

Above his visor, he pressed the transmitter which energized the burglar alarm system. He picked up his cellular phone and called the hospital again. A hollow, static noise filled his ear and transmitted itself to his soul as he sped down the road.

He turned right onto Route 17. Why was there a steady stream of traffic at this hour? Two wreckers passed him with bent and twisted cars in tow. Drunken drivers? Hey, he reminded himself, that could be you! First offenders lost their cars, second offenders their homes. After that it was definitely downhill.

Instinctively, he gripped the steering wheel as he passed the state trooper's gray and navy vehicle with its flashing blue lights. From the look of things, this must have been some night. There was an abandoned truck on the median and numerous wrecked vehicles in the grassy ditches which paralleled the road.

He grimaced to himself as the old rhyme from his high school locker room came out of nowhere and danced in his head.

"Candy is dandy, but liquor is quicker." He felt sweat trickling into his eyes and quickly wiped it away as he tried to revive himself by sticking his head out of the window. Whew! He'd better get hold of himself.

Like a basketball in the hands of an anxious Harlem Globetrotter, his thoughts bounced back and forth. So . . . what if he did drink? At least he wasn't taking drugs. And why wasn't he? Because if he did, he'd lose his job for sure, that's why. Not that cocaine wasn't legal.

At any neighborhood drugstore, a friendly pharmacist—he mentally underlined the word friendly—would access your individual computer file and duly note every purchase on your record. Regular drug users were blackballed from obtaining a job which was critical to national security or which demanded highly technical skills. In dull repetitive jobs, drug users had become the drones of the workplace, a new subclass of humans.

Of course, he mused, since he was in charge of those files, entries could be deleted. He shook his head and made a rational slam dunk. No, drugs wouldn't change anything for him or Hope. It was time to pull himself together. But saying it was one thing, doing it was another.

He checked his speedometer, then looked up from the dashboard just in time to see a trail of winding red lights ahead of him. He braked, craning his neck as the snake of cars crept around the bend where he could see a field ablaze. Silhouetted against the night sky was the fiery outline of an airliner.

What a mess! The plane must have failed in its attempt to make a landing at Dulles International Airport.

He looked at his watch. 1:15 A.M. He maneuvered his car to the right and felt the tires hit the gravel in the emergency lane. He pressed the accelerator and rushed by the waiting cars. Several drivers honked their horns in annoyance as he passed, but he didn't care. He couldn't help those poor devils in the plane, he couldn't even help himself.

With sweaty palms, he roared through the night, unable to shake off his hangover or the feelings of doom which consorted with it.

* * *

It was dawn. In eight hours the number of people in the waiting room had almost doubled. Faith had been helping process the new patients; it was better than standing around feeling helpless.

The initial panic still wasn't over, but hospital routine gave some semblance of order as patients were routed to the appropriate cubicles and examining rooms. Faith leaned against the wall and closed her eyes. She wanted desperately to go to sleep.

"Where's my baby!" screamed a hysterical woman at the admissions desk. "What have you done with her?"

A nurse put her arm around the weeping mother and whispered something in her ear, then gently led her to a chair. "Faith," she called and motioned for her to come over, then she turned to the distraught mother.

"You can help your daughter by giving this young lady the information we'll need to find her."

The woman looked at Faith with huge, blank eyes. "I can't find Clarisa . . . Is she here? She's so little—" She began to cry again in short shallow gasps.

Faith knelt down by the woman's chair and fought to keep her voice under control as she asked the questions which would help identify the baby if she were at the hospital . . . or the morgue. She'd seen enough anguish and pain in the last twenty-four hours to last her a lifetime. She wanted to cry, but she'd run out of tears.

When Faith finished, she tried to straighten up, but her knees buckled. A strong arm went around her shoulders.

"I think it's time you took a break, Miss Morgan. They've got sandwiches in the cafeteria and hot coffee. We could both use some." She looked up into Stephen Bradley's face. Like her own, it was etched with fatigue and concern. Too tired to argue, she let him lead her down the flight of stairs to the employees' cafeteria in the basement. He sat her down at one of the tables, then went to get the sandwiches.

Faith looked at the sea of faces around her, then put her head in her hands. Where were her mother and Hope? Faith closed her eyes and went over the fatal scene in her mind for the millionth time, wishing again that she could change its outcome. If she'd just waited until the July 4th weekend as they'd originally planned; but no, she'd convinced her parents to let her and Hope have the pool party the weekend after school ended.

They'd invited all their old school chums, who had winged their way to North Stafford like migrating Monarch butterflies, for one last summer of freedom before they embarked on that final road to adulthood. And what better way for Faith and Hope to confuse their guests and liven up the party, than by wearing identical blue-green bathing suits. Blue-green. Even now she could see the pool's sparkling water, water the color of Hope's eyes.

After watching the girls ride the waves in the pounding surf of the Pacific Ocean near San Diego for three years, Randy and Ruth Morgan had no qualms about having a swimming pool in the backyard when they moved to northern Virginia. Hope and Faith were finally safe from pollution, undercurrents, or the sudden stinging sensation of a jellyfish's tentacle. Safe, or so they thought.

Faith bit her lip. Only a week before the party her father had unbolted and removed the diving board because the insurance agent had said it would reduce the liability rates on their homeowner's policy. If the diving board had been in place, would the accident still have happened?

Her mind began to replay the dreadful scene. She tried to stop it, but she couldn't. She saw Hope dive in a long slow arch from the side of the pool and slip beneath the water. How long was it before anyone noticed that she hadn't surfaced?

She'd been talking to Sam—Sam with his broad shoulders and quick wit. Faith's heart began to beat louder as she heard the screams again. Even now she wasn't sure if they were her screams or someone else's, as hands frantically tried to pull the mirrored reflection of herself from the bottom of the pool. For one terrible split second she saw not Hope, but an effigy of herself.

One of the girls who'd been a lifeguard frantically gave Hope mouth-to-mouth resuscitation while someone dialed 911. Faith could still see the purplish bruise on Hope's forehead. It all came rushing back to her. Rivulets of water from her bathing suit pooled on the floor as the orange and white vehicle wailed its way to the hospital. Paramedics pushing through the double doors of the emergency room with the gurney. The stark waiting room, royal blue chairs with cold, chrome legs. She remembered the scratchy white towel they gave her to keep herself warm, and the sympathetic look from the male nurse as he talked to her parents.

"Your daughter hasn't regained consciousness. We've put her on a ventilator because she can't breathe on her own. We're doing all we can."

Stephen Bradley's voice broke through her memory.

Faith looked up at him with a questioning look.

Obviously she hadn't heard what he was saying so he repeated the comment again. "You know, you remind me of my sister, Jamie." The coffee sloshed out of the paper cups onto the steel tray as Stephen lowered it to the table. "She'll be going to the Virginia Medical Institute this year."

Small talk. He's trying to make small talk. The whole world is in an uproar, and he's talking about his sister. Her intense blue eyes studied him as if he were a rogue cell under a microscope. He was good looking in a bookish sort of way with a wide forehead and a shock of curly black hair which receded slightly above the temples. She wondered why he didn't wear contact lenses instead of those old-fashioned horn-rimmed glasses which made his eyes look enormous.

"Is this some kind of therapy, doctor? If we act as if nothing has happened, the world just goes on its merry way like before?"

"Just trying to get your mind off all of this." He took off his glasses and slipped them into the pocket of his blood-flecked disposable lab coat which strained across his powerful shoulders. Without glasses, he looked hardly older than herself. He gave her a lopsided grin which softened his square jaw. "Guess I didn't do a very good job of it, but—"

A brisk voice from the loud speaker system interrupted.

"Tonight at eight o'clock, the president of the United States will address the country concerning the recent disaster."

"Twelve hours? Why do we have to wait twelve hours before we know what's going on?" said Faith.

Stephen's memory lapsed as he noticed her pale, unblemished skin, and the freckles across the bridge of her nose. "Because—" he tried to remember her question, "it'll probably take the government that long to find out what happened or to fabricate some story that we'll swallow."

The public address system crackled to life again.

"The administrators of Quantico Memorial Hospital wish to

thank all members of its staff for their dedication in this time of national crisis."

"Dedication? I guess that's one word for it," said Stephen as he stifled a yawn and looked out of the basement window. "The traffic has thinned out some. Do you want to try and make it home?"

"I can't leave here until I know what happened to Mom and Hope. What would I say to my dad?"

"You're exhausted, you need some rest."

"*I'm* not your patient," she snapped.

"If you keep this up, you will be."

"You could be right," she said in an icy voice, "but I'm not used to having someone tell me what to do."

"With me, it's an occupational hazard." He put his glasses back on. "Look, I know you're worried, but I'll keep an eye out for Hope and your mother. They've assigned one of the relief nurses to go through and check every room on all twelve floors. By tonight we'll have a list of current patients and their rooms."

He laced his hands together, put them over his head, and stretched. "Now, will you go home?"

Her eyes narrowed. "Why this sudden concern, Dr. Bradley? Maybe if you'd been this concerned about my sister, she'd have been all right."

They stared at each other in silence.

"You're being unfair, Faith," he said quietly. "I'm a doctor. I can't perform miracles." He put his hand over hers. "Believe me, I did everything I could for Hope."

As she looked into his warm, compassionate eyes, she knew he was telling the truth. "I . . . know you did. I guess I just wanted to blame someone—" Her voice was so low he had to bend forward to hear her. "Because that way I wouldn't have to blame myself."

"Faith, it wasn't your fault. Sometimes these things just happen—"

"No, it should have been me." She withdrew her hand and rose to go. She didn't want his kindness or pity.

"Thanks for the sandwich," she said a little too brightly. "I guess I will take your advice, doctor, and go home." She turned and walked away.

3

Faith finally found her car in the crowded parking lot. A security guard helped her maneuver it to a side exit where she could enter the stream of traffic, now reduced to a single lane in each direction. Abandoned and wrecked vehicles had been pushed to the side or the middle lane. The traffic lights weren't working, and a uniformed policeman with a whistle directed her through the main intersection by the hospital's entrance.

She tried not to think about Dr. Bradley. She misjudged him, and now she was embarrassed at the way she acted. If she'd met him in another setting, just maybe . . .

She turned on the radio to halt her thoughts, switching channels while she inched along in the traffic. All she could find was the Emergency Broadcasting System with news of the president's impending speech.

She began to notice the people who wandered aimlessly by the roadside. Most of them had shocked looks on their faces. As her car passed them, several thrust their hands out towards her. She quickly pushed the button that automatically locked the car's windows and doors.

Behind her, a commuter van honked. She pulled over to let it pass. It had a cardboard red cross plastered to its side, and it weaved back and forth across the road, picking up some of the dazed stragglers before it headed back to the hospital.

The freeway on-ramp was just ahead, but a group of seedy

looking youths trying to hitch a ride blocked it. As she came to almost a complete stop, one of them dropped the bundle he was carrying in a flowered bedspread. She watched as a silver tray and jewelry spilled onto the pavement. Looters!

Faith swerved to the left to try and pass them. A red-haired boy in faded blue jeans rushed forward and grabbed the driver's door handle. He ran alongside the car and looked at Faith with his pimply face, giving her a wicked smile as he tried to jerk the door open. The seat belt tightened against her chest as she hit the brake instead of the accelerator.

He pounded on the window with his fist. In the rearview mirror she saw the other boys begin to run towards the car. She hit the accelerator and lunged forward. *Why wouldn't he let go?* The merge sign. She headed towards it, dragging the youth with her. The corner of it hit him on the shoulder, and she heard a loud thud. She sped onto the freeway; she didn't dare look back.

What if her door had been unlocked? The color drained from her face as the ugliness she'd buried for so long pushed itself to the surface, and she started to remember it all again. Her rage ignited into a blazing bonfire, and the safety barriers she'd erected to block the episode went up in flames. Her hands shook and her throat constricted as fear and anger seethed within her.

Her eyes filled with tears. Would she ever be able to extinguish the awful memories of her rape? An ear-splitting blast from an air horn shattered her thoughts. She swerved back into her lane, feeling the pull of the eighteen-wheeler as it tried to suck her into its lane as it passed. Her heart pounded in her ears. Where was her exit? She had to get home. Home—where she could lock the world outside.

What should have been a twenty-minute ride took an hour, but finally her exit loomed into sight. She was still shaking when she turned into her street. At least her neighborhood didn't look any different. But then looks were deceptive, weren't they? She hadn't looked any different the next day either.

Yet, the setting was too serene. Faith wasn't sure what she had expected but it certainly wasn't this. The neatly clipped hedges and mounds of red and white impatiens by the walkway seemed to nullify the night and the anguished moments she'd just gone through. She pulled into the driveway, and for a fleeting moment she imagined it was all a dream—until she saw Mrs. Eckworth.

Sitting on their veranda in one of the wicker rockers, Mrs. Eckworth tightly embraced a book. Streaked with yellow, her white hair lay in a single braid down her back where it swung back and forth as she crooned some tune to herself. She rocked in time to the nameless melody, her bare feet hitting the porch on the downbeat.

Faith got out of the car, plugged it into the electrical outlet by the garage, and walked up the steps.

"She's not here, is she?" Inez Eckworth called out to Faith in a reedy voice.

"Who's not here?" Faith noted that the old lady was still in her flannel nightgown, and she saw her shiver as the morning breeze drifted across the porch.

"Your mother, of course. She's gone, just like she said." As Faith approached her, Mrs. Eckworth peered intently into her eyes.

"I didn't believe her, you know. I wanted to, but something kept holding me back. Something . . . evil."

She reached out with her bony fingers and clasped Faith by the wrist. "You didn't believe either, did you? You and me, we're in the same boat, but we've still got a chance."

Faith shook herself loose from her grasp. "I don't know what you're talking about."

"That's more the pity, my dear. You'll be needing me, but don't wait too long." With a great effort she hoisted herself up from the rocker. "Your mom told me what to do, gave me this here book. It's got the answers. You come see me when you want them, your mom would want you to."

Faith watched as Mrs. Eckworth walked down the stairs, her bare feet crushing the wet grass as she made a path through the meadow and past the orchard to her house. If she hadn't been her mom's friend and their nearest neighbor . . .

The day they'd moved in, she'd shown up with a homemade peach pie. Ever since then, they'd been the recipients of not only fresh fruit but of whatever else Mrs. Eckworth's garden plot produced.

"I raise my vegetables the old–timey way, budding and grafting instead of propagating with tissue culture and computers like most folks do nowadays," she had said proudly.

Faith had heard her dad say that at one time Mrs. Eckworth's husband owned the whole area. After he died and the land reform bills were passed, she'd been forced to split up the farm and sell it. She'd kept the original 1930s white frame house and had pluckily told the authorities she planned to live there until she died.

Faith shrugged her shoulders as she took out her key to open the front door. Mrs. Eckworth was a lonely old soul and for some reason her mom had tolerated her impromptu visits. What book had her mother given her?

She opened the door and jumped when she heard the burglar alarm go off. Nothing was going right! She dashed inside, turned it off, and called the police department. "I want to report a false alarm at 113 Fernhill Drive."

"We're only answering emergency calls," a terse, hurried voice answered, and she heard a loud click as she was disconnected. She slammed the receiver down. Fine! Could she help it if the whole world was on a caffeine high? She retraced her steps, locked the front door with its deadbolt, and reset the burglar alarm. No one else was home except . . .

"Meoooooooow!"

"Oh, Thomas, I didn't mean to step on you." She reached down and enfolded the tomcat in her arms. Suddenly the tears came, a salty flood of emotions that had been dammed up ever since Hope and her mother had disappeared. She dropped to the floor and leaned up against the door of the refrigerator, burying her wet face in Thomas's black fur.

Thomas wiggled to get away, then sat by his empty bowl and let out a high-pitched yowl to get her attention. "All right, I'll get you something to eat," she said as she stood up. She read the note on the refrigerator. "At least Dad's all right. Maybe he knows what's going on," she said to Thomas. "I'll give him a call."

As a gentle reminder, Thomas rubbed up against her legs again. "Don't worry, I'll feed you first," Faith said, reaching into the cabinet and emptying a packet of dry cat food into his bowl.

She went to the bedroom and sat on her twin bed as she called her father's office.

"I'm sorry, Miss Morgan, but your father is unable to come to the phone at this time. I'll have him return your call as soon as possible."

"But this is an emergency." Faith stood up, reeling in the extra-long phone cord her father had installed for her and Hope. "My mother is missing . . . and my sister."

The voice on the other end of the phone exploded. "There are a lot of people not accounted for, Miss. I'll give him the message."

"Thanks a lot!" she cried into the dead phone. What else could go wrong?

Thomas entered the bedroom and attacked the phone cord as she hung up the receiver. She ignored him and stuck the raisin sized stereo system she'd received at Christmas into her ears. She sprawled on the floor and tucked a pillow under her head, and while she listened to the music, Thomas plopped on her stomach and began to groom himself with his sandpaper tongue.

She tried to recall her conversation with Mrs. Eckworth, but she felt herself fading away. How did Mrs. Eckworth know her mother was gone? But before Faith could come up with an answer, she drifted off into a troubled sleep where once again claw-like hands were reaching for her.

Rabbi Solomon Lowenstein, a slight, balding man in his early sixties, stood high on a hill overlooking Jerusalem, now the religious center of the world. He searched the heavens, trying to find an answer. How could people literally disappear off the face of the earth without a trace? But just days ago, on September 3, 2010, that was exactly what had happened.

Thoughtfully, his slender hands adjusted his skull cap, then caressed his long, wiry beard. He could always feel God's presence here, as the Creator with gentle fingertips brushed across the chords of his soul, disturbing him ever so slightly, pricking his conscience.

He inhaled deeply and felt swept up by Elohim, carried by the same powerful sense of a unique destiny which had been felt by every generation of Jews. An instrument of God's will, he was now part of the spearhead that would usher in the fulfillment of universal peace and brotherhood.

Would not the Messiah come when the temple was rebuilt and worship resumed?

He was overcome with emotion and wept silently, the tears streaming down his face.

And was not he blessed above other men?

He, Rabbi Solomon Lowenstein, was one of a small number of rabbis trained to use the "Ashes of the Red Heifer." What was once only a prayer was now a reality.

He thought back to the meeting he'd had that morning with the arrogant young American archaeologist, Brian Bowman.

"I've made the find of the century. Not just gold and silver, but what appears to be the vestments of the high priests and possibly the balsam oil used to anoint the Israelite kings. I've yet to find the original tabernacle built by Moses and Aaron, but the *Copper Scroll* indicates that it's in the same area," said Brian.

He had hesitated before he continued. He seemed to be trying to size up the rabbi before him. "From the markings on the outside, we think one of the sealed vessels contains the 'Ashes of the Red Heifer' which are mentioned in the Old Testament—Numbers to be exact."

Solomon had trembled at the news. He remembered how one of the Dead Sea Scrolls, discovered in 1952 in a cave in Qumran, had been carefully deciphered. The document, etched on three pieces of copper measuring nearly eight feet in length, had described a cave where the riches of the Jewish temple had been hidden over 2,000 years ago to avoid plundering by the advancing Romans.

The rabbi had forced himself to keep his voice steady and convincing. "You are aware, Mr. Bowman, that the ashes you speak of were used to purify the Jews so they could enter the Temple Mount without defiling it. If these ashes are authentic, they will allow the establishment of the third temple."

"I know," said Brian, "that a religious ruling has banned Orthodox Jews from visiting the Temple Mount because they can't walk on the site of the Holy of Holies unless they've been purified." The sandy-haired young man leaned forward and looked Solomon in the eye.

"I've got something that the prime minister or any Jew would give his life for."

"And just where did you find these ashes, Mr. Bowman?"

"Do you really think I'm that naive, Rabbi Lowenstein? My father spent almost forty years trying to locate this one cave among the thousands that dot Qumran, but he didn't live long enough to enjoy his victory. I will."

Rabbi Solomon Lowenstein had used his most persuasive tone. "These artifacts belong to the Jewish people; they are priceless." His keen eyes followed the slender man as he trotted around the room. He looked like an unsteady colt trying to stand up for the first time on wobbly legs.

"I'm sure you want to return them," he continued. "In view of the recent treaty between the Arabs and Israel, there should be no problems. You will be paid a most generous amount, I can guarantee you that."

"If the price is right, I'll turn them over. Call it extra insurance, but I don't intend to be the target for one of Israel's crack fighting forces. Since September third, a lot of people in Israel have turned up missing; I don't intend to join them. You of all people should know about self-preservation."

The rabbi passed his hand over his forehead, erasing a frown line. "There has always been chaos in the world, Mr. Bowman. We Jews are used to it, we thrive on it because we know ultimately who rules the universe. I'm not sure what caused these freak accidents and why there are so many unexplained missing persons, but I'm sure your president will try to give the world an explanation.

"Plagues, germ warfare, or perhaps," Solomon said with a slow smile, "aliens from outer space. Who knows? We have complained of overpopulation, starvation, and the pollution of our planet." He pointed to the ceiling. "Just maybe He listened, and He's helping us to take care of these problems."

"By killing people?" Brian said angrily.

"I see I've touched on a sensitive area. Please allow me to finish. You have been taught that God is a God of love, is that not correct?"

"If there is a God, He doesn't go around butchering people or whisking them off the face of the earth."

Solomon rubbed his hands together. "Please go back and read the Old Testament. The God of the chosen people wiped entire civilizations off the map in one bold stroke. I'm sure you have heard of the patriarch, Noah, and the flood? You Westerners have a hard time accepting the concept of a God of vengeance. We don't. Perhaps He is not happy with the way we have been running things. Would you concede that?"

Brian knew he was getting in too deep. He'd come to the meeting to let the high-ranking Jewish leader know what he'd found, not to get into a debate on theology. He didn't trust any of them, neither the filthy Arabs nor the pious Jews.

"The only concessions in this arrangement will be from you," he said. "I want one billion dollars."

"That . . . is impossible!"

"I'm sure the Palestinians would pay any price I asked, even though they are supposed to be your new allies. Do you really think this treaty will last? The Arabs are just buying time until they can rid themselves of the Jews once and for all. Old prejudices, like weeds, can be cut back, but the roots are still alive." Brian's back stiffened.

"Don't try to have me followed; I've removed the artifacts to a safe place. That's where they'll stay until we make our deal." Brian Bowman started to leave, then turned back to Solomon.

"After I receive my fee, you will inform the media of my generosity, then publicly you will express your appreciation to me for *donating* this historical find to the nation of Israel."

How can God work through this cocky foreigner to accomplish His will? The question hung in Solomon's mind as he gazed at the olive groves and listened to the gentle bleating of the sheep on the hillside.

His mind began to trace the history of his people. Had not God used the stiff-necked pride of Egypt's Pharaoh to accomplish the release of His people from their slavery and bondage so He could bring them into the promised land?

Yes, God could change the hearts and minds of unbelievers to achieve His purpose. Nothing could mar the happiness which welled up within Solomon, not this young American upstart or the strange occurrences throughout the world. They were all forerunners of His coming.

Songs of praise rose to his throat, and unable to contain his joy any longer, he sang the ancient psalms of David:

"If I forget thee, O Jerusalem, let my right hand forget her cunning.

"If I do not remember thee, let my tongue cleave to the roof of my mouth, if I prefer not Jerusalem above my chief joy."

Rabbi Solomon Lowenstein's voice grew in intensity as he looked down the rocky hillside towards the Temple Mount . . . waiting, waiting as his people had for centuries for the return of the Shekinah Glory.

4

Time was running out. Randy Morgan's fingers and the rest of his body, after two sleepless days, were numb. Otherwise, he would have crossed his fingers for good luck as he put the program through its trial run. He hunched over the screen, checking each phase as the computer clicked away. During the last couple of days, in a marathon of activity, he'd created a graphics program—from scratch—which would analyze the mountains of information being received.

He didn't even want to think about all the data which had been lost. Apparently, a huge magnetic field had encircled the globe, erasing information on diskettes and magnetic tapes, causing compasses to twirl erratically and electronic devices to malfunction. Artificial intelligence had been brought to its knees by a mere freak of nature.

Randy leaned over the mainframe, looked at the room full of useless computer banks, then grabbed the green apple on top of his console. He'd had too many cigarettes, too much coffee. The inside of his mouth tasted like the strip on a box of matches until he crunched into the apple's crisp skin and its tart juice squeezed through his teeth.

"Saundra, the new program is loaded," he said to the heavyset woman on his right. "Tell everyone to start feeding those lists of missing people into the computer."

Saundra turned her thick neck towards the seven foot stacks of computer paper which lined the back wall. "You mean those lists, right?" She groaned and scratched her fuzzy, copper-colored hair as the office flunky brought in another stack.

"We'd finally gotten to the point where a sliver of paper could hold a computer program or a complete medical history and now we're back to . . . this," she said indicating the reams of paper with her thumb. "It's 1990 all over again. If only everyone else's communication parameters were the same as ours."

"When this center is completed in 2013, three years from now, the entire global community will have equipment that's compatible with ours. Until then, Mrs. Swensen, welcome to what used to be the world of high-speed data networking."

He winked at her. "One day you'll tell your grandchildren that you were on the cutting edge of history."

"The only edge I want to see is the sharp edge of a knife." She made a slicing motion from her left ear to the right one.

He leaned over her and spoke with a mock German accent. "That would be too easy, Mrs. Swensen. First you must retrieve, store, and manipulate."

"Manipulate? That's what the government is doing to us." She threw up her hands. "I can't even leave to see what's happened to my family."

He put his hand on her shoulder. "The sooner we get this done, the sooner we can all go home."

Resigned to her task, Saundra Swenson started through the office assigning the work load. Meanwhile, Randy went over his instructions again. He already knew them by heart, but after years of training he'd developed a methodical checklist which he rarely altered. He started at the top, reading his instructions as if he'd just seen them for the first time.

The center had been charged with finding the common thread linking the disappearances throughout the world. When the Orange County facility began to store information in its computers, the other intelligence-gathering agencies throughout the globe wanted equal access in exchange for their cooperation. In the computer network world, not having access was like being homeless.

Equal access—to the bathroom—that's what he needed. He looked at the digital clock on the wall: 7:37. In the windowless underground building, it was hard to tell whether it was morning or evening. He tried to concentrate on the small red lighted dots on the clock which formed A.M. or P.M., but they blurred together.

His urinary tract signaled him again, and he threw the apple core into the wastebasket and got up. As he passed the receptionist, she flagged him down with a pink memo sheet.

"Mr. Morgan, your daughter called." She smiled apologetically. "I've been so busy—the phones have been ringing off the hook. I should have gotten it to you sooner."

He read the note from Faith as he walked towards the bathroom. Ruth and Hope—they were both missing!

He searched his memory for some clue. Why? Was it just random selection, being at the wrong place at the wrong time? He crumpled the note and threw it into the toilet. If only he could do that with all his problems.

He washed his face in cold water, trying to quell the anger which rose within him. This whole thing sounded like something from an old Stephen King novel. He reached up for a paper towel but the dispenser was empty. He swore under his breath, smacked the button on the hot air dryer, and stuck his face under it.

"I always knew you were full of hot air, Randy, but I thought you were more than capable of producing your own."

With a smirk on his face, Falcon Lightfoot, Randy's assistant, stood with his arms folded across his red shirt and his feet set wide apart in a pair of worn moccasins. Except for a few streaks of gray in his hair, he looked like the same eighteen-year-old youth who'd left the Shawnee Indian Reservation in Oklahoma twenty years earlier. He'd worked his way through college, joined the Marines, and met Randy in California where they had both been recruited by the CIA.

Randy laughed in spite of himself. "Falcon, I wish I could produce an answer to this whole mess as easily." He let out a sigh. "I just found out that my wife and Hope are missing. Any of your family affected by this?"

"My grandmother in Oklahoma." Falcon sucked in his breath, then slowly expelled it, trying to relieve the knot of tension which spread its tentacles like a giant web from the base of his neck to his broad shoulders. "Barring some supernatural phenomenon—which we can't rule out yet—who would be power-ful enough to pull off the vanishing act of the century?"

Randy shook his head. His assistant continued. "Here we are at the intelligence center of the world, and we don't know what's going on. What chance does Mr. Joe Q. Public have? Zip, that's what." With his blue-black hair, straight nose, bronzed skin, and lanky torso, Falcon Lightfoot looked like an Indian chief bent on waging war as he padded back and forth on soundless feet.

"At least we're one step ahead of the public, we *know* there's an intelligence center." Randy did a few deep knee bends to re-move the kinks from his legs then stood up, braced his palms against the wall, and began to push. It was a simple exercise he used to do when he was on the wrestling team in high school, but now his aging muscles rebelled at the exertion.

"We've got to get some answers and fast," he said as he turned around. "If we don't, some of the nations who've just been wait-ing to give us the kiss of death will withdraw their support."

"This 'one big happy family' line just doesn't sit well with a lot of countries, and like us, they've had a hard time camouflaging expenditures," said Falcon. He cracked his knuckles as he contin-ued. "There was a lot of opposition to a central data bank net-work where the information wealth of the world would reside."

Randy leaned against the wall. "You remember what happened to that civil liberties lawyer in Chicago when he accused the gov-ernment of moving the latest census information from one con-text to another, without informing the public?"

Falcon nodded. "He dredged up the 1986 Computer Fraud and Abuse Act."

"And they dredged him out of Lake Michigan six months be-fore the case could come to trial."

"Is the word *privacy* still in the dictionary?"

"Come on, Falcon, you're the one wearing the moccasins. The code name for this project is *Spyglass*. What does that tell you?"

The two men looked at each other for a moment, unable to voice the question which was nagging at both of them: What if the United States was the culprit?

"I'd better do a little spying of my own," said Randy, forcing a laugh, "and see if I can track down Faith."

He went back to his desk and dialed the familiar number. He heard the telephone ring twice, but before anyone could answer there was a click, then the curt voice of the head of security.

"Mr. Morgan, there'll be no more incoming or outgoing calls. Washington will be in contact with us by closed circuit television. This has the highest priority. Until further notice, all personnel are restricted to the compound."

"Wait just a minute, Pratt, I'm in charge of this operation. Why wasn't I informed?"

"You just were, *Sir*."

Randy could visualize Gordon Pratt as he talked, his huge Adam's apple bobbing up and down in the only skinny part of his anatomy. Behind his back, the staff called him "Yo Yo."

"Look Pratt, I want to make one call. If I'd made it ten minutes ago there wouldn't have been a problem."

"Yes, Sir, that's right, but you didn't. If I let you make one call, then I'll have to let everyone make a call. That would be disobeying my orders. I'm securing this line now!"

Randy was fuming as he hung up. When Gordon Pratt was picked to be in charge of security, Randy had voiced his disapproval, but he'd been overruled by the military contingency who approved of Pratt's dogmatic way of doing everything by the book. The word *flexible* was not in Pratt's vocabulary.

Randy could forget about calling Faith until the ban was lifted, or . . . would he disobey orders? In a heartbeat.

Faith Morgan struggled to wake up. For a second she thought she heard the phone, but no, it was Thomas, anxious to go out. Reluctantly she picked herself up off the bedroom floor and went to the kitchen to open the back door. With his tail held high, Thomas headed for the soft dirt of the flower bed.

It was getting dark outside. The microwave's clock flashed on and off, which meant they must have lost power for a while. She reset the microwave and plugged in the wall clock. Had she missed the president's speech? Quickly she called correct time— at least the recording couldn't hang up on her. It was seven-fifty in the evening. She had ten minutes. She transferred a bowl of leftover spaghetti from the refrigerator to the microwave.

Why didn't her father call?

BEEP!

She took out her meal and grabbed a soft drink. Thomas meowed to get back inside, so she opened the door, then sat down at the table with the cat at her feet. She took a long strand of spaghetti and held it high in the air for Thomas, who rose up on his hind feet to capture it. As the shadows lengthened in the kitchen, she buttered a piece of French bread. The normalcy of her routine helped her to conclude, between bites, that there had to be a simple explanation for the surreal events that had occurred, which she and everyone else had overlooked.

Reaching into the cupboard for a handful of chocolate chip cookies, she could almost hear her mother's voice. "Faith, you eat too much junk food. Have a piece of fruit instead."

Feeling guilty, she put the cookies back and took an overripe banana from the fruit bowl instead, then she continued to the living room to listen to the president's speech, which had just begun.

"My fellow citizens, it is with fear and trembling that I come before you tonight." President Blanco's face looked ashen in contrast to his black hair and mustache, but his hawklike eyes were riveted on the camera.

"Our entire world has faced a disaster of unknown proportions. Millions of people have seemingly vanished off the face of the earth. Few families have been left untouched by this crisis." He dabbed at his eyes with his monogrammed handkerchief. "My wife is among those missing." He struggled to regain his composure.

"All we have now are theories, but let me assure you that the most brilliant minds of our age are coming together to solve this mystery. Scientists have put forth the premise that a virus may have entered our atmosphere, resulting in the immediate disintegration of tissue in some humans. For whatever reason, those of us who are left are immune to it." He paused, letting his audience digest what he'd said.

"I have mobilized the National Guard in each state to help restore law and order. Please continue to report all missing persons to your local law enforcement agency. It's very important that you continue to report to your places of employment. It will take a combined effort to make the United States and our world whole again." He looked down at his notes, then back at the camera.

"Leaders of every nation have agreed to declare the day after tomorrow an international day of mourning. We will never fully get over the losses we have suffered, but we must go on with renewed efforts to find the source of this catastrophe and prevent it from ever happening again."

As the station switched to the NASA Space Center for a discussion by a panel of award winning scientists, the president slumped in his leather chair. He waved his advisors away, and Logan watched silently until the television crew had removed their equipment and he was alone with the president.

The president looked up and scowled at him. "What is it, Ambassador Washburn?"

"I was told that *you* wanted to see *me.*"

President Emilio Blanco removed his glasses. He didn't need them—the lenses were clear glass—but he'd read somewhere that people who wore glasses were perceived to be more intelligent. He laid them on top of his notes and looked at Logan thoughtfully.

"I understand that you're acquainted with Cardinal Mark Ryan."

"I assisted him in opening one of the first East Coast hospices for homeless AIDS victims," Logan said. He didn't tell the president that he'd been blackmailed into sponsoring the hospice. Since then, the blackmailer had met an untimely death, but the ambassador had kept up the facade of compassion. It had turned out to be a good public relation's angle.

"You are quite the Good Samaritan aren't you, Logan? Do you by any chance have a personal interest in these victims?"

"Is that why you called me here, to discuss the charities I endorse?"

"No, I just want to make sure we understand each other." The president leaned back in his chair and looked out the window.

"Have you ever heard of the Rapture?"

"The Rapture?" Logan shook his head.

President Blanco swiveled around in his chair and continued.

"It's a term that many fundamental, Bible-believing Christians have coined. Mind you, that word is never used in the Bible, I had my Minister of Religion check." He cleared his throat. "The word is used to describe a time when Jesus Christ will return from heaven and take away all His followers, leaving behind those who don't believe in Him."

Logan's eyes hardened. "You don't believe that this—"

"No, of course not." President Blanco couldn't meet Logan's eyes. "But there are many people who do. By bringing together a group of religious leaders who are well known, we can halt this rumor before it gets out of hand. Cardinal Ryan is well respected. I asked him to head the group, but he declined, saying his first priority was to assist the relief agencies he's involved with, especially now. I want you to change his mind—whatever it takes."

Logan noted that the president's hand shook as he picked up his glasses and tapped them against the desk top.

Why he believes it, Logan thought. He believes in this . . . Rapture nonsense. No wonder, his Mexican-American ancestors had been steeped in Catholicism, and his wife had reportedly set aside a room in the White House as her own personal chapel.

"I'll contact him at once, sir."

"Thank you, Logan, I won't forget this."

As Logan made his way back to his hotel, he mentally scoffed at the man who held the most important office in the United States. Any man in his right mind knew there was no God.

Influence and wealth, they were his gods, twin peaks in a mountain range of power. Religion made a man weak, vulnerable. He respected Cardinal Ryan for his dedication, but not his religion. The cardinal's efforts at playing god were futile; at best he merely put bandages on the open sores of society instead of healing them. This lower class of humanity should be expelled, not embraced.

Now was the time when men who felt as he did could come into power. Logan's heart quickened. Indeed, if there was any validity to this Rapture theory, then they were rid of the insipid believers. If the virus theory was correct, the defective and weak specimens had been removed, leaving the stronger ones to rule.

It was nature's way—survival of the fittest. He'd never understood why mankind insisted on trying to nurture the dregs of
society at the expense of the rest of the population.

He pressed the digital code into the lock and the door to his
condominium swung open. He went to the bar and poured himself a drink while he mulled over the knowledge he'd just ac-
quired. This mass exodus could be interpreted by the New Age
movement, which was slowly but surely replacing Christianity,
as a confirmation of their doctrine, which taught that those not
fit to bring in the Golden Age of Peace would be removed to
another dimension until they were rehabilitated.

He grinned like a school bully who'd just beaten up the new
kid in class and gotten away with it. No matter what the world
believed, the reputation he'd earned as a peacemaker would serve
him well in either camp.

He thought back to his negotiations a week ago. He had
achieved the result they all wanted: a seven-year treaty.

The West Bank and the Gaza Strip, now annexed to Jordan,
would be the Palestinian homeland, and in exchange the Arabs
had accepted the right of Israel to exist within newly delineated
and secure borders. During the transition period, safeguards for
both Israel and the Arabs would be implemented. A unanimous
vote by all parties had elected a unified Germany to be the world's
watchdog and to oversee the fragile peace which had been forged.

Henceforth, Jerusalem would be the capital of Israel; it would
no longer be a divided city. The expansion of Jewish settlements
would now shift towards Galilee and the still unpopulated Negev
Desert in the south. Israel's prime minister and his advisor, Rabbi
Solomon Lowenstein, had been adamant on one point. It had
been the hardest to achieve.

The Dome of the Rock and the silver domed El-Aqsa mosque
must be dismantled and rebuilt at new locations within the Palestinian homeland to enable the Jewish temple to be reconstructed
on the Temple Mount. The Moslems believed that the Dome of
the Rock was the starting point for the Prophet Mohammed's
nocturnal journey into heaven, and only their fierce desire to be
free and independent of Israeli control had made them finally
concede to Israel's ultimate demand.

Logan was grateful that the Palestinian representatives from the West Bank and Gaza Strip had never been blatantly associated with the now defunct PLO or they would never have reached an agreement.

Previously, there had been numerous attempts by the Jews to lay the cornerstone of the temple, but angry mobs of Palestinians had rioted and stoned them. Logan knew that the Jews had already prefabricated their temple, and it could now be completed in three months on the old site. For the third time in history, a Jewish temple would rise in Jerusalem.

Washburn knew this universal peace nonsense wouldn't last, it couldn't. Peace was just a pause in history, a chance to catch a collective breath and build new monuments before mankind took on fresh battles. In the end, the stronger, the smarter, and the more diligent would rule.

Ambassador Logan Washburn turned and looked into the mirror behind the bar. *Stronger, smarter, more diligent*. He knew the potential which lurked behind those ebony eyes. Yes, he was destined for great things.

5

aith looked out of the kitchen window, past the orchard to Mrs. Eckworth's white farmhouse. Like a beacon, one light shone from the upstairs window in the September darkness. She slipped on her sandals and went out the back door with Thomas, walking towards the frame structure, feeling the warm Indian summer breezes stir her hair. Thomas rustled through the rye grass as he pounced on the unsuspecting crickets and katydids squeaking out their evening melodies.

She couldn't believe or rationalize what the president had just said—it was so farfetched. There had to be another answer. Wasn't that what the old crone had said, she had the answers?

Faith walked up the creaking steps and hesitated in front of the door with its faded and peeling paint. She opened the ripped screen door, but before she could knock, Mrs. Eckworth opened it.

"Been waiting for you." She pushed a book into Faith's hands. "Read this. After you do, come back and see me." She stepped back and slammed the door.

Stunned, Faith just stood there. "Well, maybe I will and maybe I won't!" It had been a dumb idea to come here in the first place. What in the world had made her believe that some country hayseed knew more than the entire government of the United States? She had definitely been watching too many science fiction videos.

Faith began to walk back to the house, then stopped. It was

too quiet. Even the frogs and insects were mute. She waited in the darkness for a noise, any sound, but there was only silence.

She reached down and nervously picked a tall blade of grass. She put it between her thumbs and blew until an eerie whistle sound split the stillness. Suddenly the hair on the back of her neck stood up. Instantly, she knew she was not alone. Someone, something, was there, watching her.

She began to run, slowly at first, then faster as the terror pursued her through the orchard towards the pool. She heard the grass crunch behind her. Fearfully she looked over her shoulder.

Racing down the path behind her was Thomas with a field mouse dangling from his mouth.

Faith threw the book onto the webbed chair next to the pool. Relieved that the only thing chasing her was an overactive imagination, she sat there with her sandals in one hand while she dangled her feet in the silky, cold water. She looked down the path again; there was nothing.

As she watched the reflection of the stars in the pool, she heard an ambulance siren in the distance. A chill ran up her spine. She felt so helpless, caught up in something she had no power to change or halt.

The book.

She picked it up and flipped it open to the flyleaf. She recognized the handwriting of her mother, but in the pale moonlight she couldn't read the inscription. She turned on the pool lights.

To those who are left behind, this book will help you to understand what has happened. You still have a chance!

She trembled as she read the words. What was her mother trying to tell her?

Abruptly, a cold wind blew over her, ruffling the pages of the book. She looked over her shoulder and saw what appeared to be a five-foot wide dust devil of autumn leaves whirling madly towards her. She tried to get up, to get out of its way, but she couldn't! An invisible hand held her fast, pressing her to the chair and squeezing her upper body. She struggled, her mind unable to comprehend what was happening.

"Let me go!" she screamed into the night at the unseen presence.

Suddenly she was aware of the sharp, putrid smell of sulfur. She gagged as it filled her nostrils; she knew she was going to throw up.

Then she heard it.

A low, guttural howling that terrified her. A whirlwind of dust and leaves whipped over her, blinding her. She opened her mouth to scream, but she choked instead as sand and grit filled her throat. Her stomach went into spasms. She gagged and threw up.

Fingers of wind ripped the book from her grasp, and through her tears, she saw it lifted high into the air. Then it was gone, and so was the wind.

She didn't move. The pool lights shone crazily through the leaves that now covered its surface, while two deck chairs floated among the debris.

"Meow!"

With his ears flattened back and his tail drooping, Thomas clung forlornly to a chair in the choppy water. Hysterically, she began to laugh. She couldn't control herself as the tears formed and made dirty furrows down her cheeks.

Angrily she pulled off her filthy clothes and jumped naked into the pool. She swam to the deep end, making a trail through the soggy leaves, then pushed the chair Thomas was hanging onto towards the edge. He jumped up on the coping surrounding the pool, shook off the water, sat down, and immediately began grooming himself as if nothing out of the ordinary had happened.

She dove under the water to remove the debris from her hair, then began scooping up the leaves from the surface and from the skimmer, throwing them out onto the decking. She knew it was illogical but somewhere, deep within, she imagined that the more energy she expended, the further her fears would retreat.

It was almost midnight before she wrapped herself in a towel and went inside, telling herself sternly as she dried off that her terror was only a bunch of leaves and wind spurred on by her lively imagination.

But something stirred within her, and for one crazy moment she felt that her life depended on that book. Where was it? What secrets did it hold? She looked out of the window at the backyard. Except for a few leaves clinging to the fence, all traces of the horror which had smothered her were gone. She closed her eyes, and rebuked herself. It was just a bizarre series of events. It was time to get back to reality.

Disciplined is a precise word, and it described Cardinal Mark Ryan perfectly. From the time he had entered St. Mary's Roman Catholic School, where he never dallied or handed in an assignment late, until he was ordained a priest after graduating from the Catholic University in Washington, D.C., he had always disciplined his life. A six-foot, seven-inch "man of the cloth," he was not easy to ignore, and he soon became known as a "mover and shaker" on the Vatican's fast track, where his opinions were highly valued.

Social ministry was his realm, and Cardinal Ryan had learned on Capitol Hill how to play the game of politics, using both private and public funds to accomplish his social reforms. But the one-on-one contact with those who needed his help was what he enjoyed most.

There was already a long line of people outside waiting for the noon meal to be served as Cardinal Ryan unlocked the door of the rectory's basement, which served as a temporary soup kitchen. Watching him ladle out the soup wearing a butcher's apron over the black cloth of the clergy, it was hard to imagine he had earned doctorates in canon law and theology.

With his large, luminous eyes, the cardinal watched a middle-aged woman argue with one of the young priests at the door while she gripped the handle of the supermarket cart containing all her worldly possessions. He stepped from behind the serving table and walked over to her.

"Friar Tuck will be telling you how it is," he heard her say to the priest. Her face lit up when she saw Cardinal Ryan approach.

She crossed her arms and gave the young priest a smug look.

"Now, what's the problem, Mary Margaret?" Cardinal Ryan said in a soft voice.

"Friar Tuck," she said respectfully, using the name his parishioners had affectionately given him because of his girth, "he says

I can't bring my cart in. Have to leave it outside. You knows if I do that, they'll steal it—everything. I worked all day to get them newspapers and cans together, and he wants me to leave it on the doorstep for some no account to take. I won't do it, I won't." She sniffed the air, and for a minute her resolve seemed to weaken as she inhaled the aroma of the vegetable soup.

"Father Timothy, would you please bring Mrs. Kelley a bowl of soup? She can have it on the steps outside where she can keep an eye on her cart . . . and give her some of that French bread the restaurant manager just brought over." The priest's eyes widened, but obediently he went towards the kitchen.

"Bless you," said Mrs. Kelley as she ran her fingers through her unkempt hair. "It's nice to know someone cares about poor people like myself, those who's fallen on hard times."

He patted her on the shoulder, then turned to leave. He almost collided with the returning Father Timothy who screeched to a halt in front of him.

"Si . . . sir," he said, stuttering in his excitement. "There's a call for you. It's from the Vatican."

"Thank you, Father Timothy." He smiled at the eager, impressionable priest. "And don't be forgetting Mary Margaret."

What now? he thought to himself. The disappearances. No doubt there would have to be a paper issued on the Church's official position. He walked upstairs and picked up the receiver in one of the rectory's small bedrooms that he'd turned into an office. "Cardinal Ryan."

"It is imperative, Cardinal Ryan, that you come to Rome at once."

"May I ask why?" he responded to the voice he didn't recognize.

"The Holy See has requested your presence. You must leave immediately."

Surveillance cameras were located at each end of the corridor that ran from the cavernous computer room to the subterranean parking lot at the intelligence center. Randy told Falcon he had to get something from his car and headed down the long hallway.

Immediately an armed guard met him. "Mr. Morgan, no one is allowed out of the compound."

"I'm aware of that," he said briskly. "I'm just going to my car. I have a prescription in my glove compartment that I take twice a day for high blood pressure." He glanced at his watch. "I'm hours overdue as it is."

The guard looked unsure of himself for an instant. "If you'll give me your keys, I'll get it for you."

"Look, someone ripped off my stereo last week so I had a motion detector alarm installed. If you don't approach the car at the right angle . . . well, it'll make enough noise to raise the dead."

"I'll have to go with you."

"Suit yourself," he said. They started down the corridor.

"Guard, guard!" screamed Saundra Swensen. "Someone's stolen my purse." They stopped as she hurried down the passageway towards them.

"It was in my desk drawer. I usually lock it, but things have been in such a turmoil lately . . . I guess I forgot to." She twisted the rings on her chubby fingers while a single tear slid down her cheek. "I'd just gone to the automatic teller machine before this whole thing happened."

Saundra tugged on the guard's sleeve. "Since the center is sealed off, the thief must be here. You've got to find him!"

"Well, ma'am, to be truthful, if all he took was cash, it's going to be hard to catch him unless the bills were marked."

"Of course they weren't marked. How did I know someone was going to steal my purse?" she said indignantly.

"We might get back your purse and your I.D. cards, but you can kiss your money good-bye."

"Well, you have to do something! What's the world coming to when you can't even trust the people you work with?"

"I'd be glad to search the premises, but first I'm going with Mr. Morgan to his car."

"Here," Randy took his ignition key off his key ring and handed it to the guard. "Saundra's pretty upset. Why don't you go along with her? If I'm not back in ten minutes, you can send the firing squad after me."

"Maybe this is the ignition key and maybe it isn't," said the guard as he turned the key over in his hand. "Or you might have another one in your pocket. Or you could be the thief."

"Then search me," said Randy.

The guard looked towards the garage exit. Two sentries were stationed there, and it was blocked with cement pillars. "That won't be necessary, Mr. Morgan. You're not going anywhere."

"Good, then I can go to my car."

"All right, but you'd better be back here in ten minutes."

Randy raised the three fingers of his right hand. "Scout's honor." He turned on his heels and left. Saundra had been right on cue; he owed her one for that. He made his way to the car, opened the door, and got in. Keeping his head down, he looked around carefully and grabbed the cellular phone. He dialed his home number; it rang twice.

"Hello."

"Faith, it's Dad."

"Oh, Dad, I've been so worried. Did you see the news?"

"Yes. Have you been able to find your mother or Hope?"

"No, I'm afraid not. I just talked to Dr. Bradley at the hospital. Dad, I wish you were here, some really weird things are happening."

"I can't get home for a couple of days. We'll talk then. If you need anything, go see Mrs. Eckworth. There's some money in the nightstand by my bed." He heard heavy footsteps on the concrete floor. "I have to go."

Quickly he got out of the car and walked two aisles over. He recognized the short, squat figure of Gordon Pratt as it rolled towards him like a tank on a mission. "You will return at once to your work area. I said no one was to leave the facility."

Randy watched Pratt's Adam's apple play havoc with his neck before he slowly raised his eyes to meet Pratt's. *Talk about artificial intelligence.*

"Well now, I didn't actually leave the facility, did I? The garage is within the compound."

Pratt glared at him. "A technical error on your part." He handed Randy his key. "In the future, all requests to leave the building will be made directly to me. Is that understood?"

"If that's the way you want it, Pratt."

"You said you needed to get some medication." Pratt sneered at him. "Where is it?"

Randy pulled the biodegradable prescription bottle out of his pocket, and Pratt snatched it from him. He watched the sneer dissolve from Pratt's face as he inspected the label.

"High blood pressure, Pratt. That's what you get when you've worked on too many Pearl Harbor files."

Pratt dropped the bottle into Randy's open hand.

"You know, Pratt, you should have your blood pressure checked. I don't think it's normal for your eyes to bulge out like that."

As Randy walked away, he could feel Pratt's glowering eyes on his back.

"Why don't you get some sleep?" said Falcon as Randy returned to his desk. "They've got some cots set up in one of the storerooms. In six hours the president will be on the hook, and it'll be time to 'feed the bears.'"

"What have we got so far?" said Randy.

"We've keyed in approximately 25 percent of the data and a high percentage of those who disappeared had a religious affiliation . . . and brown eyes."

Randy laughed. "Two red herrings. First, dominant genes produce eye color, and second, everyone says they believe in some form of a higher being. That used to be an advantage, but now it can actually work against you in the job market."

"Yeah, it's one thing to take 'In God We Trust' off our currency but quite another to erase it from a whole generation," said Falcon. "What about you, Randy?"

"Hoping to make it to the top of the professional heap, I left that space blank on the census. Lately there's been a definite shift against the traditional religions by the government, and I don't want to give them anything they can use against me."

Suddenly Randy saw Ruth's face in his mind. He swallowed hard.

"So, we're back where we started," said Falcon.

Randy punched him lightly on his shoulder. "Keep looking, Chief. There's got to be something else."

Falcon looked at his graph again. Randy was right, there had to be something else.

6

Hannah rocked back and forth on her heels in front of Solomon, nervously wringing her hands. Her usually pasty face was flushed with pleasure. "Rabbi," she said in an awed voice, "the prime minister . . . he's sent a limousine for you." Her eyes darted from the door to Solomon and back again. "What should I do? Should I invite the driver in?"

Solomon tugged at his beard. It took so little to impress this woman; she was as subtle as a three-year-old and about as unpredictable. It had definitely been a mistake to hire her as his housekeeper when his wife died last year. Now he felt obligated, for if nothing else she was devoted to him.

He looked up at Hannah with her stout figure and ample bosom. Soft wrinkles folded together in her mottled face, and her black eyes were like ripe olives, watching his every movement.

"Tell him to wait in the car. I'll only be a moment."

Hannah Weinberg was a widow, only a few years younger than himself, but now she scampered to the door like a young girl, smoothing her mousy gray hair as she went.

The rabbi rose slowly from his chair to prepare himself. He was going to have to do something about Hannah, but what? To his horror, he'd discovered last week from the husband of one of their mutual friends that she actually entertained the notion that he might remarry someday. Apparently, she had let it be known throughout the neighborhood that she was available and willing. All Rabbi Solomon Lowenstein had to do was ask.

How could he even think of another woman after forty years of marriage to Esther? It had been a prearranged marriage, but surely it must have been made in heaven. The essence and sweetness of their life together was intact in his memory, but since her death his physical desires had abated. In their place was a spiritual hunger to see the prophecies fulfilled.

Hannah hurried back into the room. "You'll be back in time for the evening meal?"

"No, Hannah." At least he would be spared that. Along with her other failings, she was a terrible cook. "If you wish, you may go home after I leave."

He saw the disappointment on her face as he dismissed her, but he could no longer tolerate her presence. What he'd thought was an amicable arrangement for both of them had become something Solomon wasn't ready to deal with, not tonight or any other night.

The chauffeur left Jerusalem, following the ancient caravan route to Jericho. The car passed the village of Bethany and the Inn of the Good Samaritan as the road slowly descended past parched hills until they were at sea level. Solomon could see the Dead Sea shimmering in the distance below. The black car sped across the arid plain along a straight stretch of road. Near the shore of the Dead Sea the road turned sharply to the south where it followed the seashore, passing the ever-present Bedouins with their camels, who for a few shekels would allow themselves to be photographed with the tourists.

Solomon smiled as he read the words "Masada Will Not Fall Again" scrawled on the wall of a youth hostel. The Jews throughout history had wanted only one thing: freedom in their own land. Had they achieved it at last?

He looked up from the western shores of the Dead Sea to the mountains and saw the massive, cliff-top fortress of Masada, the place where many of the Israeli army tank corps now held their swearing-in ceremonies and Jewish boys had their bar mitzvahs. This lonely and barren mountaintop, a harsh symbol of Jewish determination, seemed an appropriate place to meet the prime minister.

The driver stopped and opened the door of the limousine so Solomon could board the cable car for the ride to the mountain summit. What a difference from the first time he'd come to the desert fortress as a boy to test his bravery with a Jewish youth group.

Excitedly, he'd climbed the rugged path which coiled its way to the top. He'd pretended he was a member of the small force of Jewish fighting men and their families who had retreated there in A.D. 70 to defy the Roman general Titus, who conquered and plundered Jerusalem and destroyed the temple. Unchallenged, this ragtag band had controlled Masada for two years until the Roman governor, Flavius Silva, moved up the Tenth Legion of fifteen thousand men, camped at the foot of the mountain stronghold, and besieged it.

Solomon remembered the kinship he'd felt with his ancestors as he'd climbed the ropes to assail the top. The pride in their fierce resolution to die voluntarily by their own hands, rather then submit to slavery under the Roman Empire, had become his own.

To be young again, he thought wistfully, as he worked his aching right arm back and forth. His rheumatism always seemed to flare up when the weather was going to change. He scanned the sky as the cable car climbed to the top, but only a few fluffy popcorn clouds drifted across the azure sky. Perhaps after his meeting he would have time to indulge himself at one of the spas where a hot mineral bath or the soothing Dead Sea mud would help to relieve his aches and pains.

He left the cable car and made his way among the ruins, heading towards the excavation site where some portions of the sacred scrolls had been found. Part of the area was partitioned off. As he stepped over the chain, he saw the prime minister partially hidden in the lengthening shadows. He quickened his step.

"Solomon, do you know we're standing on the site of what is believed by some to be the remains of the oldest synagogue ever found?" The prime minister stood looking out over the valley, his back to the rabbi.

"Yes, sir, I do." They seemed to be alone but he knew they weren't. In the crowd of tourists, behind the walls—somewhere there were bodyguards.

"In three months we will begin a new year, 2011—"

"Not according to the Jewish calendar," interrupted Solomon.

"We must begin to have a global outlook," said the prime minister. "The rest of the world will welcome the year 2011, and that is when the new temple will rise in Jerusalem. Tell the American archaeologist that you'll pay him whatever he wants." He turned and faced Solomon. "He won't live to spend it."

The blood drained from Solomon's face. "You'll kill him?"

"Do we have any other choice?"

"We could pay him the money—"

"And what happens when he finds another Jewish artifact? Does he want another billion or does he sell it to the highest bidder?"

"But to have his blood on our hands . . . unclean hands."

"It will be on my hands even as it was on David's when he killed the Philistine's champion, Goliath." His voice was calmer, reflective.

"Rabbis and prime ministers—we both accomplish God's will in our own distinctive way. In light of what has happened, it's more important than ever that our people be united. The temple will accomplish this. Nothing must mar its dedication." He leaned against the wall before he continued.

"Do you believe that these disappearances are a judgment from God?"

"No," said Solomon. "The Arabs are still here."

The prime minister's deep laugh echoed over the mountaintop.

"I see that we do agree on some things." He removed his sunglasses. "Jerusalem, like Masada, will not fall again. Tell the American that when we receive the 'Ashes of the Red Heifer,' he'll get his money. Let him pick the time and place for the exchange, then inform Abraham Moshe at the Tourist Information Office inside the Jaffa Gate. We'll take care of the rest." The setting sun was reflected in his eyes as he squinted at Solomon. "The Temple Mount is ours; we must begin to worship like Jews again, take our rightful place as a world leader."

Solomon nodded.

"You're one of the few good men I've known in my lifetime, Solomon. What I'm asking . . . please don't consider it a breach of our friendship." Swiftly the prime minister moved away, dissolved into the dusk, and was gone.

A good man? Hardly. I am nothing more than an insignificant pebble in the final dramatic avalanche of Jewish history. Solomon stood among the remains of the ancient synagogue for a long time, another silent stone on the rocky plateau.

Bruised clouds scurried over the top of the mountain, chased by blasts of wind, and in the rumbling thunder, punctuated by flashes of lightning, Solomon could hear the excited, legendary voices of the defenders of Masada as they scrambled to hide portions of the sacred scriptures from the Romans. They had paid the ultimate price for their faith, and if it was required, so would Rabbi Solomon Lowenstein.

Inez Eckworth lifted the cardboard box from the shelf in the closet and dumped its contents on the bed. She knew there was a Bible around somewhere, or had she given it to the Salvation Army after David died, along with his old clothes and tools? She picked through the loose photos, old greeting cards, and the musty scrapbooks with pressed flowers and newspaper clippings.

Her hand shook as she reached out to pull a folded tissue paper bundle towards her. She stroked it for a moment . . . remembering. She wanted to open it, and yet she didn't know if she could stand the pain it would bring.

Mrs. Eckworth's hands fluttered to her lap, then wavered over the wrappings like fragile hummingbirds, only to light once again on the crinkly tissue paper. Gently she unwrapped the baby gown and cap, caressing them with her rough fingertips. She picked up the creased pink rosebud print gown, then pressed it to her nose, inhaling the faint, sweet fragrance of a newborn baby.

If only Claudia had lived, it would have all been so different.

She closed her eyes and saw David again with clenched fists standing at the foot of the diminutive casket. With tears in his eyes, he had gazed at the tiny, doll-sized figure resting on the bed of white satin. She saw his face turn to concrete as he rudely sent away the preacher when he came to pay his respects.

David had told her after the burial, in a harsh voice filled with emotion, that he could no longer believe in a God who could allow this to happen. Bitter, he'd taken down the verses she'd plastered on the bathroom mirror, gathered up all the religious books she'd collected, and burned them in the fireplace. They'd never spoken of it again, and when they hadn't been able to have another child, her faith had wilted and died along with his.

Mrs. Eckworth opened her eyes and tenderly cradled the gown in her arms as her throat tightened. She could almost feel the weight of Claudia in her arms, see her cherub face with its long lashes and button nose. She felt the teardrops slide down her nose. She'd promised herself after David died that she'd never cry again, but she couldn't help herself. The old wounds she'd reopened could only be cleansed by her tears. Watered by her weeping, her withered faith began to sprout. Yes, Claudia was in heaven; she just knew it.

Wiping her eyes with the bedspread, she began to put the things back in the box. Beneath a handful of papers, she saw it: the Bible someone had given her the day she and David were married. The white cover was yellowed with age, but the sharp black print seemed to leap off the pages as she turned them.

Where to start? In the book of Matthew, yes, that was what Ruth had said. Her notes! She rushed to the living room to find the pad of paper where she'd scribbled down the information she would need.

Thank goodness she'd done it before she gave the book to Faith. Young people were so irresponsible nowadays. That story Faith had told her about the wind coming up and carrying the book off to . . . heaven knows where. Well, no matter, it just meant she'd have to reconstruct the events herself.

She sat down in her rocking chair and for the first time in nearly fifty years she began to read the Bible. She remembered some of the verses, but now she was looking for a chain of events, a chain whose first link had been forged three days earlier.

"Wake up," said Falcon as he shook Randy. "This is one pow-wow we can't miss." As Randy sat up on the edge of the cot, Falcon pushed a cup of coffee under his nose. "Compliments of Saundra. I think she enjoyed putting one over on Gordon Pratt as much as you did."

"Believe me, it didn't take much. Pratt is living proof that the garbage in–garbage out theory is correct." Randy yawned. "I'm no psychologist, but I think he tries to make up in authority what he lacks in stature."

"I think it's called the Napoleon fixation, but right now we've got other emperors to pacify."

Randy ran his hands through his hair and looked at Falcon expectantly. "Do I have to ask, or are you going to tell me what astounding conclusions we've come up with?"

"Well . . . as we assumed, it's a random pattern in most respects, but there are two notables. About 20 percent more women than men are missing and," he turned aside to check his graph, "the percentage of people with a religious tie-in has increased to 50 percent."

"I was hoping we could negate that specific group," said Randy. He thought for a moment. He looked at his watch. "We have thirty minutes to decide what to tell the president." He twisted the wedding band on his finger as he talked.

"We have two choices. We can tell him our findings aren't conclusive and stall for more time or report the trend we've discovered."

"I say give him the facts; he can decide what to tell the American public." Falcon raised his hands in the air with the first two fingers crooked to indicate quotation marks. "The buffalo chips stop here. My grandmother always said that if an Indian was elected president, she'd give him—or her—that slogan to put on their desk."

"Why is it that you can always smell manure before you see it?" said Randy. He mulled over Falcon's response while he chewed on the end of his pencil. He snapped it in two.

"We report the facts, we don't make them. Get your buffalo chips together, and we'll fax them to the White House after our oral report. Right now I'd give anything to know if that virus-from–outer space story had any merit to it. Sometimes it's easier to swallow the impossible than the plausible."

As Randy went to his locker to put on a clean shirt, he tried to concentrate on the reports. He'd have to recheck the tabulations to make sure Falcon had been right, and then run through the figures again. He couldn't shake the impression that he'd missed something. Maybe the information they were using from the census wasn't detailed enough to give them an accurate picture; there was only so much snooping the government could do. For all they knew, everyone who disappeared had eaten low-fat chocolate yogurt the night before. Randy Morgan chuckled at the thought. Now he was getting ridiculous!

7

The CIA director knew he was on the spot. It was his job to convince the president to see things the way the agency did. He was not at the Cabinet level, but in his role as intelligence advisor, John Seaton had direct access to the president. He sat across from him now with the figures the Orange County facility faxed to them. They confirmed the report that the director, Randy Morgan, had presented to them on the closed circuit television moments before.

"Do we honor the Congress's request for this information or not?" said President Blanco.

"Information is power," said John, "especially in the intelligence community. I think it's up to us to decide just how much the Congress needs to know. I'd advise you not to volunteer any information until the study is complete."

The president raised his eyebrows.

"What we're doing isn't illegal or unconstitutional. This is a covert intelligence operation that could be at risk if our speculations are incorrect and are put forth as facts."

"And if they're correct?"

"At the proper time you'll decide how much the American people need to know."

"You're suggesting that I withhold information, John. The trustworthiness and professional competence of the presidency is at stake here."

"Only if they discover you've withheld information. The

world's in an uproar now. We can give them answers if that's what they want—answers that will benefit your administration and calm down the hysteria which these disappearances have caused. If it's proven that most of these people were involved with some religious organization, it'll add fuel to the rumors of a Rapture experience, which some theologians are proposing."

John Seaton reached inside his pocket for his notes. "According to this theory, in seven years the world as we know it will end. Put forth that idea and we'll loose control. We have to squelch this before it gets out of hand."

"And how do you propose we do that?"

"Let this Randy Morgan finish the operation. Viruses are a desktop epidemic, and if the trend he's discovered remains constant, then I suggest we introduce a virus into the computer system, one which will alter or destroy all the data that's been collected."

"Without Morgan's knowledge?"

"It's better that way. We'll use the man who's in charge of security at the facility. He's got a beef with Morgan."

"Won't the Computer Emergency Response Team Coordination Center know something's been tampered with?"

"Yes, but it won't be a problem; they're financed by a research arm of the Pentagon. They know that no system is absolutely secure unless it's electronically and physically isolated from potential sources of infection. Morgan's operation hasn't had time to isolate their facilities. We should thank our lucky stars this happened before the center was completed."

"Congress will need a scapegoat."

"We'll have files and documents that will point to Morgan and one of his assistants as being members of some radical religious organization bent on converting the world by falsifying the information they've received. We have actual pictures of his wife and daughter at a recent religious gathering."

"I don't like hanging a man out to dry, especially one of our own."

"We all have to make sacrifices, Mr. President. If we can't control the people in our own country, then some other nation will come in and do it for us. The Japanese, Germans, Europeans, and Arabs have got their hands on a huge segment of our economy.

Any one of them would be only too willing to take over the government."

The president felt a migraine mushroom in his frontal lobes. "You take care of it, personally. Use as few people as possible, only those you trust implicitly."

The door closed softly behind the director as he left. The president stood up and looked out over the Capitol's reflecting pool. Seven years . . . they only had seven years left.

Faith tore through the brush outside the fence. It was thick with poison ivy, but she didn't care. Where was the book? Mrs. Eckworth had given her a tongue lashing when she'd told her she'd lost it. Who did she think she was anyway, her mother?

Mother. The word taunted her, and she sat down in the tall grass and put her head on her knees. Suddenly the book didn't matter. A single thought emerged and obsessed her. Would she ever know what it was like to be a mother?

The nurse practitioner at the clinic had refused to show her the mass of tissue they'd removed. But she'd seen pictures. She knew that even at three months the fetus was a perfectly formed human being.

"You've been raped, no one expects you to have this baby. Put this behind you and get on with your life," the nurse said to her after the abortion. But she couldn't.

Hope had stayed with her at a nearby motel. Their parents thought they were spending the weekend with a girl friend, and by Monday morning she was back at school with no one the wiser. But she could never forget the child she'd killed. Her child.

And what of the man who'd done this to her? Was he out there waiting? Would he try again?

In the library's parking lot, he'd come up behind her and clamped his hand over her mouth before she could scream. He had dragged her into the shrubbery. In the darkness she couldn't see his face as he threw her to the ground and ripped away her clothes. She'd never forget the sounds as he assaulted her.

Afterwards, she wanted to die.

Hope brought her literature from the area Rape Crisis Program, but it only made her feel worse. One in four college women were victims of rape or attempted rape, and 84 percent of those women *knew* their attackers. It could be a classmate in college, a neighbor, or a nameless male face in a crowd.

Would she ever feel safe again? Daily she struggled with her emotions. It came as no surprise or consolation that 30 percent of rape victims contemplated suicide after their attack. If she could only forget . . .

She felt something crawl slowly up her bare leg. Angrily she brushed the brown tick away. She looked towards the house as the red MGA, which had just stopped at the mailbox, turned into the driveway.

"Dad!" Thank goodness, he was finally home! She jumped up and ran towards the house, the wild berry bushes and weeds scraping her legs as she plowed through them.

Randy Morgan barely had time to get out of the car before Faith threw her arms around his neck. "I'm so glad you're home, it's been awful staying here by myself."

"You mean Thomas wasn't good company?" He reached down and picked up the tomcat who was rubbing up against his trousers.

"You know what I mean, Dad. No one seems to know what's going on. I wanted to talk to you so I could make some sense of this." She put her hands on her hips, and her eyes flashed at him.

"And just what was so important about the mail order business that you couldn't come home?"

She reminded Randy of Ruth. She even had the same inflection in her voice as she scolded him.

"I've had nothing but freeze-dried food for the last three days," he said as he put Thomas down. "How about taking a couple of steaks out of the freezer, and we'll see if I can get away with lighting the barbecue. There's been so much else going on, maybe no one is paying attention to the air quality index. I'll answer your question after I've eaten a thick, juicy steak."

"All we've got is a package of ground turkey. We're even out of leftovers."

"I can see that without me the situation on the home front is definitely deteriorating," Randy said. "It's a good thing I came home before everything and everyone disappeared."

Their eyes met. "Mom and Hope," Faith's voice faltered as she forced herself to say the words, "are they gone . . . forever?"

Randy hugged her to him, surprised at how tall she'd grown. "I honestly don't know, Faith. I wish I did."

She uncurled from his embrace. "Until then . . . Mom would want me to take care of you," she said with a tentative smile.

"Dad, what do you think happened? Do you believe that some mysterious virus made Hope and Mom disappear, or what? I mean, did some physicist develop it in a lab, or did it come from a hole in the ozone layer?"

"Let's go inside and talk," Randy suggested. As they walked into the house Randy carefully weighed the options. How much should he tell Faith? How would she react if she knew he was working for the CIA? Was she in danger if he did? Once they were seated in the family room, he cleared his throat. "Right now it's the only theory we've got. If you think about it, it's really not too hard to believe that some outside force invaded our planet or its atmosphere and brought with it the ability to destroy us."

"Even if I did believe it—and I don't—why did it happen to Mom and Hope? Why not you and me?"

"Faith, remember you asked me what was so important at the mail order business that I couldn't come home?"

She nodded.

"As you know, we have a tremendous data base with detailed information on a wide range of people. The government contacted us and wanted to combine their files with ours in an effort to find the common denominator among the missing persons. Were they male or female? What was their income bracket? That sort of thing. I hoped it would help us find out about Ruth and Hope."

Faith sat up in her chair. "Well, did it?"

"The study isn't complete yet, but when it is, I'll let you know."

"How long do you think it'll take?"

"Probably a month. By then we'll have a list of everyone who is missing, and maybe we'll have it sorted out."

"What do we do until then?"

"As mundane as it sounds, you go back to school and I go back to work after a few days' rest."

"School?" Faith said in disgust.

"Yes. I heard on the car radio that college classes will resume next week at George Mason."

"How do you expect me to go back to school after what's happened?"

"Do you think it would be better to sit around here and mope? I think we should do what the president said, get back to as normal a routine as possible."

"Normal routine. Don't you miss Mom? Things will never be normal again."

Randy reached for her hand and felt her icy fingers beneath his own. "Yes, I miss her . . . and Hope, but we're not the only ones who are hurting, honey. At least we have each other."

"Oh Dad, I wish things could be the way they were . . . before this happened, before Hope was in the hospital!" Faith tried to choke back the tears, but she couldn't. He held her as she sobbed, and for a few minutes she felt six years old again . . . and safe.

Randy stroked her hair, then placed his hands on her shoulders and looked into her eyes. "We'll get through this together, one crisis at a time."

She wiped away the tears. "Speaking of the mundane . . . will you do the grocery shopping? Hope and Mom usually did it. I hate dodging all those women with kids in their carts and coupons in their fists."

"Say, it has been a long time since you've been to the supermarket. They don't use coupons anymore. Everyone has a frequent shopper card that's electronically scanned along with their purchases at the check-out counter."

"Great. Just what the world needs—another electronic marvel."

"You'll get used to it. The card activates your personal customer file and records what you buy. When you purchase a certain item, you're automatically awarded a credit so there's no need for coupons. And if you have to wait in line, there's a television mounted above the cashier that you can watch."

"And what do they do with the kids, put them in strait jackets?"

"No, most places have a nursery at the front of the store where you can drop off the kids. It's a free service if you purchase groceries worth one hundred dollars or more. If not, there's a nominal fee."

"How come you know more about this than I do?"

"Your mother refused to buy beer, said it was bad for me, so—" He looked up at her sheepishly.

"Look, there's no reason we can't just order what we want and have it delivered. The store's master list is on my computer. We'll just punch in what we want, and within twelve hours it'll be on our doorstep."

"You're really willing to let someone else pinch the tomatoes and squeeze the toilet paper?"

"Absolutely. What I'm not willing to do is take out the garbage. I don't like separating the glass, aluminum cans, and papers. Any volunteers?"

She grinned. "Only if you empty Thomas's litter box."

He groaned. "You drive a hard bargain, young lady, but I'm too tired to argue. It's a deal."

8

The Eternal City. No matter how many times Cardinal Mark Ryan came to Rome, he was awed by it. Somehow this remarkable city, built on seven hills, retained its ancient allure, despite the modern day plagues of noise, pollution, and traffic.

It was here five years ago that the pope had officially invested him with the red hat and cloak of a cardinal. Later, at a secret consistory the pope had bestowed on him another distinctive insignia of the cardinalate: a simple gold band engraved with the image of Christ.

His fingers touched the ring reverently as he leaned back in the seat of the black Mercedes with its Vatican license plates and watched the crowds spill into the streets. Everyone seemed to be heading towards the Vatican on the Via della Conciliazione, which was now reduced to one lane of traffic because of the tourist buses on each side.

The giant dome of St. Peter's loomed into view, and gradually his eyes adjusted to the enormous dimensions of the square and the church. Emerging from the shadowy alleys, visitors today were just as surprised by the bright sunlight in the huge square as they were when it was first completed. It was what Bernini, the builder, had intended.

The Mercedes darted through open courtyards, under several arches, and past the well-groomed Vatican gardens before it stopped. The driver opened the door for him. As he stepped out, a cleric met him.

"Cardinal Erenatto, the cardinal secretary of state, said he wanted to see you, Cardinal Ryan, as soon as you arrived. Please follow me."

He was led immediately through a maze of corridors to Cardinal Erenatto's office. While he waited for the cleric to announce him, he tried to remember what he knew about the cardinal: Italian, in his early seventies, precise in his work, and from what he'd heard, the pope had complete confidence in him. He was responsible for all the Vatican's activities with the outside world and for coordinating the pope's diplomatic ventures.

"Cardinal Ryan, I'm sorry we have to meet under such circumstances." Cardinal Erenatto spoke with only a slight accent as he rose from his desk and extended his hand. "The pope admires you very much and your work in America. He said he wished the Roman Catholic church was as well represented in other nations of the world."

"Thank you, Your Eminence."

"Please sit down."

As he studied Cardinal Erenatto, he was reminded of the well-chiseled features of Michelangelo's statue of Moses; both men were monuments of Rome's antiquity.

Cardinal Erenatto's mouth barely moved as he continued in a tight, strained voice. "I have some distressing news to tell you." He laced his long fingers together and looked intently at him. "The pope died yesterday."

"What?" Cardinal Mark Ryan was startled. Why weren't the bells pealing as they did each time a pope died? Why hadn't he heard anything on the news?

"I know this will come as a shock to you, but we thought it best not to inform the world until tomorrow. The media have been clamoring for a statement from the Vatican Press Office since those puzzling disappearances took place. Many in the clergy are missing, and that, coupled with the pope's death, might give credence to the theory—" He coughed and put his hand over his mouth. "It might give the world the wrong impression."

The wrong impression? Cardinal Ryan thought silently.

"We've already sealed the papal apartments and broken the pope's ring. Usually the College of Cardinals must wait until nine days of mourning are completed before they select a new pope." He fingered the thick gold cross around his neck.

"Time is of the utmost importance. It's imperative that we make an immediate selection to replace him, so we'll forego the waiting period. You and the other cardinals will begin the selection process in conclave tomorrow."

"You mean before the pope is even buried?"

Cardinal Erenatto rubbed his hand across his eyes. "Already there is fighting among the cardinals. It's much like the American election process, isn't it? Some say he must be Italian, others want a man of vision regardless of nationality, or a conservative to keep the pope's policies and edicts intact. Who would you like to see nominated for the papal election, Cardinal Ryan?"

"Anyone but me."

"You have no aspirations to the highest office in the Catholic church?"

"None whatsoever. My Italian is less than tolerable, and it's well known that I haven't always agreed with the church's position on certain matters."

"Ah, yes." The cardinal picked up a sheet of paper from his desk. "You disagree with the church on the matters of prohibiting contraception, marriage of priests, ordination of women, and our recent policy of tolerance for homosexuals, but . . . you do not twist the knife."

"You mean, I don't rock the pontifical boat, at least not in public. Wisdom dictates that I keep quiet in order to preserve the two-thousand-year-old teachings of the church."

"That's called diplomacy, Cardinal Ryan."

"When I cast my vote, I'll try and use that same diplomacy to select the candidate who can best handle the obligations and responsibilities of the papal office."

"It's refreshing to learn that you won't be swayed by the political factions within our ranks. That's one of the reasons there will be no delay, it'll cut down on what you Americans call lobbying. The cardinals who can be accounted for are in Rome already."

He couldn't put his finger on it, but Cardinal Ryan had the uneasy feeling he wasn't being told everything. Cardinal Erenatto seemed to be waging a private war within himself as he wiped away the perspiration on his forehead with a linen handkerchief before he continued.

"It was well known that the pope was in ill health. He was seventy-nine years old, and the official statement will say that he died peacefully in his sleep. He will like in state in the Sistine Chapel—in a closed casket."

"A closed casket? That's unheard of."

"Yes, in normal times he'd be on display in his full pontifical robes, but these are not normal times." Cardinal Erenatto folded his hands in front of him and shifted his sight to the heavy draperies at the windows. "The pope told me, in confidence of course, that he would prefer a closed casket. He wanted the mourners to give their adoration to our Lord, not to him. We will respect his wishes."

"I see." He hoped the cardinal secretary of state was a better administrator than he was a liar.

"All members of the conclave will stay at the Vatican." He stood up and went to the door, thankful to get away from Cardinal Ryan's searching look. "One of the priests will show you to your room. If you haven't eaten, a meal will be prepared for you."

Cardinal Ryan followed the priest down several corridors to the spartan room that awaited him. The priest pointed to the shared bathroom down the hall. In the room there was a washbowl and pitcher, one bar of soap, and a couple of threadbare towels that even Mary Margaret wouldn't have bothered to put in her cart. A single chair and a small lamp by the bed completed the furnishings.

He lay down on the narrow bed, which creaked in protest as he shifted his weight to get comfortable. His feet hung over the end of the bed, which was nothing more than a hard mattress over a wire mesh frame. The bed was just like the one he'd had in the seminary, and as he had done then, he took his bedding and placed it on the floor. He wasn't sure what he had expected, but it wasn't this.

The room was stuffy, so he pulled back the drapes. He was surprised to find that the window was sealed and painted over. The Vatican was known for its intrigue and secrecy, but this was the only time he'd experienced it firsthand. He'd heard about the procedures for electing a pope; now he would actually be a part of it.

A knock at the door interrupted his thoughts.

"Come in."

The short, barrel-chested cardinal rolled into the room, like a tumbleweed in a high wind. "Cardinal Ryan, I am Cardinal Hampton of Great Britain. The hour is late so I will get to the point. Have you committed your vote to any candidate yet?"

"I wasn't aware that the candidates had been picked."

"True, true. But all of the cardinals have been consulting among themselves."

"You mean campaigning, don't you?"

He shook his head. "No, that's forbidden, as is active solicitation of votes. Since you were one of the last ones to arrive, perhaps this will assist you." He reached inside his robes and pulled out a sheath of papers. "This is pertinent information on most of the cardinals. It may assist you in making your decision."

"This is official information put out by the Vatican?"

"No, we . . . the cardinals from the First World countries have compiled it." He turned and tumbled out of the room as effortlessly as he had entered.

Cardinal Ryan read through the information. It was biased, to say the least. Some of the dossiers were nothing more than character assassinations. In Washington it would be called good, old-fashioned mudslinging. Why had he expected it to be any different here?

Logan Washburn knew something was going on; he had a sixth sense for picking up the vibrations of discord. Aware that Cardinal Ryan rose at five o'clock every morning, he'd skipped his first cup of coffee and the morning news in order to call him at the rectory at 5:30 A.M.

"This is Ambassador Logan Washburn, I'd like to speak to Cardinal Ryan."

"Cardinal Ryan left for Rome last night," said Father Timothy.

"Rome? What's he done, got himself in trouble with the

pope?" Washburn said jovially, hoping to loosen the priest's tongue.

"He didn't tell me, sir," replied Father Timothy. "You could try to reach him at the Vatican."

Logan hung up the phone; immediately it rang again.

"Logan, did I wake you?" It was John Seaton.

"No, I was just trying to reach Cardinal Ryan."

"Scrap that. We've just been notified that he's in Rome. We'll have to use the other religious leaders we've got lined up. It's a pretty impressive lot; should put an end to those second-coming-of-Christ reports. Anyway, we've got something much more important that requires your talents. Have you seen the news this morning?"

"No, haven't had a chance."

"About an hour ago Japan experienced one of the most devastating earthquakes in its history, a 9.2 on the Richter scale. Seventeen minutes later they had a 7.6 aftershock. The rumors are already flying that they're going to have to liquidate a sizable portion of their foreign assets so they can rebuild."

Logan was quiet for a moment as his thoughts began to crystallize. "The Japanese have deep pockets; this could change the balance of economic and political power. Germany's just been waiting in the wings for something like this to happen," he said.

"That's why the president wants you to address the Unified European Community. All the members have been pressing for a single monetary system with a common currency and a central bank in line with the central banks of Japan and the United States. In the past we've vetoed the idea, but I'm afraid we're going to have to go along with it this time."

Logan let out a low whistle. He knew that the United States had amassed over four trillion dollars in debt. Each year the trade deficit grew larger. The Japanese banks had been the principal lenders, not only to American businesses, but to countries throughout the world. If Japan pulled out now, there would be economic chaos.

"Then we're going to give it our stamp of approval?"

"A gold plated one. The agenda calls for a central banker who will be appointed to handle all the gold and silver reserves. We want that banker to be you."

The plum had fallen into his outstretched palm! Logan knew better than to appear too confident.

"There's an outside chance that I might not be able to pull this off. Then what?"

"We're cashing in all our IOU's. Eventually, there'll be a worldwide redistribution of wealth, and your influence as the central banker may well determine the future of the United States. This will take you from the number three to the number one spot."

So, he knew about that. But why wouldn't he? He was the head of the CIA.

"We're making the travel arrangements now. See you in an hour for a briefing."

Logan leaned back on his bed, and a wicked smile flickered across his aristocratic features. A world banker. Control the money and you control the world. His fingers tingled as an energizing force surged through his limbs. He would spotlight his political genius, he would be the voice of authority in the midst of chaos.

Like a pied piper, he would lead the world into a new age *without* the crutch of religion. He knew the right terminology to throw back into the teeth of those who would oppose him. He would stand on the bedrock belief that all human beings have the right to satisfy their spiritual needs, from the Hare Krishnas to crystal gazers. Spiritual needs, a hot air slogan that would swell until he could deflate it with well-placed darts of doubt and confusion.

He would replace the spiritual with the darker side, the evil that lurked in every man, desiring expression and gratification. His career had skyrocketed in the last few years, a mystery to many, but not to him. If people needed to worship a god, he would become that god. Who was better suited? The world was comprised of unsuspecting sheep, and slowly he would become their shepherd.

As John Seaton, the director of the CIA, had reminded him, the public relations firm he'd hired had done an excellent job. The last poll showed he was more popular than the president, one of the three most admired people in the world. Now it was time to exploit that popularity.

He reached under his shirt and traced the shape of the peace symbol fashioned in gold. The upside down cross seemed to pulse within his palm, growing warmer as he held it. Suddenly it was red hot.

He cursed out loud, dropping the amulet on his undershirt. The smell of smoke filled his nostrils for a moment then was gone. He looked down at his undershirt, the peace symbol was burned into it. Now the medallion was cool to the touch, as cool as the hands of the witch doctor who had placed it around his neck.

As an ambassador he'd visited many countries, but Haiti had to be one of the poorest he'd ever seen. In one of the squalid villages he had been introduced to the witch doctor, an honored, if not feared, member of their community.

When the helicopter that was to pick him up from the village was several days late because of hurricane warnings, the witch doctor had invited him to witness one of the religious ceremonies. At first he'd been frightened, then exhilarated by the actual practice of black magic with its animal sacrifices. He'd been skeptical of the real power of such machinations, but like the riverboat gambler of Mark Twain's day, he knew an extra ace in the hole couldn't hurt. Here was a force he could call upon to help him when he needed it.

Logan Washburn buttoned his shirt. It was his secret. Clothed in the guise of a social mediator, he'd meander in among the sheep, nipping playfully at their heels until the time came when he could reveal himself, and they would discover—too late—that they were surrounded by a pack of hungry wolves.

"Mrs. Eckworth." Faith banged on the farmhouse door.

"You'll wake the dead with all that racket. Now what is it?" She peered through the dirty screen door, then recognized Faith. "Oh it's you, is it?" She crossed her arms in front of her. "Well, what do you want?"

"I wanted to talk to you about the book."

"You mean the book you lost, don't you?"

"Yes."

"I reckon you can come in." Inez Eckworth unlocked the screen door and opened it.

Faith stepped back into the 1950s as she entered the living room with its armless, green nylon sectional couch, the blond coffee table, and a pole lamp with three shiny black enamel shades. Two brass water nymphs held a clock in their arms on the mantel, and books were stacked in a corner by a large overstuffed brown tweed chair in which Mrs. Eckworth, like a princess sitting on a pea, gingerly settled herself.

"Since you lost that book, I've had to do a lot of work, young lady."

"It was an accident."

"So you say. No use arguing about it, it don't change things none." She pointed to the couch that was placed next to her chair. "Sit down. I owe your mom. Since she's not here, guess that means I owe you now. She'd want us to stick together."

Mrs. Eckworth patted the books by her side. "I rounded up these books, all from folks who called themselves religious. Some of them wasn't home, so I helped myself, others gave 'em to me."

"Why did you do that?"

"I want to know what happened. You don't believe those people all just disappeared because of some critter from outer space, do ya?"

Faith laughed, a hollow, nervous laugh. "No, I guess not, but do you really think something or someone came down from heaven and took everyone away?"

Mrs. Eckworth nodded solemnly. "I've been checking it out." She opened the Bible. "Here it is in First Thessalonians, chapter four, verses sixteen and seventeen:

"For the Lord Himself will descend from heaven with a shout, with the voice of an archangel, and with the trumpet of God. And the dead in Christ will rise first. Then we who are alive and remain shall be caught up together with them in the clouds to meet the Lord in the air. And thus we shall always be with the Lord."

"Why didn't *we* see Him?" asked Faith.

"'Cause you have to see Him with your heart not your eyes, girl. Your mom named you Faith, but you sure don't have much of it."

"This . . . sound of a trumpet. I didn't hear anything."

"And why would you? He wasn't coming for you. You can be sure that the ones who was supposed to hear it, did."

"It all seems so incredible. If it's true, why isn't it on the news; why doesn't everyone know?"

"Let me see." She moved her finger over to Second Thessalonians chapter 2, verse eleven. "Here it is."

"And for this reason God will send them strong delusion, that they should believe the lie."

"This is just the start. I ain't got it all straight in my mind yet, but there's gonna be a whole slew of things come about."

She pushed a piece of paper creased in the middle towards Faith. "I listed what's gonna happen on the left and what the Bible says about the future since Jesus came back on the right. You read them verses, then you watch for it to come to pass. That's all the proof you need."

Tears sprung to Faith's eyes. "So—what if it is true? Where does that leave me? My mother and my sister are gone. I'll never see them again!"

Mrs. Eckworth smiled at her, a smile that softened her features, and for a moment Faith realized she must have been beautiful when she was young.

"I've been saving the best part for last. I know how you can see your mother and sister again!"

G ordon Pratt was jumpy and had been since he'd received the call in his office. He parked by the Occoquan Marina as he'd been told to, then walked down the pier with his fishing tackle box in one hand, his rod in the other. He checked the names of the boats as he passed them until he found the *Angler's Retreat*. He stepped on deck, put down his tackle box and rod, then opened the door to the cabin and entered.

The trim, athletic CIA agent, wearing a fishing vest, faded blue jeans, and dirty tennis shoes, turned towards him. "You're early."

"Didn't know how the traffic would be. They still don't have the bugs worked out of those commuter hydrofoils, so I drove. Better early than late," he replied bluntly as they sized up each other.

"The code name for this operation is *Rubicon*," said the agent.

"That's the river Julius Caesar and his army crossed in Italy; it started a civil war." Pratt inhaled the ocean air. "So, what are we up to?"

The agent looked surprised. Maybe this guy wasn't as dumb as he looked. "No questions, Pratt. The director of the CIA, the president, and you and I are the only ones who know about this operation. Let's keep it that way."

Pratt felt himself begin to sweat in spite of the chill October breeze that ruffled the boat's flag. *Easy,* he reminded himself, *you're dealing with the heavyweights. Act like one.* "Affirmative" he said as he lifted his eyes to the shoreline.

Deliberately he moved to the built-in seating area at the back of the cabin, looked casually out of the window, then sat down. "You got any beer in this place?"

The agent narrowed his eyes, opened the small refrigerator, and tossed him a beer. "It's light beer," he remarked as he stared at Pratt's protruding belly.

"Don't let this fool you. When I was on the football team, the other players called me BT, short for block and tackle." He flexed his muscles. "I'll get the job done."

"You need brains for this operation, not brawn. We want you to introduce a virus into the computer system at UCIC. You have access to it?"

"I'm sure you've done your homework," he said disdainfully. "You know I do."

"When we give the order, you'll type in a code word to activate the virus."

"If you don't mind me asking, why do we want to sabotage our own computers?"

"But I do mind, Pratt. You take orders just like I do." The agent opened his briefcase. "I'll show you how to transmit the virus into your data system."

He explained the operation, then prepared to leave. "One more thing." He handed a file to Pratt. "Enter these documents into Randy Morgan's 'Top Secret' file."

After he left, Pratt sat down and opened the folder. As he leafed through it, a wide grin spread across his flushed face. A swear word sailed between his teeth. "I knew that Morgan was up to something."

His Adam's apple danced up and down in perfect cadence with his eyes as he excitedly scanned the pages. "Looks as if Morgan is in for a little game of Russian roulette—with an automatic weapon." His mind reeled at the thought.

With Morgan out of the way, that cute little daughter of his would be all alone. Pratt licked his lips in anticipation. The last time he'd seen her she'd been wearing tight white shorts and one of those halter tops. Like most women he came in contact with, she'd looked right through him when he'd let her go to the parking garage to pick up her father.

After the operation was over, he'd make a point of telling her that her old man was going away—permanently. He could think of a thousand ways to console her.

Gordon Pratt helped himself to another beer and looked back at the shore where the foam was slowly rolling in and out. The tide had turned and it was his turn to ride the crest of the wave.

Randy Morgan rummaged in the back of his desk drawer, searching frantically for the emergency package of cigarettes he'd put there over a year ago. He breathed a sigh of relief when he found it. As his fingers nervously slid up and down the cellophane wrapper, his mind went in a dozen directions.

The transparent wrapper crinkled in his hands as he tore the package open and sat down. He swore under his breath, but the verbal rebuff couldn't stop his old smoking habit from rearing its ugly head.

His ragged emotions finally converged on the one bright spot left in his life. He was glad Faith had gone back to college. It would help keep her mind off what had happened—and off Inez Eckworth, who was filling her head with all kinds of religious tripe.

He slowly took out a cigarette and rolled it between his thumb and forefinger. If only Ruth were here . . .

He'd promised himself he wouldn't think about her, but sometimes late at night he couldn't help himself. Half asleep, he'd forget and roll over in bed and reach for her, longing to feel her body against his. He'd wake up in a cold sweat, and then he'd remember, and the ache would begin.

"I thought you'd stopped smoking," said Falcon as Randy lit up.

"I did."

"This isn't going to help—"

Randy raised his hands in protest. "Look, right now I'm riding a seesaw. Booze on one end, cigarettes on the other. As long as I can keep them in balance, I'll be all right."

"Sooner or later, you're headed for a fall."

Randy took another drag on his cigarette. "Maybe this is my mid-life crisis. I keep telling myself that when all this settles down, I can quit again. Ruth would have a fit if . . ." His voice trailed off into nothingness.

"You're right," said Falcon. "She'd cuss you up one side and down the other."

Randy smiled and shook his head. "Those last couple of weeks, I never heard her swear once. She just gave it up."

"I hope you haven't," said Falcon, casting a glance down the aisle. "Here comes Pratt."

Randy inhaled deeply, purposely gave Gordon Pratt a long look, then put out his cigarette in a styrofoam cup.

As Randy tossed the cup into the wastebasket, Pratt frowned at him, but backed off. He spun around and ran smack into Saundra. Pratt's face turned a deep purple as he wordlessly pushed her aside.

"A real Southern gentleman," said Saundra, giving the departing Pratt an irate look. "Now, where was I? Oh, yes. The elephants are screaming for a final report."

"Don't try to impress us with that Pentagon jargon," said Randy. "You mean it's feeding time at the Washington Zoo."

She bared her white teeth and batted her heavily mascaraed eye-lashes. "We're going to need more than bales of hay for this one. I'm happy to report that we're ready for a scrub-down on the project."

"We've entered 97 percent of the available information," added Falcon.

Randy got to this feet. "Reports will probably trickle in for years, but I'm ready to wind up this thing and go home. I figured we'd be through by Thanksgiving and here it's almost Christmas. Better let me look at the figures one more time."

Just as he'd anticipated, the religious curve had flattened as the data base increased. As far as he was concerned, the results didn't prove there was any single factor connecting those who had been reported missing.

Maybe they'd never know what had happened. A panel of eight religious leaders had issued a statement: "This is the beginning of a cleansing and purifying process for Mother Earth. God is getting rid of the less-enlightened souls so the world can move forward towards peaceful coexistence."

Right.

Although the denominations that comprised the World Church Organization had the same vocabulary, they had radically different dictionaries. Despite this, the panel proposed that the new world order should be led by the majority of countries in their organization.

After a month the initial furor and outrage about the disappearances had died down, and what should have been the story of the decade was relegated to the newspapers' back pages. The news was as stale as the cigarette he'd lit up. Short-term memory, that's what the world had. He didn't.

Even Faith had gotten it into her head that if she became a Christian—whatever that meant—someday she would be reunited with Ruth and Hope. Randy wasn't convinced. The recurring thought that had been beating its wings against the steel bars of his mind returned. Why in the world, if there was a higher being, would He want to involve Himself in the tawdry affairs of mankind? _Heaven knows, we've screwed up everything we've touched,_ he thought.

When he saw Pratt out of the corner of his eye, it only endorsed his premise.

"Good morning, Mr. Morgan. How's the project coming?" Pratt's voice was as well greased as his Adam's apple.

"Why don't you tell me, Pratt?" Randy swiveled in his chair and faced him. "I understand that you were snooping around here last night after everyone else had gone home."

For an instant Pratt's eyes betrayed him, then they were veiled again with arrogance.

"At any intelligence agency there's a constant threat of information leaks. My job entails continuous surveillance and periodic checks of the facilities."

"Leaks in my department? You're starting to believe those CIA manuals you've been reading. I handpicked every person here— except you—and they have the highest security clearance. They're all above suspicion."

"No one is ever above suspicion." Pratt ran his fingers through his crew cut. "No one."

"Spare me the details of your paranoia, Pratt. You do your job, and I'll do mine."

"You can be sure of that," Pratt said smugly as he walked away. "Bloody sure."

Jerusalem was an eclectic city built with pink, amber, and blue-gray weathered stone from the local quarries. Tonight Rabbi Solomon Lowenstein felt a special kinship with the ubiquitous rocks, for he could no more escape the Jerusalem stone than he could his tortured conscience, which hung like a weighty millstone around his neck.

Despite the light snow which had begun to fall, Solomon went to the men's side of the Western Wall at sundown to welcome the Shabbat, as was his custom on Fridays. The area was crowded as usual, but because of Israel's peace treaty with its Arab neighbors, the bus loads of festively dressed Moslems from Hebron, who used to make their way up to the Temple Mount while pious Jews gathered below at the Wall, were gone forever.

He elbowed his way through the black overcoats and placed his hands on one of the mammoth stones of the ancient wall to perform the same ritual that Jewish pilgrims, praying for the redemption of Israel, had performed for years. Here was a symbol of their past and a promise of their future that he could actually touch.

Solomon felt an energy emanate from the grey stone, chipping away at the hardness of his heart and invigorating his arthritic fingers as they inserted a piece of paper between one of the cracks in the wall. It was a prayer that God would forgive him for his part in the death of the American archaeologist.

He ignored the groups of worshipers conducting their own prayer services and the excited young seminary students as they came dancing and singing down to the Wall, rejoicing that the Temple would be completed next month. He sought solace, not company. He moved away from the Wall and deliberated on the changes which were being thrust not only upon himself, but upon Israel.

The prime minister had informed him that the European central bank wanted to locate its headquarters in Jerusalem. After merging with the World Bank, a Middle East location was chosen as a gesture of good faith to the poorer countries of Africa, Asia, and Latin America who needed assurance that there would be no competition from Eastern Europe for loans.

One of its main goals was to immediately establish a single monetary system for the entire world. Because the bank's newly elected leader, Logan Washburn, was responsible for the negotiations which enabled the State of Israel to rebuild the temple on its original site, Washburn knew the Jewish state would approve the request. Like filings drawn to a magnet, the devout and the profane would be lured to Jerusalem. *Once again,* he mused, *the wealth of the world will be at our fingertips.*

His thoughts drifted to the guest who was due to arrive at his home: a new graduate of the Reconstructionist Rabbinical College in Philadelphia—an applicant for one of the many positions at the new temple. It seemed that they must include at least one American in the temple rituals to pacify the Western faction.

It had been his idea to choose a newly ordained rabbi, one who would be like a green twig, pliable and easy to train. To avoid cries of favoritism or bias, the final decision had been reached by a random drawing. So much for tradition.

When he'd finished his prayers, Solomon brushed the snow from his overcoat and leisurely made his way to his home in the Jewish Quarter of the Old City. Because it was the Sabbath, the streets were closed to traffic, allowing him the brief period of solitude he needed to go over the tasks he would assign to the new rabbi.

Solomon had barely crossed the threshold of his house when an agitated Hannah met him.

"The rabbi has arrived—" She wrung her hands together, her dark eyes flitting around the room like alarmed magpies.

"Hannah, he and I will have much to discuss. You may leave now."

"I . . . I don't know that it would be proper for me to leave you two alone."

"What your housekeeper means," said a soft voice behind him, "is that the rabbi is a lady."

Rabbi Lowenstein whirled around and looked at the slightly built woman in a plain black dress. He was unable to speak for a moment. "You're R. B. Greenspan?" he managed to utter.

She extended her hand. "Yes, Rebecca Brenda Greenspan."

What is the world coming to? His mind was in turmoil. For over four thousand years the Jewish heritage had been dominated by men, and now this? His mind could not even explore the ramifications. He had heard that some of the more progressive Jews had decided to ordain women, but only after controversial and acrimonious debates. He disagreed violently; women should have no part in public religious life.

"I was not prepared for this," he said shaking her hand. It felt warm and smooth to his touch.

"You mean prepared for a woman rabbi, don't you? I've heard all the objections before; nevertheless, it's time for the daughters of Judaism to take their rightful place."

"How dare you speak to Rabbi Lowenstein like that!" Hannah said, putting her hand to her mouth. She stepped forward, but Solomon held up his hand and she halted. He had to admit, he admired the young rabbi's spunk.

"Let her speak, Hannah. A new age is dawning, and we must learn to be more tolerant. She has come a long way, and I will at least listen to what she has to say."

"Thank you, Rabbi Lowenstein." Rebecca straightened her shoulders, standing tall and erect before him.

"I'm prepared to serve the Jewish people. I've had six years of studying the Torah, Talmud, codes, Hebrew literature and language, practical rabbinics, history, and Jewish demographics."

"But are the Jewish people prepared for you?" said Solomon. "There is a new spirit of religious tolerance in Jerusalem . . . but still—"

"That's why it's imperative that I assist in the temple worship. It'll show the world that women have been accepted as Jewish leaders on the basis of merit, not gender," she said staunchly.

"A voice crying in the wilderness," he reflected.

"Yes, but until now our cries have fallen on ears that are more attuned to prejudice than to the voice of God."

Maybe it was the blaze of passion in her voice, the all-consuming flame of desire to serve Jehovah, that touched him. The spark that burned brightly in her eyes seemed fanned by the same winds of change that had ignited the embers in his own heart. Silently, he prayed that God would understand.

"Hannah, bring Rabbi Greenspan some food," Solomon said

as he removed his coat. "Even though it's the Sabbath, we have much to discuss."

Hannah Weinberg flounced out of the room. The idea of a woman rabbi staying in Solomon's home was preposterous and unseemly, and she'd make sure that everyone in the community knew it.

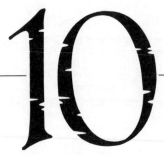

10

Two workmen were gathering up their tools from the Occoquan Bank's drive-up window as Faith counted the money the head teller, Chin Loo, had issued her. Faith had been working at the bank all year to help pay her college tuition.

"Did the drawer break again?" she asked Chin Loo.

"No, they're installing a scanning device." Chin Loo picked up one of the monthly bank statements she was getting ready to mail and handed it to her. Faith's eyes were immediately drawn to the red printing just below the customary Christmas greeting.

> The Occoquan Bank, in its continuing effort to provide better service, is introducing a scanner system which will help complete your transactions more quickly and accurately. In light of recent world events, this extra precaution will prevent access to your account by unauthorized individuals.
>
> In a painless procedure, medical personnel will insert, at our expense, a coded microchip in the palm of each customer's left hand. This will be the only form of identification needed to do business with our bank in the future.
>
> Customer service employees will be happy to answer your inquiries during this transition period and set up appointments at one of our local health care facilities.

The official statement was followed by a telephone number.

"So," said Faith, "how is this going to affect us?"

"It's supposed to make our job easier by cutting down on errors. When a customer passes his hand over the scanner, he'll be able to see his current bank balance on the newly installed monitors."

Chin Loo pulled out a headset with a small video screen attached in front. "You'll see it on this contraption."

"Whose bright idea was this? Let me guess . . . the new CEO of the bank chain."

"Right. He's decided to modernize all our systems. Not only will it cut down on bad checks and fraud, but eventually we can network into the world monetary system." She handed Faith a business card.

"It's mandatory that all employees have a chip inserted within the next ten days at this clinic. Without it, you won't even be able to get in the front door. And you'll need it for access to the safe deposit boxes."

Although there was always a constant stream of a cars at the drive-up window, Faith had been informed that next year the bank would phase out her job. The Occoquan Bank was one of the last institutions in town to have a drive-up window. Automatic teller machines were less expensive to operate, and most employers used electronic transfers to deposit checks directly into their employees' bank accounts. Checks and credit cards were becoming the coin of the realm, not cash.

At nine o'clock, after closing out more Christmas Club accounts than she cared to remember, Faith pulled down the blind. She counted her change drawer, delighted that it balanced the first time. Now she'd have time to go to the grocery store. Computer shopping was great *if* you didn't forget anything.

She stood in line at the supermarket, mentally calculating her total to see if she had enough money to pay for the dozen cans of cat food she'd put in her cart. She was surprised by a tap on her shoulder.

"Faith, how have you been?"

"Dr. Bradley, I'm . . . doing fine, I guess."

"I hope that's not what you're having for Christmas dinner," he said peering into her basket.

"No," she laughed. "We have a very large cat named Thomas

who at this moment is probably howling in the driveway because I'm not home to feed him. What are you doing here?"

From under his arm he pulled out the boxed pizza he'd chosen from the deli section. "Dinner. I just finished working at the clinic next door inserting microchip ID's." He winked at her. "Don't believe everything you hear about doctors' salaries; we can always use a few extra bucks, especially when a bank is footing the bill."

She pulled a card out of her purse. "The Hansel Clinic?"

He looked over her shoulder as he tried to stifle a yawn.

"That's the one."

"I guess I'll be seeing you next week. I'm one of the bank's employees."

His face broke into a grin. "Why not get it over with tonight? It's quick; the entire procedure takes thirty seconds, max."

"You don't mean *now?*" she said as she put the cat food on the counter.

"Sure, the clinic is just around the corner. I'll even share my pizza with you when we're through."

"Your frequent shopper card, please," said the clerk as the total appeared.

"I don't have a card, I'll just pay cash."

"We don't accept cash at this register."

"Just put it on my card," said Stephen as he handed it and the pizza to the clerk.

"Oh, no, I couldn't—"

"Don't argue," he said, looking back at the long line of people, "unless you want us and your cat to starve."

When they reached the clinic, Stephen unlocked the door and turned on the light. Faith felt a chill come over her as she trailed behind Stephen into the room; its antiseptic smell reminded her vividly of the abortion clinic.

"Hey, it's not going to be that bad," Stephen said as he saw the fear in her large blue-green eyes. He indicated the chair facing him and she sat down, her face the color of a broken eggshell.

"I'm a little nervous, I've always hated getting shots."

"This is a snap, trust me. Now take off your coat."

He pushed his glasses back on his nose. "Now what's your social security number?"

She repeated it, and he unlocked a drawer and searched through the stack of envelopes until he found the correct microchip.

The blood drained from her face as Stephen washed his hands, put on rubber gloves, and reached into the drawer for a needlelike device. Her haunted thoughts brought it all back. Her legs in the stirrups, the glaring light overhead, and the excruciating pain. She pressed her legs together.

"Relax," he said, "I haven't lost a patient yet. Now give me your left hand." It was clammy to his touch, and he hesitated as he noticed her chalky face and the line of perspiration on her upper lip.

"Faith, we can wait if you're not up to this."

"No, let's get it over with."

She squeezed her eyes shut as he cleaned her palm with alcohol. She felt a pinprick.

"That's it."

"Oh," she said as she opened her eyes and let out her breath. She looked at her hand. "I can't see it."

"But you can feel it."

She traced the outline of her palm until she felt the small bump beneath her skin.

"The chip is only as big as a pencil tip, and its made of nontoxic materials. It's sealed in biocompatible glass so it shouldn't cause any skin irritation or infection. If you do have any adverse reaction, let me know. I guess we could say that you've got the equivalent of a modern-day tattoo."

"You're looking better," he said a few minutes later as the color began to return to her face. "You had me worried for a minute. I thought you might faint."

"Morgan women don't faint," she said with a laugh. "But they are allowed to swoon on occasion. Now, how about some of that pizza?"

He took off his gloves, reached into the drawer, and pulled out a scalpel.

Her eyes widened in mock terror. "Just what did you have in mind, Doctor?"

"Please, call me Stephen."

He opened the pizza box and adroitly cut the pizza into neat slices, licking the sauce off the scalpel when he was through. He handed her a piece. "Now, tell me how its been going since—"

"Since Hope and my mom disappeared." She kicked off her shoes and tucked her feet underneath her.

"Well, I'm not sure that I've been able to accept the fact that they're really gone." She lifted a round piece of pepperoni off her slice and popped it into her mouth.

"You know, when I first tried to analyze the whole thing it just didn't make sense. It seems as if everyone has their own version of the truth." She began to recite softly:

"Truth forever on the scaffold, Wrong forever on the throne,— Yet that scaffold sways the future, and, behind the dim unknown, Standeth God within the shadow, keeping watch above his own."

"James Russell Lowell!" Stephen smiled at her appreciatively and scratched his head for a minute to awaken his memory:

"Once to every man and nation comes the moment to decide, In the strife of Truth with Falsehood, for the good or evil side."

"Why you continue to surprise me, doctor." She countered:

"New occasions teach new duties: Time makes ancient good uncouth: They must upward still, and onward, who would keep abreast of Truth."

"Your turn," she said.

"You just heard the sum of what I learned in English Lit. Now, if you want to know all the bones in the human anatomy from the anklebone to the zygomatic bone, I'm your man."

"Practicality triumphs over philosophy." Faith gave him a timid smile. Suddenly she had a new perspective—and perhaps an ally.

"Stephen, do you believe all those disappearances were just by chance?"

It was the first time she'd called him Stephen, and he rewarded her with a radiant smile which melted away the ten-year difference in their ages.

"I don't know what to believe, so like most people, I've just put the whole thing on the back burner to simmer."

"But aren't you curious? Don't you want to know what happened?"

"I have a feeling that you're going to tell me."

"Yes, but only if you want me to."

"Well, you're the professor. State your case."

She reached for her purse and pulled out a notebook and a small Bible. "I've written down all the Old and New Testament Scriptures I could find about the Lord's return and the events which are supposed to happen after that. Do you know anything about Bible prophecy?"

"You mean that end of the world stuff? I'm afraid I missed that part. I've never been an outstanding member of the Episcopal church. Before we go any further, can I ask you a question?"

"Sure."

"Am I going to have time to finish this pizza before the Lord returns?" Laugh lines played around his eyes as he picked up a slice and began eating at the point of the triangle, savoring each bit as he went.

"Stephen, you're not taking me seriously."

He wiped his mouth. "I took an oath in medical school to never be serious while I'm eating pizza, but for you I'll make an exception."

She took a deep breath, meticulously flipping through her mind like a Rolodex before she plunged ahead.

"I've found countless verses in the Bible which indicate Jesus will return to earth one day. I think that's just what happened the night everyone disappeared. He took those who believed in Him—including my mother and Hope—and they returned to heaven."

"And for some reason we didn't get invited to the party?"

"I think everyone got an invitation, Stephen, but somewhere along the line we said no."

"That leaves us in a predicament, doesn't it?"

"We still have a choice." She reached across the desk and turned over a prescription pad. She drew a straight line, then divided it in half.

"This line represents seven years. During the first three and a half years, which started the day everyone disappeared, we'll have world peace, more or less. In fact, one person will be chosen by all the countries to be the leader. He'll be the Antichrist, a man chosen by Satan."

"Satan? You mean the one with the horns and a tail?"

"He's much more sophisticated now than that, but yes. A chain of events was set in motion when the Arabs agreed to allow the rebuilding of the Jewish temple in Israel. It's been in all the newspapers; the dedication is right after New Year's Day.

"After the first three and a half years, the Antichrist will somehow break the treaty with the Jews and place himself on the throne and declare that he's God. That's when a time of tribulation unlike anything the world has ever seen will begin. It's recorded in the last book of the Bible, the Book of Revelation. I'm just getting to that part."

Stephen's interest was stirred. "And the choice you talked about, Professor Morgan?"

"I've already made it. Based on all the evidence, I believe that Jesus Christ is the Son of God and that He died for my sins. I've committed my life to Him." Faith gnawed on her bottom lip. "That decision could cost me my life."

He looked at her beautiful face, and he knew she believed fervently every word she was saying. He was skeptical, but her sincerity made him wonder. Was it really impossible?

Stephen had been brought up to believe in God when he was a child, but he'd outgrown those beliefs and tucked them away in his parent's attic, along with the model spaceships he'd painstakingly built and the collection of toy robots he used to play with.

Yet there were times in the operating room when patients who had actually died came back radiant and well and told him that they'd seen a bright light at the end of a long tunnel.

And there was Mr. Simmons, a man with a cancerous mass in his brain. In three months the mass had disappeared altogether.

"The Lord healed me," Mr. Simmons had said jubilantly.

"Here." Faith handed him the Bible. "In the front cover I've listed the Scriptures I've been talking about. After you've read them, we can discuss them."

Stephen laid the Bible on the desk, then took her hands in his own. "Faith, I can't say that I agree with what you've just told me about Christ coming back, but I'm willing to think about it."

"Believe me, I understand," she said. "A month ago if anyone had told me this, I'd have thought they were crazy."

He tapped his fingers on the cover of the Bible. "Give me some time to try and digest all of this."

Faith felt a gentle nudge from within herself to tell him everything. Her past had been forgiven; she no longer had to hide it. "Stephen, I want to be totally honest with you. I'm not even sure why."

"I think I know why." He bent down and kissed her lightly on the lips. "You're a strange one, Faith Morgan, but I'm beginning to like you."

Tears sprang to her eyes as his sympathetic eyes studied her, and she turned away. "You don't really know anything about me. If you did, you might not feel this way. Until recently, the only emotion I've felt is fear, ever since—"

"Ever since, what?" he said tenderly.

She turned and looked at him again. "Ever since I was raped." There, she'd said it. She saw the look of concern in his eyes, and he reached for her, but she stepped back. She wasn't ready to be consoled.

"I'm sorry, Faith. So sorry."

She swallowed and looked away. "I had to have an abortion. No one knew but Hope."

"You never told your parents?"

"How could I?" she whispered. "I felt so dirty, as if maybe I did something to cause it all to happen."

"No! You were a victim." He put his hands on her shoulders, then tilted her face up towards his. "Did they get the man who did this to you?"

"No, I never saw his face, so what good would it have done to go to the police? Sometimes I wonder even now if he isn't watching me—if he won't try again."

When he heard the quiver in Faith's voice and saw the pain and anguish on her face, Stephen, who'd known since he was ten years old that he wanted to be a doctor, felt an unfamiliar emotion emerge, blotting out the Hippocratic oath he'd taken.

He wanted to kill the man who had raped Faith.

Instead, he drew her to him, and she didn't resist. He felt her body shudder as she began to sob in his arms.

"I thought if I didn't talk about it, the pain would go away. It didn't. Hope was the only one I could confide in, and she's gone," she said in a muffled voice.

"You've got me now," he heard himself say.

He didn't know how long they stood there, clinging together before he forced himself to ask her the questions he knew he must.

"Faith, did you have a doctor check you after it happened?"

"Not right away. I went to the public health clinic across town about two months later when I thought I might be pregnant." She pulled away from him. "Why?"

"Did you have any kind of medical follow-up after the abortion?"

"No, I didn't have any complications—physical ones, that is." She dropped her head into her hands. "Oh, Stephen, the doctor, the nurses, everyone said that I should have an abortion." Her tortured eyes met his. "Hope tried to talk me out of it, but I wouldn't listen. Now I can't get it out of my mind. There isn't a day that goes by that I don't wonder what the baby would have looked like, what it could have become. How can one incident change your whole life?"

She smiled through her tears. "But last night after I released my life into God's hands, I felt a sense of peace about it for the first time since it happened. This year I'll be celebrating Christmas for all the right reasons. I've still got some things to work out, but with His help, I will. Yet, I'll always wonder if—"

Stephen clasped both her hands together in his, trying to infuse his strength into hers. "You did what you thought was right at the time. Don't make yourself feel miserable and guilty by re-hashing something you're powerless to change." He released her hands and paced the floor for a minute to readjust his thinking.

"I want to arrange for you to have a complete medical examination by one of my colleagues."

"But why? I feel fine."

He spoke calmly. He didn't want to frighten her. "There is always the possibility that this man had some disease that you might have contracted from him. It could take years to show up."

Her face turned scarlet. "You mean sexually transmitted diseases, don't you?"

He nodded, then tried to reassure her as he put his arm around her. "Most can be cured by antibiotics if they're detected early enough; even if we don't have a cure, we can halt their progression." He looked into her eyes.

"Tell you what, Professor Morgan, I'll share my medical expertise with you in exchange for your knowledge of Biblical prophecy."

He gave her that lopsided grin of his. "Is it a deal?"

"You might regret this, Dr. Bradley." She stood on her tiptoes and kissed him on the cheek. "But it's a deal."

11

I t was December 28, 2010, and after three months of bickering, the ninety-nine weary members of the conclave were
about to cast another vote. Cardinal Ryan didn't know
whether the cardinal who'd nominated him on the last ballot
wanted to split the vote and thus shorten—or would it lengthen
the electoral process? No matter, he was so shocked at his nomi-
nation that he'd kept his eyes on the table, unable to meet the
glances of the other cardinals as they silently dismissed his candi-
dacy.

Cardinal Ryan placed the white card on the table in front of
him and folded his roughened hands over it. He let his eyes sweep
upward to the magnificent vaulted ceiling of the Sistine Chapel
where hundreds of figures were painted in a celebration of human
beauty and energy. The frescoes had been restored in the 1990s,
and the hues were so vibrant that it was easy for him to imagine
that the stormy and sensitive Michelangelo had just finished his
last stroke and laid his wet brushes aside.

In the center of the vault, he explored God's gesture to Adam as
the Creator floated through time and space, extending His index
finger. Was Adam's face full of eagerness or resignation as he
tilted his head and stretched out his forefinger to accept the flow
of life and with it the responsibilities he would assume as the father of mankind?

Responsibilities . . .

He let his gaze drop back to the white card. The upper half

was printed with the words, "I choose as supreme pontiff." The lower half was blank, waiting for his decision.

He wrote down his choice and folded the card in half. Perhaps this time they would have the majority they needed for the election of a new pope, and tomorrow they could escape the stringent confines of the Vatican.

As Cardinal Ryan walked down the aisle to cast his vote, he was thankful he didn't have a chance of being selected. God would surely give His chosen a sign of some kind. He had faith in himself and his abilities, but now in the presence of the One who controlled the unknown, he felt submerged in the depths of a mindless think tank. For that reason alone he felt certain he was not qualified to lead the church or fill the shoes of the Fisherman. Still, the mental debate continued.

He raised his eyes, and before him on the altar wall he saw Michelangelo's violent depiction of the Last Judgment. The wall seemed to come alive as he watched the swirling mass of bodies, part of them ascending to Heaven at the sound of the last trumpet, the others tumbling into the jaws of Hell.

His eyes were drawn to the tormented figure of a man, a poor soul with his arms crossed and a hand over one eye to shield it from the sight of Hades. The other eye stared straight at . . . him! He felt the hairs on his neck stand on end.

The man made no attempt to resist the grinning demons as they wrapped themselves around his legs to drag him to his fate, but as the cardinal watched, a shiny spot appeared in the corner of the anguished man's eye, then a tear formed and slowly slid down his cheek.

This couldn't be happening! Cardinal Ryan blinked his eyes several times, then looked back at the dismal, haunted face. The tear was gone.

Bewildered, he lowered his gaze to the bottom of the fresco where the damned souls, who were being ferried to Hell, huddled together in a boat. Suddenly, his ears were filled with their terror-stricken voices. He jerked his head forward and a blood-curdling scream ripped through his head. Alarmed by the unearthly cries, he clapped his hands over his ears.

"Your Eminence, are you all right?"

The noise stopped.

He looked up at the concerned face of the cardinal.

"Forgive me, I was overcome—"

He felt a weight on his shoulders as he tried to rise, and suddenly he thought of Moses. He could envision him as he stood barefoot in front of the burning bush on Mount Horeb, shaking and faltering in disbelief, unable to comprehend the monumental task God had given him.

Fearful, Moses shouted in the face of God, "Who am I, that I should go unto Pharaoh and that I should bring forth the children of Israel out of Egypt?"

"Certainly I will be with thee," replied a mighty voice from the fiery bush which burned, yet was not consumed.

Then, as now, God's chosen were not always willing.

Cardinal Ryan rose from his knees; there was a tremor in his voice as he pronounced aloud the oath they all repeated when they cast their vote: "I call to witness Christ, the Lord, who will be my judge that my vote is given to the one who, before God, I consider should be elected."

On the altar was a chalice with a plate on it. He put his card on the plate; his hand shook as he tipped it into the cup.

Shaken, he made his way back to his seat. He could feel the tension mount throughout the room as the other cardinals went forward to place their cards in the chalice.

He watched as the cards were mixed in the chalice. The cardinal with the sympathetic face counted them in full view of everyone to make sure there were ninety-nine cards, placing them in another goblet as he did so. He turned and gave the ballots, still in the chalice, to one of the three cardinals who had been chosen by lot to count them.

Cardinal Bertollini picked up a card, wrote down the name of the candidate, then passed it to the second counter who did the same. As he passed it to the third cardinal, an expectant hush fell upon the room. He wrote down the name on his sheet, then announced the candidate's name in a loud voice: "Cardinal Sergio Rossi."

Good, they've come to their senses, finally. Cardinal Ryan tried to relax as the slow process continued.

He thought back to that morning when, in full robes with the other cardinals, he'd proceeded from the Pauline to the Sistine

Chapel. They'd had to wait while the pope's casket was removed to one of the large reception halls where tomorrow, New Year's Day, the faithful would begin to file past.

Once they were all inside the chapel, the thick door was locked behind them. Was he supposed to be impressed by the age-old rituals carried out with such pomp and circumstance? He wasn't. He was tired of a church which deferred to its hierarchy and to people in high positions, while bypassing the more important issues.

Although discussion and dissent were on the rise, the Catholic church clung to the past and stated that its teachings were inviolate and clear; they could be neither questioned nor modified.

When would it realize that it needed a more relevant doctrine, a modernized church for the many minorities it embraced, especially in Third World countries? The time had come to voice questions about the main issue which continued to divide the church: the papal ban on contraception.

"Cardinal Mark Ryan."

He winced as he heard his name read. The men who voted for him were wasting their ballots. Most of the cardinals were in their sixties and seventies; anyone over eighty wasn't eligible to vote. He scrutinized the elderly faces around him.

Which ones had actually voted for him, but more importantly, why?

The American delegation had no power or influence. What possible advantage would any of them gain if he were elected?

"Cardinal Eugenio Palermo."

That was more like it. Cardinal Palermo was his personal choice. He was a good man, complex and progressive, but not afraid to make tough decisions.

The chairs were so close together around the long tables that as Cardinal Ryan shifted in his, he could smell the sweat emanating from the cardinal next to him. The building with its overactive heating system and broken air conditioning was as archaic as the Catholic church. All of them were hot, uncomfortable, and tired. It seemed ridiculous that under these primitive conditions they would choose the next person to lead the Catholic Church.

Most of the cardinals believed that the Holy Spirit was active at the conclave, working through the humans beings who were doing the electing. That one fact made the whole business tolerable. Somehow, the right person could be chosen in spite of the antiquated conditions and personalities involved. Or could he?

Mark Ryan leaned back and looked again at the awesome and overpowering frescoes on the ceiling. How ironic that this masterpiece of world art was painted against the artist's will; Michelangelo had been furious that his work as a sculptor had been interrupted.

Cardinal Ryan sighed. It would all be over soon; perhaps by tomorrow he could catch a plane back to Washington, D.C., where his thoughts and his eyes didn't play tricks on him. He wanted to inhale the invigorating air of freedom again, shake off the pious and rigid formalities that the Vatican imposed upon him. Piety was a virtue that he did not possess.

"That's ridiculous!" said Randy.

"Keep your voice down." Falcon looked over his shoulder at the other diners in the Chinese restaurant who had gathered for a New Year's Eve celebration. He skillfully maneuvered his chopsticks and brought the last shrimp to his mouth. Falcon held one of the chopsticks in the air and whispered, "This could be one of those high-tech bugging devices."

"Now you're beginning to sound like Pratt."

Falcon took the extra bowl of fluffy rice he'd received with his meal and dumped it onto the middle of his empty plate.

"This," he said pointing to the mound of rice "is the intelligence community. And this," he said, extracting a single white grain with his fingers, "is you." He popped the granule into his mouth, then smacked his lips.

"That is what they're going to do to you, my friend. Eat you alive." He pointed to the remaining rice. "And no one will even miss you, with the exception of yours truly."

The waiter interrupted their conversation by presenting them with the bill and two fortune cookies on a small bright blue and orange plate.

"But why?" asked Randy as the waiter left with his credit card.

"Who would alter my folder to make it look like I'm a double

agent. Double agents are endangered species like the bald eagle
or the Florida panther."

The beeper on Randy's pager sounded—the light was red.
"Now what?" He excused himself and called his office at UCIC.
Saundra answered.

"Randy, you better get down here fast. Something is wrong
with the computer system." Saundra hesitated for a moment.
"The data banks are empty."

"Empty!"

"You heard me. Empty. Gone. Erased! Even the backup system. We've lost all the data from the project we just finished. If
we can't retrieve it, we'll have to reenter it."

"We can't, we shredded everything. Orders from the CIA."

"How could this have happened? You, Falcon, and the head of
the CIA are the only ones who have access to the backup system.
You don't think Falcon—"

"No, I don't."

She was silent for a minute. "Why would anyone want to tam-
per with the report? Its findings were inconclusive."

Randy hated what he was thinking. "Are you by yourself?"

"I saw Pratt's car in the parking area when I came in, but he's
nowhere around now. You don't think he had anything to do
with it, do you? Granted, the guy's a creep, but I don't think he's
got the guts or knowledge to mastermind something like this."

"Falcon and I are leaving now. Stick around until we get there."

There was a sad, yet wild look in Randy's eyes as he returned
to the table. The last time Falcon had seen that look, it had been
on his kid sister's face the morning after his high school gradua-
tion. She'd discovered him drunk and reeling in his own vomit
on the front steps.

"That was Saundra," Randy said in a harsh whisper. "All the
material we compiled—gone, erased from the data banks. Everything!"

Falcon drew in his breath sharply. "Now it makes sense. You'll
be blamed for scuttling the study, and the government can fabricate findings to support any slant on the disappearances they
want."

"They'll want you and Saundra to back them up—or else. You

know the scenario, just jump on the bandwagon and you'll probably be made head of the department." Randy's jaw twitched.

"I'm the distraction. The American public will be so busy feeding on me, they won't notice the shark fins circling the boat."

"The government's been convinced for years that the average citizen doesn't want or need to know the whole truth," said Falcon. "If he did, he might cause a ripple effect that could get in the way of the politicians."

Swiftly, Randy's mind changed gears. "You go see Saundra. Explain the situation. Faith and I have to get away—tonight."

"If we stick together, we can fight this, Randy."

"With what? I'm no hero, Falcon. I'm a forty-six-year old," he reached down and pinched the extra flesh around his middle, "out-of-shape desk jockey. Someone pretty high up wanted me to take the hit. In this game you've got to know when to stand up and fight and when to run. It's sheer luck Saundra decided to work late tonight to cross-reference the files, or I would have been left holding the bag when I walked in the day after tomorrow." He looked at his watch.

"That means I've got . . . a thirty-six hour head start before they know I'm onto them."

"Who did the CIA get to?" said Falcon.

"Pratt!" they echoed simultaneously.

"The perfect android," said Randy. "Push-button reflexes, minus reason or remorse."

"Forget him. We've got to concentrate on getting you out of here—to a place where they can't find you."

Randy's mind bounced the possibilities back and forth. "Some place illogical. I've got it! Israel. It's in chaos, bursting at the seams with all the new immigrants. It would be easy for Faith and me to get lost in the influx of people."

His eyes brightened. "Housing is critical and the government wants to jump-start construction to build state housing. I can bang in a nail as well as anyone else. Maybe some of those families I met when I was doing my research on the last survivors of the Holocaust can give us a place to stay temporarily."

"But what about the future? You're not a construction worker."

"At this point I don't have a future." Randy rolled the piece of paper that he'd taken out of the crushed fortune cookie between the palms of his hands. "Better a live construction worker than a dead agent."

"I've got some contacts even the CIA doesn't know about. I'll do everything I can to help you."

"It'll be risky, Falcon."

"Would you have walked away if they'd chosen me as the fall guy?"

There was no need for words, they both knew the answer.

"They'll be watching you like a hawk, but not for a few days," said Randy. "Maybe we can pull this off."

He unrolled the white piece of paper in his hand. With a grimace on his face, he read it aloud: "Now is the time to seize the new opportunities and horizons which appear in your future."

12

Clouds of white smoke billowed around the chimney atop the Sistine Chapel, and the people gathered in the piazza below cheered wildly.

"Attenzione," blared the public address system in the piazza. An uneasy hush came over the holiday crowd as they focused their attention on the big door above the balcony of St. Peter's. The door swung open and a cross-bearer came out, then one of the cardinals in his red hat. He raised his hands and spoke to the throng in Latin, then English.

"We have a pope."

The people began to shout, but as the cardinal raised his hands again, they quickly fell silent. They waited for him to announce the name of the new pope.

"Cardinal Mark Ryan."

The reporters from Washington, Los Angeles, and New York broke from the crowd and scattered for the phones and fax machines. An American pope! It was unheard of in the history of the Roman Catholic church. They thumbed through the biographies the church had given them, drafting their copy on their laptop computers, then transmitting it to their waiting editors.

"This one was a dark horse," said a high-strung Irish correspondent to his editor on the phone. "Came out of nowhere, he did. There's been speculation that he was a compromise candidate. Someone who could satisfy the Italians and be acceptable to the foreigners. From his bio, I'd say social justice is his angle.

"I never thought I'd live to see the day an American was elected pope. Heaven help him," the reporter crossed himself, "'cause he's gonna need it . . . and a good bottle of Irish whiskey."

Randy ripped the "For Sale" sign out of the lawn and stuffed it into the shrubs. With his car parked in the driveway, the vacant house looked like any other in his neighborhood, and no one would know that the car was out of place. He began the two-block walk to his home, slipping in and out of the pools of darkness, avoiding the houses which were still decorated with outdoor Christmas lights, despite the ban. He was glad now that his neighbors—in their quest to retain the country atmosphere— had voted against installing street lights.

He inspected his sleeping house from behind a tree across the road. He squinted at his watch. It was eleven thirty. It would be close. They'd have to break all the speed limits if they wanted to make it to New York for their flight.

Forged passports awaited them there, compliments of Falcon's contact. They were booked on a nonstop flight from New York to Israel under the same fictitious names that would be on their passports.

He hadn't been in the field for years, but instantly all of his senses were alert as he circled his house and skirted the back yard. Why was the sliding glass door ajar? A red flag went up in his mind while prickles of fear shot through his body.

Suddenly the backyard spotlights went on, blinding him.

"Welcome home, Mr. Morgan."

He tried to shield his eyes with his right hand, then saw the blurry outline of Pratt through his fingers.

"Faith and I have been waiting for you."

Faith! What had Pratt done to her?

"If you've hurt her Pratt, I'll kill you!" He advanced towards him, saw the gun in his hand, and stopped.

"Now why would I want to do that?" He licked his lips. "I have plans for her. For the crimes of espionage, you'll be locked up for life, and Faith will need someone to look after her. I'm applying for the position." He glared at Randy. "Any objections?"

The thought sent waves of revulsion through Randy and without thinking, he lunged forward. Pratt brought the gun down on his head. Everything went black as he hit the patio bricks.

A sharp kick to his groin brought him back to his senses.

"Get up," said Pratt. "I promised Faith I wouldn't kill you. I'll take you back to stand trial. She wants to say good-bye to you and after that—"

Randy could see the lust in Pratt's eyes. He forced himself to remain calm. Their lives depended on it.

"Get inside," said Pratt in a thick voice.

Randy stumbled through the door, and Pratt waved him towards Faith's bedroom.

The frightened eyes of a trapped rabbit stared back at Randy from the bed. Faith's hands were handcuffed behind her back, her nightgown was twisted around her waist.

"Did he hurt you?" he made himself ask.

"No, he just—"

"I didn't do any more than what she's done with some of her boyfriends, did I, sweetheart? Just exploring the territory before I stake my claim."

How Randy hated him! He had to keep him talking until he could find a way to overpower him.

"What do you want Pratt? If it's money, I'll get it for you."

"What I want is lying in that bed." His voice grew harsher.

"You always thought I wasn't smart enough to be at UCIC, didn't you? Yeah, I know you tried to get me thrown out. Now what was it you said? 'Pratt has a passion for the mundane and meaningless.' I did get that right, didn't I, Mr. Morgan?"

Randy tried to appease him. "I could have been wrong—"

"You were dead wrong. And speaking of dead, you'll be charged with killing Saundra. That broad started yelling at me, calling me every name in the book. Underestimated me, just like you did."

He shifted the gun to his left hand and picked up an elongated Lladro figurine of a peasant girl from the nightstand. He broke it with a large crunch. "That's what it sounded like when I broke her neck," he said, grinding the blue and grey porcelain fragments into the carpet.

Randy swallowed hard and tried to keep the anger out of his voice. "Who's behind this Pratt?"

"You're the genius; you figure it out. Whoever it is, they realize I can handle any assignment they give me." He sneered at Randy.

"Enough small talk. I can kill you here or take you back—" He looked at Faith whose eyes were filled with tears. "What's it going to be?"

"Oh Dad," wailed Faith.

Suddenly there was a large crash in the living room.

Startled, Pratt took a few steps backward. In one swift movement, Randy crouched down and tackled Pratt's knees, knocking him off balance. He slammed his opponent to the floor and pinned him. Pratt let out a chain of curses as the gun slipped from his hand. He tried to sit up, but as he lurched forward, Randy grabbed his right arm, and with a strength he didn't know he had, jammed it backwards until he heard a snap, followed by a howl of pain from Pratt.

Still on his knees, Randy grasped the bedside telephone while Pratt tried to scramble to his feet, his useless arm by his side. Randy brought the telephone down on Pratt's head, then wrapped the phone cord around his scrawny neck, freezing his Adam's apple into position.

"Don't Dad, don't!" screamed Faith as Pratt's face turned red and he choked for air, his legs and good arm flailing at his attacker. Randy couldn't help himself, he was beyond reason. He felt the sweat pour down his back as he pulled the cord tighter, a vision of Saundra's face before him.

He heard a voice like a faraway train in a tunnel, getting louder and louder, until it finally exploded in his ears.

"No, Dad. Don't kill him!"

He looked at Pratt. His jaw was slack; he'd passed out. Slowly, he looked down at his hands where the snakelike cord was biting into them, causing red welts.

Trembling, he released the phone line and brought it over Pratt's head. He rolled him over on his stomach, yanked Pratt's good arm behind him, and with the long extension cord tied a loop down and around both of Pratt's feet. He pulled it as tight as he could and tied it into a secure knot. Pratt looked like a trussed up turkey.

"Dad, it isn't true, is it?" Faith's face was as white as her night-gown.

"I'll explain everything later. We have to get out of here right away." He searched Pratt's pockets and removed the bills and credit cards, putting them in his own billfold. Extracting a silver key from a handful of change he'd taken, he sat down on the bed to unlock Faith's handcuffs.

She clung to him, her head buried in the hollow of his shoulder.

"I'd give anything if I could have prevented this, honey."

"But why—"

"Just do as I tell you, and no questions." He stood up, went to her closet, and got a suitcase. He placed it on the bed and opened it.

"Pack only the things you'll really need. We won't be coming back. Now, hurry. I'll check on that noise in the living room."

Not coming back! He left the room and Faith began throwing her things into the suitcase; she was too frightened to do anything else. She looked at Pratt and shuddered as she remembered his probing fingers touching her body.

Randy cautiously made his way to the living room, took the butane lighter out of his pocket and flicked it on. The small Christmas tree they'd set on top of the television was lying on the floor with its lights blinking. Thomas, covered with tinsel, came out from under the couch, meowing piteously.

"Thomas, this is one time I'm not going to read you the Riot Act." Relieved, he went to his bedroom and quickly packed a canvas gym bag, then returned to Faith's room. "Are you ready?"

She nodded. They went out of the sliding glass door with Thomas following them.

"Oh, Dad, what about Thomas?"

"We'll have to leave him."

"Can I take him to Mrs. Eckworth?"

She looked so forlorn that, against his better judgment, he agreed. "All right, but circle behind the house and cut through the field. Don't let anyone see you." He took her suitcase. "I'll meet you at the next corner. Hurry!"

Faith cradled Thomas against her red wool sweater and ran to-wards the old farmhouse. As if to announce her arrival, a sizzling bolt of lightning split the sky, revealing thick clouds scudding across the heavens.

She banged on the door until a sleepy Mrs. Eckworth in a flannel nightgown answered.

"Mrs. Eckworth, I'm sorry to bother you, but can you keep Thomas? I don't know when we'll be back."

"You're leaving right now, in the middle of the night?"

Faith nodded, not trusting herself to say any more as the rain began to pelt on the tin roof of the farmhouse.

"I reckon I can take care of him. Mind you, it's been a long time since there's been a male in this house." She opened the door and Faith handed Thomas to her, then kissed a surprised Mrs. Eckworth on the cheek. Just as suddenly as she had appeared, Faith disappeared into the drizzly night, along with the distance sounds of noisemakers and firecrackers as the world welcomed in the new year.

Inez Eckworth put the cat down and peered into the night as a great sadness enveloped her. "Lord, help that child. There's evil afoot, I can feel it in my bones. Evil let loose to roam . . ."

Logan Washburn stood up to address the group of leaders who comprised the European central bank. He cleared his throat and waited until all the members gave him their attention before he began.

"Russia has presented us with massive bills. Although the fifteen Soviet republics are now independent, capitalism and a free market system have not been able to salvage their crumbling economy. They hold us responsible."

Several members nodded their heads in agreement. Logan knew he would have to tread a fine line; he'd have to appear tough, yet flexible, so he could better negotiate for the good of all concerned.

Judah Midian stood up. With the dark, handsome features of his mother, a Jewess, and the cunning eyes of his Palestian father, he was a striking figure. He had been educated in the best schools in the United States and his relaxed stance with this group of influential personalities proved that he felt at ease with both Western and Middle Eastern cultures.

"The chairman recognizes Judah Midian," said Logan.

"Thank you, Mr. Chairman."

Logan realized that Judah was an oddity in this land; nevertheless, he was the perfect blend for the group he was addressing, and a tangible symbol of the coexistence which could prevail. He had a charismatic personality and was a brilliant diplomat. Until three months ago, he had been a stray thread in the tapestry of Jewish-Arab politics.

After the peace treaty, he'd risen to prominence displaying a superhuman wisdom that both nations applauded. Grudgingly, even Logan had to admit that he had met his equal in Judah Midian.

"We should not give in to the demands of the Russians," Judah said. "These natural disasters have ravaged every economy in the world. Our initial agreement when we formed this bank was to limit loans to the amount of capital a country contributed to the bank.

"The Russians and Chinese have already received that amount. China professes democracy, but it does not practice it. I suspect that any future funds we give them will be used to corner the commodities market. Then they will give the Third World countries a choice: starvation or domination. Either way, this would threaten the truce which now exists among the nations."

In a gesture of peace and supplication, he spread his hands, palms up, in front of him. "In order for reason and justice to prevail, all of us are going to have to . . ." he searched for the words, "stand fast. We have a fragile peace, we *must* preserve it."

One member rose immediately to disagree. "In all fairness, let's remember that Russia has allowed over two million Jews to return to Israel. Many of them are teachers, engineers, architects, and university graduates."

"I'm not so sure they're all Jews. They look more like militants than rabbis and technicians," said Judah. "It's a wise move on the part of the Russians—less mouths to feed, and they can keep an eye on the pulse of the world by using these . . . 'refugees.' "

Logan had to agree. Many of the so-called Russian Jews seemed more interested in eavesdropping than praying. It was almost as if they were a silent invasion force, just waiting for the right moment to attack.

He surveyed the banquet room in the National Convention Center, their interim headquarters until the new building for the European central bank was completed. The waiter who'd brought in the coffee earlier looked like one of the displaced persons they'd been discussing. No doubt any decisions they made would be common knowledge on the streets before they even left the building.

"Are we ready for a vote?" asked Logan as he looked around the table.

It was seven to three against the loan.

"Gentleman, we stand adjourned. Remember, next Thursday we are all to be guests of the State of Israel at the dedication of their new temple."

Most of the travelers who'd made a pilgrimage to the Holy City for Christmas had departed, so after the meeting Logan decided to walk back to his room at the King David Hotel in the heart of West Jerusalem instead of taking the shuttle service. He relished the thought of a cocktail before dinner on the terrace overlooking the gardens. There he would plan his next strategic move.

"Mr. Washburn," said a deep voice behind him as he strolled under the arches to the entrance.

He slowed his pace, and the voice caught up with him. "Could I speak to you in private?"

Logan turned. Judah Midian's hypnotic eyes were on his. Was it only the sun's reflection that formed a nimbus around Judah's head? A steady warmth began to radiate from the necklace hidden under Logan's shirt. He put his right hand to his chest, and in that split-second Logan's and Judah's stained souls were fused together until the end of time.

13

Where was Faith? Randy looked at his watch—it had been ten minutes. All because of that stupid cat!

A light drizzle began to fall. Would he have time to insert the side windows in his car and pull up the leather top from the hollow space behind the bucket seats before—

Then he saw her through the filmy windshield, a slim figure coming towards the intersection, her head craned forward as she searched for him. He turned on the wipers and the headlights as he pulled out of the driveway into the road.

Another car was slowly coming in the opposite direction—without its lights on. In the misty rain, he'd almost missed seeing its somber hulk. His heart began to pound like a jackhammer. Maybe it was just a coincidence . . .

He flashed his headlights and drove across the intersection as Faith ran to meet him. She opened the door and got in, just as the other car began to weave across the center line. It was headed straight for them.

"Hang on!" he shouted as he gunned the engine.

The other car's headlights came on suddenly, blinding him as he turned the wheel sharply to the right and ran up over the curb. Faith screamed, then he heard the crunch of metal on metal as the car side-swiped his door. Before it spun off to his left, his photographic memory identified one of the passengers as a CIA agent. How long had they been tailing him?

He pulled off the curb, then heard the squeal of tires as the other vehicle made a "U" turn behind him. He caught a quick glimpse of Faith scrunched in her seat.

"Are you all right?" he cried into the wind as it lashed his face with rain.

"I . . . I think so," Faith stammered.

The bewildered expression on her face spurred him on. He headed for the freeway, seesawing back and forth in the street, looking in his rearview mirror at the nondescript car in pursuit, the perfect stereotype of an undercover vehicle. For a split second he felt as if he were trapped in an old Clint Eastwood movie, but the shot which rang out was definitely from the twenty-first century.

"Faith, keep your head down!"

A spurt of adrenaline pressed his foot all the way to the floor, and his damp hair flew madly in the wind while the red sports car accelerated to 100 MPH as he entered the northbound lane of the freeway.

He checked his side mirrors but didn't slow down; they had to make it to New York. It was past midnight, but there was a steady stream of cars. He meshed between the vehicles, hoping they would provide some protection.

About two hundred yards ahead, he saw the ominous dark sedan enter the freeway and pull into the fast lane, slowing down as it located its prey. The cars behind it honked impatiently, then switched lanes. Suddenly an arm was thrust out of the sedan's window, followed by the silhouette of a head.

Randy saw the red dot from a gun's laser beam on the windshield. He ducked, and two shots rang out. The windshield shattered. He stuck his head out of the side window and swerved to the left, slid across the grassy median, and in a matter of seconds was headed south.

In his rearview mirror he saw the sedan try to follow. It entered the southbound lane and cut in front of a tractor trailer. He heard the sickening screech of tires as the truck driver braked on the rain-slicked pavement; he saw the huge rig crash into the black sedan, sending it skidding down the pavement end over end like a twisted Slinky.

Randy was soaking wet and suddenly felt incredibly tired; it was an effort to even breathe. He kept seeing double images of the white lines on the road. A warm blanket of nausea warned him that he was going to pass out. He fought it, sucking in the cold night air with shuddering gulps.

"Dad, you're hit!" screamed Faith as she stared at the growing blood stain on his white shirt.

He felt himself ebbing away. He tried to lift his foot off the accelerator; it wouldn't obey. With his last ounce of strength he pulled over to the emergency lane and hit the brakes. The car lurched to a stop on the gravel. Randy slumped over the wheel as bright orange and red pinwheels of light exploded in his brain, then there was nothing but murky darkness.

"Dad!" shrieked Faith. *Oh, God, what do I do now?* A doctor. She had to get him to a doctor. She opened her door and got out, reached over to the driver's seat and tried to drag her father to the passenger's side. The gearshift kept getting in her way. She put her arms under her father's armpits and in a final heroic effort managed to lift him into the passenger seat. Panting, she put her hand under his nose to see if he was still breathing.

"Oh, God, don't let him die, please don't let him die!" She thought of the men who'd been following them. Had they perished in the crash? A car whizzed past, spraying her with a sheet of water. It didn't matter, nothing did, except her father.

She slid into the driver's seat and turned the ignition key. The engine whined at her, then sputtered and died. Her wet bulky sweater clung to her as she pumped the accelerator desperately. With a jerk, the engine finally roared to life.

The hospital . . . Stephen.

She plunged into the flow of traffic and took the first exit as an unmarked police car with red lights flashing barreled past her on its way to the accident. She slowed down. Should she go to the police?

Pratt—she cringed as she thought of him—had said her father was a double agent. She speeded up again. How could her father, a man who built nesting boxes for bluebirds and purple martins in his spare time, be a spy? It was preposterous . . . but then, what were they running away from? Her thoughts, along with the rain, turned into a torrential downpour as she pulled up to the Emergency Room at Quantico Memorial Hospital.

She rushed into the waiting room and recognized the back of

Stephen's head in one of the treatment cubicles. She pushed back the dripping hair from her face. "Stephen!"

He turned towards her.

"My father—he's been shot!"

The Russian president was livid as he spoke to the leaders of the republics. "Every member of the European central bank knows that without economic aid our country can no longer survive. Last month the European Community met in Luxembourg and canceled a $50 billion technical aid package they'd promised us. Now they have vetoed our loan request. We have had enough! We are in worse shape than we were before the republics declared their independence from Moscow. Money and time are in short supply after twenty years of doing things to appease the West. We have to retaliate."

"Let's not forget what happened when Iraq got greedy," said the president of one of the Baltic republics.

"Unlike Iraq, we do not underestimate our enemies. The United Arab Coalition will insure our success."

"If we are such good friends with the Arabs, why are our people starving? To paraphrase an Americna cliché, 'Let them put their money where our mouth is.'"

"They will. After we help them defeat Israel."

"I do not trust the Chinese," said the acting leader of the council.

"We do not need trust, we need massive manpower. We'll take our cue from our mutual enemy, Israel. We'll attack without warning and with such strength that we will utterly defeat them. It will be a one day war."

"One day!"

"The Jews actually believe that the Peace of Jerusalem has arrived because they've completed a temple to their god." The president chuckled. "They should know that a leopard cannot change its spots. The treaty was just a stall tactic to lull Israel into a false sense of security and draw millions of them back to their homeland."

On a gigantic world map, he pointed to the ring of nations surrounding the Middle East. "Egypt, Lebanon, Syria, and Jordan will cross Israel's borders at sunset on Friday, the beginning of the Jewish holy day. With the Chinese, we will form the main invasion force from the north. We will literally forge a noose that will stangle Israel." He smiled as he pictured the havoc. "We can back them into the Mediterranean Sea if they resist.

"Our attack will be carried out with such stealth and speed they'll never know what hit them—just as the Czechs were surprised years ago. Strategic military positions are already targeted for destruction by our advance teams in Israel."

He patted his chief military adviser on the back. "Russian Marshal Yuri Valdimer's plan is brilliant. The first wave of the invasion will be on horseback, ancient tactics coupled with hand-held rocket launchers."

"The element of surprise will insure our success," said Marshal Valdimer. "Next, helicopters and tanks will swarm over the country, crushing all resistance."

Pinned on his olive-brown uniform with red piping were ten rows of decorations with a gleaming gold star perched above them. He reached up and touched one of the large gold stars on his left epaulet. "This will replace the Star of David. We want the land, its resources and ports intact; nuclear weapons will be our last resort. By the time the world awakens, we will be victorious." He rubbed his hands together in anticipation before he continued.

"As in the past, the United Nations will lodge a formal protest, but they will not risk a nuclear holocaust in order to liberate Israel." He slammed his pointer down on the conference table.

"Our policy of glasnost plunged the world into massive disarmament, and it turned the Russian bear into nothing more than a . . . tattered, hollow-bellied teddy bear. Israel will become our 'peace dividend,' and we will sharpen our claws on its defeat and resume our rightful place in the new world order." He picked his teeth nervously.

"Negotiations will be initiated using every avenue of diplomacy, but an occupied Israel will be in no position to bargain. We will have respected the world's desire for peace by a swift and complete victory without the use of nuclear weapons or lethal gas. Then the European central bank, which represents the nations of the world, will come begging to us for assistance."

"They will be grateful that Israel's resources are in our capable hands," said a Russian parliamentarian. "Jewish people have always been troublesome, a boil on the seat of history. That such an insignificant nation should cause such turmoil is ridiculous. Their dogmatic belief in a personal god has made them vulnerable. It is their weakness."

"And their strength," said the Russian president. "A man will fight for what he believes in—for the dirt under his fingernails to be his own." He paused a moment, thinking of the father he'd never known, buried somewhere in Afghanistan. No longer could Russia afford the wages of extended warfare. "A single thrust to the heart and it will be over."

"Comrades," said Yuri, as he raised his vodka glass, "to victory!" He downed the contents in one gulp, then took another to ease the dryness in his throat. If only he could rid himself as easily of the malignant premonition which stalked his conscience.

The radiologist shoved the portable X-ray machine out of his way and rushed down the hall to develop the X-rays of Randy Morgan's chest.

"Let's get an intravenous drip started and draw for type and cross," said Dr. Bradley as he put an oxygen mask over Randy's face. A nurse drew the blood in a large syringe, then began putting it into vials with red, purple, and blue tops for the lab.

Stephen tore away Randy's blood-soaked shirt and inspected the penetrating wound. With his stethoscope he listened for the breath sounds. They were absent on the left side, and he noticed that the breastbone had shifted to the right side, another indication of a collapsed lung.

Quickly he slapped an occlusive dressing on the bullet wound to prevent air from entering, then ran his fingers down the nipple line. He made a stab wound between the ribs and inserted a tube into Randy's chest so he could hook up the Pleura-Vac, a chest drainage system, to re-expand the lungs.

As he suspected, the X-rays revealed a bullet had gone in at an angle, puncturing Randy's left lung and lodging in his spine.

"Who's on call for neuro?" he asked the nurse.

"Dr. Scudder."

"Call him, get us a suite, and bring in the O.R. team."

Stephen had assisted Dr. Scudder several times; he had complete faith in his mentor, who'd helped him decide to specialize in pediatric neurosurgery.

"Sorry," she said a few minute later as she put down the phone, "Dr. Scudder's in surgery at Fairfax Hospital. You're on your own."

With the shortage of surgeons, there was no alternative. Stephen changed into clean scrubs. He passed his hands under the low-powered ruby laser which instantly sanitized them, replacing the old ten-minute washing ritual. As another member of the operating team pushed open the door, he reminded himself that he was skating on the thin ice of ethics; all gunshot wounds had to be reported promptly to the police.

In operating room number three, a nurse helped him put on his blue surgical gown while he rechecked the X-rays. Removing a bullet from the spine—it was one of those uncertain operations with no guarantee of success.

The anesthesiologist nodded to let him know the patient was under. As he made the first incision with his gleaming scalpel, Stephen tried to forget the tragic look in Faith's eyes as they had wheeled her father into surgery, but to no avail.

Faith couldn't bear to stay in the familiar waiting room. The boldly colored walls, torn magazines, and impersonal furniture flooded her mind with recollections of Hope's accident. Her nerves were stretched to the breaking point. "I'll be back—later," she shouted too loudly at the charge nurse.

With compassionate eyes the nurse watched Faith streak down the hall and through the Emergency Room doors to the outside. The rain had abated, but she was too overwrought to notice a sky full of twinkling stars.

The car! She'd forgotten that it was still parked in front of the hospital. Just how difficult was it to spot a 1958 red MGA? Hastily, she got in the car and drove round the corner to the hospital parking garage, grabbed a ticket from the automated dispenser, and made several loops to the top deck.

She got out and opened the trunk. Good. The tarp her father

used to cover the MGA in bad weather was still there. Faith threw it over the car, then took the elevator down to the first level and walked through the covered crosswalk which came out on the second floor corridor of the hospital.

With her heart pounding, she walked along the hall, averting her eyes from the curious stares of the hospital personnel. She came to the door marked *Interfaith Chapel* and stopped. How many times, when Hope was in the hospital, had she hurried by, never giving the chapel a second thought? Now she felt an urgency to enter. She pushed open the swinging door.

In the subdued lighting Faith viewed the miniature sanctuary; three rows of oak pews set on each side of a thick blue carpet led to the altar. Wearily she slipped into the back pew, savoring the solitude and tranquillity which enveloped her; for some reason she felt like she'd come home.

The street lights illuminated the two stained-glass windows that cast a soft multicolored radiance throughout the chapel. She shivered in her wet clothing. She picked up the Bible at the end of the bench, gently caressing it between her shaky hands before she opened it at random, hoping to find some fragment of comfort.

Because of the beautiful poetry, some of the Psalms had been required reading in one of her high school English classes, but she'd never thought of the Bible as a book of history or prophecy . . . until the last few weeks.

Faith pushed the matted hair out of her eyes and her breathing became slower, more even, as she absorbed the words.

"Well, Lord," she whispered, "you say here that you don't look on the outward appearance, but the heart."

She laughed gently and the lump in her stomach began to dissolve. "It's a good thing, because I know I really look a mess. But you know my heart, and if sincerity counts for anything—"

Her father's pallid face flashed before her eyes.

"Please don't let my dad die. Not before—" Her throat constricted as she wiped away her tears, "not before I can tell him about You."

She twisted a strand of hair around her fingers. "I hope you don't mind me talking to You like this, but I don't know any other way." Her voice quavered. "I read in one of the books Mrs. Eckworth gave me that there are over three hundred verses in the Bible that tell about Your return, and yet I never knew—"

Faith closed her eyes and saw the face of her mother, praying. A great shudder racked her body.

"Why . . . why am I a part of this?" she said to the empty pews. She sat there for a long time until her eyes began to close and her head nodded, jarring her awake. A muscle cramped as she tried to straighten the leg she'd tucked under her. She stood up and gently flexed her leg back and forth, then hobbled over to the window.

"I guess You don't have to sleep," she said, looking at the mosaic figure of Jesus in the window. She gingerly touched Jesus' outstretched hands with her own. "Take care of things for me, will You?"

Faith Morgan wasn't sure why, but she felt better. She took off her muddy tennis shoes, curled up on the hard bench, and fell asleep in the chapel, swaddled safely in the arms of her newfound faith.

14

Rabbi Solomon Lowenstein ran his fingertips lightly over the stones which formed the rock wall in front of his home. He swung open the iron gates and noticed with delight the freshly swept walkway and the pots filled with herbs on each side of the front door. The fragrant aroma of baked bread met him as he entered the living room.

The table was set for the Sabbath, and not since before Esther's death had his humble dwelling looked so elegant. He looked at the symbols of the holy day: the twisted loaves of bread, the burning candles, and the platter of stuffed fish which Rebecca placed on the white tablecloth.

"The rabbi is also a cook?" he asked softly.

"I couldn't stand another day of Hannah's cooking." Rebecca blushed and for the first time his old eyes saw a crack in her armor of defiance.

"I sent her home. You're not angry, are you?"

"Angry? No, I'm relieved," Solomon said as he sat down at the table, facing the window which overlooked the rock garden where, after the first frost, Hannah had removed the summer-flowering plants. Now in the dull winter twilight, only the ever-green shrubs met his gaze.

Solomon broke the bread and put a piece of it on her plate. "Please sit down so we can celebrate the Sabbath together." He cleared his throat. "Hannah means well, it is just—"

"Hannah might as well be here if we continue to talk about her."

[115]

He stroked his beard. "Your point is well taken. What shall we discuss?"

"What else but the temple? To think that I will actually take part in its dedication next week," she said as she served the fish. "I have you to thank for that. If you had not voiced your approval—"

He could do no less. Solomon had seen her passion and commitment, witnessed her unbridled zeal for God in the last month. This blurring of the lines. If she had been what he expected, a bearded man in a long black coat with gray earlocks which curled down his cheeks, he would have readily embraced her as a brother in the faith.

A fragment of a verse in the book of Esther gnawed at him: "who knoweth whether thou art come to the kingdom for such a time as this?"

Some days he almost believed that he had escaped the straitjacket of his prejudices. Now was the time to tell her.

"Rebecca, as you know, God did not allow Esther and me to have any children." He saw the creases appear on her forehead, the uneasiness in her eyes. He folded his hands in front of him and looked directly at her.

"That is . . . until now."

It took her a moment to realize what he meant, then the color rushed to her cheeks. "Rabbi Lowenstein—I—" She tried to speak again but stumbled on the words. "You wouldn't have— liked me as a child. I was very sensitive and shy, the one who always seemed to fade away into the corner."

"And as a child I was very cautious," said Solomon. "I was the truthmonger, always wanting to know the exact truth. I was popular with the rabbis, but not with my classmates." He put his fork down. "We both have grown up. Perhaps God in His infinite wisdom has allowed me in my old age to have a daughter in the faith, and you a father." He reached for her hand, held it in his own. "Miracles do happen. Isn't the temple proof of that?"

She nodded, overcome with emotion, while an apricot sun began to disappear on the horizon, heralding the beginning of another Sabbath.

As he poured the wine into the silver goblets, Solomon heard the rumbling of thunder in the distance. Strange. He hadn't noticed any clouds.

Rebecca took a sip of wine and her dark eyes glistened in the candlelight. "Isn't it exciting? Israel is once again the heart of the Jewish nation. We're no longer a scattered people, but a united people in our own homeland. For the first time in centuries, we don't have to live in fear. Terrorist attacks are a thing of the past, and women and children can laugh in the streets as they rejoice at their good fortune."

"Yes," said Solomon, "I noticed today that many of the walls around the city have been torn down and new orchards and fields planted."

"Oh, Solomon," she squeezed his hand, "it's been such a long time since the Jews have known peace—real peace—that sometimes at night when I'm alone, doubt creeps in under the covers . . . and I think that maybe it won't last."

"God will continue his grace towards Israel," said Solomon. "It is our time. No longer will the world be able to label us the 'Wandering Jews.'"

A blast of cold air rattled the open window and blew across the dining room table, bringing with it the rumbling Solomon had heard earlier, but now it sounded like the earth was being pounded with a thousand angry fists. "I'll close the window," he said.

As he pulled the casement towards him, he looked beyond the rock garden to where immense brown clouds of dust, whirling over the countryside, were plainly visible on the darkening skyline.

"A wind precedes the rain," he said. "A thunderstorm must be on the way."

How was he to know that it was the horror of war unleashed on horseback?

Judah Midian squinted at the clouds of dust which swirled across the horizon. As the long spikes of sunset spread across the lush Jezre'el Valley, he stood with the binoculars around his neck on one of the lookout points on Megidda. Three major arterial roads crossed the valley following the contours of a natural pass, and at the mouth of each path, where it joined the Jezre'el Valley, stood a city. Megidda, where thirty-five centuries of history had been uncovered by archaeological excavations, was the city at the end of the central road.

Judah wasn't sure why, but ever since he'd been brought to Megidda as a child by his mother, he'd been fascinated with the place. Maybe it had been her vivid tales of the battles fought in this place throughout history, from the time ancient Egyptians and Israelites were pitted against each other to the defeat of the Turks and Germans in 1919 by the British. Even now he could imagine the clash of arms, but—perhaps it was something more. He'd heard the American tourists describe this place as Armageddon, the site of ultimate battle.

Judah looked to the north at what appeared at first to be a long line of black ants, slowly surging forward across the plains in the deepening gloom. He readjusted his binoculars and gradually the swarming figures grew until he could make them out. Horses, more than he'd ever seen at one time. Thousands of them—with riders!

An electric current, brought on not by terror but by foreknowledge, tore through his body. With a heavy thud the binoculars fell to his chest. He didn't have to look again. He'd recognized the Russian and Chinese uniforms and the familiar turbans of the Arabs.

The temple! The people would flee to it, and he had to be ready to lead them. Wasn't he the Chosen One? He raced to his car, jumped in, and sped down the road. Behind him he could hear the thin high wail of a woman, then shrieks amid the throbbing sounds of hoofs which surged forward like the sea at high tide.

The buildings behind him swayed and toppled. He slammed on the brakes as the road buckled in front of him, and the earthquake rumbled on its maddening course. An uprooted tree came crashing to the ground just inches from him. He felt one of its branches scrape across his face as he bypassed the unheaval in the earth. He had to get back to Jerusalem.

He drove like a madman, swerving to miss the boulders in the road, ignoring the cries of those trapped in the rubble. Outside Jerusalem, hordes of hysterical people blocked the roads. He abandoned the car to join them as they pushed their way towards the temple area.

"It's the Chinese," shouted one group.

"No, the Arabs," howled an irate merchant. "We should never have trusted those dogs of Mohammed."

"They will take the airport next, we are trapped," yelled a

butcher waving a knife in the air. "They already have the coastline along the Mediterranean."

"We will fight," said a youth.

"No," his mother screamed. "They will kill everyone who opposes them. What good is a dead Jew?"

"They have broken international laws. They signed a peace pact," said a stalwart student of the Talmud. "The world will come to our rescue."

"How will they know? The Russian Jews have destroyed all lines of communication."

"There are millions of armed men! What can we do?" lamented an elderly rabbi. "I knew it was too good to be true!" He spotted Judah in the crowd and pointed an accusing finger at him.

"What shall we do, Judah? Use your wisdom now to help us defeat our enemies before they spill our blood on the temple steps and kill us all. You said God would protect us."

Judah climbed the steps and pushed his way through the fear-stricken crowd. He raised his hands to the darkening skies, and their cries fell to a murmur. "Oh, Great Jehovah, show these Your chosen people that I am their redeemer by raining upon our enemies pestilence and death so they may know that I am the Chosen One."

He could hear the low roar of tanks in the distance, the shots of automatic weapons, and still he stood on the steps of the temple as the others in horror fled through the streets, trying to avoid the approaching army. He feared no one. The power was his.

The screams of pain and death did not send chills up his spine; on the contrary, they were the first notes of the rhapsody which would eventually underscore his advent. Despite the icy rain that began to fall, he stood there, drenched, his arms uplifted, waiting for his answer, not from heaven, but from hell.

The name Cardinal Mark Ryan was gone forever like a paper cup which had served its purpose and had been discarded. Officially he was Pope Timothy I, a title he'd chosen when he'd read II Timothy, chapter 1, verse 9: "Who has saved us and called us with a holy calling, not according to our works, but according to His own purpose and grace which was given us in Christ Jesus before time began."

In a few hours it would be dawn, and the Vatican would awaken like an old man, wheezing and rubbing its stiffened joints, moving slowly through its routine. Garbed in his new papal robes and duties, Pope Timothy I would enter a unique phase of his commitment to the Catholic church.

The pope looked at himself in the full-length mirror and saw a large, powerful stranger. His robes, like the thin layer of gold applied to the mirror, covered a multitude of sins. He expected someone to come in at any moment and tell him that it was all a mistake.

For some reason the Vatican actually thought that because of his past association with Ambassador Logan Washburn, he would be able to influence him to release funds from the European central bank to many of the Third World countries which were predominantly Catholic. To his chagrin, he hadn't been informed of that point until after the election.

He shook his head. "Did God choose me?" he said out loud to the reflection in the mirror. There was no answer. It makes no difference, he convinced himself as he straightened his finery. Whether it was God or greed, he was the pope, and he was entitled to some answers.

He had to know how the former pope really died. Now.

Rarely was he ever left to himself. Always a group of advisors or cardinals prowled his four-room apartment, and the reporters were often in the corridors beyond. He hadn't slept all night for the question, like a festering splinter, had abscessed his mind. He left his desk and stepped into the hall.

He held his breath, then laughed at himself. He had no need to skulk around in the semidarkness—he was the pope. Still, he could trust no one in this matter.

He continued along the hallway, down the stairways until he reached the reception area where mourners were allowed to view the closed casket of the former pope from six in the morning until midnight.

The two Swiss guards in their helmets and swashbuckling uniforms designed by Michelangelo snapped to attention as he approached.

"I would like to be alone to pray for his soul."

It was the new pope's first request, and the Swiss guards, after a glance at each other, did as he asked. They were well aware that the Vatican was an independent state, and as such the pope possessed full legislative, executive, judicial, and military powers here. They were his to command.

As their steps receded, the pope put his hands on the casket and bowed his head. The white candles on either side of the casket flickered in the darkness as slowly he tried to shove the coffin lid aside. The eerie sound of chalk on slate screeched through the night. He held his breath. When no footsteps sounded in the corridor, he leaned over and looked inside the casket.

He couldn't make out what was inside, so he slid his hand in, touching the soft fur of the ermine blanket which covered the pope. He closed his eyes and his fingers explored the soft outline of a body, then the purple veil which shrouded the pope's face. Maybe he'd been wrong after all.

He had to be sure. He reached over and took a candle from the lampstand and held it over his head so he could see inside the casket. He pushed the ermine blanket aside.

He'd been right!

A body of flour sacks. Three fifty-pound sacks of flour.

Pope Timothy didn't feel the hot wax searing his fingers as he replaced the candle. He put his shoulder to the casket lid and pushed it back into place. This time it didn't protest, there was no reason to. It had already given up its secret.

Russian Marshall Yuri Valdimer watched his advancing armies from his position on the hillside of the Jezre'el Valley. It was dark, but by the light of the quarter moon he could see the tanks moving. By now, the first wave of horses would be in Jerusalem.

He pulled the wool coat tightly around himself as the rains began, mentally making a note to reprimand the meteorologist. He may not have been able to predict the damnable earthquake, but nothing short of incompetence could be his excuse for not forecasting the rain which battered the invading armies.

The rains increased; suddenly he felt something hit him sharply on the head and neck, something hard and icy. The other officers shouted curses as they ran for cover. He put his hand to his neck and, drawing his hand back, saw a glob of ice, sticky with his own blood. He hurried inside the stone house.

"You're hurt, Yuri," said one of his aides as he rushed forward with a towel.

He brushed him aside. "It is nothing. What is a hailstorm compared to the winters in Russia, eh comrade?" He looked at the core of men surrounding him.

"If I were a religious man, I would say that the God of Israel is upset with us. But since we all know there is no god, we will use this panic provided by the forces of nature to assist us in our victory. Confusion in the enemy is always advantageous."

As if the storm agreed with him, the hail pelted the roof so loudly he had to cover his ears. All at once, part of the roof crashed in and the men raced for the door, barely making it outside before the entire roof collapsed.

Like a pack of frightened jackals, they ran under a tree, trying to shield themselves from the frozen balls of ice which were now six inches across. Two officers dashed for the side of the hill, and Yuri followed the glow of their flashlights as he ran across the grass and into the cave they'd discovered. Just as he took cover, another earthquake ripped through the valley. Even from inside the cave he could hear blood-curdling yells and cries as enormous boulders rolled down the hills, crushing tanks and men in their deadly path.

15

Someone pounded on the door. Pope Timothy lifted his head from his desk. He must have fallen asleep. He stood up and a shaft of light fell across him; the sun was high in the sky.

"Enter," he said.

"Your Supreme Pontiff," said the aging cardinal, wringing his hands together as if he were in pain, "Russia and her allies have attacked Israel! You must make a statement immediately!"

He put his head in his hands. *Why, why have I been chosen for such a time as this?*

He sighed. "Bring me the reports from the Vatican news office and send someone to brief me on them."

He splashed some water on his face and combed his hair as he tried to prepare himself for the ordeal ahead.

"I have tried to put the facts together in a logical arrangement," said the priest from the newsroom, his voice quavering. He'd only recently been assigned to the Vatican because of his command of English, and he was visibly awed by the presence of the pope.

"Not that you couldn't have put them together yourself—"

The pope leaned back in his chair and closed his eyes. "Father Paul, begin at the beginning."

"You mean you don't want to read the reports?"

"I assume you have already done that. I expect you to summarize what has happened."

"Yes, sir."

Behind his closed lids, he could hear Father Paul shuffle the papers, then he began in a strained voice, like a schoolboy giving an oral book report in front of a classroom.

"Last night Russia, China, and the Arab Coalition attacked Israel at sundown." He cleared his throat. "The invaders were on horseback, followed by tanks and helicopters. This attack was a blatant violation of the recent treaty they'd signed." He paused.

"And?"

"There were a series of . . . some say . . . supernatural events, things that can't be explained." The pope could hear the excitement in the priest's voice.

"First an earthquake followed by giant hailstones—but the skies were clear—and part of the invasion force was killed. Tanks and horses were bogged down in the mud and . . ." He stopped momentarily to catch his breath.

"Please continue," urged the pope as he sat forward in his chair, his eyes still closed.

"The helicopters crashed!"

"So, Israel did have a chance to retaliate?"

"No, sir. The Israelis were completely surprised. It was the locusts. A swarm of locusts flew into the helicopter blades."

He opened his eyes. "At night?"

Father Paul nodded.

"Everything but fire and brimstone."

"Well, Your Holiness, some people said that fire and rocks blazed through the heavens," said the wide-eyed priest.

"And what was the outcome of this . . . invasion?"

Father Paul looked down at the paper in his hand. "These reports haven't been verified by us, but eyewitnesses say that the invading soldiers were so confused they killed each other by mistake. They thought they were under attack by the Israelis. Estimates are that only 15 percent of the attack force survived."

"And the Israelis?"

"Some casualties, of course, but they've taken captive or routed what's left of the hostile forces."

"I see. You're telling me that in less than twelve hours Israel has completely vanquished her would-be captors and conquered her enemies?"

"It looks to me, if I might take the liberty, Your Holiness, as if they had some help from . . . outside sources. Heavenly sources."

The pope was thoughtful for a moment. "The things which are impossible with men are possible with God."

"Then it was a miracle, wasn't it?"

"A miracle? Sometimes God does intervene into the affairs of man. At this point . . . well, I would not classify it as a miracle yet. Some might see a correlation—"

He saw the shadows of doubt fall on Father Paul's features.

"Personally, I don't believe in coincidences, I believe in predestination," the pope said.

A smile broke across the priest's eager face. "Is there anything else I can do for you, Your Holiness?"

"No. Thank you for your report. Keep me informed."

Pope Timothy mulled over the events after Father Paul left. He refused breakfast, and his lunch he left untouched on the table as he waded through the bulletins Father Paul fed to him.

God had intervened. It was a sign, the sign he'd been waiting for. The Arab Coalition had been the main dissenters when a plan had been introduced to headquarter the World Church in Rome. Now they were defeated. The proposal could become a reality.

He knew the rumors that would soon be flying in the Vatican. What was it a rabbi had told him once? A rumor in Jerusalem during the day usually becomes a fact by nightfall. Maybe it would be the same in Rome.

Who would head the World Church? A man they could respect . . . perhaps the leader of the Roman Catholic church.

No doubt Israel would be occupied with rebuilding. Then they would enjoy the spoils of war, conquering the oil-rich lands and the ports of Iraq, Kuwait, and Saudi Arabia. No one would protest. The Russian agnostics had failed, and already China was denouncing their actions, stating that only a small faction of rebel Chinese had joined forces with them.

With the Russian and Arab countries under control, they could merge all religions into one, laying the framework for a single world church that would fulfill all of man's hopes and dreams— during his lifetime.

The voices of experience and prudence whispered to him that this was too good to be true. He tried to silence the voices, but the realist inside him argued that utopia could never be achieved this side of the grave. He could only wait and see.

Marshall Yuri Valdimer crept through the fields, his leather boots caked with mud, his soul caked with defeat. What did it matter now that his once-immaculate uniform was torn and blood stained, that the stars on his epaulets had been ripped off by his aide so he could slink out of Israel like a snake on its belly?

He hated himself because he was still alive. Tears streamed down his cheeks as he saw the bodies of his soldiers, lying like broken matchsticks over the muddy fields of Israel. He could not return to Russia.

Quickly, he made the final decision of his life. He almost envied the Israelis and their god. If he could believe that there was life after death . . . but he couldn't, not even now when death was imminent. He'd die as he'd lived—an atheist.

A thought skyrocketed through his gloom. What if he'd been wrong all his life?

He drew the gun from his holster, put it to his head, and fired. Now he knew the answer, but it was too late.

"Faith, wake up."

Faith stirred in her sleep and opened her eyes, blinking at the face above her until it came into focus.

With a jolt it all came back to her. She sat up in the pew, her heart racing. "Is my father all right?"

Stephen smiled his slow, reassuring smile and sat down by her. "I think I got the bullet out without damaging the spinal cord, but we won't know until the swelling goes down. If everything went well, the feeling in his legs will gradually come back."

She buried her face in Stephen's chest and he held her, stroking her tangled hair as she sobbed.

"Tell me what happened," he said.

"Someone tried to kill us. If they find out we're here . . . you won't say anything to the police will you, at least not until I can talk to my dad?" she pleaded. "Please."

"Why would anyone want to kill you?"

"I'm not sure, but it's got something to do with the CIA."

"Maybe you better start at the beginning."

She looked up at him sheepishly. "You want to know everything?"

"I think you owe it to me, don't you?"

"Yes, you're right. I didn't mean to be ungrateful . . ." Faith kept her eyes downcast. She told him about the wild chase on the freeway, and haltingly she told him about Pratt—she didn't mention his probing fingers.

"All right," Stephen said, measuring his words, "I'll admit your father to the hospital under a false name until we can get to the bottom of this."

"Stephen, I can't go home. Could I stay in Dad's room?"

He nodded, surprised that he wasn't thinking about her father, just the fact that he'd get to see her every day.

"I'll get a cot for you."

All at once, life seemed very complicated.

"Faith, remember those books and verses you gave me to read?"

"Yes. Have you had a chance to read them?"

"Not everything, but there was something in one of the books about Russia invading Israel. Well . . . it's happened."

"When?"

"Yesterday. I don't know all the details but the attempt failed. Mother Nature rebelled, and Russia, China, and the Arab Coalition have been left with only a handful of their original forces. All Israel has to do is pick up the pieces. They'll probably become the stabilizing influence for the oil-producing countries in the Middle East."

Faith clutched his hand. "Don't you see, Stephen, what the Bible says is true. You have to believe now, before it's too late."

Did he? Stephen felt as if he were balanced on the brink of a cliff and events were slowly but surely pushing him over the edge. In a world gone wild, what difference could his decision make in the scheme of things? He didn't know, but he had a feeling he was about to find out.

★   ★   ★

The Israeli prime minister put a handkerchief over his nose. The stench of decaying bodies overwhelmed his senses. Even now, days after the attack, he couldn't believe his eyes.

They had given up trying to estimate the number of dead—it was in the millions. Corpses, like the crimson leaves of autumn, littered the landscape. In some places they were so numerous that not a blade of grass nor a clump of dirt could be seen beneath them.

The sky was black with scavenging birds that cartwheeled through the blue canopy, making touch-and-go landings as they ate their fill of rotting carcasses. They were joined by carnivorous animals, attracted by the smell of rapidly decomposing flesh made more putrid by the warm climate.

After his inspection, the prime minister knew it would take every able-bodied person in Israel to bury the dead in a valley east of the sea. He turned to the man next to him.

"Solomon, I agree with you. The land must be thoroughly cleansed, but it'll take months, maybe a year to complete the job." He pointed to where several men wearing masks were loading the bodies on trucks.

"This putrid odor, the foul breath of death, must be dispersed before I can send in more workers to speed things up."

Unlike the prime minister, Rabbi Solomon Lowenstein didn't cover his nose, instead he inhaled deeply and held his queasy stomach in check. He recorded every vivid aspect of the horror and carnage on the videotape of his mind so that he would never forget. Tears welled up in his eyes.

"You're moved by this slaughter which God has rained down upon our enemies?" inquired the prime minister.

"No . . . I'm thinking of my grandfather."

"Ah, what a sight for him to have seen. Perhaps it would remind him—he was at Auschwitz wasn't he?"

"Yes. When I was a boy, he'd make me listen to his stories about the wretched conditions in the camp. 'Remember,' he said, 'remember so it can't happen to your generation.' Until now—this minute—I didn't understand." He swept his hand towards the landscape.

"Why did God choose such an ordinary race of people like the Jews to be His people and inhabit this land? Perhaps that's why mankind has continually tried to destroy us; they don't think we're fit to be the recipients of His love. Why else do they seek to destroy, not only our lives and our dreams, but our very souls?" He shook his head. "Now they must see. God has reversed our roles; we are no longer the hunted, but the hunter. We're burying them."

"Yes, and using what the dead left behind," said the prime minister. He picked up a gun stock. "We've discovered that all their weapons, even the tanks and helicopters, are made of a new type of rustproof material; it's as strong as steel but much lighter. I've never seen anything like it. Watch this."

He walked over to one of the open fires that burned continuously to rid the land of the trash that had accumulated since the disaster. He threw the stock into it. It began to melt, then it burst into flames.

"It's combustible when exposed to an open blaze, but it will take hours before it's consumed. Never again will we have to depend on outside sources for fuel; we'll burn their tanks and helicopters. Eventually, we'll capture the oil fields."

He turned to Solomon. "But you didn't come here to discuss our cleanup operations. We haven't spoken since the slaying of the young archaeologist. What's the real reason you asked for this meeting? What do you want of me, Solomon?"

"Judah Midian."

The prime minister's eyes narrowed. "He's a saviour to the people of Israel. They're convinced that Judah's pleas to God on our behalf saved the country." He looked out over the fly-covered corpses in the valley before he spoke. "There's no other explanation for this grisly massacre. Don't you agree?"

"I agree that Judah has chosen God for his own purposes; I am not so sure that God has chosen Judah. There's been a persistent march of 'saviors' in every century, but there's something about this one that disturbs me. First he claimed he was a prophet, but now he states he's part god."

"Is not God a part of all of us, Solomon? You're the master of the Talmud, not I, but if God breathed the breath of life into us, then we must have some of His attributes. Can we help it if Judah displays them better than we do? The Jewish people have made him a national hero, and yes, I have heard the rumors that many say he is the Messiah."

Solomon clenched his hands into tight fists. "He's too presumptuous! He now gives audiences in the temple each day with that American, Logan Washburn, by his side. Our people listen to him instead of the rabbis. What does he know of our faith? He's never fully embraced it, how could he with a Palestinian father? It's an abomination!"

"Times are changing, Solomon, and we must change with them. The pavilion of faith shelters many religions. It doesn't surprise me that Judah and Washburn are inseparable; it's a good business relationship. Washburn with his reputation as a peacemaker is an excellent public relations man with the right connections throughout the governments of the world. He'll see that Judah stays in the public's eye." He backed away from the fire.

"I know what you think of Judah, so I hesitate to tell you this, but Washburn has arranged a world tour for Judah. He's billing Judah as God's anointed and himself as the minister of religion."

"You approve . . . of . . . of this?" stuttered Solomon.

"They don't need my approval. Or yours. They've been granted an audience with the new pope. Finally the world will listen when Israel speaks."

Solomon covered his nose with his hand as a breeze brought the sickening sweet odor of death across the valley. "Have you ever looked into Judah's eyes? It's like falling off a precipice into a bottomless pit. I warn you, he and Washburn will leave a stink in the nostrils of Israel which will make this smell sweet by comparison."

"You make too much of it, my old friend. Don't worry, I'll keep an eye on Judah Midian. His 'Goodwill Tour' can only strengthen Israel's position in the new world order."

"But at what price?"

"Solomon, those who dance with the devil must pay the price of admission."

Together they drove back to Jerusalem in silence. One battle was over, but in Solomon's heart there raged a spiritual warfare which could not be defeated by mere words.

D ad, I'm here."
Randy Morgan heard his daughter's voice and
opened his eyes. He was still on his stomach. All he
could see was a rumpled sheet and the gray floor tiles in the corner of the room. He licked his lips, tried to speak, but he could
only manage an inaudible whisper.

"Don't talk yet, let me get you some ice chips." Faith got the
pitcher from the table, knelt down, and put the ice in his mouth.
He sucked on the wet, cold slivers and felt the water dribble
down his chin. He raised his right hand and saw the tubing from
the intravenous drip.

"You were shot, Dad. Through the lung." She dabbed at his
chin with a paper towel.

"Stephen—I mean, Dr. Bradley—took out the bullet that was
lodged in your spine. That's why you're on your stomach. You'll
have to stay that way for at least a week, until the wound heals."

She sat down on the floor and leaned her head against the mattress so he could see her.

"How long have I been here?"

"Three days," she replied.

"Are you all right?"

She nodded.

"We have to get away from here, Faith." He heard the door
open, then the soft squish of rubber soles on the floor.

"Dr. Bradley said you're not in any condition to leave the hospital."

"That's right," said Stephen as he came around the side of the bed. "You're lucky to be alive."

"We must leave. If anyone found us . . ."

"Dad, I told Dr. Bradley everything. He hasn't reported anything to the police yet. He's agreed to help us."

"We need all the help we can get," Randy groaned. "I guess I owe both of you an explanation." He closed his eyes, trying to collect his scattered thoughts.

"Faith, I work for the CIA."

Her eyes widened in disbelief.

"I was working on a top-secret project investigating the recent disappearances which occurred throughout the world. I reported our findings directly to the White House, and it was my understanding that they would be made public." A trickle of sweat broke out on Randy's forehead. "Apparently, the government has decided to squelch the report and everyone involved with it. Someone conveniently erased all the data from our computers, then planted evidence to prove that I'm the fair-haired boy who did it. Now they want to kill me."

"That's a pretty incredible story," said Stephen. "What you're suggesting . . . I thought it was illegal for the CIA to participate in murder."

"It is, but that hasn't stopped them before." Randy pointed to the ice pitcher, and Faith put some more ice chips in his mouth. "And it won't now."

"What did you find out?" said Faith.

"Absolutely nothing." Randy moaned as a burst of excruciating pain tore through his back.

"I'll order something for the pain," said Stephen as he reached for the call button.

"This whole thing is so insane . . ." Randy's voice trailed off.

"If they want to kill you, you must have found something. What was it, Dad?" said Faith.

He tried to concentrate on her question. "After 50 percent of the data was entered, it looked as if a majority of the people who'd vanished had a religious affiliation." He closed his eyes. "Then we got an influx of new material, and eventually even that trend flattened out. There really wasn't a common thread in the whole study."

The nurse came in and injected him with painkillers, 100 milligrams of Demerol and 50 of Vistaril. As Randy felt himself rising higher and higher, one thought floated through his mind and made its way to his lips. "Why was there such a time lag between the first and final data we received?" he said with a great deal of effort.

"Oh, Dad," said Faith, "don't you see? For thousands of years the Christians have anticipated that Christ would return and take them to heaven. That's what happened when all those people disappeared. If everyone knew that, it would cause a panic. People would read the Bible, and then they'd know the rest of the prophecy . . . like I do."

"Now you sound like your mother, Faith. This religious tie-in is a pretty outrageous idea."

"If it's so absurd, why has the government gone to all this trouble to try and keep you quiet?"

"Your daughter has a point there," said Stephen. "What you've just said makes her theories seem even more plausible."

"I'm in no condition to argue the point." A numbing wave of relief came over Randy. "One thing is certain though, as soon as I can travel, we're leaving for Israel."

"Israel?" said Stephen. "You can't take Faith there . . . not now. Russia and a few of her friends just got soundly defeated trying to invade the country."

"What?"

"I'm not the squeamish type, but the satellite pictures are gruesome. It's literally an open graveyard. The area will probably be rampant with disease before they can dispose of all the bodies properly."

"That makes it even better . . . for us. Who in their right mind would go there?" He twisted his head to look at Stephen. "You said you'd help us, Dr. Bradley. Will you see that we get the right shots and vaccines before we leave?" Randy felt as if there were bricks on his eyelids.

Stephen nodded grudgingly.

"Good. We'll have new identities, and maybe we can start over again. I'm hoping that out of sight is out of mind, but with the CIA, you never know."

Randy closed his eyes, his strength depleated. He never even heard Faith and Stephen leave the room.

Solomon hurried to the temple, hoping that Judah and Washburn wouldn't be there. As he entered the outer courtyard, he heard a powerful voice behind him.

"Who is on the Lord's side? Let him come unto me."

He whirled around and stared at the two men clothed in coarse sackcloth, their faces and hands black with ashes.

One of them carried a staff in his hand, and he raised it as he spoke to the curious throng that had gathered.

"Behold the Lord cometh with ten thousand saints to execute judgment upon all, and to convict the ungodly amongst you of the ungodly deeds which you have committed, and to condemn you for all the harsh speeches which you have spoken against Him." The man's long white hair streamed over his shoulders as the January wind rustled through the temple courtyard.

Where did they come from? Jewish immigrants probably. With the defeat of the invading horde two weeks ago, the dedication of the temple last week, and the resuming of the temple sacrifices, Jews from every corner of the earth were coming back to Jerusalem.

"Take off your sackcloth, old man," replied one of the seminary students to the orator. "This is a time for rejoicing, not for grief and suffering. God has defeated our enemies."

The other man with a weathered face, pulled his cloak tightly around him, then lifted a hairy arm and pointed his finger at the student. "We're witnesses of Him whom you rejected. Though the number of the children of Israel be as the sand of the sea, a remnant shall be saved." He spoke with the voice of authority and the crowd grew quiet as he continued. "If thou shalt confess with thy mouth the Lord Jesus, and if thou shalt believe in thine heart that God hath raised Him from the dead, thou shalt be saved.

"For the Scripture saith, Whosoever believeth on him shall not be ashamed.

"For there is no difference between the Jew and the Greek, for the same Lord over all is rich unto all that call upon Him.

"For whosoever shall call upon the name of the Lord shall be saved."

"You believe that Jesus was the Messiah?" scoffed the student. "The Messiah is Judah Midian."

"No! You're wrong," shouted Solomon, but his words were lost in the angry voices of the hecklers in the crowd. From the corner of his eye he saw a remote television camera recording the event.

Undaunted, the prophet's eyes burned into his audience. "As the Lord God of Israel liveth, before whom I stand, there shall not be dew nor rain these years, but according to my word so that ye may know what I have spoken is true."

"I'm not going to throw away my umbrella yet," quipped the lighthearted student as he rejoined his friends.

Solomon moved away from the self-proclaimed prophets, but he noticed that a knot of men stayed to listen. It was part of the legacy they would all have to pay in the global year 2011, as Israel regained its position as a world leader. The rich and the poor, the confused and the wise, all would come through her gates.

Pope Timothy readied himself for his audience with the two most important religious leaders from Israel. He removed the heavy ring from the second finger of his left hand as he washed his hands. He picked it up and looked more closely at the emblem of a fish head and the words "the keeper of the bridge" engraved on it.

He dried his hands and put the ring back on. He recalled that during Babylonian times, the symbol of the bridge had had a different meaning; it had signified the connecting link between a worshiper and Satan in the false religions. Perhaps it had been true before the Roman emperor Constantine had become a convert to the Christian faith, but later the phrase had been adopted by the Christians, and now he was the "keeper of the bridge." Its significance had changed just as his own had.

The pope walked to the reception room where he was to receive his visitors, wondering what the outcome of the meeting would be. He admired Washburn's diplomatic achievements, but contrary to what the Vatican believed, he'd only met him a few times at fund-raising events in Washington. Father Paul had to brief him on Judah Midian's background.

Closely he watched the two men as they came forward and kissed his ring. He gave them both a benign smile as he sat down. He'd learned that everyone liked a smiling pope—it made them feel better.

"Your Supreme Pontiff, thank you for granting us this audience," said Judah.

"Perhaps I should thank you. It's not every day that one gets to meet a god." He studied Judah's face as an expression he could not name flickered across his dark countenance. Judah did not deny the claim.

"You know how easily people are led. They are sheep, looking for a shepherd. I'm sure you understand my position better than anyone else."

The pope was amused. "You consider me a shepherd, then?"

"That is an understatement. I meant it only in the most simplistic terms."

"You're right, Judah, we are responsible for the care and feeding of billions of sheep. It can be a heavy burden."

"That's why I've come to ask for your help."

"How can I, a mere mortal, help you? We are at opposite ends of the spectrum." He glanced at Washburn, surprised that he stood silently by Judah's side.

"Not really, Your Holiness. I propose that Rome be chosen as the center for all the religions of the world. We and the other leaders from the major denominations will form a board to administer the religious functions for the World Church.

"Israel has taken over much of the Arab world. Will there still be a place for the Moslems under this umbrella of religion?"

"Yes, we will not discriminate."

"Why have you come to me?"

"If you sanction it, the others will follow."

So that was it. He looked at Judah and saw under the unruffled exterior, not a shepherd, but a ravenous wolf in sheep's clothing.

To keep this wolf at bay, he must first thrust his personal feelings aside. The plan he'd carefully thought out could be put into place using Judah Midian. The revenue from the World Church would make the Catholic Church solvent again, and the Vatican could be refurbished at its expense.

"Is this perhaps a stepping stone to your leadership of the European Common Market?" he said.

The pope was more astute than Judah thought. He had a bargaining chip, and he intended to use it.

"It's being discussed," said Judah.

"But your appointment to that position would be assured if you could get this religious center underway in Rome, wouldn't it?" The pope leaned forward in his chair to make certain he heard Judah's reply.

"Yes, it would, but the Vatican would also benefit. Money would flow through Rome like water in the ancient aqueducts."

"Flow through . . ." murmured the pope. "I prefer that it stay here. These are my conditions: The Vatican will require a 20 percent administration tax from each sect that falls under the banner of the World Church. The monies these sects previously spent on social programs for the poor will be relinquished to us. We will distribute it on their behalf throughout the world. Then you will have my blessing." He stood up to dismiss them.

As they left the reception room and walked through the maze of corridors, Judah Midian and his minister of religion, Logan Washburn, discussed the pope's conditions.

"But how can you get the others to agree to his demands?" said Logan.

Judah's ebony eyes stared straight ahead. "My power and your influence will persuade them. The World Church will be established here in less than a month." Logan's arm tingled as Judah touched it. "We must be circumspect for a while, but the stage is set. It's my time to rule the world, and you'll be at my side."

Logan's heart skipped a beat. He believed in the man walking next to him and the destiny that was ahead of them. They'd harnessed the forces of darkness, and there was nothing in this world that could stop them, not even death.

★   ★   ★

"Stephen, it's been a long three weeks, but dad's doing great now, isn't he?" asked Faith as they sat in the hospital cafeteria having lunch.

Stephen nodded. It had been the fastest three weeks of his life. "Your father will have to walk with a cane for a while, but the prognosis for a full recovery is excellent."

Faith felt joy bubbling up inside of her. Her father was well, and they were actually going to Israel! Her prayers had been answered.

"I'll miss you," said Stephen, sitting across from her. He looked around the dining room, took a drink of his coffee, and played with the tofu meatloaf on his plate. "I'll always think of this as 'our place,'" he teased, but there was a note of sadness in his voice.

"You could come with us, Stephen."

"That's impossible. I have my work here, and I promised my parents I'd keep an eye on my sister, Jamie, until she got through school."

"But we only have the next seven years before this earth, as we know it, will be gone."

"So you tell me. I'll just have to make them the best seven years of my life . . . but I would enjoy it more if you stayed."

Her eyes blazed like emeralds in the sun. "Stephen, don't try to placate me, I'm not a child. If you really believed, nothing could stop you from going."

"You're right," he said, "but I've never been good at making snap decisions, even medical ones."

"Come with us, Stephen."

He felt his resolve begin to crumble. He didn't understand himself anymore. He'd just told her father that going to Israel was irrational and illogical, and now he was actually entertaining the same idea.

He linked his fingers in hers, startled by the realization that seven years with her would be worth a lifetime. Nothing had changed since he'd walked into the lunchroom, except the most important thing of all, his heart.

Gordon Pratt didn't trust anyone or anything—except his own instincts. Now they screamed in unison that Faith and her father were somewhere in the tri-county area. The surviving CIA agent had said he'd shot Randy Morgan, but from some place deep in his gut, Pratt knew that Randy was still alive. He was looking forward to the ensuing game of cat and mouse.

Morgan didn't know how to play hardball; otherwise he would have killed Pratt when he'd had the chance. He'd forgotten a rudimentary principle: Don't leave an enemy alive to come after you again.

Pratt mulled over his options as he took a letter opener out of his desk and slid it down the side of his cast to stop the incessant itching. His broken right arm was a painful reminder to never underestimate anyone's ability, especially in a crisis situation.

Faith and her father would have to seek medical help. He'd already been to the police station to run through the reports, but nothing matched up. He'd spent weeks dogging the CIA's investigation which included checking the local emergency clinics and all the John Does in the morgue. They were missing something; he'd just have to dig deeper. He'd do whatever it took to find Faith, even if that meant examining the hospital admission records personally.

The thermostat was set at sixty-five degrees, but beads of perspiration broke out on Pratt's upper lip as he thought of Faith.

Ever since he'd first followed her home last spring, familiarized himself with her routine, then waited until that night at the library when she was alone . . . Faith was all he could think about. Longing rose up in him as he remembered the touch of her velvety skin.

Pratt wiped his lip and swept his emotions aside. He had to concentrate on the case. Find Randy Morgan and he'd find his daughter.

Once again, his instincts told him that Falcon Lightfoot could be the key. He'd been too cooperative in the subsequent investigation which had pinned Saundra's murder on Morgan. Nothing had surfaced despite a wiretap, the interception of his mail, and constant surveillance, but it was just a matter of time before Falcon slipped up. Until then . . .

Pratt spread the Prince William County map in front of him and circled the hospitals. As he refolded the map with his left hand and put it in his pocket, he looked again at the month-old newspaper on the desk beneath it. Splashed across the front page was the caption; "Double Agent Still at Large" and a picture of Randy Morgan.

In a fit of rage, Pratt seized the dagger-shaped letter opener and thrust it through the picture, nailing it to his desk in one swift movement. It was the first nail in Randy Morgan's coffin.

Thirty days—wasted. A thousand pinpricks tap-danced up and down Randy's legs as he limped across the floor of room 439 in the Isolation Unit. Nightingale, the six-feet tall robot who'd been assigned to him so he would have minimum exposure to the hospital staff, glided behind him in case he should fall.

"How are you feeling?" Nightingale said in his electronically processed and synthesized voice.

Randy had become accustomed to the robot's large twinkling "eyes" in an oval-shaped head which could rotate 360 degrees, but when it spoke, that mechanical voice still unnerved him. He turned and looked at the sleek, one-piece body whose torso featured a flat, liquid crystal display panel which could play video and stereo tapes.

"I'm fine. Go do something."

"Your command is too vague. I am unable to distinguish 'something.'"

"See if you can get the maintenance man to fix the light panel above my bed."

"I can do that." Nightingale extended its two-fingered, clamplike hands and unscrewed the flickering fluorescent tube. He glided out of the room with it.

"Lady with the Lamp," Randy muttered. The lack of company had not improved his disposition. His legs still felt like Jell-O, although Dr. Bradley had assured him that in time the soft tissue damage would heal, and he'd be able to resume his normal activities. Normal activities. Did fleeing for your life come under that heading?

He rubbed his hand over the stubble on his face and adjusted the steel-rimmed glasses Faith had purchased for him at the local discount store. After seeing his picture repeatedly on the nightly news, he'd tried to change his appearance to avoid recognition. He glanced up as he shuffled past the mirror, startled, yet pleased, by the *skinny* eccentric who stared back at him.

His hair was now a scraggly mass that curled over the top of the insipid hospital gown, giving him the appearance of an impoverished college professor rather than the country's most wanted double agent.

"I got everything, Dad," said Faith as she hurried into the room with an instamatic camera in one hand, a brown shopping bag in the other.

"Good." He looked with dismay at Faith's boyish, cropped haircut. "I'm sorry you had to cut it, honey."

"It'll grow back." She sat down on the bed and emptied out the contents of the shopping bag. "Stephen helped me buy these, I hope they fit."

She divided the clothes and disappeared into the bathroom with one pile.

Randy pulled on the blue jeans, buttoned the red and gray flannel shirt, and put the charcoal gray sweater over it. *I look like an undernourished Scotsman or a footsore camper,* he thought to himself as he pulled on the hiking boots.

He heard the water running, then the hair dryer. Twenty minutes later, Faith emerged in a man's oversized sweater and shapeless corduroy pants, her face scrubbed free of any makeup, her once-blond hair now a russet color and parted to the side.

"How do I look?"

"If I had a daughter, I might introduce you to her."

He walked around her slowly. "Something's not quite right." He put one finger under her nose. "A mustache, that's what you need."

"Why not a cigar, then I can look like Groucho Marx?" she said bitterly, pushing his hand away.

"Or Adolph Hitler. Don't get testy, honey. In this Halloween contest, the prize is our lives."

"I know," she said, collapsing on the bed. "It's just that it all seems so incredible. It's like a weird video where suddenly the audience is thrown into the film, and they become the actors. Is it really me in these clothes, or some impostor?"

"Until we get to Egypt, it's an impostor. Now stand up and walk around the room."

She did as he asked.

"An agent would spot you a mile away. You have to walk differently," he said, "bigger strides and more klutzy."

She practiced loping around the room until he was satisfied.

"Guess I won't be needing this." She threw the purse with her lipstick and a small bottle of perfume into the trash can and put the remaining comb and some change into her pockets.

"Dad, is this really going to work?"

"I'm counting on it," he said soberly. "This isn't the first time I've been responsible for getting someone safely out of the country. We'll be in New York by tonight. After I'm sure my contact isn't being watched, we'll appear on his doorstep and have him forge our passports and some phony identification—while we wait.

"Tourists and immigrants can't get into Israel officially until they clean up the mess from the invasion. We'll take a flight to Egypt, and one dark night we'll unofficially cross the border into Israel."

"Stephen said he'll drive us to New York in one of the ambulances. That way we shouldn't be stopped."

"You're going to miss Dr. Bradley—I mean Stephen—aren't you?"

She shrugged her thin shoulders. Her voice had a soft, dream-like quality. "If things had been different, it could have been—" She gave him a timid smile. "I asked him to come with us, but . . ."

She'd asked Dr. Bradley to accompany them? Randy was surprised and uncomfortable. He'd had the same reaction when Pratt made those suggestive remarks about her. It was hard for him to think about Faith with any man.

When was he going to accept the fact that his daughter was grown up? Somehow, like countless fathers before him, he'd been too busy to notice the subtle changes during her transition from adolescent to woman. This time a stinging sensation pricked his heart, not his legs. Ruth would have known what to say to Faith at a time like this, he didn't. For the first time in more than a month, he wished he had a cigarette, a drink—or both.

"I guess you're stuck with me," he said apologetically.

She got up and hugged him. "With crazy glue."

"I hope I'm interrupting something," said Stephen as he entered the room with a fiberglass cane in one hand.

"Just a father-son talk," said Randy glibly.

Stephen leaned up against the door and eyed Faith from the top of her reddish hair to the tips of her brown loafers. "I guess I better not call you Faith anymore. What's your new name?

"Louis . . . Louis Bitterman." She stuck out her hand and he shook it.

"And let me introduce you to my father, Russell."

"Well Louis . . . and Russell, we'll take the service elevator to the parking garage while the evening shift is coming on duty."

Stephen handed the cane to Randy. "You'll ride in the back of the ambulance, Louis can ride up front with me."

"I appreciate what you're doing for us, Stephen."

Stephen smiled. "Believe me, sir, I'm doing this as much for myself as for you." He reached over and took Faith's hand, holding her slender fingers between his own. "Your daughter has changed my life in more ways than I can tell you."

"Dad, will you take a picture of Stephen and me?"

He nodded—what else could he do?—and she handed him the camera. They smiled self-consciously as he snapped the picture.

"How about one last dinner at 'our place'?" Stephen said to Faith.

She looked at her father's untouched tray. "Do you want to go with us, Dad?"

He shook his head. "After this hospital food, I'm actually looking forward to an in-flight meal. You two go along, enjoy your last evening together. And remember, even in this day and age, if you hold hands you're going to get some odd reactions."

Gordon Pratt parked in front of the Quantico Memorial Hospital and looked at his watch. It was eleven o'clock. He yawned and wondered if he should wait until the morning. No, might as well get it over with. People on the night shift always seemed more talkative.

He stretched as he got out of the car, absentmindedly ran his hand over his short bristly hair, then tucked in his shirt. He tightened his belt a notch, pleased that his efforts to lose weight were paying off. He'd never been vain, but there was no reason he couldn't look his best for Faith.

He heard the wail of a siren as he walked towards the main entrance. He paused before he entered the hospital to watch the ambulance leave the garage and race past him with its crimson light flashing. For a brief moment the etchings of the night were turned into a red canvas. The hackles went up on his back and he stared into the night sensing . . . what? Conditioned reflexes, he convinced himself—like Pavlov's dogs.

The double doors slid open, and he made his way to the unoccupied information desk where a sign told him to proceed to the registration office. Pratt showed his badge to the sleepy clerk who was on the phone. He observed that she wasn't wearing a wedding ring.

"I need to see records of all your admissions and discharges between January first and today."

She pointed to two baskets on top of the metal filing cabinet. "They haven't been filed yet, but they're in alphabetical order so we can put them in the computer." Her voice hardened. "Be sure you leave them that way." Obviously annoyed at being interrupted, she went back to her conversation.

He grunted, sat down at a vacant desk and spread the admission papers across it. First he separated them into two piles, one for females, one for males. Then he took the male admissions and checked the ages, winnowing out those men below age thirty and those above fifty. About 150 folders were left.

Slowly he sifted through them, noting the time of day each had been admitted, and funneling the emergency and unusual cases into another pile.

He had twelve names left. He checked those discharged, matching their names against the admissions, jotting down the room numbers of those who were still patients.

"I've got three rooms I need to check," he said to the typist, as he replaced the file baskets. She put her hand over the mouthpiece. "I'll be with you in a min—u—te." Ignoring him, she went back to her conversation.

How he hated the clerks of the world! He let out a curse, grabbed the receiver from her, and slammed it down so hard a stand-up desk calendar went flying through the air.

"Did anyone ever tell you that you could lose your job for making personal phone calls?"

"Well! Who died and put you in charge?" She shot him an angry scowl as she reached into her drawer and pulled out a badge, then pushed a form at him. "Fill this out and be sure to return the badge when you leave," she said disdainfully.

Angrily, he crumpled the form in his fist, then reached over to the baskets on top of the filing cabinet and dumped them on the floor, scattering the contents with his foot.

"You can't do that!" the clerk shouted as she got to her feet.

He left her fluttering like an irate chicken.

Pratt bypassed the elevator and took the stairs so he could avoid the nurses' station in the center of each floor. If he found Morgan, he wanted no witnesses.

The first two patients on the third floor were sound asleep when he poked his head inside the door. He walked to the fourth floor, ignored the "No Admittance" sign on room 439, and pushed the door open. The room was empty, the covers thrown back on the bed.

"Just what do you think you're doing in here?" an angry voice said behind him.

He spun around and looked at what he assumed was a nurse. She was covered from head to toe in a green cap, mask, gown and gloves. "This is an isolation unit, no one is allowed in here without the proper attire." Her accusing eyes looked like brown slits in an ocean of pea soup.

"I'm looking for the patient in this room. Where is he?" he asked, flashing his badge.

The nurse went to the foot of the bed and looked at the chart.

"He's been transported to New York for further evaluation."

"What was the matter with him?"

"If we knew that, he wouldn't have been taken to New York," she snipped.

"I need to look around the room."

"Suit yourself, but this room hasn't been scrubbed down yet," she said turning on her heels. "It's on your own head if you get something contagious."

Pratt checked the room, picked up the wastebasket and dumped it on the bed. What was a man doing with a purse in his wastebasket? He opened the purse and took out the half-used bottle of perfume and unscrewed the top. He held it to his nose and a smile broke across his face.

He'd never forget that smell! It was the sweet, yet spicy, fragrance Faith had worn.

They couldn't be far away. Hurriedly he searched the bathroom; he pulled the empty film carton, then the package of hair dye out of the garbage. He left the room and found the nurse who'd harassed him.

"Did you know the patient in room 439?"

"Well," she sniffed, "Dr. Bradley seemed to take him under his wing. He assigned one of the robots to take his vital signs. I got the feeling Dr. Bradley didn't want anyone in the room. Personally, I think there was something fishy there."

"How so?"

"He was registered as John Doe, but then what John Doe has a young woman who spends the night on a cot in his room?"

"Where did they take him?"

"After Dr. Bradley made a copy of his chart, he said he was going with him to New York for the evaluation. That's highly unusual. Generally, the doctor just refers the patient to another physician. Also, I noticed on the chart that Dr. Bradley didn't record the name of the hospital where the patient was being transferred. I pointed it out to him. He said not to worry about it."

Without another word, Gordon Pratt raced down the hall.

It was six o'clock and forty-five minutes remained until their flight to Egypt would depart from New York's Kennedy Airport. Randy Morgan glanced through the terminal's coffee shop window at the people asleep in their chairs, then checked his inside breast pocket again; the passports were still there.

Everything had gone smoothly. He'd whisked Faith in and out of the old brownstone apartment to have her picture taken, then he'd deposited her with Stephen in the ambulance around the corner while he finished the transaction—permanently. They were almost home free.

He took a sip of his coffee. Stephen and Faith were sitting across from him in the booth blissfully unaware of his presence while they savored their last moments together.

"Stephen, you don't have to wait if you don't want to," said Faith as she nibbled at her English muffin.

"I want to."

"Will you write to me?"

"Sure, as soon as you send me your address. It's not everyone who has a girlfriend with a mustache."

She stuck out her tongue at him.

"You'd better sign those letters with the name Louis, just in case someone is snooping around," said Randy as he stood up. "I'm going to get a paper before we leave."

He scanned the paper, but for once there wasn't a story about him in any of the sections. Good. His notoriety had been short-lived; he was yesterday's news.

He looked at the front page where the main story was a world-wide drought. From the color map, Eastern Europe seemed to be suffering the most. It's lakes and reservoirs were contaminated with lead and other heavy metals.

Randy remembered when massive changes had shaken the former Soviet-bloc nations in the 1990s. In their disregard for the environment, the emerging democracies of Rumania, Bulgaria, Czechoslovakia, and Hungary wouldn't acknowledge pollution. They'd failed to switch to less toxic fertilizers and pesticides; they had been too busy producing basic food items for the present to worry about the future.

Leaning on his cane, he walked back to the coffee shop. There were storms of controversy throughout the globe and there seemed to be no answers to the problems. He thought of Ruth and Hope and of a world gone berserk. Was it too much to ask for a hideaway where they could seek refuge from all the madness?

Randy walked over to the booth where Faith and Stephen were sitting. "All right you two," Faith said, looking up at her father, then at Stephen, "I have to go to the bathroom and I can't go to the women's restroom dressed like this without causing a panic. Any suggestions?"

"Follow me," said Stephen, "I'll give you a guided tour of the men's lavatory."

Faith felt herself blush as she answered him. "I hope you don't expect me to use one of those urinal things."

"Nothing as primitive as that. They have stalls."

With his back throbbing again, Randy cautiously lowered himself onto the padded seat. "I'll read the paper and wait for you here," he said with a grimace.

"This has really been hard on Dad," said Faith, as she stopped in front of one of the gift shops on their way to the restroom. She smiled as her eyes fell on a turquoise ring in the window. "Oh, look, isn't it beautiful?"

"Come on," said Stephen steering her past the jewelry display, "shopping is not on your itinerary. We've only got thirty minutes before your plane leaves, they'll be boarding any minute." He stopped in front of the men's restroom. "Wait here."

In a minute he was back. "The place is empty except for the last stall. "Go on, I'll wait for you out here."

She rolled her eyes, then pushed open the door.

Stephen rushed back to the gift shop. "That turquoise ring in the window—can you wrap it up for me? I'm in a hurry."

★ ★ ★

Faith went to the first stall and locked the door. She heard the main door to the bathroom open again. Had Stephen come back or was the man in the last stall leaving? She felt ridiculous, but nevertheless, she quickly got up on the toilet so her feet wouldn't show beneath the door.

"I know you're in there. Come out and no one will get hurt."

The blood drained from her face. Gordon Pratt! What was he doing here? She held her breath. Where was Stephen?"

Pratt couldn't believe his luck. He'd spent the last five hours at JFK watching all the arrivals and departures. From the one-way mirror in the security office, he'd spotted all three of them when they'd first come in. He'd thought about taking Morgan at the magazine stand but his first priority was Faith. Even with her haircut and those shapeless clothes, he'd recognized her. When she'd gone into the men's bathroom, he'd decided to make his move. The guy at the gift shop must be the doctor. He'd take care of him next.

He stood outside the last cubicle. "Come out. Now!"

There was no response.

"If you don't come out, I'm going to break this door down."

He heard a movement behind the door and smiled to himself. She didn't have a chance and she knew it. He tried to push open the door but it was locked.

"All right, we'll do it your way," he said in a menacing voice. He stepped back and raised his right foot to smash in the door.

Pratt heard the gunshot blast an instant before it burst through the door and hit him in the chest. He reeled backwards, a look of amazement on his face as he hit the floor.

Faith screamed. She pushed her stall door open and a beefy man with a gun and a parcel sprinted by her, knocking her down as he dashed for the exit.

In front of the last stall, Pratt was on his back, clutching his stomach. Faith scrambled to her feet and saw the door with a hole in it the size of a baseball. Cautiously, she walked towards Pratt. She stood over him with her hand over her mouth, cringing as she saw the blood spattered on the white tile floor.

Pratt opened his eyes, and she stood there, frozen, unable to move as his eyes met hers.

He tried to speak but the words came out in jerky syllables.

"It wasn't . . . you. You wouldn't hurt me—" He smiled at her, gasped for breath as his Adam's apple flailed in his throat.

"Faith!" Stephen ran towards her.

"It's Pratt," she said, her voice trembling.

Stephen bent down and felt for Pratt's pulse. It was erratic, then there was nothing. Gordon Pratt's sightless eyes stared at the ceiling.

"He's dead, let's get out of here," said Stephen, dragging her by the hand. She stumbled after him into the terminal. They walked down the corridor, then leaned up against the plate glass window pretending to watch the airplanes land and take off.

"Are you all right?"

"Yes," she answered in a frightened voice. She wrapped her arms around herself to control her shaking. "He thought it was me in the last stall. That awful man was coming to get me."

She saw Pratt's face again. "Before he died, he looked up at me . . . and he actually smiled, a sad . . . pathetic smile. He didn't look evil anymore, he just looked . . . like a hurt animal."

"He'll never bother you again, Faith."

"No, but someone with a different face and the same motives will take his place. We're going to be hunted down for the rest of our lives."

She turned to him, leaned on his arm. "I feel overwhelmed, as if somehow I'm responsible for this whole mess."

He shook his head. "We're both upset, but that's no reason to blame yourself for what happened."

She exhaled slowly, trying to release all the pent up anger she'd suppressed for so long. "Political assassinations, governments being overthrown—I never thought those issues could touch me . . . until now. They were just spectator sports I watched on the news. You know, I never even registered to vote. I figured, what difference could my vote make?"

"Is this the same girl who told me one person can make a difference?"

She nodded. "Maybe this time I can."

"You're right. We can't change the past, but we can change the future."

"Oh, Stephen, I wish we could, but it's going to get worse, a lot worse."

Randy saw the airport security guard run past him. He hoped it wasn't another bomb threat, he wanted nothing to delay their flight. Faith and Stephen came towards him stiffly, their faces set in masks of concrete. Instantly, he knew something was wrong.

"It's Pratt," whispered Stephen as he sat down beside him. "He's dead. In the restroom."

"Flight 986 now boarding for Cairo," said a voice over the intercom. Randy stood up and put his arm through Faith's. The three of them walked down the corridor to the boarding area. No one looked back.

18

While Randy Morgan waited impatiently for Faith and Stephen to say good-bye, he scrutinized the airport crowd. What if Pratt hadn't come alone? He knew it was corny, but he felt like they were reenacting the final scene of *Casablanca*.

People milled around them, but Stephen saw only Faith's downcast face as she blinked back the tears. *How could he let her walk out of his life like this?*

He scratched his five o'clock shadow, pushed back the glasses on his nose, and unwrapped a stick of sugarless gum, crushing the foil wrapper into a ball which he rolled nervously between his thumb and forefinger. He cleared his throat. "Faith?"

"I'm going to miss you," she said, not trusting herself to look at him. "I told myself I wasn't going to get emotional about this. It's best for both of us but—"

She concentrated on the tips of her brown loafers. "When you find someone you really care about . . . it's . . . hard to let go." A tear rolled down her cheek as he cupped her chin in his hand and tilted her face towards his.

Ignoring the quizzical looks of the other passengers in line, he took her hands between his own and lost himself in her blue eyes. All at once, he was tumbling hopelessly through the sky in a free-fall. Maybe it was only a knee-jerk reaction, but suddenly the parachute of commitment unfurled and buoyed his spirits.

"It'll take me about six months, but as soon as I can wind up my work here . . . I'll come to Israel."

"Oh, Stephen—but you'd be leaving everything."

"No," he said in a gentle verbal embrace. "I'll be gaining everything."

He pressed the jewelry box into her hand. "This will have to do until I can get something more appropriate. Don't open it until you get on the plane."

"Last call for flight 986 to Cairo."

Faith hugged him and felt his heart beating next to hers. "I'll be waiting for you in the summer," she whispered in his ear.

She turned to join her father, and suddenly they were gone.

Stephen ran to the rail to catch a final glimpse of Faith. As he did, an incredible joy mixed with the sorrow of parting filled his heart, and with it came the realization that love was a coupling of the mind and heart, not just the flesh.

"Gordon Pratt was shot to death in the men's restroom at JFK Airport in New York." John Seaton, the director of the CIA stood in front of the president's desk waiting for his reaction.

"And Morgan?"

"My guess is he skipped the country. Pratt had a map on him with all the local hospitals and clinics circled on it." John looked at the papers in his hand. "He was last seen by one of the nurses at Quantico Memorial Hospital where he asked a lot of questions about a patient who was listed as John Doe.

"This John Doe was sent to New York for an evaluation, and Dr. Stephen Bradley, who's in charge of the case, went with him. I've got a man waiting at the hospital to pick up the doctor for questioning as soon as he returns."

President Emilio Blanco sighed deeply. "Drop it."

"Sir?"

"You heard me. Forget it. Even if Morgan talks, who'll listen to him?"

The president's right eye twitched as he tried to keep his taut facial muscles from revealing that he'd looked at Morgan's file and seen his exemplary record, along with pictures of his family.

He'd learned early in his political career that it was dangerous to show any outward signs of weakness or compassion.

"Morgan's obsolete," he said. "No one cares about him anymore. What we need are solutions to our current problems. In case you haven't noticed, Russia's defeat has changed the balance of power and our nation's priorities. The United States is no longer the world's front-runner. Liberty and democracy have spread throughout the European core, and a unified Germany, Japan's technology, and now Israel's victory have redefined our position. We're a poor relative in this new global relationship."

"So, our past is beginning to catch up with us."

"Every president knew it would happen sometime, they just didn't want it to happen on their watch. We've imported more goods than we've exported, accumulated debts which could never be paid off in our lifetime or our children's, and invested our money in welfare programs instead of education. Now we're paying for it.

"Our most recent poll shows that if we want the party to stay in control and if we want to regain our leadership position, we have to win back the public's trust and seek more peaceful pursuits."

The director's mouth curled like a rattlesnake poised to strike. *He's giving a campaign speech!*

"But he killed two men. We can't just let him get away with that!"

"You're forgetting something. We set up Morgan; he was just defending himself. I don't want you wasting anymore time or energy on this investigation. I want you to let this one go, John. Close the file."

President Blanco went to the window and looked out at the dying, brown lawn. "Water reserves are at an all-time low. We can't even rely on our rivers and streams for drinking water unless we use chemical additives." He drummed his fingers on the thick, bulletproof glass of the window.

"Once the food chain is disrupted, we're in trouble. We'll have a whole new set of problems: extinction by famine, not warfare. We have to take care of the business at hand."

"We've got the best scientists in the world; they should be able to come up with something," said John.

"We *had* some of the best scientists. No, there isn't a quick fix for this situation. We're back to seeding clouds or distilling sea water. Either one will only give us minimum results."

Until he'd been appointed CIA Director, John Seaton had been a simple, basic, down-to-earth guy who enjoyed radio talk shows, hot dogs, and flea markets. He'd traded these in for wire-taps, roast beef on whole wheat bread, and covert operations. John Seaton actually believed he was making the world a safer place for democracy; that was what worried Emilio.

"One more thing," said the president. "Logan Washburn has turned in his resignation. He's looking for greener pastures. He's decided to team up with that self-proclaimed peacemaker and messiah, Judah Midian. Apparently, he's convinced Logan that they're both some kind of holy men on a mission."

"So, now we have the God Squad to contend with," said John sarcastically.

"I would have preferred the Russians or the Chinese. At least we'd know what we were up against." The president reached into his desk drawer and withdrew a box of Cohiba cigars. He flipped open the lid. "Washburn gave these to me as a parting gift. When Fidel Castro was alive, it was his favorite brand, and they're almost impossible to get." He clipped the end of the seven-inch long cigar and rolled it between the palms of his hands as he talked. "I've heard it costs three hundred to five hundred dollars now for a box of twenty-five. Washburn has expensive taste."

He was thoughtful for a moment, choosing his words carefully. "Logan Washburn has traded in the presidency for a larger sphere of influence. He must have something up his sleeve, and I want to know what it is."

"I wouldn't put it past him and that Jew-Arab heretic to somehow maneuver their positions with the World Bank so that they control the currency of the world," fumed John.

"But there are safeguards in place—"

"Just like the safeguards in the JFK conspiracy, but that operation finally blew up in our faces didn't it?"

The president lit his cigar. He changed the subject to an issue he could do something about.

"In the past, Israel has been one of our allies, but eventually they'll control the oil. It's an explosive combination. Keep an eye on Israel and Washburn. Pull your men off Morgan and get them started on this."

President Blanco inhaled deeply as the director left the room, but this time he derived no pleasure from the tobacco as he exhaled. He wasn't sure of the part the United States would play in the coming years, but scraps of a conversation he'd had with his wife two decades ago came back to haunt him.

It was during his stint as a Navy lieutenant that the United States had been pressured by the Arab League to cut back on weapons and armaments to Israel. To strengthen their position, the Arabs aired a documentary on American television highlighting the violence in the West Bank and Gaza strip. Needless to say, it was a biased account, presenting graphic footage of the atrocities inflicted by Israel on the Palestinians, but it caused many of the voters to cry out against the United States' policy of aid to Israel . . . until the war with Iraq.

Over breakfast, Carmelita had listened as he voiced his concerns to her. She'd been silent at first, but he knew by the way she twisted her napkin, she had definite ideas on the matter.

Finally, she had said, "One of the reasons America has been blessed is because of our continued aid to Israel. In the Bible, God said that he would bless the nations that bless her and curse those who curse her."

"What about the sweat and tears of the immigrants who built this country?" he replied indignantly. "Or the democratic process? Don't they get some of the credit?"

"Now you're talking like a politician, Emilio."

She knew him too well, that was why he enjoyed debating issues with her. She was one of the few persons he couldn't intimidate.

"A country is a lot more likely to be blessed if the men who run it use wisdom and prudence," he answered.

"Men come and go," she said flatly. "Only God remains steadfast. If we support Israel, we'll prosper. If not, we'll receive a spiritual reprimand."

Even now, her words were like salt on an open wound. Whenever she'd brought up the name of God, using it like a battering ram, he'd felt only anger, but now her words came back to him, incessant drops of water steadily wearing a trench in his thoughts. Perhaps it was wiser and easier to believe in a God who controlled the universe than to believe that one's own abilities, devoid of God, made a difference.

He sat back in his chair and let his thoughts, along with the cigar smoke, rise to the ceiling.

As the plane reached cruising altitude, the warning sign went off and Faith undid her seat belt. She fingered the bow on the present Stephen had given her and closed her eyes for a minute, trying somehow to accept Pratt's death and her separation from Stephen.

"I'm sorry that you've had to go through this," said Randy as the Egypt Air jet streaked through the stratosphere towards Cairo. "When you were a little girl, I could 'make it all better' for you. I wish I still could."

She opened her eyes and with her fingertips felt the fake mustache under her nose. "As you may have noticed, Dad, technically I'm not a girl anymore, and this isn't the land of Oz. If it were, I could click my heels together and everything would be the way it used to be." She reached for his hand.

"Well, I've felt a lot like Dorothy lately. I've been picked up by a tornado, and it hasn't decided where to put me down yet. I have a feeling it isn't going to be Kansas."

They burst into laughter as the steward stopped to give them their breakfast trays.

"I don't know much about politics, but I was wondering," said Faith as she devoured the stewed prunes and apricots, "why didn't Egypt join Russia to attack Israel? There certainly isn't any love lost between them."

"You're right. Through most of history Egypt was Israel's perennial enemy, but in the latter part of the 1980s Egypt established a peace agreement with Israel. My guess is that if Russia and the other Arab nations had been successful, Egypt would have jumped on the victory wagon soon enough."

Silently, they finished their breakfasts, lulled into a false sense of security by the consoling hum of the engines in the background and the quiet efficiency of the stewards.

After they finished eating, Faith brought the gold-wrapped box out of her lap and put it on her tray.

"What's that?" asked Randy.

"Stephen gave it to me." She carefully unwrapped the paper and stared at the jewelry box. Slowly she lifted the velvet lid. The circular, blue-green turquoise stone, which was set in finely wrought silver, sparkled in the light. She put it on the third finger of her left hand.

"Look—it fits perfectly." Her voice bent like a slender bamboo reed. "He said he'd come to Israel in the summer."

"So that's the way it is," said Randy pensively. "I wouldn't hold him to it, you could be disappointed. A lot can happen between now and then."

"He'll come, Dad, I know he will. We don't have much time left, and we want to spend it together."

"You've got your entire lives ahead of you," he said, patting her arm. "Don't rush things."

She looked out the window. The bright blue sky seemed to reinforce her thoughts—now was as good a time as any to tell him.

"No, Dad. We have a little less than seven years, maybe not even that long."

"You really believe that?"

"With all my heart. Can I show you why?"

Randy nodded. Anything was better than thinking about the last couple of months.

Faith brought out her canvas bag from under the seat and pulled her notebook and Bible from it. "Promise me you'll keep an open mind. At first I didn't believe any of this either."

Randy Morgan listened as Faith began, hoping sublimely in his subconscious that maybe there was an answer to all the events which had occurred, some master plan behind them that would soon be revealed.

"Do you really think this is a good idea?" said Logan Washburn as Judah Midian arranged his long white robe in front of the full length mirror.

"It's been a month since the temple was erected. It's time."

"But to call the news media here . . . what if—"

"You still doubt your abilities and mine?" Judah turned and once again Logan felt the intensity of Judah's energy, like a pulsating aura that inspired, then consumed him.

"No," he replied as he felt himself fusing with Judah's will. "I'm ready."

Rabbi Solomon Lowenstein was agitated, and it didn't help matters that the fish he'd had for lunch was trying to swim upstream. He burped as he pressed against the newspaper reporters and made his way among the camera crews. He hoped Judah Midian would make a spectacle of himself; only then could this nonsense be over. The outer courtyard of the temple was so crowded that people spilled into the adjoining streets and shops.

Huge video screens had been installed outside the area so everyone could witness this media event. Washburn hadn't missed a trick. Judah was already fifteen minutes late, no doubt a ploy to heighten the enthusiasm of a frenzied and anxious crowd of supporters.

Ripples of excitement began at the temple steps and spread over the waiting audience as Judah Midian appeared at the edge of the platform. He walked across it to the front of the altar where the sacrifices had been resumed after the rebuilding of the temple.

Judah looked over the mass of people before him, quietly waiting until the clapping ceased and until everyone's attention was focused on him. He stepped forward to the edge of the platform where the microphone was located and hesitated for a moment before he spoke: "Behold, I will send you Elijah the prophet before the coming of the great and dreadful day of the Lord. And he shall turn the heart of the fathers to the children, and the heart of the children to their fathers, lest I come and smite the earth with a curse."

Judah stepped back and extended his right arm. Logan Washburn appeared and the crowd cheered again.

Solomon shook his head. Was there no end to this man's impertinence?

Logan raised his hands to the heavens. "So you might know that I am God's anointed." His eyes locked with Judah's.

Suddenly, a bolt of fire from the cloudless skies struck the altar behind him.

Logan jumped back, as surprised as the throng below who were watching. Quickly he regained his composure. If Judah could command the heavens, they really were invincible!

"It's impossible," said Solomon as his nostrils inhaled the scorched air. The crowd, who had cowered at first, now began wildly applauding. As Judah raised his hands again, the noise died down.

Solomon searched the heavens. This must have been contrived, but how? The multitude surged forward to hear what Judah had to say, taking the rabbi with them.

The people were silent as they waited to hear Judah. He opened his mouth to speak, but before he could utter a single word, a shot rang out. Judah staggered and fell backwards, collapsing into a heap on the platform.

There were gasps in the crowd, then shouts of indignation ripped through the multitude as they realized what had happened. Dazed, Logan bent over the body as people scrambled onto the platform.

"I'm a doctor," said a shaggy-haired man with a British accent. "Let me through."

Logan tried to push back the crowds to give him room to work. The doctor bent down and saw the bullet hole between Judah's eyes. He felt for his pulse. There was none.

"He's gone," he said as he stood up.

Logan's stony features registered neither surprise nor sorrow.

Falcon walked three aisles over to the house and garden center and pretended to be interested in a paint roller. He heard the woman come up behind him, but he didn't look up.

"Mr. Lightfoot?" said a low throaty voice.

"Yes." He glanced up. Randy was right. She looked more like a contestant in a beauty contest than an attorney.

She dropped her gaze and seemed intent on the can of high-gloss, enamel paint in her hand. She distanced herself from him, and began to examine some brushes as she talked.

"You know the authorities are still looking for Randy."

"He said you could be trusted to be discreet."

She looked at him shrewdly. "In November, Randy had me put all his financial assets in the name of a dummy corporation. I dissolved the corporation last week, and sold off the assets as he instructed."

"And the money?"

She tapped the paint can. "Inside," she said. "All in the new universal currency. Good luck, Mr. Lightfoot." She put down the can and walked away. Falcon looked around as she left, then picked up the paint can and a roller and headed for the checkout counter.

As he walked to the parking lot, he buttoned his buckskin jacket to ward off the February chill. As was his habit, he checked the rearview mirror when he got in the car. For some reason, he hadn't been followed for the last couple of days, or if he had been, the guy was so good, he hadn't spotted him.

Falcon Lightfoot smiled to himself. The warrior blood that once flowed through his ancestors still surged through his veins.

The cardinals had discreetly told Pope Timothy that a computer would be more efficient for his writing tasks, but the pope had learned in the seminary to think with a pen in his hand, not a keyboard. He had no desire to have every word he spoke appear instantly on a screen. The new Verbiage Computer sat unused in the corner of his office with its cursor blinking angrily as he prepared his speech.

He lifted his head as Father Paul charged through the door. "Your Supreme Pontiff, Judah Midian has been shot!"

The pope put down his pen. "It seems you have only bad news for me lately."

Father Paul shifted from one foot to the other as he stood in front of the pope. He wasn't sure whether to continue speaking or not. A slight nod from the pope unleashed a torrent of words. "They don't know who the assassin was; he disappeared into the crowd! The World Church—who will take Judah Midian's place?"

"Just because Israel's prophet"—Pope Timothy choked on the words—"has been murdered, it doesn't mean that our goal of world peace has been destroyed with him." He fingered his rosary. "Peace—is it only a tattered illusion? It seems to slip away every time we try to capture it."

"What'll we do?"

"We'll send the Vatican's condolences and see who steps forward to replace him."

"Oh." It was apparent that Father Paul was disappointed with his response.

"You expected me to perhaps send a legion of cardinals to help track down the murderer?"

The young priest felt himself flush. "No, sir. I guess I . . . didn't think at all."

"As the head of the Catholic church, Father Paul, I cannot indulge in that luxury. It is just as bad to overreact to a problem as it is to ignore it."

"Yes, sir." Father Paul colored again and backed out of the room. When he reached the door, he spun around and hurried down the corridor and back to the safety of the press room.

Logan Washburn felt intoxicated, but he'd had nothing to drink. Judah's assassin had lost himself in the hysterical crowd, and with the inflow of new people into the Holy City, the investigation could go on indefinitely. Although the police had looked at films of the crowd and tried to pick out suspects, their efforts so far had proved futile.

Logan looked down at Judah's face, trying to draw strength from it. He'd washed away the blood, and except for the bullet hole between the eyes, Judah looked as if he were sleeping. The public was already demanding to see the body of its slain hero, but he could not allow other hands to touch Judah's flesh.

Painstakingly, he removed his own garments and turned on the two-minute shower in the hotel room. The prime minister and other officials had come and gone, shaking their heads when he wouldn't allow them to remove Judah's body from the room.

"Overcome with grief," he'd heard them say. "Out of his head."

They were wrong.

He dried himself, then put on one of the white linen robes he'd had brought over from Judah's home. Only then did he approach the body again. He'd never seen Judah naked before and as he tenderly undressed him, he was surprised to see that he had not been circumcised.

He sponged the lifeless body with lukewarm water, letting the washcloth linger a moment on a small tattoo on Judah's left thigh. He bent closer to examine it more carefully, running his fingers over what appeared to be three numbers in the center of a pentagram. He felt lightheaded as he stared at the final evidence of Judah's birthright. How could he have ever doubted?

He patted Judah's body dry with one of the thick towels in the bathroom, then he slipped a shimmering white robe over the naked body. He lifted the head reverently from the pillow, combed Judah's raven hair into place, and kissed the place where the bullet had entered.

They were both ready.

Logan knew he would be openly criticized for not allowing Judah's body to be embalmed or his followers to view the body, so he announced to the press and wire services that he would hold a news conference at the grave site prior to Judah's burial.

He placed a bodyguard at the door of the hotel room and refused all attempts by the media to talk to him about the assassination, even though he knew the media were eager to pump him for information because of the rumors that he would assume Judah's position. If there were no "exclusive" stories, the world would be hungry for what Logan Washburn had to say.

It was going just as he and Judah had planned, maximum coverage beamed to the world—their world.

The immigration official at Cairo International Airport scrutinized Randy's business visa and the student visa in the name of Louis Bitterman.

"I'm sorry sir, but Egypt is a member of the World Health Organization. We adhere strictly to its immunization requirements. You and your son will be quarantined until you have had the proper inoculations. It's for your own protection."

He looked squarely at Randy. "Frankly, Mr. Bitterman, I'm surprised that you and your son were not aware of these regulations."

"We were," Randy assured him as he turned to Faith. "Louis, I thought your mother put our health cards in your duffel bag."

Faith dumped her bag on the counter and began to rummage through it, searching for the two yellow cards which Stephen had given them after they'd had their shots. Where was the magazine she'd put them in so they wouldn't get bent? Finally. She flipped through the slick pages, retrieved the cards, and handed them to the Egyptian official.

He seemed almost annoyed that she'd found them. A frown settled on his features as he stamped the passports with a flourish, then loudly snapped them shut.

"In the future may I suggest you keep your passports, visas, and health cards together so you will not delay the other passengers on your flight." He flashed them a dazzling smile. "Enjoy your stay in Egypt."

As they walked down the hall of the terminal at Cairo International Airport, Faith was fascinated by the people who swirled around her. Very few of the Muslim women wore veils, but they peeked discreetly at her from under lashes as black as the long dresses they wore. The traditional ankle-length robes worn by the Egyptians mixed with the more contemporary Egyptians in Western dress. It was a blending of the old and the new, and it was apparent that both were welcome in Cairo's society.

"Dad, I feel like we've stepped into another world."

"We have," said Randy, "and I'm going to show it to you. I see no reason why we can't act like tourists for a few days. I was just about your age when I came here, bright-eyed and bushy tailed—and ready to change the world."

"Really?"

"Don't act so surprised. I was young once, you know."

"What happened?" she laughed, nudging him in the ribs.

"Just like you, young lady, I grew up. Things went from black and white, right and wrong, to shades of gray."

He stepped on the escalator which would take them downstairs to the luggage area. "You get one shot at life, and I'm beginning to wonder if I missed the mark." He rubbed his forehead.

Randy couldn't tell his daughter, not even now, how he felt. Sometimes having a photographic memory was a curse; it wouldn't let you forget. The Scriptures she'd shown him kept reverberating in his head. He'd always figured that death was the end of everything; now he wasn't so sure.

She seemed to know what he was thinking. "It's pretty incredible, isn't it, Dad? I mean, God has His workers and His plans clearly mapped out. He's revealed His will for us in the Bible."

"It's . . . a little frightening when you think about it."

"Dad, the antidote for fear is faith."

He wasn't as eager as she was to believe. It would mean that he'd have to view everything he'd done in his life from a whole different perspective. Until now, he'd been comfortable in his rut of self-sufficiency.

Randy watched the luggage go around endlessly on the carousel. If someone didn't pick a bag up on the first pass, it came around again and again, giving the passenger another chance to claim it. Second chance. Maybe that's what he was being offered.

He lifted the suitcase from the merry-go-round and showed the baggage ticket stub to the guard. Randy searched the crowd for anyone suspicious, then headed for the exchange office where he converted his money into Egyptian pounds and piasters.

Afterwards, Randy and Faith followed the arrows toward the terminal exit. When they walked outside into the brilliant sunshine, a zealous dark-skinned man in a wrinkled robe ambushed them.

"I will give you a better rate on the American dollar than the banks," he said smiling widely at both of them. His hands darted back and forth as fast as the broken English he uttered in a rapid-fire dialect. "We both make money."

Randy brushed him aside and tried to hail one of the dark blue and white cabs that whizzed by.

Fearlessly, the young man stepped off the curb, throwing himself in the path of a taxi. The driver squealed to a stop and with a bold, sweeping movement, the young man opened the cab's door for Randy and Faith to step inside.

As Faith got in, Randy tried to give the man a few piasters, but he refused them.

"We will meet again," he said, "if Allah is willing." He melted into the teeming ant hill of humanity that was Cairo.

"Cairo Marriott," Randy said to the driver, who pushed the flag down on the meter. Within minutes they were in a noisy traffic jam. Horns honked and drivers wearing fezes yelled in Arabic and gestured wildly to each other.

"It's not always like this, is it, Dad?"

"I'm afraid so. Rapid transit and modern technology have a hard time getting a foothold here. The buses are even worse."

As they inched their way through the streets, Randy began to point out the stately mosques among the modern buildings and the shady parks overlooking the Nile.

Faith and her father were so caught up in the pulse of the sprawling city, where one out of three Egyptians lived, that neither one of them noticed the taxi behind, weaving in and out of the traffic to keep them in sight.

20

Burt Calhoun vehemently cursed the Cairo traffic jam. The taxi driver, who'd learned long ago that Americans possessed money, not patience, turned up the volume on the radio and smiled, showing his tobacco-stained teeth to his passenger.

In front of the gasping taxi, a donkey strained to pull a cart piled high with scrap metal, and to the right, a battered bus which had stalled was belching clouds of black smoke while its passengers overflowed into the street to join the other pedestrians who habitually walked in the roadways.

Calhoun knew he'd been sent to this "litter box" of the world because his Afro-American features enabled him to blend into the culture more easily than his white counterparts. The fact that he'd picked up a smattering of Arabic while on a six-month assignment to Alexandria had clinched it. He'd hated Egypt then, despite Alexandria's excellent climate and beaches, and he hated it now, in the winter.

It was a small consolation, but he knew that a few vehicles ahead of him, Randy Morgan was embroiled in the same bottleneck.

Accustomed to the quirks of the traffic and his passengers, the driver, with one hand on the steering wheel, lazily cracked nuts with his teeth and spit the shells through the open window while the cab, which had been in one too many fender-benders, inched forward like a dented turtle.

Thirty minutes later, Randy's taxi turned off and skirted a square, finally stopping at the entrance to the Cairo Marriott.

Calhoun motioned for the driver to pull over. *At least Morgan has good taste,* he thought as the hotel's lattice porticos loomed over him.

The CIA had definitely not gone all out when it booked his accommodation at the Tulip. The acid of resentment welled up within him and ate away at his pride. His room didn't even have a private bath. Last night, out of curiosity, he'd leafed through a bookstore's recent copy of Fodor's guide to Egypt. It came as no surprise that the Tulip was recommended for the budget traveler.

Calhoun waited until Randy and Faith entered their hotel, then mingling with the other arrivals in the lobby, he followed them. He grabbed a newspaper and sat as close to the main desk as he could from where he inspected the slender youth by Morgan's side who kept scratching his mustache. The way he touched Morgan's arm—yes, it had to be his daughter.

"Is this your first visit to the Cairo Marriott, Mr. Bitterman?" inquired the clerk cordially.

"Yes. My . . . son and I are looking forward to our stay."

"And well you should," he said clapping his hands together in obvious delight. "Forgive me for sounding like a commercial, but the management requires that I give each customer a brief overview of our facilities." He launched into his spiel with good humor. "Our hotel is a pleasant combination of today's amenities and yesterday's charm. Let me inform you, if you are unaware, that the heart of the hotel was a famous palace built as a guest house in 1869 for Empress Eugenie and other European royalty during the festivities surrounding the opening of the Suez Canal. As you can see, it's been restored to its former grandeur, although we have had to make concessions by adding two modern high-rise towers."

"It's beautiful," exclaimed Faith.

"We are located on twelve acres overlooking the Nile. We have tennis courts, swimming pools, a health club, and an assortment of retail shops so that we can meet your every need." Satisfied that he'd welcomed them properly, the clerk turned to get the key to their room.

Randy looked up from the guest registration card and pointed to the carved marble staircase of the main entrance hall.

"Since 1960 this place has been famous for its wedding receptions," he whispered. "Not that I want you to get any ideas, but the blushing bride usually comes down those stairs."

The clerk handed Randy the key but not before Faith gave her father a huge grin. As they walked through the lobby, she stared in awe at the high ceilings and elaborate arches. "Can we afford this?"

"For a few days. I know it can't make up for what's happened, but we can try, can't we?"

Faith bit her lip. "For a minute, I almost forgot . . . I wish Mom was here—and Hope."

"So do I, honey, so do I."

Calhoun folded and refolded the paper while Randy and Faith made their way to their room. The president had called off the search for Morgan, but John Seaton had resumed it without the president's knowledge. That lousy room at the Tulip—no doubt it was the CIA director's doing. Cheap lodgings didn't arouse suspicions and were easier to explain in the budget.

Sulkily, he approached the desk clerk who, for a pound note, gave him Morgan's room number. Calhoun sat down in the lobby to calculate his next move. Years ago he'd learned to think of murder as an impersonal act, done swiftly and humanely whenever possible, but he'd never had to kill a young woman. The thought disturbed him, but he knew he was going to eliminate Morgan and his daughter as quickly as possible so he could leave this city, crammed with thousands of worshipers and brawling markets, and return to the sanity of his apartment in Maryland.

All he wanted to do now was reach retirement, and if he picked up some extra cash along the way, all the better. Too late, Calhoun realized that he'd given his all for an organization which didn't give a straw about him. It was a bitter pill to swallow.

Engrossed in his own thoughts, he didn't notice that the Egyptian who'd approached Randy at the airport was studying him from across the room with an amused expression on his face.

Although both men were bent on accomplishing their respective missions, only one could survive.

★ ★ ★

"Solomon, don't get so excited. Judah Midian is dead. He can do us no harm," said Rebecca as her heart tightened into a painful knot.

"It's not over. I feel it in the marrow of my bones. You were not there—you didn't see the bolts of fire which crackled and leaped from a cloudless sky to the courtyard of the temple." Rabbi Solomon Lowenstein put his hands behind his back and paced around the enclosed garden at the back of his home.

"His death proves that he was only a man. Now the people will turn their hearts to the arrival of the true Messiah. I am . . . we are rid of him," said Rebecca, running her hands through her dark, curly hair.

"Perhaps you're right." Solomon stopped his pacing and leaned against the garden wall. "Still, before he was shot, I looked into the eyes of the crowd and what I saw frightened me. Rabbis, elders, old women and young people, even foreigners—all would have followed Judah anywhere, done anything for him—it was written on their faces. Blind obedience . . . it reminded me of—"

"Of what?"

"Of the stories my grandfather told me of Hitler's conquest of Europe. Hitler promised his followers a world based on anti-Semitism, and he almost delivered it."

"But Judah is . . . was . . . half Jewish."

"Some people still believe that Hitler had Jewish blood in his veins."

"Enough," said Rebecca shaking her head. "In every culture there are class distinctions, social barriers, even here in Israel. Despite the treaties, can you honestly say that the Arabs are not discriminated against by the Jews or vice versa?"

Solomon shook his head sadly.

"You dwell too much in a past that we cannot change. The future . . . that is where we must place our efforts and our hopes."

Maybe she's right, thought Solomon as he let her lead him inside for the evening meal. He had noticed lately that Rebecca seemed distracted, but then who wasn't after the events which had taken place in Israel?

He made a mental note to keep his ideas to himself. Even though Rebecca was a rabbi, first she was a woman. No matter how hard the world tried to convince him otherwise, women, in his opinion, were still the weaker sex. It was the way God in His wisdom had planned it. He made a promise to himself not to involve her in his personal holy war.

He drank more wine than usual, hoping it would blur the faces of Judah's admirers, but still he could not rid himself of the feeling that he had not heard the last of Judah Midian.

Dr. Stephen Bradley turned over the postcard with its picture of the three Pyramids of Giza and read the short note on the other side and the interpretation beneath it: *"Aleikum as-salam wa rahmat Allah wa barakatu" (Upon you be peace and the mercy of God and his blessings).* It was signed, "Louis."

He'd felt uneasy since Gordon Pratt's death, and although he was glad Faith had sent the card, he wondered if it had been wise. He turned on the front burner of his electric stove. When it glowed cherry red, he held the postcard to it; quickly, it burst into flames just as his life had.

He was living in two worlds. He'd handed in his resignation at the hospital with the explanation that he wanted to go to Israel to give medical assistance to those injured in the invasion and to help the hordes of new immigrants who were arriving. The chairman of the board, impressed by his dedication, said he would arrange to have the hospital pay his expenses while he lived abroad.

Stephen was floored by the proposal, and the chairman took his momentary lapse into silence for acquiescence, informing him that it was an excellent public relations angle; all Stephen would have to do was send in a quarterly report.

Stephen knew he couldn't turn down the offer. What would he say? That he was leaving everything to run away with a girl he barely knew to a place where he'd never been? It sounded ridiculous even to him.

He made his rounds as usual, but for the first time in his career he felt fractured, at odds with himself. Medicine had always been foremost in his life. Now something else had emerged, intruded into his—familiar, if not orderly—world of human illness.

His patients were no longer just bodies in need of repair, but human souls in need of redemption. For the first time in his life he was looking at the whole person, body and soul. It was disconcerting, but somehow it made sense. People were not one-dimensional; they were more than just craniums, femurs, ribs, and vertebrae—much more.

He tried to trace the origin of these new, and somehow startling, revelations. It had begun with his own bare-bones faith, a mere skeleton that Faith had helped him flesh out with Scriptures from the Bible, but it was his own research and prayers which had finally convinced him.

"The only verse I know by heart is John, chapter three, verse sixteen," he'd said to Faith at the hospital when they were having one of their discussions before she left.

"I was six years old and Miss Pennyworth, my Sunday school teacher, promised me a gold star if I memorized it. I was madly in love with her. You know, you remind me of her."

She had squeezed his hand. "The gospel is so simple, Stephen, that a child can grasp it, and so complex that the wisdom of all the ages is contained in it. The verse you mentioned is a good place to begin. It's God's plan for mankind in a nutshell. 'For God so loved the world, that He gave His only begotten Son, that whosoever believes in Him should not perish, but have everlasting life.'"

"But most people want to work their way to heaven, pull themselves up by their own . . . stethoscope," he had said.

"Yes, but it's not necessary. Everlasting life is a gift which God gives to us in the form of His Son. All we have to do is receive Him and ask Him to forgive us for all the wrong things we've done. Then with His power, we can live for Him."

"But, you and I are finding all this out after—what did you call it—the Rapture?

She had nodded.

It's sort of like we missed the main event," he said.

"That wasn't the main event."

Stephen looked down at the feathery gray ashes around the

burner, then bent down and blew them into the air. They scattered, and like his questions, disappeared into the larger circle of his new existence. He still didn't have all the answers, but at least now he knew where to find them.

So, the charlatan had one more trick up his sleeve. Solomon didn't tell Rebecca where he was going; she would only have told him to leave well enough alone. He wanted to see how Logan Washburn was going to slither out of this predicament. Even he couldn't raise the dead.

Rabbi Solomon Lowenstein grumbled within himself as he hurried to the summit of the Mount of Olives, wondering why, of all places, Logan Washburn had chosen it for a press conference.

As he stopped to rest for a moment while the crowd of people swept past him, he looked down and saw the sacred Jewish cemetery where many of the ancients were buried. They were waiting, as he was, for the Messiah. Jewish tradition declared that the dead would be resurrected from their graves when He appeared and would follow Him into Jerusalem through the Gates of Mercy.

As the rabbi looked at the graveyard which spread around the western side of the Mount of Olives, he wondered if one day he too would lie there . . . waiting. It was considered a privilege to be buried in what was believed to be the oldest cemetery in the world still in use. He wanted no such privilege.

He rubbed his aching knees and continued trudging up the mountain, suddenly aware that perhaps Logan Washburn had received permission to intern Judah Midian there. He felt a surge of righteous indignation tear through his stiff limbs. Yes, it was just like him; even in death the mongrel would attempt to shape events to his liking.

The swarm of people thickened as he neared the summit. Solomon circled to the far right on the fringe of the crowd so he could see better. He thought he saw the Israeli prime minister and once again felt the heat of anger. By coming here, he had lent dignity to this man's lies and blasphemy. It never occurred to Solomon that perhaps his presence could be viewed in the same light.

He craned his neck, and above the bobbing heads he could see Logan Washburn standing in a roped-off area. Armed officers in front of it kept the people back.

His eyes widened as he saw a casket on a raised platform behind Washburn. Washburn should have been a filmmaker.

A woman behind him began to sob, and Solomon turned and looked at her in disgust. The crowd was so tightly packed that he was afraid to sit down. There was the possibility that he would be trampled if their mood changed.

"Ah, Solomon," said one of his childhood friends, as he spied him in the crowd and edged closer. "You have come to see the burial of God's anointed."

"Surely you must be joking, Johnathan. I have come to see a false prophet and his deceptions buried. I grant that he was a world leader who captured the hearts of our people with signs and wonders, but he was nothing more. He was not the Holy One of Israel."

"You are very certain of this."

"Does this not prove it? If he were the Messiah he would have called down the very angels from heaven to protect him from a madman's bullets." Solomon wagged his arthritic finger at Johnathan. "You should have known better than to put your trust in him."

"He has not been buried yet. There is still time."

"Time for what?"

The sound of clapping drowned out Johnathan's answer as Logan Washburn stepped forward to a portable microphone. *They look like flies.* Solomon waited for the throng to quiet down. *A swarm of black flies hovering over the mountainside in search of the spiritual garbage they think Logan Washburn can offer them.*

Logan put his hand on the casket. "Judah and I wish to thank all of you for coming."

Muffled sobs and high-pitched wails echoed throughout the still morning air amid the hum of camcorders.

"You have come to mourn one who is dead, but your weeping shall be turned into laughter."

Two newscasters looked at each other and raised their eyebrows.

"You have to admit," one mumbled to the other, "Washburn always puts on a good show."

"We'd like to ask you some questions," shouted a woman reporter from Paris, dressed in a tight black dress with a fur jacket. "Why has no one been allowed to see his body except the coroner and yourself?"

Logan ignored her question, took a deep breath, and put his hand again on the casket. The reporter and the crowd grew still in anticipation of what he would do next.

Logan Washburn cried out in a loud tormented voice, "Judah come forth!"

Shivers went up Solomon's spine.

For a moment all eyes were on the casket.

Nothing happened.

People nudged each other, and slowly whispers of ridicule and disbelief, like loose kites, floated above the audience.

He's gone crazy, thought Solomon.

Then he heard it. A collective intake of breath as the coffin lid began to move.

No! No! This can't be happening!

The muscles in Solomon's neck sent a throbbing pain down his collarbone as he jerked to the right so he could see past the corpulent woman who had shifted her position in front of him.

The casket lid began to open. A pair of slender hands emerged and pushed off the marble lid. It landed with a thud on the rocky hillside, and for a moment, in the stillness which followed, all Solomon could hear was his own heart pounding in his chest.

Languidly, like a sleepwalker returning after a long journey, the translucent, robed figure of Judah Midian sat up.

The woman in front of Solomon screamed, then fainted, falling backwards into his arms and knocking him to the ground.

Roughly he pushed her limp body out of the way and jumped to his feet so he could see.

"I told you," said Johnathan, wringing his hands together as Solomon crowded to his side.

Like a wild bird caged for the first time, Solomon's heart beat frantically against his ribs as Judah put his legs over the side of the casket. With the help of Logan Washburn, he stepped out of his death bed on shaky legs.

Judah faced the astonished crowd with his magnetic eyes.

Rabbi Solomon Lowenstein pushed his way through the crowd, fighting for a closer look. He saw the pale face and the round hole between Judah's eyes where the bullet had entered. He felt weak, and even as he trembled in disbelief, Judah's mesmeric eyes met his and held him upright.

Burt Calhoun heard the loudspeaker in the pencil-thin minaret crackle the call to prayer as it did five times a day. Why in the world were they going to a mosque . . . and at prayer time?

He removed his shoes before he stepped over the threshold of the sanctuary of Ibn Toulun. He'd read that it was one of the best examples of pure Islamic architecture in the world; that must be why Morgan had included it on his itinerary. Calhoun had no desire to soak up the local culture; he wanted to soak in a hot tub, even if it was down the hall—and two people before him had used the same bathwater.

He hadn't slept well last night and after following the Morgans all morning as they toured the historical area of the Citadel, situated on the slopes of the Mokkattan Hills, he was weary. If Morgan had wanted to show his daughter the spectacular view of Cairo, the Nile, and the Pyramids of Giza from the hillside, why couldn't he have taken a cab or bus for a sightseeing tour like everyone else instead of walking?

Burt Calhoun spied them at the back of the mosque. He wiped the sweat off his brow with the corner of his robe as he positioned himself not far from them, then he folded his robe under him, turned to face Mecca, and squatted with his forehead on the prayer mat. From the corner of his eye he watched the two of them, straining to hear what they said.

It took Faith a moment to shut out the noise of the many buses, braying donkeys, and pushcarts that comprised the bustling traffic outside, along with the percussive crafts of the nearby tinsmiths and furniture makers. It was fainter now, but she thought she could still hear the voices of shrieking housewives as they yelled at each other from the second and third floor latticed windows.

She breathed deeply, and the sweet pungent scent of incense filled her nostrils. She felt herself begin to relax.

"I feel like we've stepped back into the time of the *Arabian Nights*," Faith said in a hushed voice as she looked around at the kneeling Moslems in prayer. "But . . . I still can't get used to the crowds in the streets. All those people jostling together—it frightens me," she admitted.

"Cairo is one of the *safest* cities in the world. Despite all the noise and the teeming population, street crimes are almost unheard of," said Randy. "Traffic accidents—now that's another story."

"Why is it different here?"

He pointed to the men at prayer. "That's the reason, moral solidarity."

"You mean because they're Moslems?"

"Yes. If a person were attacked on the street, the first passerby would stop and immediately come to his aid. It would be inconceivable for him to do anything less. You wouldn't dare go out at night by yourself in New York or Washington, D.C., but you can in Cairo. In fact, the word *Islam* comes from the Arabic root *salima,* to be safe."

"Safe. I hope you're right." She gnawed one of her fingernails. "Do you think they've given up trying to find us?"

"It's too soon to say, but now that I'm out of the country maybe I won't be perceived as an immediate threat any longer."

"Does that mean I can get rid of this?" She wrinkled her nose to ease the prickly heat rash that had broken out under the fake mustache. "When can I be the 'opposite sex' again?"

"In three days when we cross the Sinai Peninsula into Israel."

"Will we be able to see Mount Sinai?"

"It's definitely the longest way to get to the border crossing at Rafah, but if you've got your heart set on it—"

"I'd love to see where God gave Moses the Ten Commandments."

"In that case . . . we'll spend the night at the tourist village, then walk up the path to St. Catherine's Monastery to the site of the burning bush. Just behind it is a trail to the summit of Jebel Musa where most people believe the Ten Commandments were delivered to Moses. But until then I need to fortify you, young lady, with a real Egyptian meal. Believe me, it will in no way resemble the continental breakfast we had in our room this morning."

Burt Calhoun pondered the facts he'd just gleaned as Randy Morgan and his daughter left the mosque. If he'd believed in God, he would have thanked Him. Depending on which route they took, the Sinai region afforded several barren and remote places where he could accomplish his mission and dispose of the bodies.

Silently Calhoun stood up and followed them back into the land of the *Arabian Nights*.

Fouad glanced around the street cafe until he spotted Burt Calhoun trying to blend into the potted palm he was standing behind. If this was the best the American intelligence community had to offer, he was not impressed.

He focused his attention on Randy Morgan and his daughter, who were sitting at one of the outdoor tables shaded by a leafy vine. The ground had been sprinkled with water by the owner to keep the dust down, and inside the cafe he could see the clouds of sawdust rise from the floor as the customers made their way to the counter at the back where they puffed on water pipes and read the paper.

Instead of the mannish clothes she was wearing to disguise herself, what would Faith Morgan look like in a galabieh, the long flowing robe many Cairenes wore, he wondered. In a mosque controlled by fundamentalists, Fouad had been taught that if a wife disobeyed her husband, she was condemned to hell. An Arab woman's role was to pray, wear the veil, and care for the children.

Egyptian women did not frequent the street cafes. They knew it was a man's domain where men came to exchange quips, have endless conversations, drink strong Arabic coffee sweetened with sugar, and perhaps play a game of backgammon. Faith's father had brought her to this cafe, perhaps to show her the "real" Egypt after they'd visited the marketplaces.

Out of sight, Fouad had followed them through the old bazaars on Mouski street as they sniffed the spices and perfumes, inspected the workmanship of the goldsmiths and textile merchants, and haggled over the price of an inlaid box. A small mound of neatly wrapped purchases was piled on the chair next to the girl as she sipped her Arabic coffee.

Fouad sat down, gave his order to the waiter, and thought back to his meeting with Falcon Lightfoot last week at the secluded town of Petra in Jordan. While they'd talked, they'd ridden horseback through the winding canyon that led to the Treasury, the Corinthian Tombs, and the Monastery.

Falcon. It was an unusual name for an unusual man. This American reminded him of Horus, the god of the sky, who, in Egyptian mythology, was depicted by a falcon's head on a man's body or by a winged sun disc. Reincarnation, maybe it was possible.

Falcon had entrusted him with Randy and Faith's safe passage to Israel and with a large amount of money from the sale of Randy's property in the United States. After paying Fouad well for his services, this man, who had seemed one with his Arabian stallion, had galloped back into obscurity. He hadn't given Fouad any explanations; they both knew that money was the universal coin of illumination and enlightenment.

Money, that was what Fouad needed to establish himself.

When he was twelve years old he'd decided he didn't want to be a fellahin, a peasant farmer, like his father and brothers. Surely Allah had smiled down upon him years ago when, as a struggling student at the Al-Azhar University, he'd been chosen as a guide for a group of foreign government officials visiting his country.

He was twenty-seven years old, and when he completed this task, he would make his first pilgrimage to Mecca, then he would marry and live in the middle-class Dokki neighborhood. His father had three wives who squabbled constantly, and a tribe of hungry children who were dependent on the cotton crop he planted. Although Fouad would be allowed four wives under Islamic law, observation had made him desire only one.

He thought again of Falcon. His resemblance to the ancient god of Egypt—was it just a coincidence?

Faith and her father rose to go.

Fouad observed the CIA agent. This man was all that stood between him and his future. He wished even now that he was at the desert valley of Mina where, with the other pilgrims, he would hurl pebbles and rocks at the three pillars which symbolized the devil.

He saw clearly the face of Burt Calhoun superimposed on one of the columns, and in his mind he picked up a bolder and heaved it with all his might, smashing the last obstacle in his pathway to success.

22

Pope Timothy I pushed the button on his private elevator, and it started its climb to his apartment on the third floor of the Apostolic Palace, where he would meet with his secretary of state. *There is never enough time for everyone,* he thought.

In the past six months, his hand had been squeezed, pulled, and kissed by hundreds of people in numerous audiences, but he found that he had given them more than his hand; he'd given them his heart. He'd listened to their needs: for faith, reassurance, courage, healing. Inevitably, their faces were mirrored in his soul, and their words bruised his ears.

He'd heard some of the cardinals say that he'd borne the weight of the papacy with remarkable endurance. He could not have done it without the people who were now a part of his life: Carlos, his valet and chauffeur, who served him his meals dressed in a white jacket with gold buttons; his two personal secretaries; the four nuns who ran the kitchen, cleaned the apartment, and washed his clothes; and the confessor, before whom he got down on his knees at least once a week.

The elevator door opened and he stepped out. The disturbing news of Judah Midian's so-called resurrection made him painfully aware of his responsibilities. It was necessary, once again, for the head of the Catholic church to make a move in the chess game of church politics.

Rabbi Solomon Lowenstein crumpled the telegram in his hand. He could barely remember Randy Morgan. Now he was asking for asylum in his home. He scratched his forehead, trying to awaken his sleeping memories.

Let's see . . . he'd met this American when Randy was a student, doing research on the Nazi involvement in the Holocaust. Solomon remembered that his father had volunteered to let the young foreigner stay in their home. At the time, Solomon had protested about this to his aging grandfather who lived with them, but he'd been overruled with a statement about hospitality to the stranger in the land.

Later, Solomon discovered that this had been only one of the reasons. His grandfather confided to him that the Holocaust needed to be documented, not only by Jews, but by outsiders, so that future generations could not dismiss or forget what had happened. Along with many other private contributors, his grandfather had helped finance the five-story, 265,000 square foot United States Holocaust Memorial Museum, located in Washington, D.C., just a few hundred yards from the Washington Monument and the Smithsonian museums.

Still, Solomon hadn't liked Randy Morgan. He'd seemed almost clinical in his studies, showing no passion as his grandfather related the terrors of the concentration camps. The rabbi was torn between his own feelings and his respect for his deceased father and grandfather. Nervously, Solomon rubbed the bald spot on the back of his head.

"Rebecca?"

"What is it, Solomon?"

"We will be having guests soon." He handed her the wrinkled telegram. "A friend of my father and his daughter."

"For how long?"

"I don't know." He paced the floor. "This is not the time, not now."

"You mean because of Judah Midian?"

"Yes. I must expose him. The whole thing has to be a fraud. You cannot put new wine in an old bottle."

Rebecca looked lovingly at this man who had become a second

father to her. He was so stubborn. She was certain that Judah was not the Messiah. He was an opportunist, but now he was an important man in Israel, and his words must be heeded. She glanced at the telegram. "Perhaps this Randy Morgan can help you expose him."

Solomon's eyes widened. She was right! He nodded his head thoughtfully. Morgan's dispassionate and impartial approach could be put to good use. But he'd promised himself that he would not involve Rebecca, a promise he'd already broken.

"I know you and some of the elders must think me an obstinate old man, Rebecca, but I must be sure. For years God has been angry with the Jews. An Islamic mosque stood on the only spot where we could make animal sacrifices, and according to Leviticus, chapter seventeen, 'It is the blood that makes atonement for the soul.'

"Now that we have resumed the blood sacrifices, we must not anger God again by worshiping Judah Midian. He stands in the way of the true Messiah's appearance."

Rebecca would not argue with him. His beliefs were rooted as deeply as the well from which they drew water. Now water rationing had forced them back to the methods used by their ancestors in Jerusalem and perhaps to their form of government.

"Some people want to make him a king."

"Do they never learn?" he said angrily. "Centuries ago the Israelites demanded to be ruled by a king, like the other nations around them. It was a mistake that divided our nation." He stroked his beard while thoughts tumbled through his mind. "Yes, we may make a Righteous Gentile out of this Randy Morgan."

"A Righteous Gentile?"

"The name given to those Gentiles who risked their lives to save Jews during World War II."

"Surely you do not believe it will come to that," Rebecca said in an alarmed voice.

"One must be a realist. Power is not easily overthrown."

"Promise me you will be discreet." She moved closer to him. "If and when you discover evidence to prove that Judah is a . . . fraud, then we will take it to the prime minister, together. Promise me!"

"It would be unwise to try and take on the pride of Judah by ourselves. We will go the proper authorities together."

Satisfied, Rebecca went to prepare the rooms for their guests while Solomon looked out the window, reminiscing. They were "the chosen people." Chosen by God to carry the burden of His commandments. It was a weight on his poor shoulders, and if Rabbi Solomon Lowenstein was not careful, he would be crushed beneath it.

There was a knock on the hotel door. "Who is it?" asked Randy as a shot of adrenalin ripped through his body. He reached under the mattress, pulled out his gun, and put it under his jacket.

"Come in," he said, stepping away from the door.

When the door opened, he was surprised to see a young Egyptian, the one who'd approached them at the airport. A chance encounter? He doubted it. He looked into the man's eyes, trying to fathom any signs of deceit in their murky darkness. "We've met before, haven't we? At the airport. The first day we arrived.

"Perhaps you'd better come in and we'll talk further," said Randy, still brandishing his gun.

"I assure you my intentions are to do you good, not harm," said Fouad as he shut the door behind him, then faced Randy and Faith.

"I'll be the judge of that," said Randy. "Sit on the bed, and keep your hands in front of you." He stood in front of Fouad. "Who are you working for?"

Fouad raised his right hand slowly to his head. "If you will notice, I am wearing a white turban, not a black one. That makes me, as you Americans would say, one of the good guys." He smiled broadly.

"You didn't answer my question."

His smile melted away. "I was hired by Falcon Lightfoot."

"How do I know that? It was no secret that Falcon and I were friends."

"Precisely what he said you would say. If you will allow me, I will tell you something which will convince you that what I say is true."

"Go ahead, it's your thirty seconds."

"The last night you saw Falcon, he turned over his bowl of rice at a Chinese restaurant and said that it represented the intelligence community. He extracted one grain and put it in his mouth. He said that solitary grain was you; they were going to eat you alive and no one would miss you, except him."

Randy lowered his gun. "And he was right. Good old Falcon. Still trying to take care of me halfway around the world. I assume he sent you here to help us get to Israel?"

"Yes, and to take care of anyone who might get in your way. You're being watched by a CIA agent named Burt Calhoun."

"Black, late thirties," said Randy as Calhoun's face flashed through his mind. "We'll have to get rid of him."

"They'll just send someone else," said Fouad. "I have a plan that will halt their efforts once and for all." He stood up. "I understand that you're trying to engage a guide to take you across the Sinai Peninsula to Israel."

Apparently this young man was adept at his job, thought Randy, but then if he wasn't, Falcon wouldn't have used him.

"Yes. This morning I rented a four-wheel drive for the trip. I'll pick it up tomorrow."

"I will be your guide." He winked at Faith. "If the gods smile upon us, we will be successful. Now I suggest you both go down for dinner. Afterwards, you will go to the reception desk, where I will meet you. We will argue loudly about the fee for my services, so that even Mr. Calhoun, from behind his newspaper, will know the time of our departure."

"We'll have to make sure we don't give him the opportunity to do anything until we get to the desert," said Randy. "We want to play this game on our timetable, not his."

"Mr. Calhoun has only been stalking his quarry; he is not yet ready to pounce," said Fouad. "I have seen many men like him. They enjoy the hunt more than the actual kill, but when it comes down to it, he will kill—ruthlessly and without feeling—because he must in order to survive, like the fabled gladiators of Rome."

"Or be eaten by the lions," said Randy.

"True," said Fouad, "but remember that the female lion is the best huntress, not the male."

Faith's short, reddish-brown hair framing her pale face glis-

tened in the lamplight, and for a brief second Fouad saw before
him a Sphinx with the head of a woman and the body of a lion.

Fouad could barely see the road through the clouds of choking
dust and sand which seeped in through every crack in the roof,
doors, and windows of the jeep, showering Randy Morgan and
his daughter with fine particles which filtered through their
clothes and made them gasp for breath. With scant warning, the
desert of northern Sinai had exploded into a swirling mass—a
gigantic piece of sandpaper that buffeted everything in its path.
It was nature at its worst.

Fouad stuck his head out the window as he pulled the jeep off
the main road. His face felt like a piece of chopped liver as he
unwrapped the long piece of brown cloth he'd used as a turban
and rewound it around his head until only his bloodshot eyes
were visible. They smarted and Fouad blinked rapidly, trying to
dispel the grit that had invaded them.

"How long do you think it'll last?" shouted Randy above the
roar of the storm.

"The desert's fury is like a hot-blooded woman. It may be over
in five minutes or five hours, one never knows."

Faith leaned forward from the back seat. "Are we very far from
Abu Rudeis?"

"Maybe a half hour. We'll turn east there and start up the
mountain to the monastery."

"If there are no objections," said Faith as she pulled a blanket
out from under the backseat of the jeep, "I think I'll get some
sleep."

"How can you sleep with all this racket?" said Randy.

Faith smiled at him from under her blanket. "Compared to
most of the music today, this is a lullaby." She lay down on the
seat, closed her eyes, and immediately drifted off to sleep.

Randy shook his head. "The last thing in the world I could do
right now is fall asleep."

"She has entrusted her life to someone she has complete faith
in, therefore she does not fear," said Fouad.

"Entrusted? Who? Do you mean . . . me?"

"No. She told me that her God guides her. Do you believe also?"

"Oh, that." Randy squirmed in his seat, wishing he could terminate the conversation. Fouad's candidness pricked Randy's conscience, and he was forced to recall from his memory everything he and Faith had discussed on the plane.

Fouad sensed his uneasiness. "People seek solutions to their problems in their own way. That is why every year hundreds of Egyptians go to the Giza Plateau near Cairo to absorb the mystical vibrations trapped inside the pyramids of the pharaohs Cheops, Chephren, and Mycerinus. They believe that by doing this they can find positive, not negative, solutions to their problems. Perhaps because the pyramids have remained for more than four thousand years, they attract the seekers of the unknown."

"You mean people think that the pyramids have some kind of psychic power?"

"Yes. Some believe that the secrets of Atlantis and the knowledge of the future are buried under the right front paw of the Sphinx at the foot of the Giza Plateau."

"Back in the States I kept hearing the phrase, 'pyramid power.'"

"The Japanese bring tour groups that come to tap this pyramid power. Some of the visitors sit in the lotus position and hum or seek extrasensory powers, while others are content to meditate or dance."

"I guess people still want to believe in magic."

"Do you?"

"No. To me, magic is just a synonym for deception. The pyramids are nothing more than giant tombs for ancient Egyptian rulers. You know," Randy said, more to himself than to Fouad, "every great religious leader in the world is buried somewhere, except for one—Jesus Christ." Like a Rubic's Cube, the squares of Randy's mind began to fall in place.

"He had no family to bury him?"

"He *was* buried after His death on the cross, but He actually came back to life. That's what the Bible says."

"He must be a very powerful god," said Fouad reverently. "Do you believe in this Jesus Christ?"

"I'm . . . not sure . . . but for the first time in my forty odd years, I'm beginning to realize that maybe I've been wrong." He turned to Fouad. "What if the foundation I've based my life on is nothing more than"—he looked at the landscape outside his window—'shifting sand'?" Suddenly his eyes lit up at the implications of his allegory.

"Then you must replace it with a solid foundation."

"Yes, but can it really be that easy?" Randy slumped down in the front seat and closed his eyes, trying to shut out the storm which wailed and shrieked around them. The Bible verses he'd read on the plane pushed their way through the incessant noise and penetrated his thoughts. This time he played them over and over again, digesting them word by word, phrase by phrase, and as he did so, each one became a building block which would form the basis for his new life. He felt bone-tired, yet he was elated with his newfound knowledge, which in its very simplicity had unraveled the complexities of life. Unbeknown to him, the hard-fought battle for his soul was over, but Satan, never at peace with himself and constantly on the prowl, was preparing for an even bigger battle.

It was too quiet. That was what woke her . . . the silence. Faith yawned and unwrapped herself from the blanket. Fouad turned and put his right forefinger to his lips for her to remain quiet. He pointed to her father. She sat up and saw that he was sound asleep, his head leaning against the window. He looked different somehow, so untroubled, as though he didn't have a care in the world.

She stretched and looked out the windows at what seemed at first to be a moonscape, complete with craters and barren stretches of wasteland, covered with an endless carpet of beige sand. The storm was over.

"I've got to go to the bathroom," she whispered. Fouad nodded. Faith reached in the back of the jeep, got a roll of toilet paper, and opened the door. Her boots sank into the sand that had drifted up against the car, and she felt as if she were plowing through snow as she headed for the privacy of a sand dune. She pulled her pants down, then squatted in her sandy outhouse.

"Finish what you are doing, then get up very slowly."

She froze. Faith felt her face flush to the very roots of her hair. Angry and embarrassed, she pulled her pants up hastily. She turned to see a middle-aged black man pointing a gun at her.

"Come with me," he said in a low, menacing voice. "If you utter one word, I'll kill you."

Something was wrong. Fouad shook Randy.

"What's the matter?" he said groggily.

"Your daughter left fifteen minutes ago to go to the bathroom. She hasn't returned."

Instantly, Randy was wide awake. "You let her go by herself?"

"I did not think that she would want an audience."

They scrambled out of the jeep and followed the heavy indentions in the sand that indicated the direction Faith had gone.

"She was here," said Fouad, pointing to a damp spot in the sand, then at the two sets of footprints which trailed out into the desert. "It must be Calhoun."

"He wants us to follow them, that's why he left those tracks. He's using Faith as bait," said Randy.

"You'll follow them," said Fouad, "but this episode will not end the way Mr. Calhoun has planned."

The global food and water shortages, coupled with the recent outbreak of the bubonic plague in Europe, had killed one-third of the world's population. The nations of the world were anxious for a savior, and Judah Midian was more than willing to oblige them.

He felt confident in his new role. He'd been careful to keep the right touch of humility towards his accusers so his image would not be tarnished by arrogance.

"Skeptics are the accountants who keep the balances in the ledger of life. When I am weighed in the balance, I will not be found wanting," he said to the constant stream of people from around the globe who came to solicit his advice and counsel.

Like an ancient sage, Judah dispensed his philosophy from a West Bank office building which one of his admirers had given him for his operations. It was being completely redecorated, and

Logan Washburn scurried through the thirteenth floor, keeping an eye on the staff he'd recently hired. Eighteen secretaries were necessary to handle the correspondence and donations which kept pouring in. Judah was more than just a prophet or king, he was a multi-billion dollar organization.

Wisely, Judah Midian had declared that he wanted only to use his supernatural abilities and the enormous funds at his disposal to insure that mankind could achieve a literal heaven on earth. Of course, in order to do this, he would have to implement some changes to rid the world of the discord which had crept in.

Judah was glad this day was over. He was weary of the petty arguments and requests of the emissaries who had passed through his office. He placated them because he knew he needed their loyalty, but soon they would outlive their usefulness.

"The sculptor is here," said Logan Washburn as he entered the office and closed the door.

"Has everyone gone?"

"Yes."

"Then show him in and . . . Logan, we want to be alone."

Judah exchanged glances with the handsome young man who was standing awkwardly at the door with his sketch pad in his hand. He motioned for him to come forward.

"Mr. Nicene, I've heard that you are a gifted and very promising Swedish sculptor; that's why I've asked you here."

"Thank . . . you . . . ," stuttered the nervous youth as he gazed in awe at Judah.

"You have some sketches to show me?"

"Yes, sir." Lars opened his sketch pad. "You understand I had to do these on the plane from newspaper pictures, there was so little time after you summoned me."

Judah said nothing as he flipped through the pages to examine the drawings.

"I work better from an actual model . . . if you would have some time for a sitting—"

Judah lifted his hand. "These are excellent. When can you begin?"

Lars swallowed hard as he answered. "Immediately."

"Good. I will have Logan arrange a place for you to stay."

Judah handed the sketches back to him, and for a brief instant their fingers touched. Unnerved, Lars dropped his pad on the rug in front of Judah's desk.

As he bent down to pick it up, Judah saw that his body was firm and supple. Good. He smiled to himself. Mr. Nicene would be able to serve more than one purpose.

"Judah, as leader of the Common Market, can control the food supply of the world." Solomon was beside himself. "Am I the only one who can see what is happening?" Primed for an argument, he stood up in his seat in the Knesset, Israel's parliament.

"Judah Midian has promised to protect Israel and he has. What he does with the rest of the world does not bother me," said a bearded elder named Ezekiel as he addressed the 120 members of the Knesset.

"It does not bother you that we are being branded like cattle?"

"You make too much of it. A small, invisible mark on our foreheads. It is like a ration card. It only means we have pledged our allegiance to Judah and therefore are entitled to special privileges. It is like separating the wheat from the chaff."

Contemptuously, Rabbi Solomon Lowenstein crossed his arms in front of him and stared at the members who had recently been elected. "I will not allow Judah Midian to label me. Have you forgotten the number that was tattooed on my grandfather's arm—and your grandmother's?" He pointed an accusing finger at Ezekiel.

"How can I forget? You won't let me." Ezekiel shook his head. "Do as you please, but when you're hungry don't come begging at my door. All I will give you is a stone to remind you of the hardness of your heart."

Like a small, spewing volcano, one man with a florid face erupted. "Solomon, we all know the old joke: Six rabbis equal seven opinions. But you have carried it too far. Now, as never before, we need unity. If you are not with us, you are against us."

Ezekiel rose from his chair, and the other men who'd come to the meeting began to leave the chamber. They did not want to listen to the ravings of an old man who would not fit in with the new programs for their country. They would do Judah's bidding without Solomon's help.

Solomon's heart was heavy as he stood outside the entrance of the Knesset where the eternal flame honoring Israel's fallen soldiers burned brightly. He adjusted his prayer shawl. It was useless; the members of parliament were animals returning to their own vomit. God forgive him—had he actually called them swine?

He looked across the road at the huge, bronze Menorah, the seven-branched candelabra which was Israel's national symbol. Solomon remembered the Hebrew inscription from the prophet Zechariah which ran along the outer arms. "Not by might, nor by power, but by my Spirit, says the Lord of hosts." Only Jehovah's intervention could alter the path Israel had chosen.

Even though it was late, he decided to walk to the Old City instead of hailing a taxi or riding the bus. Time was irrelevant. By the time he had labored up the hill towards his house in the Jewish Quarter, only a handful of people were on the streets. He stopped, then whirled around in the darkness. There was no one there, but he still felt it. Eyes . . . watching him.

"Rabbi Solomon Lowenstein," a voice whispered. He searched for its source and saw a figure in the shadows. "Please keep walking. You are being followed."

Followed? Solomon continued his steady pace up the hill.

"I must speak with you," the voice said from a doorway. "Go to the Damascus Gate at sundown tomorrow. I will meet you on the bridge."

For the first time, the thought came to Solomon that he might really be in danger. This thought was rapidly pursued by another. *What difference does it make? If I am to die waiting for the Messiah, so be it.* He was not the first, nor would he be the last Jew to die because of his beliefs.

23

Was it just the wind playing tricks on him, or had he really heard laughter? Randy stopped and listened, but all he could hear was his own rapid heart beat, his own uneven breathing.

The sun was setting, and as he watched it slipping below the horizon, he saw two black specks moving from west to east across it. It had to be Faith and Calhoun.

"God," he prayed, "what am I going to do?" Immediately he felt a warmth spread throughout his body, calming his feverish spirit. He basked in it for a moment, then began to head for the ant-sized figures which had now stopped.

"Your father has found us." Calhoun looked out across the desert at the approaching figure.

"Why didn't you just kill us back there on the road?"

"Too many travelers use that road. I'm a professional killer so murder must never look like murder. This way it will look like you wandered out into the storm, got lost, and—I'm sure a smart girl like you can guess the rest."

The shadows lengthened and endless ridges of sand melted into the darkness, playing tricks with Randy's depth perception as he trudged across the desert. It was another twenty minutes before his wobbly legs brought him close enough to make out the faces of Faith and Calhoun. Randy hesitated, then staggered towards them, planting himself in front of Calhoun.

Burt Calhoun's expressive face reflected the anxiety and tension he felt. At one time, Randy had considered Calhoun decent and competent, if not dull.

"Where's your're driver?" asked Calhoun.

"I left him with the jeep."

"How can I be sure of that?"

"Look Calhoun, I hired a driver, not a bodyguard. By now that jeep is probably halfway back to Cairo, and tonight some Arab will be bragging to his friends about how he hoodwinked an American."

"Put up your hands." Calhoun pointed his gun at Randy, then patted him down and backed away. "Take your boots off and throw them over here." He ran his hand inside one of the boots.

"Did you really think I'd miss this?" he said as he pulled out the razor sharp knife. "I'm disappointed in you, Morgan, I expected something more original. They told me you'd gone soft, been sitting on your laurels for too long; they were right."

Faith wrapped her arms around herself as the desert began to cool in the semidarkness. She looked at Calhoun's face, then at the wave of sand behind him which seemed to shimmer and move in the twilight. Would she see her mother and sister sooner than she had anticipated? She reached for her father's hand.

Calhoun felt himself waver when he saw them together. No— he had to do it, unless he wanted to end up as an overweight guard with a stun gun at one of the isolated penal colonies.

"Sit down," he ordered them. With their shoulders touching, Faith and Randy eased themselves into the sand and faced Calhoun.

Calhoun reached into his pocket for the hypodermic needle. At least it would be painless. Once injected, they would have about three minutes before they died. Then he would bury them in the sand for some camel driver or scavengers of the desert to find. If an autopsy was performed, it would show that they had been buried by the storm's shifting sands and had suffocated.

Randy saw the needle in Calhoun's left hand. *I'm not going to just sit here and be murdered without a fight. Maybe I can save Faith.* He sat back on his haunches. If Calhoun came towards them, he'd kick sand in his face and try to get the gun.

"Morgan, for some reason the CIA wants you out of the way, permanently," said Calhoun. "This is nothing personal. If you'd been ordered to kill me, you would have, so let's make this easy on everyone."

Randy perceived that maybe Calhoun was a reluctant villain. He seized his opportunity. "And my daughter, where does she fit in? She has nothing to do with this."

"It's unavoidable. You know I can't let her go." His voice hardened. "The girl first." He looked at Faith. "Stand up."

With tears in her eyes, Faith squeezed her father's hand. "We almost made it," she said. She felt no anger or regret, just acceptance. Her dreams for the future with Stephen had been fragile ones. Now, like butterfly wings, they were being torn to shreds by the fierce winds of change and hatred. But none of that mattered now. She started to get to her feet.

The sand dune behind Calhoun shimmered in the lingering rays of twilight. Suddenly it exploded! Fouad lunged out of it, his cinnamon eyes shining through his sand encrusted face.

"What the—!" Calhoun tumbled down the bank of sand as Fouad tackled him, knocking the gun out of his right hand.

Randy scrambled to his feet. "Stay here," he shouted to Faith, picking up the gun. His socks slipped in the sand, and he was on all fours as he tried to follow the path of the entangled bodies down the embankment. In the dusk he strained to make out who was who.

Calhoun held onto the needle tightly. It was the only way he could rid himself of the man who'd landed on top of him and was hammering at his kidneys with his fists. He tried to turn over in the sand, but as he did, Fouad kicked him in the face with his boots. He grabbed his assailant's leg, and the needle went flying through the sand. He balled his hand into a fist, slamming it into Fouad's groin.

Fouad doubled over and rolled down the hill of sand. Calhoun could taste the blood in his mouth as he stood up on shaky legs.

Where was Morgan?

He looked up just as Randy leaped at him from above. He tried to duck, but Randy fell squarely on top of him. Calhoun staggered and sprawled on the sand, the breath knocked out of him. He squirmed beneath his attacker's body and gasped for breath. Then he felt it—the sharp jab of the needle in his back.

"No!"

Faith heard a blood-curdling scream, a primeval sound which sent quicksilver chills up her spine. Then there was an ominous silence, a pause between life and death. She looked over the ridge, but in its shadowy darkness there was no movement, no sound. The silence became unbearable. She waited. Was her father dead?

"Faith, get down here," a voice echoed up the ridge.

Relieved, she moved towards her father's voice. "What happened to—?"

"He's dead. The needle."

They clung to each other. She could make out a crumpled figure a few yards behind her father. Fouad lifted his head as they ran towards him.

"Playing the part of a mole has its down side." He winced as they helped him up. "Just a few broken ribs and some unmentionable bruises. I will mend."

"Wait here," said Randy. "Faith and I will bury Calhoun."

Using their hands, they scooped out a shallow grave in the sand. Faith couldn't look at Calhoun's face. They'd been spared and she was grateful, but once again their freedom had been purchased at the price of another's life.

Randy dragged Calhoun's body into the trench and covered him. He started back up the hill. "Come on," he said as Faith hesitated by the graveside. "We've done everything we can for him." He could see the struggle going on within her. For the first time, he felt it also. It had never bothered him before, this taking of another life, but something had changed.

Faith shoved her hands in her pockets. "Give me a minute."

She bowed her head, but there were no tears in her eyes as she reached into her pocket and pulled out the olive wood cross she'd bought at one of the markets. Gently, she laid it on the mound which covered Burt Calhoun.

In the desert silence, Faith looked up into the heavens, and the stars, like a thousand glimmers of hope, twinkled back at her. Sadly, she realized that even in death Burt Calhoun would never be free.

Rabbi Solomon Lowenstein mingled among the people who were on the bridge. He looked at the faces, trying to determine which one belonged to the nameless voice in the dark which had brought him there.

"Continue to look towards the Damascus Gate," a voice behind him said. "It is better if you do not see me."

Solomon did as he was told.

"Judah Midian has compiled a list of people to be exterminated. You are on it."

Solomon felt as if someone was squeezing his heart with an iron fist. Exterminated! A word used to describe the killing of insects. He felt anger overwhelm the fear which had first pierced his heart. He did not turn around; instead, he massaged his hands, rubbing the stiffened knuckles as he addressed the unknown informant.

"Why do you tell me this? One Jew's death in the scheme of things—why is it important to you?"

"I am one of the sealed children of the tribes of Israel."

"Sealed? I don't understand."

"God has put his mark upon us. We are to bear witness to our countrymen that Christ is their Savior and Messiah, not Judah Midian."

Another radical, Solomon thought. He would counter with reason. "The original twelve tribes of Israel have been lost, intermingled for centuries; now we are all just Israelites."

"God has kept the genealogical records."

Solomon couldn't argue with that, so instead he bickered with himself. He must not be so harsh; after all this man was probably putting his own life at risk to tell him of this death list.

"I can't agree with you that Christ is the Messiah, but I know Judah Midian isn't."

"It's a beginning. You are a reasonable man, Solomon. Look around you—put the events together, and you will arrive at the truth. There is very little time left."

"What do you mean?"

"Earthquakes, volcanic eruptions, meteorites which fall from the sky—these calamities are God's judgment upon the earth prophesied in the Scriptures. Death stalks the land, accompanied by drought, famine, wars, and disease. They are all forerunners of Christ's return as the Messiah. Read the prophet Daniel in the ninth chapter. *The midst of the week is swiftly approaching.*"

"We have always had these misfortunes in the world." Solomon stroked his beard. "Granted, never with such intensity, but I do not fear the future."

"If you want to know the future, read the book of Revelation."

"Read the Christian Bible? Never!"

"You are a scholar, Solomon. Examine the evidence."

Solomon stood there, gripping the top of the bridge until his knuckles turned white. His thirst for knowledge was piqued. He whirled around, no longer able to contain his curiosity.

To no avail, he scanned the faces of the people around him, looking for a clue to the mysterious identity of the man who had revealed Judah's scheme. He felt nauseated and he moved woodenly as he began the journey home; there was nothing else he could do. Was history repeating itself?

In the 1990s Russia and several Eastern nations had spread the lie that the collapse of communism had been engineered by a "Zionist" conspiracy. Russia's fanatical anti-Jewish group called Pamyat had searched through four hundred years of Russian genealogical tables in an attempt to harass anyone with Jewish blood. No wonder one and a half million Russian Jews had emigrated to Israel.

And what were the Israelis to do—turn the immigrants out as the American president suggested in order to appease the Arabs?

Even in the "land of the free and the home of the brave," a wave of anti-Semitic sentiment had caused a flood of Jews to emigrate to Israel.

Stupid! Stupid! Stupid! So many people were willing to believe the lies because they were desperate to blame someone for their failures. But then it was the same tactic Hitler had used: He had blamed the economic collapse of postwar Germany on a conspiracy led by international Zionist bankers. Government leaders originated the lies, and the people believed them.

Had he, Solomon Lowenstein, been labeled an extremist, and, therefore, been targeted for extermination? Did Judah Midian resent anyone who disagreed with him? He was convinced that Judah was not above using "social engineering" to bring about the utopia he had promised.

The Jews would never give up Jerusalem. Judah Midian knew that. It was a non-negotiable piece of real estate. Then what was up the sleeve of this eloquent demagogue who so easily led the global community in their quest for peace?

And what of world peace—the treaties that had been signed? He knew only too well that they were only temporary bridges of communication between Israel and her enemies, bridges which could be flicked away like a spider's web once they'd served their purpose.

For the first time he felt utterly alone, abandoned not only by his people, but by his God. He straightened his shoulders.

What was he to do with the news he'd just heard? Someone would listen to him. If not his own people, then he would go where he would be listened to and accepted. Yes, tonight he would go to the meeting in the caves.

24

The offshore oil rigs belched flames into the darkening sky as the jeep sped towards the Gulf of Suez where Abu Rudeis, the center of Sinai's oil fields, was located. As the road left the coast and headed inland, Faith took one last look at the fiery spirals which leaped and pirouetted into the air like ballerinas.

They passed through mountains of pink sandstone veined with green, then into the southern Sinai Desert. Its rugged valleys warned them of the desert's lack of hospitality, but they pressed on, anxious to reach their destination. A few wandering Bedouins, who eyed them curiously, seemed to be the sole inhabitants of this wretched land with its chaotic masses of bare rocks interspersed with patches of green.

Within a half hour, the dry gulch around them suddenly blossomed into an oasis of date palms. Jagged reddish cliffs bordered the sides of the valley at the Oasis of Feran.

"How far is it to the monastery?" asked Faith as the sharply dropping temperatures prompted her to throw on a sweatshirt.

Randy noticed Fouad's grimace as the young Egyptian turned in his seat to answer her. "It's about twenty miles from here," he said, trying to change his position to ease his discomfort.

"I'll drive the rest of the way," Randy said as they came to an open plain. Fouad didn't protest; his whole body was beginning to stiffen, and his joints ached as the two men changed places.

As the jeep approached the fourteen-hundred-year-old St.

Catherine's Monastery, only the arches of a few buildings inside could be seen above its imposing stone walls. Did the walls keep the invaders from entering or the monks from leaving? Perhaps both, Faith reasoned, viewing the fortress from another vantage point when they stopped at the tourist village to pick up their room key.

"Egypt has been a refuge for many people," said Fouad. "Did you know that your Jesus Christ fled with his mother and father through this very area? And it is said that the Christians came here to escape the Roman persecution."

"At least we're in good company," said Faith.

Fouad looked at his watch. "We will not be able to see the place where God gave Moses the Ten Commandments until the morning. Tomorrow, God willing, you will cross over into Israel." A look of pure pleasure spread over his features. "Ah . . . to immerse my whole body in steaming hot water."

"Not here," said Randy, pointing to a sign in the restaurant window. "Water rationing is in effect."

"Some days Allah smiles upon you, some days he doesn't." A rakish smile crossed Fouad's face. "May I suggest that you both have a good night's rest? I have no doubt that I will." He limped towards the natural stone cottage they'd rented for the night, leaving Faith and Randy to admire the vast desert sky.

Her full lips were cracked and dry from the sandstorm, but Faith didn't notice; she was too excited. Tomorrow they'd be in Israel, "a land flowing with milk and honey." They'd be home at last.

He'd fired her! Solomon had fired her like a common Arab laborer. Hannah Weinberg paced up and down the sparsely furnished room she'd rented since her husband's death, her vexation multiplying with each step.

She'd been replaced by that Rebecca, a woman young enough to be his daughter. There was no doubt in her mind that Rebecca intended to become the next Mrs. Solomon Lowenstein.

It was indecent, that's what it was. Solomon had been tricked by this woman who had come in the guise of a rabbi. She visualized Solomon in bed with Rebecca, and her scrawny face twisted into a mask of ugliness and hatred.

What did they care that from now on she'd never be able to show her face in the marketplace? Hannah could see it now—the women pitying her, tittering behind their hands about her predicament as she walked by the bunches of leeks and piles of melons. Everyone knew Solomon was meant for her. Hadn't her late husband been his best friend?

But it was more than that, much more. Secretly, she'd loved Solomon since he was a boy. She'd been livid when Solomon's parents had chosen Esther for his wife, and she was given instead to Hezekiah, the bookseller. Although Hezekiah was a good man, she didn't love him, and the only way she could endure his touch was to pretend that he was Solomon. Perhaps that was why they'd never been blessed with children; it was her punishment for living a lie.

When Esther and Hezekiah died within six months of each other, she knew that it was only a matter of time before she and Solomon would be together at last. God had seen fit to bless her not with beauty, but with tenacity.

She wouldn't give Solomon up without a fight. There had to be a way. Hannah's soul shriveled inside her as she realized that if she couldn't have Solomon this time, no one else would either.

The monk who'd given them a tour of St. Catherine's led Randy and Faith behind the monastery to where two paths led to Mount Moses.

"The well worn and less tedious path curves behind the southern slope and requires climbing 800 steps to the summit," he said. "The more difficult cliff to the right has 3,750 stone steps carved into the rock. As in life, you must choose which path you will travel." He bowed slightly as he left them to contemplate their decision.

"I'd like to climb all 3,750 steps," said Faith, peering up at the rugged stairway above them. "You can take the easier path, Dad. I'll meet you at the top."

"Don't worry about me." Randy tapped his cane against the dirt. "I have this third leg to help me, and I haven't smoked for almost three months. If Stephen is as good a doctor as you say he is, your old dad will be able to keep up. I'm not going to wind up in the Skull Room, not yet."

The Skull Room. As she started to scale the steep, uneven rock steps, Faith thought about the ossuary where the skulls of the former monks lay piled together on the floor and ledges built into the wall. They'd both been speechless as the vacant eye sockets of the abbots stared back at them. She'd tried to visualize the faces that were now reduced to chalky skulls with gaping holes, but as she did, the thought came to her that soon Burt Calhoun would resemble them.

"At one time, I thought that's what I'd come down to—a pile of useless bones," her father, who was standing next to her at the ossuary, had said with a catch in his throat. "Now I know death isn't the end; it's just a jumping off point to another life."

Faith thought she saw tears glisten in his eyes. Surprised and unable to think of anything to say, she'd only smiled and nodded her head.

Her father's dark eyes had met hers. "Do you think God can still speak to us today, as He did to Moses?"

"Yes, Dad," she'd answered. "But we have to be willing to listen."

As they approached the summit, Randy looked up at the cloudless indigo sky; his life in Virginia seemed an eternity away. He felt himself swept back in history as he viewed the massive mountain range with its pinnacles and valleys.

"Last night I read in Exodus about what happened up here," he said. "One morning the Israelites, who were camped below, heard a crack of thunder pealing down from Mount Sinai. They saw a thick cloud at the top—maybe at this very spot. While they watched, flashes of lightening crackled on the mountain, and then they heard the blast of a loud trumpet." He grinned. "I guess you could say God was trying to get their attention.

"By the time Moses scrambled up the slopes to meet with God, everyone was eagerly awaiting what he'd have to tell them when he came back down."

"With the Ten Commandments?"

"Yes. But he took longer than they'd anticipated, so they became impatient and made a calf of gold to worship."

Faith was thoughtful for a moment. "Why is it, Dad, that even when people know the truth, they still prefer a lie?"

He had to tell her now. Somehow this seemed the perfect place. Randy took her hands and squeezed them so tightly that he could feel the imprint of her turquoise ring in the palm of his right hand.

"Faith, a lie is something you get comfortable with. When the truth comes along . . . then you have to admit to yourself that you weren't as smart as you thought you were; it's like shooting yourself in the foot. You have to rethink everything. Most people aren't willing to do that."

"Are you, Dad?" She glanced up at her father's subdued face and saw reflected in it a quiet strength and understanding which hadn't been there before.

"Yes, I am . . . now. For the first time, I'm seeing the world through God's eyes. This new relationship with Him is more important than my career—or our lives." He laughed awkwardly. "I'm not sure where to go from here, but I know He'll be going with us."

Randy could only equate Faith's smile to that of the dazzling sunshine which flooded the mountain, casting light where once there had been only darkness.

"A nude sculpture?" Lars couldn't believe what he'd just heard.

"Yes." As skillfully as a snake shedding its skin, Judah languidly took off the red silk robe he was wearing and stood, clothed only in his silk underwear, before the young sculptor's easel.

Without thinking, Lars stepped back. He had done nude sculptures before, but why in the world would Judah Midian, of all people, want a nude sculpture of himself?

Judah turned slowly, displaying his muscular body in the sunlight that streamed through the studio's north wall of glass.

"You desire that the sculpture be bigger than life—six times your normal size?" said Lars as he tried to pull his eyes away from Judah's body. Judah's eyes seemed to mock him.

Lars tried to avert his eyes, but he found himself scrutinizing the small tattoo on Judah's left thigh.

"I've been studying the block of marble," Lars began while his confused thoughts churned back and forth. "It is . . . almost as magnificent . . . as you are." The words slipped out before he could stop them. Surely, this man who possessed everything the world had to offer was not interested in him and yet . . .

Shyly, he lifted his eyes again to look at Judah, and as he did so he felt his face flush.

Judah was pleased to see Lars's distress.

"This statue," said Judah as he walked towards the trembling youth, "will be your masterpiece."

25

Pope Timothy I looked out over St. Peter's piazza from the corner bedroom he occupied on the top floor of the Apostolic Palace. He coughed into the handful of tissues he carried and wondered if he should call the Vatican pharmacy for some cough syrup. No, they would want a doctor to see him, and then he'd be poked and prodded and asked a million questions. He just wasn't up to it.

He told himself that he did not have time to be sick. In just an hour the decree would be read at St. Peter's before the College of Cardinals, numerous bishops, and countless of the faithful and *not*-so-faithful followers of the Catholic church from around the world.

Officially, he was the head of the World Church Organization, but it was just too unwieldy for him to handle with any real control. Like a flooded river, the church picked up all obstacles in its path and carried them along until it crested in the high tide of its own dogma. Eventually, all those who opposed it were either shoved aside or left to a watery grave.

Somehow, he felt they were all being swallowed up by this organization, and he was helpless to stop it. At first, the funds they had collected from the participating churches had put them in a sound financial position. Sadly, this had been short-lived. The church's efforts to aid the famine victims throughout the world were draining the treasury.

And the natural disasters! They occurred one after another

with such precision that there was hardly time to recoup from one before another arrived. Earthquakes, hurricanes, sickness. Had anyone ever lived through such a time as this?

And to top it all, if he believed the church's reports, there had been a 71 percent increase in the number of exorcisms since he'd taken office. Nature and Satan were both on a rampage. When would it end?

He sat down on the edge of his bed; his forehead felt hot to the touch. He reached for a glass of water and swallowed a couple of aspirins. At least he could take them without any fear of reprisal from the medical personnel who constantly guarded his health.

This morning he'd gone down to one of the four Vatican post offices, much to the surprise of the cardinals, to see for himself the gigantic volume of mail received since his announcement about Judah Midian.

He'd towered over the postal workers as bulging sacks of mail and faxes addressed to the Vatican from all over the world were being tabulated and sorted into two piles. One pile for those who believed in this so-called miracle resurrection, and one for those who did not. Public opinion was running two to one for those who believed in a miracle. It should have made what he was about to do easier, but it didn't.

What the cardinals had first suggested to him the day after Judah Midian's resurrection had, at first, seemed unthinkable. Attempting to sort out his thoughts, he stretched out on his bed as the fever began to abate.

Canonization of a living person was unheard of; canonization of one who did not claim to be a Roman Catholic was equally preposterous. Yet, in less than an hour, on March 1, 2011, that was exactly what was going to happen in one of the most glorious ceremonies of the Catholic church. It would be followed by the singing of the Mass for the new saint, Judah Midian.

The pope had already commanded public veneration of Judah by the universal church. In light of the miracles which Judah had performed, he had no other choice. As a saint, Judah would be honored and venerated, but the rumors that he was God incarnate would be ended. God alone would be adored.

He'd met with Judah yesterday, and although Judah had tried

to conceal it, the pope had detected a glimmer of contempt in his Jewish-Arab counterpart. He'd received the subtle impression that, as far as Judah was concerned, the pope's position was no longer one of strength but perseverance. They'd been polite, even conciliatory with each other, willing participants in a chess game in which they swapped pawns, each trying to gain the advantage.

He shuddered as he thought of the people who would flock to Judah, trying to use him as an intercessor between themselves and God.

There was a knock on the door.

"Enter."

It was his valet. He looked concerned as the pope got up from the bed, then perplexed when he saw that he was not dressed in the ceremonial robes he had laid out earlier.

"Are you all right, Your Holiness?"

"Yes," he said with a wave of his hand. "Just trying to forestall the inevitable."

How he wished he was merely Cardinal Mark Ryan again, but he knew there was no turning back; forces beyond himself controlled not only his, but Judah Midian's, destiny.

The Gulf of Arabia was to their right as the three occupants of the jeep headed towards Israel. After nightfall they would slip silently over the border at Elat, Israel's southernmost town. There was a sweet sickly aroma in the air as they began to pass bleached bones and equipment left behind by a defeated army.

"What's that smell?" said Faith, wrinkling up her nose.

"Only some of the dead from Israel's war with Russia and her allies have been buried," said Fouad. "Wild animals have eaten much of the flesh, but many bodies are still decomposing. That's why this road is almost deserted. The stench used to be unbearable. In Jerusalem, I hear, it is better."

They rode along in silence, the presence of death, as in the ossuary, was a grim reminder of their own mortality. They stopped only once to refuel the jeep from the five gallon containers they had filled at the tourist village. As they did, Fouad said, "The

Suez Canal is open to Israeli shipping, but once Elat was Israel's only port on the Red Sea."

It was dusk when they left the main road to avoid the border checkpoints. Soon they were driving across Israel's border towards Elat.

"You have heard of the Six-Day War?" asked Fouad.

"Yes," said Randy.

"This is where it started." Fouad pointed to the gulf waters, shimmering in the moonlight on his right. "Egypt blockaded the Gulf of Aqaba and Israel retaliated."

"So this is Israel," said Faith. Somehow she felt let down, but she wasn't sure why. Perhaps she really had expected an angel from heaven to greet them as they entered the sacred land of promise; instead, she saw only desolation and carnage. The blackened restaurants and gutted nightclubs of Elat were now the only sentinels of the once-thriving vacation spot.

"Since Russia's invasion, the beaches, which were once crowded with Europeans on holiday, are deserted," said Fouad. "The port is open again, but the town is now largely occupied by Israel's navy."

"This isn't what you'd expected, is it?" said Randy to Faith as the jeep came to a stop. He got out of the vehicle and stretched. "As we get closer to Jerusalem, it'll look more like the Holy Land and less like a combat zone."

"Elat is one of the last places that will be rebuilt," said Fouad. "Like a wheel with Jerusalem as the hub, the spokes of rebuilding began in Jerusalem and will work out from there."

The gulf breezes carried the stench away from them, and while Fouad spread out a map on the hood of the jeep, Faith discovered she was hungry. She rummaged through her duffel bag and brought out some dates and black figs sticky with juice.

"You will take the jeep and follow the path I have marked for you," said Fouad as he handed Randy the map. He reached inside his robe.

"These are entry visas which will allow you to travel through the country now that we have crossed the border and . . ." he undid a thick belt which he had been wearing, "this is the money that Falcon received from the sale of your property and possessions."

Fouad turned over the belt and undid the zipper on the back, revealing stacks of bills concealed inside.

"I . . . didn't expect this," said Randy.

Fouad handed him the belt with a broad grin. "Falcon entrusted me with your lives and your money. Now I give both of them back to you."

"But how will you get back?" said Faith, looking at the remote area they were in.

"Do not worry. Like the camel, I am a child of the desert. I will find my way."

"Then this is good-bye," said Randy. "We can't thank you enough—"

"It is not necessary. Now I have paid my debt, and I will marry and have many, many children." He looked fondly at Faith, his warm sepia eyes resting on her lovely face. "May I wish the same good fortune for you." With that brief statement and a wave of his hand, he disappeared into the night.

Lost in contemplation, Solomon dropped into his wife's rocking chair in the living room. When she was alive, Esther had said that the gentle motion of the rocker helped her soothe her nerves no matter what crisis she faced. Would it work for him? It was worth a try.

"You must tell the authorities," said Rebecca who sat across from him on the couch.

"Tell them what?" said Solomon. "Members of the Knesset have labeled me a troublemaker, one who does not agree with Judah's so-called reforms, or what used to be called purges."

The rabbi muttered to himself, "Giving new sanitized names to old sins, that's the least of Judah's transgressions." He rocked faster.

"I'll go with you."

"What will I tell them? That I am marked for death? Who will listen? I have no proof. 'Meshugah' they'll say . . . the ravings of an old man."

"Then you must leave!"

"And go where? I am a Sabra, a native-born Israeli Jew. This is my home. If I am going to die, it will be here, in my own land, if not in my own bed."

"You are being unreasonable."

"And you are forgetting that the sabra is a cactus plant, one that, in spite of its sharp spines, bears not only flowers but an edible fruit."

"Please, Solomon, I am in no mood to try and figure out your allegories. Sharp spines are no match for a bullet."

"A bullet?" He stopped rocking. "Who would want to waste a perfectly good bullet on an old rabbi like me? But just in case, perhaps you should leave."

"What?"

"My only regret would be if you were harmed in some way because of me."

"And what of this American and his daughter?" said Rebecca. "You think they will be safer here than me? No, I will stay. We will not discuss it again."

"Now who is being stubborn?"

Through her bedroom wall Rebecca Greenspan could hear Solomon's raspy snores as they punctuated the crisp night air. For hours she had fought a silent battle, but she could be still no longer. Quietly she got dressed and, drawing a shawl around her head, left the house. The streets were empty; only a stray dog accompanied her to her midnight rendezvous.

Finally, the temple loomed before her, and she felt her emotions vacillate again. Was she doing the right thing? She saw the death angel standing in the shadows by one of the pillars. With a heavy heart she approached him.

"He will not leave," she said, and her voice cracked like slivered glass in the still night air.

"He must."

"He said he would rather die here than leave."

"So be it." The figure stepped out of the shadows. "You know what you must do."

"I . . . don't think I can."

"What?" the voice sneered.

"He's been good to me. I care about him."

"That's your problem. You make the decision—Solomon or your son. Which is it to be?"

Rebecca Greenspan fought back the tears. He was right. Solomon was sixty-five years old, he'd lived a long life. She had to give her son that same chance. *God forgive me for what I am about to do,* she prayed.

"I will take care of it," she replied in a trembling voice.

"Good. Then we will discuss your son's future. One more thing. Randy Morgan and his daughter have a price on their heads. If they do not cooperate with us, we will collect it."

She could not swallow the lump that was in her throat. They had gone too far; they were asking too much of her. "I will have no part of that."

"You'll play whatever part we tell you and don't you forget it." His harsh voice softened slightly.

"It is necessary for the common good. You know that as well as I do. You have seen the enthusiasm, the drawing together of this nation. Dissenters must be removed."

"And what of the followers of the two so-called prophets? Each month that it does not rain, they grow stronger. I hear that throughout Jerusalem there are more than a hundred thousand Jews who believe as they do."

"At the right time, in the right place, they will become martyrs."

She had to play her trump card, there was nothing left. "And just what do you think would happen if the world knew that its new savior had a five-year-old son?"

His icy, dispassionate reply sent fear racing through her. "The world would grieve with Judah after his son was killed by one of the extremist groups."

Aha! She knew Rebecca was up to something. Hannah slid into the shadows. She was too far away to hear their conversation, but it was obvious that they didn't want to be seen together. Why else would they be at the temple after midnight? She rubbed her eyes as she tried to focus on the obscure figure who loomed above Rebecca. A smile played across her thin lips, revealing her uneven, yellowed teeth. The moon came out from behind the clouds, and in its faint light she recognized—Logan Washburn!

So, Rebecca was not content with a mere rabbi. The girl was nothing more than a whore, just as she'd thought. Men. They were all such fools. Solomon would thank her when she told him. Of that, she had no doubt.

26

Rebecca could hear Solomon snoring as she reentered the darkened house. For some reason the sound comforted her, as the familiar often did when she was faced with change.

She went to the kitchen and put on water for tea, a domestic routine which engaged her body but left her agitated mind free to roam endlessly in its quest for an escape. The simple, everyday habits were only temporary buffers against the unavoidable, but at least for the moment they helped her to believe that everything was normal.

She measured out the loose-leaf tea. Her hand trembled so much that instead of going into the teapot most of the tea leaves spilled onto the table. Methodically, she scooped them up in the palm of her hand, then pressed her nose to the dry spicy leaves. She inhaled their sharp scent before she returned them to the kettle and added the boiling water. Rebecca looked aimlessly at the kitchen tiles while she sat at the table, letting her thoughts steep along with the tea.

She'd almost forgotten why she'd come to Jerusalem. She'd actually begun to postulate that the Rebecca Greenspan who existed in this house was a separate entity from the woman who'd left Chicago three months ago.

Picking up her purse from the table, Rebecca pulled out the dog-eared snapshot. Minus his two front teeth, her five-year-old son's face grinned back at her, and in spite of her own despondency, a smile tugged at the corners of her mouth.

To give him up . . . it was the most agonizing choice she'd ever made. There had been some consolation in meeting the grateful, middle-aged couple who adopted him. They were Methodists, and each year on her son's birthday they dutifully sent the agency a new picture of him. In turn, the agency forwarded it to her.

"Donald," she said softly, caressing the photograph between her hands.

If she'd kept him, he would have been an Abraham or a Joseph, but she'd purposely given him a name which would in no way reflect his Jewish heritage. It was better this way, for weren't the Jews the litmus test which God used to determine the worst in people? At least she could spare him the rancor and acrimony which her race had inherited.

She shuddered—even though it had occurred over two decades ago—at the vivid memory of when she'd reached down in the hallway of her high school to pick up a shiny quarter from the waxed floor.

A chorus of students, who'd hovered nearby to see who would pick up the money, screamed at her, "Jew! Jew!" Even now her face flushed at the thought of it.

The harassment had increased. Swastikas had been scratched on the lockers belonging to some of the Jewish students, then obscenities were smeared on the walls of the local Jewish community center. This festering bitterness towards the Jews had re-emerged in the United States with the same intensity as it had once inflamed Europe.

Rebecca poured the steaming tea into a china cup and watched the vapor rise and evaporate in the warmth of the kitchen. If only her past could disappear as easily. Had it been only six years since she'd first met Judah? It seemed a lifetime.

Judah Midian had been a guest lecturer at the college—charming and witty, fluent not only in English, but in Hebrew and Arabic as well. At a reception following his lecture, she'd been flattered by his attentions, but now in retrospect, she could see why he'd singled her out. He'd detected her innocence and vulnerability, two traits he didn't possess.

He'd been gentle and charming at first as he slowly chipped

away at her reticence, but as she stepped into the wider ripples of his life, their relationship changed. His obsessive personality absorbed her like a paper towel absorbed water. When they were together, she seemed to have no will of her own; she wasn't Rebecca Greenspan, only an extension of Judah. She gravitated towards him as his personality made her a willing, if not helpless, prey.

He questioned the validity of her Old Testament studies and exhausted her with an intense zeal which consumed everything in its path. She told herself that what they were doing was wrong; it went against everything she'd been taught since childhood. Judah insisted that he'd merely ignited the repressed sexual passions which had smoldered beneath the surface of her personality for years. After he'd made it clear that marriage had no place in his life, she'd wrestled with her own integrity, only to find that the more she struggled the more entangled she became in the web of their relationship.

Physically they had melted into one another, but real intimacy, that rare blending of the spiritual and physical, was impossible. Judah would allow her to get only so close, then withdraw to some place where she couldn't reach him. Questions about his family brought only vague responses, and she began to wonder what he was hiding. In the middle of the night she'd awaken and find him gone. He gave no explanations when he returned, rejuvenated from his midnight wanderings.

She'd always clung to the fact that at one time he must have loved her, but the years of separation and tonight's threats made her realize that Judah was incapable of loving anyone but himself. Now she understood his reaction on that fateful day.

"Pregnant!" he had shouted. "You really are stupid. How could you let this happen?" He had paced back and forth in the bedroom, a coyote baying at an eclipse.

"You'll have an abortion, I'll arrange it."

"No!"

He'd turned on her, then slapped her across the face so hard that he'd knocked her down.

"Nothing must interfere with *my* plans. If you insist on having this baby, I'll walk out of that door."

Slowly, she'd picked herself up, laid her hands across her stomach to reassure the small life within her that it would have a chance. She had walked to the door and opened it, daring him to walk through it.

He'd grabbed his few belongings and started throwing them into an empty pillowcase, tossing her one final insult as he left. "You don't really expect me to believe it's *my* child, do you?"

He'd slammed the door behind him and disappeared from her life as quickly as he'd entered it. She'd never heard from him again until a year ago.

Her choice to be a rabbi—made during the six month sabbatical she'd taken from college to have Donald—was supposed to set things right, make up for what she'd done. But it hadn't. Nothing had turned out right. The voice of conscience continued to torment her. Would she ever be free from it?

Rebecca began to cry, and the tears ushered in thoughts of her mother. A year after he had been adopted, she finally told her mother about Donald. She'd begged for her mother's forgiveness, and for a moment they cried together, but Leah's sympathy was short-lived.

With her black eyes flashing, she'd placed her work-worn hands on her ample hips and retorted, "You've given away my first grandson. With such a large dose of chutzpa you need God's forgiveness, not mine."

Rebecca heard Solomon's slippers shuffling down the hall. Quickly she shoved Donald's picture back into her purse and wiped the tears from her face with the back of her hand. She'd need more than mere chutzpa to get through this.

"What is so important, Rebecca, that you must get up before the birds?" Solomon said playfully as he looked at her through sleepy eyes. He saw her red-rimmed eyes, the fine lines etched around her mouth.

"I hope you're not worrying about me again."

"I was thinking about life and . . . death. The death list your name is on—you don't seem to be frightened by it, but I am."

"Why? Our whole life is one long preparation for death, so you tell me, so why do we act surprised when it comes?" He sat down across from her.

"I . . . don't know."

"Of course, maybe I would not feel this way if I were thirty-five again, like you." He patted her hand.

They were both silent as the sun rose in a graphite sky tinged with flecks of rose. Rebecca felt the warmth of his hand on her icy fingers. She wanted to draw her hand away, but she didn't.

Slender, golden pencils of illumination scribbled across the kitchen table as the yellow shafts of light pierced the pearl gray dawn. Solomon lifted his hands from the table and let them move in the waves of sunlight.

"Like the dawn, there are some things we have no control over. The day we step into eternity is one of them. Until then, we must live life to the fullest."

Rebecca shrugged her shoulders. "You are right, as usual." She tried to keep her voice even. He must not suspect. "I'll get you a cup of tea."

As Solomon reached for the cup she offered him, his elbow knocked her purse on the floor, scattering the contents. "I'll get it," she exclaimed, but Solomon had already reached down and picked up the picture of Donald.

He held it in the light. "A nice-looking boy."

"Yes," she said hurriedly, "my sister's son."

"So, you are an aunt." He handed the picture back to her.

"You know it is not forbidden for a woman rabbi to marry. You could have children of your own."

He saw the color rise in her cheeks. "I wouldn't think of such a thing," she blurted out.

"In order to understand life, Rebecca, one must live it. Death has no such requirements."

She looked down at him. There was no laughter in his eyes, only concern.

She put the picture of Donald back in her purse, then quickly snapped her purse, and her heart, shut.

"Faith, you drive for a while and I'll check the map," said Randy as he halted the jeep. They both stretched before they switched places.

"We should be on Route 25 to Beersheba, then we pick up

Route 60 to Jerusalem." He squinted at the map bathed in a circle of pale light from the flashlight he held in his hand.

"How far?" asked Faith as she put the jeep in gear and took off through the Negev Desert.

"We've probably come a hundred miles. I'd say about another twenty to thirty miles and we'll be in Beersheba. We can get a room there, grab a couple of hours sleep, and still make it to Jerusalem by late tomorrow afternoon."

"I've lost all track of time," said Faith as she tried to stifle a yawn. "What day is it anyway?"

"Not that it makes any difference," Randy said as he shone the flashlight on his watch, "but it's March third."

Faith plucked the seventeenth century words of the English poet, Andrew Marvell, from her memory. "But at my back I always hear, Time's winged chariot hurrying near. And yonder all before us lie, Deserts of vast eternity."

Eternity. Everlasting life. Heaven. The new words in Randy's vocabulary tumbled through his thoughts, footnotes to a chapter which was just beginning.

Judah Midian tipped back in his leather chair, closed the book he was reading, and swung his feet up on the massive desk made of lacquered rosewood. He looked past Logan Washburn to the picture window where he had a panoramic view of the West Bank, the modern political designation for Judea and Samaria. "Put this away for me," said Judah, handing Logan his book.

Logan looked at the title as he walked towards the bookcase which covered one entire wall of Judah's office on the thirteenth floor. He placed John Milton's *Paradise Lost* among the other rare first editions, running his fingers lightly over the book spines of Dante's *Inferno,* Goethe's *Faust,* Arrigo Boito's *Mefistofele,* and *The Screwtape Letters* by C. S. Lewis.

"Literature proves that the Christian world has always needed a focal point for their spiritual fears," said Judah with disdain.

Logan walked past the fire crackling in the grate and stood at the door. "They're waiting outside," he said.

Judah looked into the flames, closed his eyes, and pulled his mind from the past. He ran his hand slowly around his collarless shirt. "I remember reading about their master computer years ago. Does it really deliver what it promises?"

"Yes," said Logan as he reached into a manila folder and pulled out an old newspaper clipping from the *The New York Times*. "It was first announced in 2002." He proceeded to read the article aloud:

> Swiss Forge Swords Into Cheap Electricity
> "ZURICH, August 23 (Reuters) — The Swiss government has devised a high-tech plan to use plutonium, salvaged from the former Soviet Union's nuclear arsenal, to generate cheap electricity to power its master computer. By applying the concept of recycling to the world's most dangerous trash problem, radioactive nuclear material will be put to peaceful use. In cooperation with members of the European Common Market, Swiss diplomats and engineers have proposed that the stock exchange be replaced by computer transactions from their offices."

"So," said Judah, "by interfacing with their technology, we can organize our worldwide financial system. No doubt, you have someone in mind to make these adaptations?"

"One of our sources in the CIA gave me the name of Randy Morgan."

"Randy Morgan. I've never heard of him."

Logan handed Judah a folder. He stood silently as Judah leafed through the information he'd compiled on Randy Morgan.

"So, the CIA wants to dispose of him. That could be all the impetus he needs to join us."

"The last page," said Logan, clearing his throat, "you will find very interesting."

Judah's head lifted slightly as he tried to keep his voice under control. "He sent a telegram to . . . Rabbi Solomon Lowenstein?"

"Apparently they met when Morgan came here to do his graduate studies years ago. Morgan has asked him for asylum."

Judah's jaw hardened. "Have you talked with Rebecca yet?"

"She only knows that we want to use Morgan or . . . lose him. She'll cooperate."

A dark cloud passed over Judah's features. "I do not trust Solomon, my old nemesis."

"Why does this one old Jew irritate you so much?"

"I have my reasons!" Judah replied, slamming his fist down on the desk in a rare display of anger. Seething, he stood up and put his hand on a bronze statue of the archangel, Michael, which was on his desk. His fingers tingled as he caressed the sword the archangel held in his uplifted hand.

"I have put Rabbi Solomon Lowenstein on the list, along with these 'witnesses' who seem to have sprung out of the woodwork," said Logan, trying to placate Judah. "It is only a matter of time before your foes are destroyed."

"Yes," said Judah as his confidence returned. He marched to the window again to survey his domain. "I must be patient. Remember what I told you—for a while let these two witnesses do or say whatever they want. As we slowly draw the noose tighter, they will be blamed for certain 'events' which will cause havoc in the world." Judah laughed. "People will beg us to get rid of them, to remove the 'curse' which has been put upon the earth."

"The proverbial scapegoats," said Logan as he crossed the carpet printed with the signs of the zodiac to where Judah stood.

"Well put. It has worked in the past, it'll work now. History does have a way of repeating itself," said Judah, who was wearing a custom-made, three-piece Italian suit for his meeting with the businessmen from Switzerland. Western dress would put them at ease and make it easier for them to accept his proposals.

He picked up the open package of Swiss chocolate on his desk. "A nice touch, Logan. Now . . . show the gentlemen in, we don't want to keep history waiting."

27

As Faith rolled over in bed, she could hear the usual clatter of road sounds, highlighted by the occasional braying of a donkey. She opened her eyes and closed them tightly again as the blinding sun poured in through the hotel window's wooden slats. With a great deal of effort, she pulled herself into a sitting position and forced her eyes open. She let out a scream as an enormous grasshopper leapfrogged across the bedspread.

"Oh!" she groaned, falling back on the bed as the strained muscles in her neck and back tied themselves into knots. She looked over at the other bed. It was empty.

"Good morning," said Randy as he swung the bathroom door open. "Was that a scream I heard?" He was dressed in clean clothes, and the fresh pine scent of his favorite after-shave lotion filled the air.

"Yes, a grasshopper was using my bed as a runway."

"I've already killed a few of the pests in the bathroom. Seems as if they've laid siege to the town because of the drought."

"Couldn't we just give them a drink and get them out of here?"

"Not unless you want to give them your water rations. I'm not that sympathetic."

"What time is it?"

"It's almost nine."

Faith groaned again as she got out of bed. "I think bouncing over sand dunes in a jeep has finally gotten to me. Every bone in my body aches. I guess a hot shower is out of the question?"

"Sorry, but you'll have to make do with a basin full of luke-warm water. The desk clerk informed me that the government has curtailed the flow of water through the irrigation system which brings water from the Sea of Galilee to the Negev Desert."

Her father lifted his armpit and made a face. "I'm just thankful I had a bottle of after-shave with me. Otherwise, I'd have to stick with the goat and sheep herders today."

"Do you think we'll be facing the same situation in Jeru-salem?"

"By tonight, we'll know. Do you need anything? We're not far from the market."

She winced as she stood up. "Just some liniment."

An hour later they were at the market that was held every Thursday morning in Beersheba. Here the Bedouins, who still dwelt in tents as their ancestors had for centuries, mixed easily with the city people who lived in the modern housing units built to minimize the intolerable summer heat. Both the ancient and the modern merchants swatted and kicked at the grasshoppers that invaded their wares.

"Which one do you think will look best?" said Faith to Randy. She finished the shriveled apricot she'd just purchased from a fruit vendor, then held up a blue-striped native robe and a cream colored one. Randy pointed to the blue robe.

"This time," she said with a glint in her eye, "let me do the haggling."

"I thought we were looking for liniment."

"Very sorry, but I must close," the shopkeeper interjected in broken English. He impatiently snatched the robes from Faith and bundled up his goods in a large basket.

"That's the first time I've seen one of these fellows intention-ally kill a sale," said Randy. They watched as the proprietor scur-ried through the compound, stopping at the other end of it to join a crowd which had gathered.

Curiously, they drifted towards the gathering. Randy peered over the crowd and saw what appeared to be the object of their attention. Dressed in a robe the color of whipped butter, a man with an ageless face raised his hands and motioned for everyone to sit down. Dropping on the dusty ground, the crowd formed a circle around him.

Randy and Faith looked at each other in surprise as he began to speak in English. "Maybe he's a teacher," whispered Randy as they stood at the back of the circle of listeners. "Ben Gurion University isn't far from here."

"I am Aaron of the tribe of Levi," said the man boldly. A murmur went through the audience as he lifted his head and looked directly at them with his piercing green eyes.

"Look . . . look at his forehead," said Faith.

Standing out in stark relief from his pale forehead was what appeared to be a cross traced in dried blood.

"God's people are enduring famine, wars, earthquakes, unrest in the Holy Land, betrayal, and," he bent down to pick up a locust, "pestilences. I am a believer in the Messiah of Israel who is coming for His bride." His eyes fastened on Faith, then moved to Randy.

"This is the common heritage of those who reside in Israel. We have lived to see the fulfillment of Ezekiel's prophecy. Did not Russia come up against the people of Israel like a cloud covering the land, and did not God in His anger send fire and destroy His enemies? These are the latter days spoken of by the prophets of Israel. Harken unto me! Jesus Christ is the Messiah, and He will return to claim His bride. What God has begun, He will finish."

The tall, rugged-looking man reached into a leather pouch at his feet, drew out a stack of pamphlets, and handed them to the rotund shopkeeper Faith and Randy had encountered earlier.

"Read for yourselves the portions of Scripture which prove these claims."

Aaron pointed to the sky. "Look up, for your redemption draweth nigh."

"And just what do you get out of this?" a disgruntled man said, hobbling to his feet. As he tried to gain his balance, it was apparent that one leg was shorter than the other.

"Brethren, my heart's desire and prayer to God for Israel is that they might be saved." With these final words, Aaron stepped into the crowd. As he passed the fretful heckler, he lightly touched him on the shoulder; the man recoiled from Aaron's touch. The mysterious prophet plunged into the crowd which was now getting to its feet, and by the time Randy and Faith had made their way to the front, he had vanished into the swirl of the marketplace.

"Look—look at me!" The lame man cried out in amazement. He was standing on his feet. "My leg—it's all right!"

The crowd swarmed around him as he danced up and down by Abraham's Well on two perfectly formed legs.

"They've begun their ministry on earth," said Faith excitedly. "Aaron must be one of the 144,000 witnesses."

"Witnesses?"

"Yes. The Bible says that after the Rapture, the mark of God's seal will be placed on twelve thousand people from each of the original twelve tribes of Israel. They'll tell the Israelites how God has fulfilled all of His promises through Jesus Christ so they will know He is the Messiah, the one they've been waiting for."

As Faith and Randy surged forward with the other listeners and reached for a booklet, the shopkeeper recognized them.

"A thousand pardons," he said. His English was halting as he searched for the words, then a smile broke across his face. "It would be easier for us to talk in Hebrew."

"I'm afraid our knowledge of Hebrew is very limited," said Randy.

A puzzled expression appeared on the man's face. "But you were listening to the prophet so intently that I thought you understood what he was saying."

"We understood," said Faith, using the tone she reserved for the children whom she used to babysit, "because he was speaking in English."

"No," said the shopkeeper. "He was speaking in Hebrew."

"Hebrew? He was not speaking in Hebrew," said an old Arab who had been eavesdropping. "He was speaking in Arabic."

Faith looked down at the pamphlet she held. It was written in English. Her eyes darted to the pamphlet the Arab held shakily in his right hand—it was in Arabic. Even before she looked, she knew that the shopkeeper's pamphlet would be written in Hebrew.

President Blanco looked down at the messages he'd received from the CIA. Phrases like *worldwide domination, threat to national security,* and *possible dictatorship* leaped at him from the freshly printed pages.

He paused to reflect on the last decade, which had seen the spread of democracy throughout the world. Even China had achieved a government which, if not totally democratic, was at least tolerant of the demands of its people. Equality between blacks and whites had been accomplished in South Africa, but a white backlash in America had set civil rights back twenty years. Still, the United States was finally beginning to remedy that situation.

Since the invasion, Russia and her allies were no longer a threat. In Britain, William, Prince Charles's elder son, had brought the United Kingdom into the twenty-first century under the tutelage of his mother, Diana, even though she had divorced Prince Charles ten years before he died. Central America had settled down into a model of industry since drugs had been legalized, and even his own beloved Mexico, he mused, finally had a stable economy.

For the first time in a century, the United States was pouring more of its tax dollars into research and welfare programs for the general public than into defense. Why then, was he so uneasy?

He was waiting for the other shoe to drop.

And it had. He looked down at the paperwork on his desk. Rumors. It could all be conjecture and sour grapes. No one wanted to go up against a man who had been proclaimed a saint by the pope. How he wished Carmelita was alive. He knew the answer before he'd formed the question, but he had to ask it anyway. How would all this fit into her biblical promise of the end times?

President Emilio Blanco opened his desk drawer, unwrapped his last cigar, and lit it. This time it gave him no pleasure; the acid taste of fear in his mouth remained. What part would he play in this arena, this unrehearsed yet scripted drama that was unfolding rapidly, scene by scene? At least he had an advantage; he knew the director, the plot, and now he knew one of the main characters.

He reached for the dictionary in the bookcase, flipped through the A's until he came to it. *Antichrist: An enemy of Christ. The epithet of the great antagonist who was expected by the early Church to set himself up against Christ in the last days before the Second Coming.* As he pushed the dictionary aside, the president thought of all the evil men throughout history who had been tagged with the word *antichrist.*

His eyes fell on the last and most incriminating communication he'd received from the CIA. He folded the paper into neat even squares as he thought. What he needed was hard evidence. He barked into the intercom. "Rose, get the director of the CIA, immediately."

Fifteen minutes later John Seaton arrived, his hair still damp from his interrupted shower at the health club. His sinewy body rippled beneath his suit as he stood before the president, a testimony to the body-building routine he began six months ago.

"John, this 'Grim Reaper' list you talk about in your report. Do you actually have such a list or is it just hearsay?"

"I brought it with me." The CIA director put his briefcase on the desk, opened it, and handed the thick stack of papers to the president.

Chewing nervously on the end of his cigar, President Blanco scanned the list, pausing now and then to shake his head. Fifteen minutes passed before John heard the president suck in his breath; he knew he'd seen his own name. There was an ominous silence in the oval office, an internal balancing of emotions before he spoke.

"I don't know whether to be flattered or insulted. I'm almost at the end of this list." President Blanco put his glasses back on and drummed his fingers on the desk. "How accurate is your source?"

"One hundred percent."

"Has anyone on this list been killed yet?"

"Not to our knowledge. Our informant said that it is phase four in a five-phase operation. From what we can gather, phase one was the defeat of Russia and her allies. Phase two, the centralization of the world's finances, is the current project."

"And phases three and five?"

"We're a little sketchy on those, but we think phase three has something to do with the World Church, phase five with the State of Israel."

"Is there anything we can do to stop this—?" He couldn't finish. He put his head in his hands, rubbed his forehead, and tried to fathom the monumental task which was before him. He knew it was no use; no matter what he did, there was no stopping Judah Midian, not now.

The president barked into the intercom again. "Rose, set up a meeting of the Joint Chiefs of Staff for tomorrow morning."

He turned to John. "Maybe we can't kill a saint, but we'll give him so much grief that before we're through he'll wish we had."

"I don't know if that's a good idea, sir."

"You have a better one?"

"I'd rather deal with one rational leader who speaks for all the countries of Europe and the Middle East than a dozen hotheads. If it comes to it, we can always cut the head off the snake and replace it with our own man."

"An assassination?"

"Whatever it takes, sir. Meanwhile, we'll double up on your security."

"You ever thought of running for president, John?"

"Yes sir, I have."

In a flash of silent understanding, their eyes met. They both knew they couldn't stem the tide of terrorism which was going to engulf the world, but at least they could delay it.

28

ervous?" asked Randy as they stood together at the Jaffa Gate. Faith nodded.

Her whole body trembled with anticipation; she felt as she had on Christmas morning when, barefoot, she and Hope used to tiptoe quietly down the stairs to the living room while their parents were still asleep. There, the culmination of all their excitement waited for them in a fir tree aglow with lights and the avalanche of gifts beneath it. Now, it was Jerusalem that invited her to open and explore its treasures.

Joyfully, she and her father passed through the Jaffa Gate into the city. Neither of them was aware yet that in the hearts and minds of its people, Jerusalem, the hub of Israel, enjoyed a privileged status. It was truly God's earthly gift to those who inhabited it. Even with its unfamiliar sights and sounds, Faith readily accepted the gift, for she saw Jerusalem through the eyes of a weary traveler who had come home at last.

Randy Morgan also accepted the gift as he surveyed the crowded streets. *So this is the City of Peace,* he thought—that's what the name *Jerusalem* literally means. What a contradiction! Since Israel had gained its statehood in 1948, erratic periods of peace had been overshadowed by blood and violence. But even as he rationalized his feelings, Randy too felt the presence of an unseen hand upon the thriving city.

The old city was bristling with life as they walked down David Street through the maze of shoppers at the Arab Bazaar, and veered right, past the Armenian Quarter and Zion Gate. Gaping holes in several of the stone buildings were the only visible traces left of the Russian invasion. Unlike the rest of Israel, Jerusalem seemed almost untouched by recent events.

"Rejoice with Jerusalem, and be glad with her, all ye that love her." The sentiments of Isaiah, spoken more than 2500 years ago, echoed in Faith's mind. She realized that Isaiah wasn't speaking only of Jerusalem's physical dimensions, but of its spiritual dimensions, which were boundless.

Silently, she made her way towards the Jewish Quarter while the fragrant smell of baking bread, exotic fruits, and sizzling meat filled her nostrils. Like an artist intent on capturing every detail on the canvas of her senses, Faith concentrated on absorbing the sights and smells of Old Jerusalem with its vaulted, covered bazaars, crowded market alleys, and Middle East flavor.

For a moment she stopped and leaned against a stone wall. She closed her eyes and listened to the heartbeat of the Holy City. Mingled with it, she heard the voices of Jesus and His disciples as they walked through the dusty streets.

As if he'd read her mind, Randy said, "I have a feeling that when Jesus was here, it looked almost the same as it does now."

She nodded and opened her eyes. Now they could see the area between the Jewish Quarter and the Wall. It had been laid out in a series of ascending terraces which created a gradual transition from the regal scale of the Wailing Wall to the smaller and more complex dimensions of the Jewish Quarter.

Faith's eyes swept upwards, past the Wall to where the sun glinted off the newly built temple. As she gazed at it, she felt as if one of the monumental Herodian blocks which formed the western wall had been lifted from her shoulders.

"For awhile, I wasn't sure we were going to make it to Jerusalem," said Randy. With renewed energy, they began to climb a flight of steps that led to Solomon's home.

"Ah, here it is," he said, stopping before an iron gate. "It hasn't changed much." Randy pushed the gate open, walked under the archway, and pounded on the thick wooden door. There was no response.

"I hope you haven't been waiting long," said a female voice behind them. They turned to see a handsome woman with dark wavy hair coming up the stairs, a basket filled with loaves of bread in one hand, a sack of fruit in the other.

"I'm Randy Morgan, and this is my daughter, Faith."

"We've been expecting you, but we weren't sure when you'd get here. Your telegram was a little vague." The sun's reflection bounced off her hazel and gold-flecked eyes, and although she smiled, Randy depicted an air of sadness about her.

A feeling he hadn't felt in months rushed over him, and he was both surprised at himself and shocked. Granted, she was beautiful, but she was either Solomon's wife or daughter; either way, he was a Gentile with a rather bleak future. He'd lost almost everything. *Everything,* he reminded himself, *but that which really counted.*

Randy tried to put her out of his mind, and to atone for his wayward thoughts, he tried to conjure up a picture of Ruth. He could see her blond hair, but the rest of her face remained a shadowy outline without form or definition.

"My name is Rebecca Greenspan," the woman said, pushing the door open with her hip. "Solomon has allowed me to share his home seeing we have . . . mutual interests." They followed her inside as she put the groceries on the kitchen table.

Mutual interests. That covers a lot of bases, thought Randy. He had to admit he was happy she wasn't related to Solomon.

"I hope you don't mind, but there are only two bedrooms so you, Mr. Morgan, will share a room with Solomon and," she turned to Faith, "you'll share a room with me."

So they weren't sleeping together. Talk about jaded—he hadn't changed. "Faith and I appreciate your hospitality" said Randy. "I hope it isn't an inconvenience."

"Oh, but it is," she replied matter-of-factly. "But in Jerusalem, most things are. You get used to it." She saw the look of surprise on Randy's face. "I usually speak my mind. I hope you will do the same; we'll get along better that way."

Randy had the distinct feeling that this no-nonsense woman disliked them, and for some reason he felt it was important for him to find out why.

"You'll need food and water ration cards. If you have passports, we can register with the magistrate tomorrow," she said as she motioned them to sit down in the living room.

"It would be best if no one knew of our arrival," said Randy. "I don't know what Solomon has told you, but our circumstances are a little unusual."

"Apparently, someone knows you're here." She reached into the pocket of her dress. "This letter came for you this morning." She placed it on the table. "It was posted in Israel."

Rebecca saw the fear and apprehension on their faces. "This letter was probably mailed weeks ago," she tried to reassure them. "The symbol of our postal system is a white deer on a blue background, but it's a common joke that it should be replaced with a snail."

Faith gave her father a weak smile. "Why don't you open it?"

Randy tore open the envelope, noting there was no return address on it, and withdrew the single sheet of paper. He read it silently, then handed it to Faith.

"Is it good news or bad?" Rebecca said, feigning an interest in the letter. She knew every word of it by heart.

"I'm not sure," said Randy with a perplexed look on his face. "I've been offered a job and political immunity."

El Al, the Israeli national airline, is definitely losing money on its flights, thought Stephen as he looked around at the vacant seats; the plane was almost empty. The Israeli government's restrictions on incoming traffic had drastically reduced the number of tourists. Stephen put the armrest down between the seats and stretched out in the first class section of the "Star of David," one of Israel's newest commercial planes.

In the clear light of morning, the fears Stephen had encountered last night in his bare apartment were nonexistent. Instead of six months, it had taken him only six days to wind up his career. He'd given part of his furniture to his sister, Jamie, and sold the rest by putting an ad on the hospital bulletin board. It had been almost too easy.

Maybe that's why last night at 3 o'clock, he'd sat up wide-awake in the sleeping bag he'd put on the floor of his apartment. He'd turned on the light and looked at the picture of Faith he'd propped up in front of the traveling alarm clock, the picture which was now hidden in the secret compartment of his wallet. He'd dug the Bible out of his luggage and reread what had become one of his favorite verses: "Therefore, if any man be in Christ, he is a new creation; old things are passed away; behold, all things are become new."

Well, he reminded himself as a wave of nostalgia swept over him, *things will definitely be new and different.* This morning he'd picked up his lone aluminum suitcase, opened the door of his apartment, and walked through it to a new life. Where he was going there was no room for excess baggage.

Stephen took the headset off his curly black hair and was amazed again at how quiet the interior of the aircraft was. He could actually hear the stewardess fluffing the pillow as she came towards him. For lack of anything better to do, she'd pampered him with offers of bottled water and the latest bestseller, which could be read on a laptop computer that had replaced the magazine rack. Johann Gutenberg would have turned over in his grave, he thought. As plugged-in publishing expanded, they were on the way to becoming a paperless society.

The stewardess handed him a card of safety instructions. "Can I get anything else for you?" she asked, offering him the pillow.

"No, thank you." Stephen gave her that irrepressible grin of his and replaced his headset. He wasn't really listening to the music, but perhaps if she thought he was, she'd leave him alone. He read the card and located the red button which would jettison his seat and automatically inflate the parachute attached to it. In the headrest was a built-in oxygen supply. Heaven or Jerusalem. One way or the other, he would see Faith again.

He reached for the picture of her in his wallet. Stephen had looked at it a dozen times since he'd left home, unable to believe even now that she was waiting for him. While he apprehensively massaged the hockey scar under his chin, he turned the picture over and studied the name written on the back in Randy's bold scrawl: *Solomon Lowenstein.* A phone number was beneath it.

Overhead he saw the red letters of the seat belt sign light up, and the airplane began its final approach to Israel's Ben Gurion Airport. As he fastened his seat belt, Stephen felt his stomach do hand springs. Was it caused by the change in the plane's altitude or the change in his attitude? As a trained physician, he knew there was no physical reason for what he felt, but as a man in love, he wasn't sure of anything anymore.

"Midian Enterprises has been able to pinpoint and classify the major causes of dissension," said Logan Washburn, "but now we must provide concrete solutions or our supporters will turn to someone who can." His eyes traveled from the bronze statue on Judah's desk to the bookcase and back. "Things are getting worse." Nervously, he twisted a strand of grey hair around his index finger as he continued.

"Disease and fighting follow this famine like a child clinging to its mother's skirts. Almost 25 percent of the world's population has been destroyed. Wild animals are so thrist-crazed that they come into the cities and attack anything that moves."

Judah spun around in his chair. "Fear and panic, two of my favorite emotions. They always spawn irrational actions and build momentum.

"Get me all the footage you can on the prophets. I want that piece the networks did when those two misfits first appeared in Jerusalem. Especially the segment in which they stated that it wouldn't rain for three and a half years."

Judah began to line up his targets. "With a little creative help from our media staff, we'll convince everyone that these prophets and their followers are, in fact, responsible for this drought and everything that goes along with it."

His eyes glittered. "The prophets have ignored my warnings. 'Doom and gloom' is their prophecy to Jew and Gentile alike." His ears seemed to flatten against his head as he crouched in his chair. "What gives them the right to go around screaming that God's judgment is come upon the world?"

"Most people are too sophisticated to swallow this judgment theory," said Logan.

"Thank heavens." Judah smiled at his own joke. "And yet . . . the miracles they've produced have convinced some that they're the genuine article." Hatred narrowed his eyes and his cunning mind ejected its poison. "It's time to have a televised, head-to-head confrontation. We'll concede that possibly the prophets are on the right track."

"But—"

"Then," he fingered the amulet beneath his shirt, "as a spokesman for world peace, I'll appeal to them to call upon their God to end the drought. Surely He does not plan to come back to a world devoid of people. Who would worship Him?" He laughed then, secure in his own power. "And, of course, the drought will continue, despite our pleas to the prophets. We will have no other choice but to get rid of them and their companions."

"People will say you're going off on a witch-hunt."

"You really are the devil's advocate, aren't you, Logan? On the contrary, who can fault us for doing everything within our power to end these hardships?" He pointed at Logan. "It will be your painful duty to see that somehow our list of the prophet's converts and associates is leaked to the media."

He ignored the buzz from his intercom.

"Special consideration will be given to those who assist us by turning in the names and whereabouts of believers. In return for their cooperation, we'll promise them better job opportunities, education, and priority in housing. The gambit of privilege has been used throughout the centuries to divert *good* people from the real issues.

"To those who need miracles to seduce them, we'll provide demonic ones. They'll never know the difference."

"But the Jews—"

"Forget about the Jews. They're fighting among themselves. The more educated ones have refused to participate in the offering of bulls and goats on the sacrificial altar at the temple; they call it an anachronism. I find that very amusing, don't you?" A sinister smile of satisfaction flickered across his dark features.

"If the truth were known, the Jews and other religious groups want a saint they can see and touch, not the promises of an illusive God."

"But how will this—"

"After we've presented the country with these sacrificial lambs, I will be thrust into the position of ultimate power which I have always deserved. As the world's only living saint, I will bring an end to the drought and become God in the process."

Judah Midian leaned back in his chair and closed his eyes. For a brief moment he saw the brightness of heaven before he felt himself hurled back to earth. His eyes snapped open. The sand in earth's hourglass was running out, but he'd turn it over and begin again . . . his way.

The dazzling March sunshine filtered through the branches of the sycamore tree in Rabbi Solomon Lowenstein's rock garden promising an early spring.

"It's good to see you after all these years," said Solomon to Randy Morgan as they sat together on a wooden bench surrounded by shrubs.

Randy brushed his fingers across a tender green bud on one of the oleander bushes. "Why? We never got along when I was questioning your grandfather about the Holocaust. I got the impression that you only tolerated my visits for his sake. Rebecca has made it quite clear that we are an imposition at best."

Solomon was surprised; it wasn't like Rebecca to be so inhospitable. "You haven't changed much. Always the skeptic, eh?"

Randy's features softened. "No, I have changed, Solomon. My life . . . well, it's been turned around so to speak."

"Whose life has not in these last few years?"

They were both hedging, trying to sound out the other. Although they needed each other, neither one wanted to be the first to admit it.

"So, what are your plans while you're in Jerusalem?"

"I've been offered a job here."

Solomon's curiosity was aroused. "Not as a rabbi, I hope." He chuckled at his own joke. "Two in this house are enough."

Something clicked inside Randy's head. Mutual interests. "You mean Rebecca is—"

"A rabbi."

He savored the thought for a moment. "I always thought of rabbis as old and ugly with long beards and—" He stopped as he realized he was describing Solomon.

"It's true," said Solomon, shrugging his shoulders. "Perhaps Jehovah thought He could attract more bees with honey than vinegar. There have been many changes in the Jewish community, Rebecca is but one of them. Now this job you speak of, what will you be doing?"

Randy pulled the letter out of his pocket and handed it to Solomon.

Solomon's hands began to shake as he saw the letterhead on the stationary. Judah's fingers reached into everyone's pocket.

"Well, what do you think?"

A pause. "It could be useful."

"Useful?"

"If you and I are willing to put away our former prejudices and work together."

"Work together? To what end?"

"To unveil the treachery of Judah Midian."

"Logan Washburn, former Nobel Peace Price recipient and assistant to Judah Midian of Midian Enterprises, has issued a formal challenge today to two men who, along with their followers, continue to condemn the new world order."

The film clip of the two prophets in their robes rolled across the television screen in the newly painted dormitory room the hospital had prepared for Stephen. Moments before, he had been anxious to unpack and get in touch with Faith and her father, but now he sat on the bed, unable to believe what he was seeing. As he watched the story unfold on television, everything else seemed unimportant.

The international news program that was broadcast in English continued as the tanned, humorless face of Logan Washburn flashed on the screen.

"As a representative for Judah Midian, I have been asked to address the 'prophets' and those who support them."

"You proclaimed over a year ago that there would be no rain upon the earth until _you_ deemed it. Therefore, it is time for you to accept full responsibility for the drought which has crippled the globe."

The station spliced in a clip of the event as Logan continued.

"We personally implore you and your followers to end this drought. We concede that your conclusions, based upon the text of ancient scriptures, may be correct, but we find it impossible to believe that the God you say you worship would allow this suffering to continue. What will He come back to?" At this point pictures of starving children and dead and diseased animals flitted across the screen.

"We challenge you to call upon your God to bring rain once more upon the earth. If this does not happen, we'll be forced to ask the following questions: Is it possible that your God is displeased with *your* actions, and therefore *your* arrogance and defiance have caused the catastrophes we are now experiencing?"

"By ridding the world of you and your followers can we not end these natural disasters, just as by throwing Jonah out of the ship the rest were spared?"

The question hung in the air like an ominous premonition, and Stephen felt his heart sink. He did not know how long it would be before the slaughter began, but he knew it would.

Quickly, he turned over Faith's picture and called the phone number on the back.

Faith put on the blue robe she'd bought in Beersheba, then tried to do something with the short crop of hair which insisted on plastering itself to her head. She bent her head over and vigorously brushed her hair, hoping it would fluff out around her face.

"Can I help you with anything?" said Rebecca.

"What I really need is a shampoo."

Rebecca shook her head. "Hair washing is only allowed once a week; in this sector it's done on Monday. Today is Wednesday." She walked out of the room, ending the discussion.

Faith scowled at her reflection in the mirror that was on the wall behind Rebecca's bed. She removed the scowl. It was a definite improvement.

She leaned against the door jamb and acknowledged the breathless, funny feeling in the pit of her stomach which wouldn't go away. Once again she felt as though she was hanging suspended at the highest point of the roller coaster ride at Busch Gardens. She looked down, frozen in that one terrible instant before the roller coaster plunged downward at breathtaking speed.

What would Stephen think when he saw her?

She dropped an earring as she tried to put it on. Great! She was not only nervous but incredibly clumsy. *This is ridiculous,* she told herself as she scrambled on all fours looking for the earring. After all she'd been through—her mother's and sister's disappearance, the flight from the United States, and the hardships of the desert—why did she feel even more unsure of herself than ever? It just didn't make sense.

She slid her hand under Rebecca's bed, groping for the smooth feel of the pearl earring. Instead, her hand touched something cold and hard. She stopped and bent down, then lifted the edge of the bed quilt so she could see. Something gleamed as the light hit it. It was the barrel of a handgun! To the right of it lay the earring.

She heard the click of Rebecca's shoes on the stone floor as she came towards the bedroom. Quickly Faith scooped up her earring and stood up, dropping the bedspread into place.

"Faith," said Rebecca as she entered the bedroom, "if you want to wash your hair, go ahead. Considering the circumstances, I think we can bend the rules this time."

"Could I really?" squealed Faith.

"I didn't mean to be so harsh before," Rebecca said apologetically. "At this point, obeying the water conservation mandate is a matter of self-discipline, not law enforcement, but we do have to be careful. We're luckier than most countries. For two consecutive years before the drought our annual rainfall was higher than normal."

"Thanks. I want to look just right," said Faith as she put on her other earring. She put her hand on her throat. "I've never been so nervous before."

The resentment dissolved from Rebecca's face. "Why are you so worried? It's only been a week since you've seen this Stephen of yours."

"Yes, but—" Faith drew her breath in sharply. "What if he's changed? What if I don't feel the same way about him?" She wrung her hands together. "My stomach is so churned up that I feel like I'm going to—" She put her hand over her mouth and raced for the bathroom. Rebecca heard her throwing up.

"Are you going to be all right?" asked Rebecca as she heard Faith brushing her teeth.

"It's just a case of the jitters; I'll be fine. There's nothing left to throw up."

Rebecca almost envied Faith as she remembered how her first blissful months with Judah had kindled her hopes and aspirations. Now they were shattered and broken, impossible fragments which could never be put back together.

She wanted to hate this girl and her father, but she saw too much of herself in Faith. Everyone had a right to a little bit of happiness.

Faith came into the bedroom and tried to smile; Rebecca put her arm around her and pushed her gently down on the bed. "Now, what's the worst thing that could happen?" she said to Faith, posing her grandmother's favorite question for all of life's absurdities.

"I guess . . . he could say he doesn't love me. And then . . . I'd have to convince him that he did."

They laughed together, and for a moment Faith forgot what she'd discovered under the bed and all it's implications. Tonight her love for Stephen cast its glow over any suspicions she might harbor, and not only Stephen, but Rebecca could bask in its light.

They both heard the knock on the front door at the same time.

"It can't be Stephen, he just called," exclaimed Faith.

"Don't worry, I'll get the door. You wash your hair. If it's Stephen, I'll entertain this young man of yours until you're ready." Rebecca smiled and hurried to the door feeling more lighthearted than she had in weeks.

She swung open the door. Her smile quickly vanished as she was greeted by Hannah's sour-apple face.

29

At the sight of Rebecca Greenspan, Hannah's courage fled, and the wrinkles in her forehead deepened into front-line trenches. What was *she* doing home? She usually went to the market at this hour.

"Yes?" said Rebecca curtly.

Hannah cleared her throat and looked past Rebecca into the living room. She was pale beneath her dark complexion as she tried to compose herself. "I must speak with Rabbi Lowenstein, immediately."

Rebecca just stood there.

"Please tell him I'm here," Hannah insisted. Her pulse was racing and beads of perspiration began to form on her upper lip.

"I'm sorry, but he has a visitor. I don't want to disturb him."

"*You* don't want to disturb him?" Hannah glared at the brazen woman before her. Her voice trembled. "So now you decide when he can see someone. Don't you think you're overstepping your bounds?" Her voice began to rise. "You are nothing more than a boarder in his home. You are not his wife," she said indignantly.

"And neither are you."

Something inside Hannah snapped. "I . . . I want to speak to Solomon, now!" She tried to push her way past Rebecca, but Rebecca stood her ground, blocking the entrance.

"Hannah," said Rebecca as a wave of pity for the distraught old woman swept over her, "I am sure Solomon would want to give you his full attention; he can't do that now. Why don't you come by tomorrow afternoon?"

Hannah's eyebrows knitted together. "Will you be here?" She raised her chin. Was that a phone she heard ringing, or was it the pounding of her own heart?

Their eyes met. "No," said Rebecca, "not if you don't want me to."

"Why would I?" said Hannah. She turned to leave, then cast a hate-filled glance at Rebecca. "Things would have turned out differently if you hadn't shown up." She rolled her words tightly together and squeezed them out like the final dabs of toothpaste from a tube. "They still might."

The huge block of marble from the island of Paros in the Aegean Sea had been sculpted into a remarkable likeness of Judah. The waxy properties of the Parian marble gave it a beautiful sheen as Lars Nicene rubbed the snowy white marble with a cloth, watching with delight as the delicate veins and cloudy hues appeared.

Each day he'd worked for twelve to eighteen hours with his mallet and chisel, consumed by a passion which he couldn't explain. The sculpture was in the final stages of completion. Despite the ache across his shoulders, he continued to polish the statue lovingly. In just a few days the best work he'd ever done, his masterpiece, would be completed.

Lars leaned against the sculpture, letting the cloth drop to the floor as he closed his bleary eyes. His fingers fondled the marble, and it felt warm to his touch, almost like human flesh.

He opened his eyes and stepped back to look at his creation. In this light it looked so lifelike. The head—he rubbed his eyes—did it turn ever so slightly?

He must be hallucinating. Lars massaged his greasy forehead with his thumb and forefinger. He needed sleep, food, and a bath, but he couldn't stop now.

He glanced up at the statue. Its unblinking eyes stared back at him. He studied the lips he now loved, captured in a half smile. Then he heard it. Not again! He put his hands to his ears, but the voice that had begun as a whisper grew louder and louder.

He couldn't shut out the demanding voice. Was he losing his mind?

"No!" he screamed into the deserted studio. The voice subsided.

Lars felt light-headed as he approached the figure and put his hands on the chest of marble to reassure himself. Suddenly, beneath his long tapered fingers he felt the breast rise and fall! He gasped and stepped back, tripping over his tools. Above his withered and sunken cheeks, Lars's eyes blazed with the intensity of a man possessed.

Now he knew he was sick.

Judah would make him well. Judah could do anything.

He ran his finger along the inside of his mouth, felt the loose teeth in their sockets and the blisters which had formed on the soft inner lining of his cheeks. Lars Nicene stood up and picked up his cloth. He must think only of his work now.

It had to be ready—? He searched for the calendar, found it beneath the marble chips, and put his aching finger on the circled date. In just one week the statue would be put into storage until . . . when? Even now, he didn't know where its final destination would be, but it didn't really matter. What mattered was that Judah was pleased with the sculpture.

Stephen left the Hadassah-Hebrew University Medical Center on the western edge of Jerusalem and took a cab to Old Jerusalem. He fumbled with the coins in his pocket, fingering the shekels and the coins of the new universal currency. He took both currencies out of his pocket as the Arab driver came to a halt.

"Take your pick," he said as he got out of the cab.

The Arab turned over the newly minted tin coins, shook his head, and picked out the shekels from among them before he sped off in his Mercedes to pick up another fare.

Stephen touched his nose to push back his glasses, only to realize for the umpteenth time that he had contact lenses. Old habits, like unwanted relatives in July, were hard to discourage. As he blinked rapidly and began to jingle the coins in his pocket, he wished he'd kept his glasses.

What if Faith didn't like the new Stephen Bradley? The thought came out of nowhere and tortured his frail ego for a moment before the brilliant sunshine helped him to dismiss it.

As Stephen walked along the street, following the map that one of the doctors at the hospital had drawn for him, he straightened his tie and buttoned his jacket. Maybe it was too much—maybe he should have worn something more casual. No. When you're going to ask someone to marry you . . . well . . . he really was just a traditionalist after all.

He grinned as he thought of his sister, Jamie, who would never have believed that her older brother was actually going to take the plunge. He'd been too cowardly to tell her about his plans to get married. It would have to wait until later.

Jolted by the news report he'd just heard in his room, he'd concluded that it was no use postponing his marriage to Faith. Intertwined with his love for her was a fierce desire to protect her from whatever terrors were lurking in their future.

Another dart of doubt struck him. What if she said no? He'd given her the turquoise ring and she'd promised . . . He tried to think of her exact words.

"I'll be waiting for you in the summer."

Those words, they didn't really mean anything. She could have said that to anyone—an uncle, a friend, or a complete stranger. He was thinking of a real commitment, but maybe he'd read too much into that final kiss.

His steps were slower now as he turned into the street and walked up the steps to the houses perched at the top. He was oblivious to the view of the Temple Mount and to the strident noises which besieged Jerusalem.

Stephen continued cross-examining himself. If Faith were as eager to see him as he was to see her, why hadn't she talked to him when he'd called on the phone? He watched the scuffed toes of his shoes lead him to the gate of Solomon's house. While still outside the gate, Stephen heard the iron gate swing open. He looked up, but not quickly enough to avoid the gate as it hit him on the right shoulder.

"Ouch!" he exclaimed to the woman in a blue dress who was just leaving.

"Excuse me. I didn't see you standing there, I had other things on my mind," said Hannah. She looked Stephen over, from the top of his neatly cut black hair to the imitation leather shoes he was wearing.

"You have business with Rabbi Lowenstein?" she inquired tersely.

"Why, no, I've come to see a young lady who's staying with him."

"I thought as much!" Hannah wagged her finger in his face. "Take my advice young man and forget about her; she will cause you nothing but trouble." Without further explanation she marched down the street like an angry blue jay flapping its wings.

What in the world was that all about? Before he could answer this question the door burst open.

"Stephen, I thought you'd never get here."

Faith was more beautiful than he remembered. He stood there, staring at her, tongue-tied for the first time in his life.

"Well just don't stand there, kiss me."

A slow grin spread across his face, but before he could move, she threw her arms around his neck and hugged him. Instinctively, he wrapped his arms around her, nuzzled her neck, and felt once again the warmth of her body against his and the sweet smell of her hair. He knew he had to ask her now before he lost his nerve.

"Faith," he whispered in her ear, "will you marry me?"

He felt her arms go limp as she stepped back and looked at him with a solemn expression on her face. She gazed down at the stone walk.

I should have waited, he thought to himself as a feeling akin to panic began to overtake him. Marriage to me is probably the last thing on her mind—she can't even look me in the face.

Faith slowly raised her head. Their eyes met.

"Why, Dr. Bradley . . . I thought you'd never ask."

"What? You will?" With a great sigh of relief, he bent down and kissed her smile softly, then more intently, and his doubts took flight like a flock of desert larks.

For a few minutes Randy Morgan stood outside the pyramid-shaped building that housed Judah Midian Enterprises before he pushed open the glass door and entered the large reception area. A thick emerald green carpet swept across the room and ended a third of the way up the walls where it met a series of vividly colored murals depicting lush tropical scenes, bright with flowers and animals.

He felt as if he'd walked into a jungle; there were groups of live plants and potted palm trees scattered throughout the area, and a floral fragrance wafted through the room from the overhead vents. Chattering birds in cages were suspended from the glass ceiling. Fountains and pools with fish in them completed the jungle effect. He was duly impressed.

He gave his name to the shapely receptionist, then went back to study the murals while he thought about Faith and Stephen's engagement.

"I see that you appreciate fine art," said a voice behind him a few minutes later.

He turned round and immediately recognized the speaker.

"This series is entitled *The Garden of Eden*. I think the artist did an excellent job recreating it, don't you?"

"I really wouldn't know," said Randy, "but it is impressive."

"Yes, first impressions tend to set the tone of a relationship. We want the public and our employees to realize that Judah Midian Enterprises is synonymous with eloquent, yet basic, New Age values. We hope that you will join us in our endeavors, Mr. Morgan."

"I'm definitely interested," said Randy.

"Good. Why don't we go to my office where we can discuss the details in private? My name is Logan Washburn. I'm vice-president of the company."

"I've seen you on television, Ambassador, many times." They shook hands.

"Please, call me Logan. I used to work for the government, but as you probably know yourself, it's very easy to get disillusioned with the establishment."

"They say you could have been the next president of the United States. Why did you walk away?"

"Why did you *run* away, Mr. Morgan?"

They both left the questions unanswered as they entered

the elevator, and Logan punched the button for the thirteenth floor.

"It's rather unusual to have a thirteenth floor in a building," commented Randy as the elevator rose swiftly.

"Only if you're superstitious, Mr. Morgan. Are you?"

The doors opened.

"No, I don't think so."

"Then you have nothing to worry about, do you?" A mechanical smile appeared on Logan's face, but his hard eyes were riveted on Randy's before he led him to a chair in his office overlooking the West Bank.

As he sat down, Randy noticed that the entire wall behind Logan's desk was covered with a world map where colored pins had been stuck. Strange, he thought he smelled baby powder.

"Let's get to the point, shall we, Mr. Morgan?"

Randy nodded his head.

"Someone in the United States has offered a reward for one million dollars for you and your daughter's return, dead or alive—no questions asked."

Randy felt a surge of anger course through his veins, but outwardly he remained calm, his eyes never straying from Logan's face. His personal feelings would have to be put aside if he was to be of any use to Solomon and the others involved. He must appear cool and calculated.

He leaned back in the chair, laced his hands together, and rested them on the back of his head while he crossed his legs and assumed a nonchalant position. "Only a million . . . You're right, I am disillusioned. I thought it would be at least two."

For a moment there was an awkward silence, then Logan threw back his head and laughed. Randy joined him as he drew his chair closer to the desk. He lowered his voice. "May I assume, Logan, since I'm in your office now, instead of being escorted back to the States in a pine box or an urn for someone to display on a fireplace mantel, that I'm worth more than a million to Midian Enterprises?"

Logan's penetrating gaze swept across Randy's face before he answered. "You could be. If you accept our offer, you'll be paid well, and the advantages of working for us far outnumber any negative aspects. Your every need—and desire—will be met."

Raw greed. That's the common factor which will make this deception work, thought Randy. "My daughter is getting married in a couple of weeks. She and her husband will need an apartment, and I'll need a place to call my own. Living with two rabbis is not exactly conducive to . . . having female companionship." Randy flashed Logan a knowing look.

"That can all be arranged, but I must stress that this assignment cannot be taken lightly. It requires that you take a blood oath."

"A blood oath?" said Randy, taken aback. Quickly he tried to make light of it. "Like selling your soul to the devil, eh?"

"Some might say that," said Logan, with a glimmer of sarcasm.

"Well . . . I did that when I joined the CIA." Randy stood up. "Where do I sign?"

"Follow me," said Logan as he headed for the elevator. "Our personnel department is in the basement," he explained. As the elevator began its swift descent, Randy felt his thoughts plunging wildly to the bottom with it.

The doors opened to a long corridor dimly lit by candles in decorative wall brackets. "As you can see, we're not hampered by the traditional way of doing things," said Logan.

Randy nodded and looked at his watch. It was three-thirty. Where were the other employees?

As they headed down the corridor toward the end room, it seemed to be getting darker; Randy could barely make out Logan, who was ahead of him.

Logan stopped at the last door, opened it, and waited for Randy to enter first. The only light in the cavernous room was a six-armed candelabra that illuminated a pentacle-shaped table with three chairs around it. As Randy got closer, he could see that someone was sitting in one of the chairs. The figure rose and came towards him. Randy looked into the face of Judah Midian.

"I'm glad that you're going to join our organization," said Judah. He didn't offer his hand. "Logan has given you my stipulations?"

"Yes," said Randy. It was too warm and he loosened his collar as he inhaled a faint whiff of—charred wood mixed with lily of the valley?

Logan picked up a contract from the table and handed it to

him. Randy scanned the figures on the five-year contract. He whistled under his breath.

"I assume our offer is acceptable," said Logan.

"You've just bought me lock, stock, and barrel," Randy said.

Judah picked up a quill pen. "Your left hand," he demanded. Randy gave it to him, and Judah pricked his forefinger with the pen's sharp tip. He handed the pen to Randy.

Randy brushed the point of the quill across the red droplets which oozed from his finger. When he leaned over to sign his name on the contract he heard a loud buzzing noise, like the sound of a thousand angry flies. When he looked up, Judah was gone and so was the noise.

"Now," said Logan, giving no explanation for Judah's swift disappearance, "I'll show you the rest of our operation."

This is ridiculous, thought Randy as the elevator rose to the fourth floor. This whole "signing your life away" procedure was just a psychological ploy, and yet he couldn't shake the feeling that somehow he'd been compromised. With every fleeting scratch of the pen, he'd felt a part of him perish.

"Recently we incorporated olfactory science into our technology," said Logan as they got off the elevator.

"Olfactory science?"

"It's called the fifth sense. Molecular biologists have proven that smell is subtly but intimately connected with our mental and emotional well-being."

Randy inhaled deeply as he followed Logan through the work spaces. "Apple blossoms?"

"Yes. That scent improves work performance on computer vigilance tasks."

"What does baby powder do?" prodded Randy.

"You noticed," said Logan appreciatively. "It's the one smell almost universally accepted as safe and secure."

So they wanted him to feel safe and secure. "And lily of the valley?" he asked.

"It triggers relaxation and reduces stress."

Randy ran his thumb over his forefinger, felt the tiny pin-prick where he'd actually squeezed a drop of blood to sign his name on the contract. He popped his knuckles and tried to pay attention to Logan as he trailed him through the fourth floor where the computer system was installed, but he couldn't con-centrate.

Results. That's what counts, he told himself. But if what he was doing was right, why did he feel as if his soul had just been put through a paper shredder?

30

Hannah crossed her thick ankles and sat back on the sofa in Solomon's living room while he went to the kitchen to bring her a cup of tea. She ran her fingers across the coffee table making long streaks in the dust. A smile of satisfaction crept across her features. It was just as she'd thought—Rebecca was not a good housekeeper, another reason for Solomon to get rid of her.

"Now, Hannah, to what do I owe this visit?" said Solomon as he put the tray on the table.

"I must talk to you about Rebecca."

"Rebecca?" He eased himself into the rocking chair.

Hannah picked up her cup and took a drink. It would give her strength to go on. "Since you dismissed me—"

"That is too harsh a word to use," said Solomon. His kind brown eyes looked into hers. "Now that Rebecca and I have a mutual understanding—"

"A mutual understanding! Can't you see what's happening? She has made a fool of you. Everyone is talking about how Rabbi Solomon Lowenstein has been seduced—"

"Seduced!" Solomon stared at her, unable to fathom her accusations. When he did, a tide of crimson spread across his face. Slowly, he rose from the rocker. "Hannah—" his voice broke. "I have treated Rebecca as a daughter and nothing more." His face searched hers. "How could you possibly think—"

Hannah's hand shook as she put her cup down. If Solomon was telling her the truth . . .

"What else could I think when suddenly after forty years—" She burst into tears.

"There, there," said Solomon as he sat down and patted her on the shoulder. She leaned against him and a shudder went through her body. He handed her a tissue from his pocket.

"If I have misjudged you, Solomon, I apologize," she said wiping her eyes.

"Maybe we have misjudged each other," said Solomon with a sigh. "Esther and Hezekiah would have wanted us to remain friends."

"Then we can see each other again?"

"Yes, Hannah." He must use tact and grace. "But I can promise nothing more."

"It's a chance to start over, that's enough for now. I know you'll do the right thing, Solomon."

Would he? Solomon felt himself sinking into the mire and quicksand of a life with Hannah, a life that would destroy his soul.

The pope ran his fingers through his iron-gray hair. Instead of working on his Easter message, he forced himself to reread the latest news releases. It was too incredulous!

He looked up at the picture above his desk. A beaming Pope John Paul II dressed in a white robe was clasping former Soviet leader Mikhail Gorbachev's hand. Held in the winter of 1989, it was the first meeting between a Kremlin chief and a Roman Catholic pontiff. "A promise-filled sign for the future," Pope John Paul II had declared, and he had expressed the hope that all mankind would be able to practice their religious life freely. That promise had been a reality. Until now.

Judah Midian had clothed religious persecution in the guise of saving the world from extinction. Last week Pope Timothy had watched with interest, then dismay, when the two prophets appeared on television. They steadfastly refused to end the drought, stating that it was God's judgment upon the earth.

Three days ago, the Vatican's intelligence had informed him that tonight Judah would get rid of the estimated half million followers of this sect. Could no one but he see that everyone's religious freedom was at stake—that by doing nothing to stop Judah they were condoning his actions? Even the Pontifical Academy of Sciences, which contained some of the greatest scientific minds of the world, had turned a deaf ear to his pleas.

He reminded himself that as the pope he was the personal representative of God on earth. This lofty thought did nothing to ease his guilt. When he had declared Judah a saint, he had unwittingly become part of this plot to exterminate those who did not agree with Judah.

He must confront Judah in person; there was no other way. He pressed the buzzer on his desk and gave orders to the monsignor to make arrangements immediately for a trip to Jerusalem.

"These things take time, Your Holiness. The security, the press—"

Like dry tender waiting for a spark, the pope's words blazed through the room, scorching the amazed black-robed cleric. "I *must* be in Jerusalem *tonight!*" the pope demanded.

Dr. Stephen Bradley looked down at his watch. "We'd better get going if we want to meet your father on time." He took off his stethoscope, emptied the pockets of his lab coat, and placed his penlight on the desk in his room at the university.

"Can you believe that dad actually found an apartment for us? Everyone told me that with all the refugees, housing was impossible in Jerusalem." Faith snuggled closer to him. "I had visions of us living in this room with just a hot plate and a mattress."

"Well, now—that wouldn't have been so bad, would it?" he teased as they walked outside to catch a bus.

"As long as we're together in Israel," she said, rotating the turquoise ring on her left hand, "I don't care where we live."

"Whose arm did your father have to twist to get this apartment?" said Stephen as they boarded the bus and sat down. "I heard there was a waiting list a mile long."

"He said it was one of the perks when he took the job with Judah Midian Enterprises." With a lurch the bus headed into the afternoon traffic.

"Just what does he do there?"

"You know, I'm not sure—must be something to do with computer technology. I've been so busy thinking about our wedding that I'm afraid I've neglected dear old Dad. Not that he would have noticed."

"What do you mean?"

"Rebecca and he always seem to have their heads together. He says she's helping him brush up on his Hebrew." Furrows appeared in her forehead as she continued, "It's really weird to see my father . . . I mean to think about him with someone other than my mom."

"You think it's serious?"

She sighed. "I could be overreacting. At first Dad and Rebecca barely tolerated each other. Even Solomon commented on it." She flashed him a smile as her thoughts congealed. "Maybe like us, he wants to pack as much happiness as he can into the next few years, and if Rebecca is a part of it, you won't hear any complaints from me. I'll be too busy trying to take care of you."

"You—taking care of me? I thought it was supposed to be the other way around."

She punched him playfully in the ribs and for the next fifteen minutes they forgot everything but their own happiness as they bantered back and forth while the bus picked up and let off passengers.

"This is our stop," said Faith as the bus squealed to a halt. "Dad said he'd be waiting for us at the cafe across the street."

They both saw Randy at the same time, but he seemed unaware of their arrival. He was absorbed in the newspaper, his cup of coffee untouched as he sat at the outdoor table.

"Hi, Dad."

Randy Morgan looked up at his daughter with sadness in his eyes, then back at the newspaper. "Have you seen this?" He pushed a copy of *The Jerusalem Post* across the table.

Without thinking, she read aloud the bold black print: *"Capture of Prophets and Followers Imminent."*

Tears welled up in her eyes. She'd been so caught up in her own happiness that the tragedies throughout the world had seemed far away. Now they had lighted once again on Jerusalem's doorstep.

★   ★   ★

"Stephen, I want to get married now—today."

Surprised, Stephen put down the X-ray he was holding.

"Faith, are you sure? We can't even move into our apartment until next week."

"I don't care. April 21, 2011, is as good a day to get married as any other."

"This isn't exactly the way we'd planned it."

"Nothing is the way we'd planned it. If we don't get married now . . . well, maybe we never will."

"But your father—"

"I'm marrying you, not my father. He'll understand." She put her hands on her hips. "Are you by any chance going to stand me up, Doctor Bradley?"

"Not on your life," he said with a dazzling grin. "In fact, I think we can be married right here."

"At the medical center?"

"Yes. They have a synagogue. I'll have to make a few phone calls, then we'll go see it."

Twenty minutes later Stephen and Faith walked down the steps of the Hadassah synagogue, a rectangular building designed by the American architect Joseph Neufeld in 1962. Once inside, they were awe-struck by the stained-glass windows.

Stephen gazed at the twelve windows as the sunlight played through them, scattering the jeweltone colors. "Each window commemorates a son of Jacob and the tribes the sons founded. I discovered that human forms are never used in Jewish religious art; that's why Marc Chagall, the artist, used symbols such as birds, animals, trees, and fish to represent each tribe's personality and achievements."

Stephen paused. "They're really stunning, aren't they? It's hard to believe that Chagall was seventy-two when he accepted this commission. I guess artistic expression is ageless."

"They're magnificent," said Faith.

"Just like you," he said as he tilted her chin upward and kissed her soundly.

Faith felt almost dizzy as she reluctantly pulled herself away. "Oh Stephen, I'm so happy. Sometimes I almost forget why we're here and what the next three or four years will bring, don't you?"

"Yes," he said as he put his arm around her shoulders, "but just being together will make it easier."

They stood there, neither one speaking, mesmerized by the brilliant array of red, green, yellow, blue, and purple colors which danced in the light.

"Do you think they'll allow us to be married here—today?" said Faith. "I mean, since we're not Jewish."

"I've already gotten their permission," said Stephen squeezing her hand. "It's a little unorthodox, but a lot of things in Jerusalem are these days."

Two hours later, the bride was beautiful in a white silk suit, and the groom was nervous as he slipped the platinum wedding band on her finger. With a stray rabbi who was visiting a family member at the medical center and two witnesses they'd never met before, Faith Morgan and Dr. Stephen Bradley became husband and wife.

As dawn's invisible fingers began to deftly peel away the layers of darkness, Faith rolled over in bed and looked up at the ceiling where shafts of daylight, the color of freshly squeezed orange juice, began to trickle across it.

She glanced lovingly at Stephen while the blazing edges of a tangerine sun began to sift through the lone window in the room. With his hair tousled, he reminded her of a little boy; only the stubble of a beard betrayed her illusion. She listened to his even breathing and felt the contour of his strong body next to hers. He was asleep now, his passion spent along with hers.

Why had she been so frightened at first? She had feared his closeness would awaken the terrifying memories she thought she'd re- pressed, but Stephen's patience and tenderness had helped her blot them out, replacing them with a love which transcended the mere coupling of two bodies. This wasn't what she had expected. It was more, much more.

Stephen stirred and opened his eyes. "Good morning, Mrs. Bradley," he said with a mischievous smile. He propped himself up on one elbow. "You look like Eos, the goddess of the dawn."

"Good morning," she said, pulling up the sheet to cover her

naked body. Suddenly she felt shy again, as if the light of day had somehow changed what had happened last night.

Stephen slid his arm under her, drawing Faith to him. He kissed her and they melted together. Once again they were caught in a time warp where neither the past nor future existed, only the present.

31

After three years, the parched, cracked earth and its inhabitants longed for rain, but as each cloudless day appeared, hope languished and hatred for the two prophets who had predicted the drought increased. But in 2013, no longer did the sickly-sweet aroma of death fill the nostrils of those in Jerusalem, and despite the lack of moisture, the faint fragrance of spring hovered over the Holy City.

Faith Bradley had promised to help Rebecca with preparations for the Passover. Perhaps the fact that the celebration fell on her and Stephen's second wedding anniversary had something to do with her willingness to participate in this time-honored Jewish custom. She smiled secretly to herself. No, it was more than that.

Faith inhaled deeply, and the promise of a new beginning stirred within her, for even the lack of rain was unable to keep the earth and her heart from its seasonal celebration. The soft breezes of April gently lifted the curtains at the open window, bringing not only the clean scent of spring into the kitchen, but the insistent bleating of the male lamb that was tethered in the garden behind Solomon's house.

"The house must be spotless for Passover," Rebecca reminded Faith. She reached for the towel as she finished washing her hair in the kitchen sink.

"If the Lord wanted the house to be immaculate, He would have given us some rain," replied Faith.

"We'll have to make do with what we've got," said Rebecca,

picking up the precious bucket of sudsy water which remained. She carried it to her bedroom, and the dirty water sloshed across the dusty tile floor as she emptied the bucket and began to push the mop through it. To clean under the bed or not . . .

She moved the bed and caught sight of the gun; it was a grim reminder of Solomon's reprieve. Why had Judah decided to spare Solomon? Rebecca leaned on the mop handle. Springtime almost made her believe in miracles. Almost.

She sighed deeply and went to the kitchen to combine the ingredients for the bread of affliction. The old and the new, could they exist together? She thought of the elderly women who still threw the dough on the side of a hot brick oven to cook it; they were still wedded to the past, but she wasn't. Their outdated and unsanitary customs had no place in the new world order or *her* Passover preparations.

Patiently Rebecca mixed the bread along with her thoughts until slowly they both began to take shape. The leaven of her imagination multiplied as she began to spread the dough in the flat pans for baking. Could she have killed Solomon? Her hands shook so violently that she had to grip the edge of the sink to steady them. Why had Judah given her and Solomon a second chance?

She gazed out the window at the lamb that was now contentedly chewing the sparse clumps of grass that had managed to push their way through the earth's dry, hard crust. Faith, who had been sweeping the patio, knelt down and rubbed its woolly head. Today, as had been the tradition for centuries, the lamb would be killed and the shank roasted for the Passover.

"Good morning, Rebecca," said Rabbi Solomon Lowenstein as he entered the kitchen and joined her at the window. "You're not feeling sorry for that lamb, are you? Esther always did."

"Maybe, a little. But then, not every lamb is chosen for Passover, only the best, the one without spot or blemish." Rebecca smiled at the man who'd become a second father to her as she washed the unleavened matzo dough from her hands. Her eyes twinkled. "Of course, the lamb might not see it from the same perspective."

"Speaking of perspectives . . ." Solomon's voice trailed off.

"What is it, Solomon?"

"I would like to invite one more person for the seder."

"Who?"

"Hannah Weinberg."

"Hannah?" Rebecca twisted the dish towel. "Why isn't she spending it with her family?"

"What family? Her husband is dead, she has no children, and like me, she's outlived most of her friends and relatives."

"You feel sorry for her?"

He rubbed his forehead. "Maybe I do, but that's not why I asked her to join us. Remember when she insisted on seeing me, just after Faith and her father arrived a couple of years ago?"

"I've tried to forget. I still can't believe she actually thought you and I—"

"When one is lonely, things get exaggerated. I promised myself then that I would see to it that she had someone to talk with. We've worked things out."

"And just how have you managed to keep her on the hook for so long—without tying the knot?"

Solomon raised his hands. "Now I promised her nothing more than the chance for us to get reacquainted. So far, it has been enough. No one can ever replace Esther, but Hannah and I are friends; that's why I asked her to join us for the seder. Since Randy Morgan and the Bradleys are coming, what is one more?"

Unconsciously, Rebecca smiled at the thought of Randy, and for the moment she forgot Hannah. No one had ever accused Rabbi Rebecca Greenspan of being an incurable romantic, but knowing Randy had changed her. She could afford to be magnanimous.

"Well, I haven't purchased the bitter herbs to mix with the apples, nuts, and wine. If Hannah is coming, I won't have to."

Solomon chuckled. "Good, I will see you this afternoon, after my meeting."

"You know, Solomon, you're hardly ever home. What have you been up to lately?"

"Now you're beginning to sound like a wife," he said, avoiding her question. He kissed her on the cheek and hurried out the door.

Rebecca found herself thinking of Randy as she watched Solomon make his way down the street. She'd always considered herself sensible and sane except for her brief interlude with Judah. After it, she'd kept a tight rein on her emotions, until now.

The Hebrew lessons had brought them together. She couldn't remember now if they'd been her idea or Randy's; it didn't really matter. It had taken almost two years—no one could say she'd rushed into anything—but he'd gradually made inroads into her life. He'd made her uncomfortable at first, grated on her nerves with his honesty and lack of pretense, and left her feeling defensive because she couldn't—wouldn't—respond in kind.

She'd drawn the line, and Randy wouldn't cross it, not until she was ready. He'd only kissed her once, but she could see the longing in his eyes, as if he were waiting for her. What held her back?

Religion. They both believed in the imminent return of the Messiah, but they disagreed on who He was and just about everything else. Tonight they would celebrate the Passover which marked the Israelites release from Egypt and the birth of Israel as a nation. Did this mirror of the past hold a reflection of her future? Biting her lip, she contemplated the options as her resolve and her spine stiffened.

Tonight would also mark the rebirth of Rebecca Greenspan.

Judah was annoyed when his secretary lumbered into his office; he'd told her an hour ago that he didn't want to be bothered.

"Until when?" she'd replied in her broad Boston accent.

"Until—a man can see his own faults," he'd replied tartly.

Now she was back again. He'd chosen her as his personal secretary because she had a mind and a mouth like a steel trap. It hadn't hurt that she was in her fifties, the grandmotherly type in a size sixteen dress; hence her appearance fueled no rumors of impropriety. She was also a Presbyterian, a tangible symbol that there was a place for all religions in his organization.

"What is it, Marion?" he growled. He noted her flushed face.

"Why . . . ah . . ."

It was unlike her to be flustered. Normally she was precise and forthright. He waited.

"The . . . ah, the . . . pope wishes to see you," she stammered.

"What's so difficult about setting up an appointment?" he said.

"You know the procedure. Find a date when I can get away for a few days and make the arrangements with the Vatican."

"Sir, he's—" She pointed to the door she'd just walked through. "He's outside."

Judah Midian savored the moment. This was the fourth time in the last two years that the pope had walked in, uninvited. The delicate balance of power was shifting in his favor as he had known it would.

"Give me a minute, then show him in."

He cleared the posters off his desk, putting the one he thought had been the most effective on top of the pile. It was by Kim Su Young, a political cartoonist whose work had already appeared in almost every major publication.

The slogan, *"No Rain? Prophets are to Blame!"* blazed at him. Under the caption, the muscular hand of God held a watering can that was tilted to water the nations of the earth below it. Each drop of water contained the picture of one of Judah's spokesmen.

Beneath this, a huge black tarpaulin stretched over the globe. Although the life-saving moisture pooled on the tarp, the water couldn't reach the earth because the corners of the tarp were held up by two leering caricatures with hook noses who were easily recognizable as the two prophets. In bold, shiny red letters which dripped like blood, the words *Selfishness and Sin* were scrawled across the coal-black tarp.

It definitely wasn't subtle, but it was effective. The campaign had placed the blame for the world's catastrophes squarely on the shoulders of the two prophets, and it had unleashed a torrent of hate towards them and the remnant of their believers.

Judah was exhilarated. His campaign had gone even better than he'd planned; the prophets' followers were forced to travel in packs in order to protect themselves. He closed the drawer in which he'd put the posters and looked up as the pope, without his usual entourage, entered the room and shut the door behind him.

"Your Holiness," Judah said, rising from his chair. His eyes slid over the pope's face, searching for any telltale signs of weakness. He was met instead by the steely eyes of an adversary, the same Irish eyes that had fought their way through the tough streets of inner Chicago and survived. The straight Roman nose was flared above the tight-lipped granite mouth as they stared at each other across the desk. *So that's how it was going to be. No kid gloves, just bare, raw knuckles.*

"Please sit down," said Judah with a touch of vinegar in his otherwise oil-slick voice.

"One does not sit down in the presence of Evil."

Judah could read the hate and anger in the pope's face, but it came too late. The same venom coursed through his own veins, but unlike the pope, he knew how to channel it to further his own ambitions. Why shouldn't he? He was on intimate terms with its source. The pope was no more than an ephemeral mouse toying with a perennial cat. Although Pope Timothy recognized his enemy, he was now powerless to stop him.

"Good versus Evil . . . a rather frayed cliché don't you think?" said Judah. "I prefer to clothe it more in today's terms, the 'Good Prophet—Bad Prophet' routine."

"This war isn't against the flesh, it's against the Father of Lies. I won't let you get away with it."

"Oh, but I am getting away with it. That's why you're here, isn't it? After centuries, the church has failed. You've had your chance, now it's my turn."

Judah leered at the pope, leaning across the desk, and gave him a chilling smile. "Which means, Mark Ryan, that you have failed. You're not a spiritual leader, just a puppet that I ultimately will control—or destroy."

The pope wanted to smash Judah's face, to rid himself of the aberrant personality who taunted him, but he restrained himself. "You must stop this . . . this . . . genocide immediately!"

"I explained to you two years ago why the world must rid itself of the prophets. Nothing has changed."

"The world will hold you accountable for the slaughter of thousands of people, all innocent victims of your treachery."

"Innocent? Hardly. You yourself teach that all have sinned and come short of the glory of God. I've just been getting rid of those who have missed the mark. I hear no cries of outrage."

Judah tapped his upturned palm. "I have the global community right where I want it." His eyes bored into the pope's. "You either stay out of my way or—"

"Is that a threat?"

"I don't make threats, I remove them."

"What the—"

With a jolt, the floor swayed as massive plates of earth moved past one another, and the world abruptly shifted.

"Look out!" shrieked Marion from the outer office. They heard a loud crash and the tinkle of glass as the chandelier in the reception area plunged to the floor.

Both men continued to stare at each other, neither one moving despite the turmoil around them.

The earthquake lasted for ten seconds.

"Your reign, like that tremor, is over." said Judah. "I suggest you leave immediately for the Vatican's lakeside retreat in Castel Gandolfo."

"My place is in Rome," retorted the pope.

"This is not a request, it's an order. Perhaps the cool Alban Hills will help you to see things more clearly. If not, I'll have you replaced by one of the self-serving members of your staff. The name Cardinal Galiano comes to mind."

"God is the one who chooses the pope," Mark bristled.

"Not anymore. You have overestimated your power and underestimated mine," said Judah as he sat down. "After this week, I will be the leader of the world's new economic order. I will be God."

He would not tolerate this blasphemy! The pope pointed his finger at Judah. "I will denounce you for the madman you are."

Judah's bellowing laughter roared through the room as he swatted the globe on the corner of the desk and sent it spinning.

"The world is full of madmen—haven't you noticed? Some people have even called you one. How else can they explain why the pope would declare Judah Midian a saint?"

A red flush swirled over the pope's face. "There are still decent people in this world, uncorrupted by power," he said as his eyes swept over the statue of Michael, the archangel, on Judah's desk.

Judah stood up and glared at the pope. "Don't you understand yet, you fool? Decency has nothing to do with it. The moral frontier no longer exists; it's been eradicated by wealth, sex, drugs, and power. Mankind is anxious to enter an uncharted frontier where spirit guides will help him unlock the magical forces within himself."

"Magical forces? You mean diabolical forces, don't you?" shot back the pope. "You have no authority—"

"Don't you recognize me, Mark Ryan? I am the *only* authority. No one has need of your god and his Christ. Until now, the two prophets have escaped us, but we've captured most of their followers. Soon the world will gladly submit to my authority. In fact, they will beg me to be their leader—their God."

Awareness exploded in the pope's eyes, and Judah saw in them the aftershock of his revelation. He was triumphant.

32

"Are you expecting more guests?" said Faith as she looked at the two empty chairs and place settings at the table.

"Hannah Weinberg is coming, and we always set an extra place at the dinner table for Elijah, the prophet, during Passover," said Rebecca. "We even fill his wine glass, and sometime during the seder we'll throw the door open for him. When he enters, he will bring news of the coming of the Messiah."

"If Elijah comes tonight he will not recognize the Holy City," said Solomon, striking the table with the flat of his hand. He retreated to the rocking chair.

"Jerusalem is no longer the city of God, but a city of wickedness." The fruitless meeting he'd had that afternoon with Logan Washburn underscored his feelings of frustration and indignation.

"We've been inundated with tourists and political adventurers, so what do we do? We build new hotels and entertainment complexes to accommodate them. And riding on prosperity's coattails are crime, prostitution, gambling, and greed—all legalized. We're like Sodom, cultivating our vices instead of weeding them out." He rocked faster.

"And Judah Midian Enterprises has a controlling interest in all of these activities," said Randy. "Solomon, I think it's time we let everyone here know what's going on."

"Yes," Solomon nodded, "before Hannah arrives. What better time than now, the season of Passover? If Judah had his way, he would smear the doorpost with our blood to mark us, not for salvation, but execution."

A trickle of fear began to rise in Faith. She crossed her arms and placed them protectively across her stomach. "What are you talking about?"

"Judah has compiled a list of, shall we say, expendable persons throughout the world." Randy pointed to his leather briefcase. "I have a copy." They stared at the briefcase as though it was a coiled snake, poised to strike.

Stephen swallowed hard. "What are you going to do with it?"

"We have an obligation to warn those on the list," said Solomon.

"How?" said Rebecca. "Who will believe you?"

"We've thought of releasing it to the media, but they are peppered with Judah's followers. It'll take time to ferret out someone we can trust."

"When do these . . . annihilations begin?" said Faith.

Randy cleared his throat before he answered. "They've been going on for quite sometime now."

"You've looked at the list?" asked Rebecca.

"Just a few pages," he lied. "I only broke the access code this afternoon." He couldn't meet her eyes; he'd promised Solomon that at least for tonight she wouldn't know.

"We've got to look at it—now. Maybe we can save someone's life," said Stephen.

"No. If Judah becomes suspicious, he won't hesitate to get rid of us all. It's taken me two years to gain his trust, and I don't want to jeopardize that until we're ready to break this story worldwide. It sounds harsh, but these deaths will substantiate our claims."

"Dad! You can't mean that. We'll be as reprehensible as Judah Midian."

"Faith, I didn't want this responsibility, but it's been thrust upon me. When you cut through all the emotion, this is the best course of action."

"Your father is right," said Stephen. "In the long run, we'll be able to do more good if we wait."

A hush fell over the room as the Angel of Death, who until

now had waited outside the door, glided into their hearts and fanned their fears with its outstretched wings.

There was a knock on the door.

"We will celebrate Passover," said Rebecca crisply as she stood up. "Things must remain as normal as possible." Her eyes pleaded with Solomon.

Reluctantly she opened the door. "We're glad you could come," she said to Hannah, forcing a smile.

The crow's feet around Hannah's eyes seemed to fade away. "Thank you, Solomon invited me. I hope it isn't too much trouble."

"Of course not. Come in, let me introduce you to our other guests." They approached the table, and Hannah spied the sprig of parsley and the egg on it, which represented spring and re-birth.

"This is Dr. Bradley, and his wife, Faith."

"I met Dr. Bradley when he first arrived," said Hannah as the color rose to her face.

"And this is Faith's father, Randy."

The loving look Rebecca gave Randy did not go unnoticed by Hannah as she felt the hand of jealousy which had been clutching her heart loosen its grip.

"Sit here," said Rebecca, indicating the chair next to Solomon.

"I will read the Haggadah," Solomon said with a nod to Hannah as the smell of the roasted lamb wafted through the house.

"This is the story of the Israelites' exodus from Egypt. Our ancient forefathers were slaves, and tonight we will celebrate their freedom—and ours—from the intolerable conditions of slavery in Egypt."

Faith closed her eyes. She was already grieving for those who would be sacrificed in the aftermath of the tribulation. A verse consumed her thoughts: "See, I have set before thee this day life and good, and death and evil." She no longer feared death. She feared instead that she wouldn't live to tell others about the One who had transformed her life, just as centuries ago, He had trans-formed the lives of the Israelites.

Solomon did not have to look at the book before him. Instead he began to recite from memory the age-old story of a nation's escape to freedom.

As Faith listened she could almost hear the doubtful voices of the budding Jewish nation as they planned to leave Egypt.

"Hurry, hurry," a father had said while his family gathered their belongings for the journey. "Tenacious Pharaoh can change his mind. What we'd prayed and hoped for could be postponed again."

Apprehension and anxiety had mingled with their joy as they hurriedly prepared for their expedition into the unknown. They had filled their carts and tried to ignore the skeptical voices of the cynics among them. Faith put her hands over her ears to stop their strident voices. It didn't help—they kept growing louder and louder!

Suddenly, the front door was thrown open with a deafening crack that splintered the air in the room like a sonic boom.

Faith's eyes flew open. She saw a solitary figure in the doorway, silhouetted against the evening sky. Was she still dreaming? No! Stephen was sitting next to her. She turned to him, but as she started to speak, a mighty rushing wind filled the house and tore the words from her.

The prophet's robe clung to his lean body as he looked wildly around the room and lifted his staff. He opened his mouth to speak, and instantly the room was calm. His eyes fastened on Solomon.

"The Messiah whom you have waited for, Solomon, comes."

Astonished, Solomon sat rooted to his chair, unable to move. Next to him Hannah sat speechless, with her mouth wide open. For a split second, time stood still.

Then they heard the voices in the street; the accusing, angry voices of a mob intent on revenge. The clock began to tick again.

"Quickly—you can escape through the garden!" said Rebecca as she rose to her feet. The boisterous voices were closer now, reverberating through the night, picking up intensity.

The prophet's sad blue eyes melted into hers; she felt her whole body bathed in their warmth.

"We have finished our testimony, the days are completed," he said with quiet dignity.

"Look! There he his!" shouted a youth as the hysterical mob surged toward the door.

"Stop them!" cried Faith. But it was too late. Like enraged hornets, the crowd swarmed over the prophet, dragging him into the street.

"Stay inside," shouted Randy as he raced to the door, followed closely by Solomon and Stephen.

"I wouldn't be interfering," said a burly man blocking their path. "Not unless you want to be next. We're doing what needs to be done. Getting rid of the vermin that's caused all the trouble."

Solomon stepped forward. "I am Rabbi Solomon Lowenstein, and I demand that you release that man."

With one blow, the man sent Solomon crashing into the street. Hannah screamed. Quickly, the man pulled a gun from under his coat.

"Wait a minute," said Randy. "He was just trying to—"

"You two"—he pointed the gun at Randy and Stephen—"back into the house, or I'll save the mob the trouble of making a return trip."

From her vantage point at the front window, Rebecca could see the crumpled form of Solomon, then the man's revolver. She ran into her bedroom, bent down, and with trembling fingers scooped up the gun from under the bed.

"I'm a doctor," said Stephen to Solomon's attacker. "Let me take him inside."

The beefy bully seemed confused for a moment. "Back in the house like I told you and shut the door. You leave the old man where he belongs, in the gutter."

Randy and Stephen looked at each other. The mob was gone now, headed towards the temple with their prey. Why wouldn't this man let Solomon go? With their backs to the doorway, they slowly inched their way through the door and reluctantly shut it.

Outside, Solomon let out a low groan as he began to regain consciousness. He put his hand to his head and felt the wet stickiness of his own blood. He tried to push himself up on one elbow, but the ruffian kicked his arm and sent him sprawling again. He felt the barrel of a gun pressed to his back as the man bent over him.

"I know who you are, Rabbi Lowenstein," he uttered in a gruff whisper. "Judah sent me. Remember him? The boy you wouldn't allow at the orthodox religious school because his father was an Arab?"

"Judah? So long ago—I . . . don't remember."

"Senile, are you? We'll try something more recent, you Jewish slug. Do you remember this afternoon when you were asking Logan Washburn all those questions? You won't be asking any more questions—ever." He jammed the gun against Solomon's temple.

Was this how it was going to end? Solomon almost felt relieved. He heard the click of the gun, then a distant shot rang out. He heard his ribs snap as the thug fell heavily against him.

But wait—he was still alive! Solomon sucked in the night air and felt a crushing pain in his chest, then the gun exploded at his temple and the bullet ripped through his senses. He felt a great heaviness, then a final sweet release from all that held him to the earth. He would meet the Messiah at last.

"Solomon!" screamed Rebecca.

Randy flung open the door, and Rebecca hurled herself past him and raced into the street followed by Faith and Stephen. In a state of shock, Hannah stumbled behind them, her heart beating wildly as they drew closer to the bodies.

Rebecca bent over both lifeless men and frantically tried to move the thug's body. The gun in her hand clattered to the cement. She felt something warm and wet on her knees as she knelt on the cold pavement. It was blood! Solomon's blood. "No!" she wailed into the silent night, "No."

Randy knelt down beside her and felt for Solomon's pulse.

"Rebecca . . . he's dead."

"He can't die like this—I won't let him!"

"There's nothing you can do."

Gently he put his arms around her and lifted her like a limp rag doll to a standing position. He looked into her tragic eyes, saw the tears on her cheeks.

"You tried to protect him . . . it might have worked if—" He looked down at the gun still clenched in the thug's enormous hand. "If he hadn't squeezed the trigger—"

"You killed him!" Hannah screamed at Rebecca. She looked down at Solomon. He was gone . . . gone forever and all because of that . . . that hussy! She'd never feel his body next to hers—

she'd never know his love. Tonight was supposed to have been the beginning, not the end. Through her tears she saw Randy holding Rebecca, smoothing back the curly hair from her face as great sobs racked her body. White-hot rage coursed through Hannah, and there was no doubt in her mind that, given the chance, she'd use her own two hands to strangle Rebecca.

Rebecca pressed her face into Randy's shoulder. She took a final looked at Solomon's limp body. A ghostlike fog whirled above it, forming itself into the jeering face of Judah.

She collapsed against Randy who picked her up and carried her gently into the house. Hannah stood over Solomon's body, unable to accept what had happened.

The street was empty, but Faith felt a dozen pairs of eyes focused on them. It was common knowledge that if you wanted to stay alive, you had to placate the new government; now, at the first sign of trouble, the citizens of Jerusalem locked their doors, feeling no twinges of guilt at their behavior. The attack on Solomon only reinforced what they knew: Go with the flow, or be drowned by it. No doubt, someone had anonymously called the police.

Faith shuddered as she watched Stephen roll the thug's body off Solomon. He picked up the gun Rebecca had dropped and put it into his pocket. Faith's voice quavered, "Are we going to be next, Stephen?"

He couldn't answer her. He thought he'd recognized one of the men in the mob who attended the secret meetings they held in their apartment each week to study the Bible. Was he a spy?

He grabbed Faith's hand, and they both looked down at Rabbi Solomon Lowenstein and saw in his slack face their own mortality—a frail, eggshell existence which, with a single gunshot, had been shattered and consumed.

From out of nowhere a clap of thunder shook the earth. Hannah cowered and raced back into the house. Faith jumped as lightning crackled in the clear sky. Suddenly they were drenched as the heavens split open and poured forth their life-giving rain upon the earth.

A few hours later Jerusalem was in an uproar. The rain flooded the world for three days, there was dancing in the streets, and a holiday celebration was declared throughout the *Global Village,* the newest term adopted to describe the unity of the nations. Gifts were exchanged as the world celebrated the executions of the two prophets. It was Christmas in April.

No more would mankind have to contend with the scathing accusations that God was pouring out His wrath upon the earth because of man's unbelief and sinfulness. Guilt had lost its final champion. Although one tribulation was over, a greater tribulation was beginning.

"Did you know that at Passover a drop of wine is spilled for each of the ten plagues that forced Egypt to release the Jews from bondage?" said Rebecca to Randy. It was the day after Solomon's death, and tears filled her eyes as she thought of him. "Judah has replaced the wine with blood. Now we have an eleventh plague: Judah.

"I don't understand why Solomon's or the prophets' murders raised so few objections," said Faith to Stephen as they sat in the living room at Solomon's home.

"Because those who dared to voice any were promptly killed, labeled as conspirators, or thrust out of the city. The news reports, with Judah's guidance, have convinced the world that before a utopian age can be ushered in, we must be purged of the cancerous taint which the prophets introduced."

"Yes," said Rebecca bitterly. "Logan Washburn suggested that, as a warning to others, the prophets' bodies should be left on display in the square where they were beaten and killed."

"This has united Judah's supporters," Randy said, turning to Stephen and Faith. "It's the day of emancipation for them."

"Now they're free to systematically round up and kill the prophets' followers," said Stephen.

"And anyone else who doesn't agree with him," added Faith.

"The world's moral compass has been rendered useless," said Randy. "We're reaping the harvest of an entire generation that's been raised by electronic babysitters. The media have captured their minds, emotions, and senses."

"I heard a newscaster today praising Judah for his wisdom," said Stephen. "The sad part is, he actually believed what he was saying."

"Judah is a leader they can follow," said Randy. "Unlike the prophets, he praises their triumphs and forgets their transgressions."

"You're an international hero," said Logan to Judah. "The drought and epidemics are over, and an indebted world wants to show you their gratitude."

"And I will let them."

"The three-day holiday celebration was the crowning touch," said Logan. "Literally."

"It pleases you that the leaders of the nations have voted to give me the title of Worldwide Ruler?"

"Yes. We'll have unlimited powers, just as you promised."

"Like royalty, I'll have a coronation," he said. "You'll arrange it."

"Where?"

"The one place that the world's greatest religions revere—the Dome of the Rock, the Jewish temple."

Logan raised his eyebrows. "The priests will never allow it."

"Not allow it!" said Judah, his voice choked with pride. "They have no choice. The god they worship is dead. The Messiah they wait for is nothing more than a remnant of an old way, abolished. Judaism and the Christian system have disintegrated. We will build upon the bedrock of a new world, and dissenters will be crushed beneath it."

33

"Are you sure you want to do this?" said Stephen to Faith as they drew near to the square that was overshadowed by the temple. "The prophets have been lying in the sun for more than three days; it's not going to be a pretty sight."

"It's going to happen sometime today, Stephen, I know it is." Her voice was filled with excitement. "The prophecy says so in Revelation, chapter eleven, verse eleven. I know it's true, but I want to see for myself."

On a hastily erected scaffolding above them, the television camera crews, who kept a daily vigil at the scene, prepared to broadcast again the spectacle of the two dead prophets sprawled in the street. They were accompanied by the crowd who thronged around the square, jubilant, pushing and shoving their way to the front, some of them to get a better view of the bodies, others hoping to be captured on camera by the Worldwide News Broadcast System.

Stephen held on tightly to Faith as they jostled through the brash crowd to get in line. The police, who had roped off the area where the prophets had been killed, now monitored an endless queue of spectators. The line rippled through the streets and snaked past the square like an enormous throbbing dragon at a Chinese New Year's Day parade.

A bizarre carnival atmosphere, together with the elated voices of a dozen different languages, swirled around Faith and Stephen while they stood in line amid the jovial faces. As they inched to-

wards the fatal spot, Stephen put his arm around Faith and tried
to shield her from the converging crowd.

"Look," said the portly Englishman in front of them, "am I
seeing things or is one of them blokes moving?"

"You must be in your cups," said his companion. "Them fellows ain't going nowhere. Take another look."

Curious, the mass of bodies crushed against Stephen and Faith,
propelling them forward until they were pressed against the
ropes.

"Stephen, look!"

Was it just the breeze that stirred their clothing or . . . The
crumpled bodies of the prophets slowly began to twist and
stretch in a grotesque ballet.

"It can't be!" exclaimed a pulpy-faced woman, clutching her
hand to her heart.

But it was.

The crowd watched in open-mouthed horror.

"It's a trick, it has to be a trick," shrilled an outspoken critic
of the prophets. An unearthly hush fell over the Jerusalem mob.
Shocked, the critic shrank back in astonishment with the rest of
the throng as the battered and bruised bodies of the prophets,
clothed in blood-spattered sackcloth, rose and faced their accusers.

Quickly, an ambitious cameraman zoomed in on the prophets'
faces. Billions of television viewers saw the piercing eyes which
days earlier had condemned them. A riptide of panic swept
through the mob. Shrieks penetrated the air.

Suddenly, a thunderous voice from heaven shook the earth and
silenced the hysterical voices.

"COME HITHER."

Paralyzed with fear, the crowd could only watch. With upturned faces they saw the prophets gradually rise into the sky,
enveloped in a misty cloud. The now mute spectators craned their
necks and stared, transfixed by the miraculous resurrection of the
two bodies which only moments before had lain in pools of dried
blood.

Faith's expectations soared as she and Stephen squinted into the
brightness where the two men slowly disappeared from view.
Everything they'd read in the Bible was true, it was all true!

They were still gazing into the sky with awe and amazement when suddenly, without warning, the earth let out a great shudder and the pavement buckled beneath their feet.

"Faith!" Stephen grabbed her, and they clung together as buildings crashed around them, spilling bricks and glass into the streets.

Faith saw the camera crew clinging to the scaffolding as it tottered, then collapsed, hurling them and their equipment into the crowd. A second quake rumbled through the city. Howls of pain erupted as the chastened but rebellious throng broke loose, trampling those who'd been unlucky enough to fall during the first tremor.

Dragging Faith along with him, Stephen scrambled for safety. Glass crunched beneath his feet, and he stumbled on smashed bricks as he pulled Faith into a doorway. "Are you all right?" he gasped, his face red from exertion.

"I think so. Oh, Stephen, we just saw a miracle!"

"We'll need another one to get through this mess."

"Look, look over there!"

Ignoring the frantic crowds around them, a group of God's chosen people were on their knees. Spurred on by fear, they began to loudly praise the God of heaven.

"Forgive us, forgive us!" shouted a young man with his hands outstretched to the sky.

"Come on," said Stephen. "We have to get out of here." He pushed Faith towards the spot where the prophets, only minutes earlier, had risen into the sky. The temple loomed over them, and quickly they were swept along with the tide of people who, in their terror, once again were seeking the God of their fathers.

Impeachment! President Emilio Blanco, the forty-sixth president of the United States, stared at the members of the House of Representatives. He'd been blindsided. In this vague and uncertain state, he wondered if this was how Andrew Johnson, the seventeenth president of the United States, had felt when he was impeached in 1868.

"On what grounds?" he heard himself ask. He was presented with nine articles of impeachment. The words treason and bribery jumped off the pages as he scanned them. Emilio blanched. The charges were false, but that didn't make any difference. His trial was just a formality to get him out of office. The House had impeached him because they already had from the Senate the two-thirds vote necessary for a conviction.

So . . . Judah Midian had killed him without using a bullet.

"We should be thankful we escaped with only superficial cuts and bruises," said Stephen to Faith as he finished setting a splint on a youth's leg in the emergency room of the Hadassah–Hebrew University Medical Center. He helped the boy back to his mother, returned to the triage area, and looked down at his rumpled clothing. He needed a bath and about forty-eight hours of uninterrupted sleep. "Trying to stem this flood of earthquake victims is like emptying out the ocean a teaspoonful at a time."

"The Emergency Broadcasting System estimates that one tenth of the city is in ruins and more than seven thousand people have been killed," said Faith. "It was the worst earthquake in Israel's history." She handed her husband another bottle of antiseptic, then scrutinized the scores of injured people still waiting to be seen by medical personnel.

"Déjà vu," she said in a weary voice.

"What?"

"I feel like I've experienced all this before."

"We did," said Stephen. "But last time neither one of us understood God's timetable."

"I still don't understand everything." Faith smiled up at him. "It seems that these tragedies are the glue that keeps us together."

"If I'd never met you—that would have been the real tragedy."

Their eyes locked and for an instant the rest of the world became a blur. He reached out and touched her hand, revitalizing her spirits, if not her exhausted body.

"Doctor, you're needed over here," yelled a nurse.

Reluctantly, he let go of her slender fingers.

Solomon's funeral was brief and without ceremony; just one of many in a nation consumed with grief and death. Faith and

Stephen were not surprised that the mourners were few; to pay tribute to an enemy of Judah's was to invite adversity and misfortune.

As the remains of Rabbi Solomon Lowenstein were lowered into the earth, Hannah stood apart from the others on the Mount of Olives. Her body sagged, and only the emotional crutches of anger and sorrow kept her from throwing herself into Solomon's grave.

She had done the right thing, she reminded herself. Rebecca Greenspan had killed Solomon, and Rebecca must pay for it. It was only right. Hadn't the newly appointed magistrate agreed with her? Oh, Solomon's death had looked like an accident, but then, what better way for Rebecca to rid herself of an old man she no longer had any use for?

She knew she was right when she learned that Solomon had bequeathed his house, which had suffered only minor damage in the earthquake, to Rebecca along with the rest of his meager belongings. No doubt Rebecca had talked him into it with promises of—she couldn't allow herself to think of that, not now.

Hannah looked around at the handful of mourners. This pitiful group was an affront to Solomon and the life he had lived. It was all because of Rebecca. Acting in the guise of a rabbi, she had poisoned him with her radical ideas. Hannah had almost been fooled by Rebecca's crocodile tears, but now she saw her for what she really was: an opportunist.

A light drizzle began to fall, and heartbroken, Hannah left the funeral to go back to her rented room. She started to put up her umbrella, then stopped. What difference did it make to anyone if she came back wet or for that matter, whether she came back at all? What good was this wonderful utopia they'd been promised if she had no one to share it with?

Hannah's warm tears mingled with the cold rain, forming lukewarm drops on her cheeks. Lukewarm! Yes, her whole life had been tepid and indifferent—until now. As a final tribute to Solomon, she would see that justice was served.

Logan Washburn, in his capacity as minister of religion, paced the floor in front of Judah's desk while the candles he'd lit flickered in the darkened office. "There's a great spiritual revival sweeping the country. It seems that the ascension of the prophets into heaven has given some validity to the prophecies they extolled."

"This newfound faith is rooted in fear; it will fade away as quickly as it came," said Judah as he stood in front of the fireplace. "The world is vulnerable and ready for my charismatic leadership. Whether the masses believe that God has intervened in the affairs of the human race or not isn't important.

"My coronation will focus the world's attention once again on the future and the one who controls it. Didn't *I* promise that the prophets would be removed? Now, in 2013, we're on the brink of having the entire world at our feet."

The candles flared brightly and jumped towards the ceiling, casting elongated shadows on the bookcase. The smell of burning flesh filled the room as Logan and Judah touched the sizzling amulets hidden under their shirts. The medallions singed their fingers, but they experienced no pain as the three shadows on the wall merged into one and mushroomed into an atomic cloud until the room could hold it no longer.

34

he list . . . what good is it now? If Solomon had let us know he was on it—if you had—maybe his death could have been prevented," Rebecca said to Randy as she finished folding Solomon's clothes.

"Who would have thought they'd come after him on Passover—"

"I know, I know." She crossed her arms and looked at the floor. "I'm just so angry. At myself, at you, at Solomon . . . at Judah. I thought I had everything figured out, but now the puzzle I put together has been knocked over. For the life of me, I can't put it back together again—there are too many missing pieces."

Rebecca picked up the black-and-white prayer shawl and held it to her face. She couldn't bear to give it away. The other things could go to one of the agencies that was collecting clothing for the earthquake victims, but not this.

"The President of France is dead," said Randy in a flat voice.

Rebecca spun round and faced him. "He was on the list?"

"Yes."

She sank down on the bed. "How did it happen?"

"They said it was heart failure."

"You don't believe that, do you?"

"Stephen said there are several drugs which can induce heart failure, but they're virtually undetectable in an autopsy."

She stood up. "Oh, Randy . . . I don't know what to believe anymore." She shook her head. "I'm so confused."

He held her close, then pulled her down with him onto the bed. "You know Rebecca Greenspan, I'm in love with you."

She didn't know whether to laugh or cry. Why was he telling her this now? He gently held her face between his hands.

"Randy . . . I—"

He kissed her. "I've been wanting to do that again for a long time."

They were interrupted by a knock on the front door.

"Someone is supposed to pick up this box of clothing," she said.

"Let's ignore them," said Randy. "I want to make an honest woman of you," he buried his face in her neck, "before this goes any farther."

"They'll only come back." Rebecca struggled to her feet and picked up the box. "Don't go away."

Randy heard her open the door.

"Rebecca Greenspan?" inquired a curt voice.

"Yes."

"You will come with us, now! You are under arrest for the murder of Rabbi Solomon Lowenstein."

Rebecca traced the pattern on the bedspread with her finger and wondered why she was sitting in a hotel room instead of the police station. There was something strange about this whole ordeal; no one had even asked her about Solomon's death since her arrival, and the lone guard posted outside her room stoically ignored her questions. Did Randy know where she was?

A clash of voices erupted through the crack under the door. She heard the snap of a coded plastic card as it was inserted into the door's locking mechanism. It swung open, and Logan Washburn entered the room.

"What do you . . . want . . . with me?" she stammered.

"Judah wants you to attend his coronation."

Judah? Then this didn't have anything to do with Solomon's death.

"Why?" she replied in a guarded voice.

"He wants both you and Donald to be there."

"Donald!" So he'd known all along about Donald. Her palms

began to sweat and her stomach compacted into a hard, tight fist. Why? Why had he decided to acknowledge their son now? She couldn't think straight; her emotions rapidly rose to a flash point. "You leave Donald out of this!"

Logan turned back to the guard. "Bring him in."

It was Donald.

No longer a picture in her memory, but a flesh-and-blood little boy wearing blue jeans held up by rainbow suspenders, a polo shirt with the words "Bike Today, Turbo Tomorrow" on it, and high-top tennis shoes tied with glow-in-the-dark laces. His mouth drooped and her heart went out to him.

A smattering of freckles wrinkled across the bridge of his nose, and he bit his lip and shifted from one foot to the other in front of her.

"Say hello to your mother, Donald," said Logan in a mocking voice.

Donald's startled eyes looked into hers. She could see the question and uncertainty in them.

"Are you my . . . real mom?" he said, his high, sweet voice cracking.

She inhaled slowly, trying to regain her composure. "Yes, I am."

"Oh."

She wanted to take him in her arms and hug him, but she couldn't. It would just give Judah fuel for whatever diabolical scheme he had in mind. Somehow she knew Judah was going to use Donald—just like he'd used her—for his own gratification.

"Are you going to the . . . coro . . . nation too?"

"It seems that I've been invited," she said, giving Logan a cool glance. "Maybe we can keep each other company—get to know each other a little better."

A timid smile flittered across his face. "I got to ride in a jet," he said in a quavery voice. He fought back the tears, but one escaped and slid down his cheek. "I miss . . . everyone back home. They wouldn't let me say goodbye."

Bitterly, she looked up at Logan.

"I wanted to bring my dog." Donald's face lit up. "His name is Hoagie." He chewed on his lip. "But they said he'd get sick on the plane. You know, throw up." He plunged his hand into his pocket and pulled out two pieces of strawberry bubble gum, a crystal sun catcher, and two marbles. "Wanna piece of gum?"

"Not now, but maybe after we get something to eat. Are you hungry?"

He nodded.

"After this is all over, I'm sure they'll let you go back home. You can tell Hoagie and everyone what a good time you had."

"Really?" Relieved, Donald threw his arms around Rebecca, and she hugged him to herself, relishing the feel of his body next to hers, wondering now why she'd ever given him up seven years ago.

"You'll wear this at the ceremony," said Logan, throwing a black linen robe on the bed.

Rebecca glanced up at the controlled face of Logan, and suddenly her heart was filled with fear, for herself and for Donald.

Hasty repairs were made to the Jerusalem hotels which had been damaged in the earthquake, and laborers worked frantically to clear the streets of rubble, while dignitaries, heads of state, political hopefuls, and celebrities arrived for the coronation.

Judah was ready. Skillfully cloaked in the garb of religious tolerance, he was the very personification of a world dictator ready to usher in an age of prosperity and peace. If the cloak was threadbare, no one cared. He gave people what they wanted, platitudes to shore up their frail faith in tomorrow and a leader who did their thinking for them.

"People are saying that it's a miracle that the Jewish temple wasn't damaged," said Logan as he sat on the corner of the desk in Judah's office. "Not so much as a hairline crack in any of the walls."

"There are other ways to destroy a temple," said Judah, as he tracked the path of the May sun as it sank lower into the sky. "In two hours the Jewish Sabbath will begin and so will my reign. You will be at my side, Logan, when I officially become ruler of the world."

Logan smiled. He no longer felt that they were two separate identities; they had fused into one with the master of darkness.

Judah's power surged through both their lives. Still, a couple of problems needed to be resolved.

"Morgan has a copy of the list."

Judah whirled around. "After tonight, everyone will. Add Randy Morgan and his family to it. We'll pay a bounty for each person turned in to be . . . reeducated so they can inherit this new earth we're preparing."

"Reeducated?"

Judah's eyes glittered in the setting sun. "Words like ethnic cleansing and death are too harsh to use yet. Speaking of death—where is Rebecca?"

"I've had her arrested. She'll be brought here to witness the ceremony."

"Good." Judah hesitated. "My son—?"

"Everything has been arranged."

"We must rid ourselves of the past before we can step into the future," Judah said as he put on the red silk cloak, emblazoned on the back with a picture of the world encircled by a snake. "Let's not keep it waiting."

The orthodox Jews and the rabbis were nervous. Normally on the Sabbath, the priests entered the temple from the East at the entrance hall. It was almost sundown, but tonight they had been ordered to wait in the courtyard for Judah Midian and Logan Washburn before they could enter.

"It's a desecration of the temple to allow this," the other Jews muttered as they were restricted by the high priest, Eli, to the courtyard which surrounded the temple complex. Jostled by the crowd that had come to see the coronation, they had to strain to see Judah and Logan arrive at the entrance hall.

It was an unusual request, but Eli was pleased that Judah had chosen to be crowned in the temple—the Jewish position in the world community would be strengthened.

Representatives from more than sixty nations and a camera crew had already been allowed inside the rectangular temple, which was divided into two rooms: the Holy Place, where the representatives sat, and the Holy of Holies, where no one was allowed.

The golden bells on the skirt of Eli's blue robe tinkled as he walked into the temple in his priestly attire with Judah at his side. A stab of conscience pricked him when he saw silk banners draped over the stone walls, which were covered with cedar and overlaid with gold, but he rationalized that it was only a temporary situation. After this, the Jews would be left alone by the unclean Gentiles to worship as they pleased; Judah had signed the agreement proposed by the elders.

"We have the lamb ready for the sacrifice," said Eli to Logan.

"We have brought our own sacrifice," Logan replied. "When it is time, it will be brought forward."

Eli was taken aback; this was not the way they had planned it.

Judah stopped at the front row where a dark-haired woman sat dressed in a black robe. Eli thought he recognized her—wasn't she the rabbi from America who'd taken part in the temple's dedication?

Judah bent over and whispered something to her that Eli couldn't hear. The high priest wondered why the woman's eyes attacked Judah, but, like him, she seemed powerless to stop the events which had been set in motion.

Steps leading to a recently constructed throne were behind the laver, a large basin where the priests cleansed themselves before making an offering. Judah mounted the steps while Logan followed at a respectable distance. Judah turned and stood in front of the throne. The cameras began to roll.

"My fellow members of the global community, I applaud your wisdom in choosing me as your leader. I say this, not as one who is arrogant, but as one who is worthy to hold the earth's future in his hands. I have proven myself.

"Each country represented here has agreed to acknowledge me as its supreme commander. As such, I will control the dispensation of food and water, the regulation of currency, the price of oil, and the weapons to launch attacks against those who would oppose us. Granted, the factions are few, but they must be dealt with immediately.

"You have shown your faith in me, and now, before I am crowned, I will show my faith in you. I will make the ultimate sacrifice to prove that I am worthy of your loyalty."

Eli watched as, from behind the throne, a small boy dressed in a white robe appeared. He couldn't have been much more than seven years old. He seemed dazed, as if he were walking in a trance; Logan helped him make his way to Judah's side.

"This is my son," said Judah, putting his hand on Donald's head. "Has there ever been a leader in history who was willing to sacrifice his son in order to prove his devotion to his country?"

_No!_ Rebecca tried to get up. _I can't let this happen!_

Together, the people drew a sharp breath as they realized what Judah was suggesting. It was shocking and yet . . . they had grown accustomed to death in the last three and a half years. Somehow the death of Judah's son would make it more palatable when they, as world leaders, informed their citizens that they would be required to wear a mark on their forehead or right hand to identify themselves as members of the new world order. What was that compared to Judah's sacrifice?

Stop! Rebecca screamed the word in her head, but no sound came from her throat. She demanded her legs to move so she could stand up and stop Judah, but they wouldn't obey. That glass of orange juice—she'd been drugged!

All her limbs felt like water. She'd been stupid to underestimate Judah. The faces around her became fuzzy, but she couldn't close her eyes to shut out what was about to happen.

No one uttered a word as Judah, with Logan following, slowly led the boy down to the brazen altar. Judah motioned for Eli to come forward.

Eli's face was as white as the boy's robe. He could not do this horrible thing in the Lord's house! Human sacrifice—it was an abomination fit only for those who worshiped the devil! As Judah placed the knife in Eli's shaking hand, the high priest looked into Judah's ungodly eyes, eyes seared by a blazing fire kindled in hell. He dropped the knife and it clattered to the floor.

Logan bent down and picked it up. He pushed himself next to the priest and spoke in a voice so low that only Eli could hear.

"Your supreme commander is waiting. Falter and it will be your life." He thrust the knife back into his hand, and Eli felt the sharp blade nick his finger.

Judah picked up the boy and laid him on the altar. Eli shuffled towards them, stopped, and looked at the innocent face of the boy. What man could kill his own child? His hands trembled as he put his hand on the boy's throat. This was not a lamb or a bullock, but a human soul. He paused with the knife in mid-air. No—he couldn't do it!

Disgusted, Judah reached up and grabbed the knife. He pushed the high priest aside. Without a shred of emotion, Judah looked down at Donald. The boy made no sound as, with one swift motion, Judah slit his son's throat from ear to ear. He watched as the blood spurted from the tender flesh of his son's neck, staining the white garment and spilling onto the altar. He left Donald's unseeing eyes open.

Rebecca fainted.

A wave of dismay swept over Eli as Judah walked to the basin and washed his hands slowly, almost methodically, as every eye watched him. He gaped in horror as Judah made his way towards the Holy Place where the golden altar of incense was flanked by the golden lampstand and the table of shewbread. Twelve cakes of bread gleamed on the table.

Judah bent over the lighted lampstand, which had three branches on either side of a center stem, and with one great blast from his mouth he extinguished the dancing flames. He strutted towards the Holy of Holies, the inner room, where only Eli, the high priest, was allowed to enter once a year.

"Stop!" screamed Eli. He raced forward, but one of Judah's men caught this arm and held him back.

Winged cherubim, fashioned from olive wood and overlaid with gold, stared down at Judah as he reached up and yanked down the veil which divided the Holy Place from the Holy of Holies.

Eli blinked and a shiver ran up his spine. He was speechless, unable to focus on what he saw. The cherubim, who were positioned as guards over the ancient Ark of the Covenant in the Holy of Holies, now guarded not the Ark of the Covenant, but a life-size statue of Judah. A nude statue that revolved!

A roar of applause welled up from the audience, and the video cameras closed in on the jubilant faces of the crowd as Judah turned and mounted the steps to the throne. Logan followed and handed him a jeweled crown. With an air of finality, Judah Midian placed the crown on his own head and sat down. He was the anointed one.

35

With her head pounding, Rebecca came to in the hotel room. She shivered, and as she drew the bedspread around her, she realized that she was wearing only her underwear. She struggled to sit up, but a thick blanket of grogginess threatened to smother her. Somewhere in the recesses of her mind, the instinct for survival surfaced, and with an explosion of effort, she rolled out of bed and staggered to her feet. She had to get away!

She stood there, swaying, until the room came into focus. Her head began to clear as she leaned against the wall, then zigzagged over to the closet. Where were her clothes? For a brief interlude she was spared the pain of remembering, then her mind unwittingly began to replay the horror she'd witnessed.

Rebecca saw Donald's innocent face again, the glint of the knife blade in Judah's hand. She slumped down on the bed. As sorrow engulfed her, she put her head in her hands and sobbed. Why Donald? She was the one who deserved to die.

She sat there contemplating what had happened, trying to make sense out of a senseless act. Slowly the sorrow began to be replaced with a knuckle-sized rage, which started in the pit of her stomach and rapidly spread until it became so powerful she began to shake. Like a cold shower, it awakened her, pushing her back from the brink of despair to action.

Someone had to stop Judah. He'd proved to her and the world that he was capable of doing anything to achieve his own ambitions; lawlessness would replace order. She didn't know how, but someway she'd see that he paid for what he'd done—with his life.

Once again Judah had become her reason for living, but first, she had to escape. She was no match for the man standing guard outside the door. Rebecca switched on the bathroom light, and a plan began to form in her mind as she splashed cold water on her mottled face.

She turned on the sink faucet, pushed the lock down on the door, stepped back into the bedroom, and closed the bathroom door. She turned off the lamp and wedged herself under the bed, making sure the bedspread hid her presence. It was almost an hour before she heard the door open.

"Where is she?" Logan exclaimed to the guard.

"In there," said the wary guard as he spied the light under the closed bathroom door. They both headed for it; Rebecca could see the soles of their shoes as they passed the bed.

"You promised that I could have her," said the guard as he licked his lips, "for one night."

"Tomorrow," answered Logan, "you can do whatever you want before you dispose of her."

Dispose of her! She had to move, now, before it was too late. Logan hammered on the door as Rebecca rolled out from under the bed, and, with one smooth, catlike movement, flew through the open door and down the corridor towards the fire escape door. In the stairwell, she quickly grabbed a sheet from a maid's cart and wrapped it around herself. She heard angry yells above her and half ran, half stumbled in her bare feet down three flights of stairs to the basement. Her breath came in short, hard gasps, but she didn't dare stop.

Rebecca ran past an empty maintenance shop and several cluttered storerooms. There had to be a way out! The laundry room. She bolted past the woman folding sheets and darted through the back door, which had been left open to let the heat escape from the dryers. Panting, she looked at the narrow alley which ran behind the hotel. Now what?

She had to find Randy.

★   ★   ★

Randy paced back and forth in Solomon's bedroom. His mind was reeling. Where was Rebecca? He'd just returned from the local police station. They said they had no record of her arrest. They suggested that he check in Tel Aviv, and no, they couldn't do it for him; their computers were still down from the earthquake.

He flipped on the television. Film footage of Judah's coronation dominated the news. He started to turn it off, but his eyes widened as he saw Judah lift his hand and—oh, no! It was unbelievable!

With a bright smile the news commentator began to compare Judah's actions to those of a deity.

Why isn't the world outraged? wondered Randy. *Maybe, like the rest of humanity, I'm losing my mind.* He actually thought—but he must be mistaken—that he'd caught a glimpse of Rebecca at the coronation. He shook his head. What would Rebecca be doing with a psychopath like Judah?

He turned off the television and walked out to the rock garden, hoping the fresh air could lift his spirits. Too preoccupied with his own thoughts, he didn't notice the tender green shoots which the recent rains had brought forth. He looked over the garden wall and let his mind drift, searching for an anchor.

His gaze met Hannah's.

"Mr. Morgan, I want to talk with Rebecca. I knocked on the door but no one answered, so I thought I'd look back here."

"She'll . . . be out of town for a few days." At least he hadn't lied about that.

A smug look appeared on her wrinkled features. "Oh, I think she'll be gone longer than that, don't you?"

The inflection in Hannah's voice made Randy look at her more sharply.

"What do you—"

"It's amazing how men are so easily fooled by a pretty face. I've done you a favor, Mr. Morgan, one that someday you'll thank me for, just as Solomon—if he were alive—would."

"Why you old—" He reached across the stone wall, but she stepped back, and with a triumphant look, walked briskly down the street.

Stunned, Randy just stood there. The expression on her face was the same one he'd seen on the faces of the crowds in the news clips he'd been watching. The frenzied crowd who'd approved of Judah's depraved act . . . and Hannah . . . they possessed the same cold vacant eyes. A fragment of memory pricked his conscience. The herd instinct, mass hysteria. Wasn't that what Solomon's grandfather had called it?

"People who follow a good example can just as easily follow a bad one," he'd said as he had struck his chest with his fist. "Unless there's something in here."

They'd been visiting Yad Vashem, the Museum of the Holocaust in Jerusalem. As they felt their way through the dark passageway of the Memorial to the Children, which was lit only by the mirrored reflection of candle flames, Solomon's grandfather had continued:

"A few good citizens can't stand alone against the strong currents of hatred which inundate a nation. Add a dose of fear and eventually they're not only unwilling, but unable to offer resistance to the experts of violence. Decent people do nothing while other humans are being humiliated and destroyed—until it happens to them. Then it's too late.

"Listen," the elderly rabbi's faltering voice had said as the names of the youngest of the six million who died were called out. "What if one of them was your child?"

The words flashed through Randy's mind together with brutal scenes of the Holocaust which Solomon's grandfather had described to him. He could still see the old patriarch's spotted hands as they writhed together in his lap, reliving the agony of their past.

Oh, Randy had listened politely, but he'd chalked up the tales as mere skeletons of an old man's failing memories; now those same ghosts of the past had returned to warn him of a genocide that would encompass the world. He felt sick to his stomach as the truth hit him. Was history repeating itself with a new cast of characters?

Then a startling thought came to him. Satan had been as surprised as the rest of the world when the Rapture occurred! Yes, Satan knew Scripture, knew that it would happen someday, but he hadn't known when. That was why, throughout history, Satan always had a man in the wings whom he could control. Hannibal or Napoleon or . . . Hitler . . . Stalin . . . Saddam Hussein . . . and now—

"Randy!"

Rebecca, looking like a terrified apparition, raced through the garden draped in a sheet which billowed around her slender body.

Why in the world was she dressed in a sheet?

"I'm so glad you're here," she said, holding her side as the ache in it began to subside. Her face was drawn, and in the harsh May sunlight the fine lines around her mouth were more pronounced than he remembered.

"What happened? I was just getting ready to go to Tel Aviv to look for you."

"I escaped. We have to get away! Faith and Stephen are in danger too."

Randy looked into her reddened eyes—the distraught eyes of a cornered animal. He held her and saw the trail of red spots on the garden pebbles behind her; her feet were cracked and bleeding.

"What did they do to you?" he said gently.

She pushed him away and ran toward the house. "Hurry, they'll be there any minute."

"Who?" he said catching up with her in the kitchen. He put his hands on her heaving shoulders to quiet her and made her turn and face him.

"He sacrificed Donald." Rebecca ran her fingers through her tangled hair and tears streamed down her face. "We have to stop him before he destroys all of us."

The phone rang.

"Do we have to answer that?" said Faith as she snuggled up to Stephen. She didn't want to leave the nest of warmth they'd created.

"No, but they'll just send someone to bang on the apartment door." Stephen picked up his wristwatch. "I've got rounds in an hour." He kissed her, then swung his legs over the side of the bed.

She made a face at him as the phone buzzed again.

"Hello," she said into the receiver, then winked at Stephen. "The Bradleys are not at home right now. At the tone please leave a message, and we'll get back to you."

There was silence for a moment.

"Faith?"

"Dad . . . is that you? You sound funny."

"Listen, you and Stephen have got to get out of there as fast as you can. We've joined that elite group on Judah's hit list."

"What?"

"I can't explain now. Get your stuff together and meet us at the Jaffa Road, just before the turnoff for the bus station."

"But where will we go?"

"Rebecca says there are some caves we can hide in until we decide what to do. Bring blankets, food, and candles . . . and hurry."

It was a sleepy morning despite recent events, and Randy stood silently in the slow-moving line to purchase four bus tickets aboard Egged, the Israel bus cooperative which crisscrossed the whole country. The fact that the tickets were cheap and the seats comfortable didn't matter; he just wanted to blend in with the locals and not draw attention to himself.

While Faith and Stephen waited on a nearby bench, Rebecca leaned against the wall and gave Randy a weak smile as he inched towards the counter. Dark smudges, like fingerprints of pain, underscored her hazel eyes. She'd told Randy everything about herself and Judah . . . and Donald. There had been no tears; the time for tears was over.

In return he'd told her about his work for the CIA and the reason for their flight to Israel. With an open Bible in his hand, he'd presented her with facts and ideas she was still trying to grapple with. Randy was certain that Satan was trying to exterminate every believer on earth through the reign of Judah, whom he called the Beast, and Logan, his False Prophet.

He'd shown her verse after verse in the book of Revelation which described events that paralleled the happenings that had taken place in the last three and a half years. The evidence was there . . . or was it just coincidental? It was too much for her to digest. They had agreed only on one point—the imminent and final return of the Messiah, the One he called Jesus Christ.

Rebecca rubbed her forehead. Were they on different paths which would end ultimately at the same destination?

She didn't want to think anymore. She was too confused and exhausted. She only wanted to sleep; in sleep she could escape the memories and questions that plagued her.

Stephen took the tickets Randy handed him as they boarded the bus. He and Faith made their way to the back, and Randy and Rebecca sat on the left, two seats ahead of them. Faith spread out the newspaper she'd just purchased.

"Oh, Stephen," she whispered as she skimmed its columns, "it's all happening, just like the Bible said it would."

"Which means that these next three and a half years will be the worst." He tilted her chin towards him. "The authorities will kill anyone who doesn't worship Judah or pledge their allegiance to him. You know where that leaves us."

She looked deep into his eyes before she spoke. "Do you think we'll live to see His return?"

"I honestly don't know." Stephen wanted to change the subject; he couldn't bear to think of being without her, not now. He took a lighter note.

"Before I asked you to marry me, I went through the Bible concordance and looked up all the verses that had your name in them." He grinned at her. "Don't ask me why; men in love do crazy things. Until then, I didn't really understand what faith was."

"And now?"

His voice sobered. "It's acting upon God's promises even when you can't see a foot in front of you. It's complete and utter trust in Him to do what is best for you, no matter what the circumstances. I've had to let go of all my preconceived ideas about what's really important."

"Will we have to let go of each other, Stephen?"

He thought for a moment before he answered. He looked out of the window. He couldn't meet her eyes. "I hope not."

"I'm afraid," she said in a tiny voice as she crowded closer to him. "Oh, not of dying . . . just when it'll happen . . . and how."

"So am I. Didn't someone say that in order to conquer your

fears, you have to acknowledge them?" He pressed her cold hands between his. "I want to hang on to my life with you as long as I can." His eyes clung to hers. "Our future is now, one day at a time, by faith, until His return."

36

Randy sat up as outside the bus a group of militant young men appeared. A youth with peach fuzz on his cheeks and a gun slung over his shoulder jumped aboard the bus. He seemed to be the one in charge as he spoke rapidly to the driver then turned his attention to the passengers. In rapid-fire Arabic, the youth began to speak.

"What does he want?" whispered Randy to Rebecca.

"He wants everyone to get out, so they can search us."

"For what?"

"Anything that will prove we are outside the pale of the accepted political party. No doubt they have the list."

Randy was glad he'd taken the aisle seat. He leaned back against it, comforted by the feel of the handgun he carried in the small of his back under his jacket. With a single shot he could drop the boy on the steps, then force the driver to take off. Maybe he could do it before any of the youths outside knew what was happening. It was a long shot, but it was the only one they had.

Oh God, I don't want to do this, he pleaded silently, *but if I have to . . .*

The youth motioned for everyone to stand up.

Randy got up along with the others, moving his body so he would have a clean shot. He looked back down the aisle and saw the resignation in Faith's eyes.

The group started to move forward. Randy arched his back and stretched, sliding his right hand under his coat and around to his gun. He could smell his own perspiration as his fingers gripped the butt of the gun. Rebecca was behind him, and she touched his arm lightly, somehow aware of what he was going to do. He didn't have any particular desire to be a human shield, but perhaps he could give the others a chance.

"Saeb, Saeb," shouted one of the adolescents excitedly as he ran towards the bus.

As the leader of the group conferred with one of his teenage companions, Randy relaxed his grip. For a moment the youthful leader seemed confused, then he stepped off the bus and banged the door for the driver to go on.

The bus rumbled into action but not before a couple of the youths had pelted the bus with rocks. The passengers returned to their seats, shaking their heads.

"What happened?" said Randy, wiping the sweat from his brow as he sat down again.

"It seems they found a group of dissenters hiding in the Citadel." Rebecca laughed nervously. "Apparently they believe that old proverb, 'a bird in the hand is worth two in the bush.' "

The bus driver squinted through the dust on the windshield, his mind going back twenty years. Then he'd driven a commuter bus between Jerusalem and Hebron. It was only a one-hour trip, but he'd rarely finished it without Palestinian youths pounding his bus with rocks and bottles in defiance of the soldiers who tried to enforce Israeli rule in the territory. They'd even dropped small boulders on the roof and hurled iron bars through the windows. He'd been injured more than once, along with many of the passengers.

He hummed as he headed along the Jerusalem corridor, the road from Jerusalem to the coastal city of Tel Aviv. This temporary show of force they'd just experienced would end when all the believers were rounded up. He wouldn't mind finding a few himself—he could use the extra money. He was so caught up in his thoughts that before he knew it, he had traveled the twelve miles to the Kibbutz Bet Gurvin.

"We want to get off here," yelled Rebecca to the driver. He brought the bus to a screeching halt at the first left turn.

"Nobody is at the kibbutz anymore," he grumbled. "Everybody is either in Tel Aviv or Jerusalem, that's where the food distribution centers are. Just what are you going to do up here anyway?"

"My daughter just got married," said Randy, indicating Faith and Stephen with a wave of his hand as they got off the bus, "and they wanted some place quiet to stay."

He eyed Faith's ash blond hair suspiciously. "Well—if quiet is what you want—that's what you'll get. Haven't dropped anybody off here in months."

With these final words, the door hissed shut and the bus roared off down the road. Strange, the driver thought, parents don't usually accompany their children on a wedding trip. What if—

He braked to a stop, then glanced at his watch. He was already fifteen minutes late. Tomorrow. Maybe he'd have time then to see if they were telling the truth. An irate passenger shouted at him, and he temporarily forgot his curiosity as he cursed him, then sped off into the desert.

"It's this way," said Rebecca as she started down the road. They adjusted their bundles and followed the route she indicated until they reached a fork in the road.

"Where are we?" asked Faith.

"We're near the Ela Valley," said Rebecca as she branched to the left. "There's a brook which crosses the main road there. It is said that David probably selected the stones for his slingshot from it." She pointed in the direction of the valley. "That's where David had his confrontation with the giant, Goliath."

Stephen looked down at Faith. "Sometimes the little guy *can* outwit the giant," he said with a shallow laugh.

"If God's on his side," she replied.

Ahead of them they saw the caves. "At one time this was a lime quarry," said Randy. "The lime was used to make cement during the Roman period. Be careful where you walk."

He pulled out two flashlights and gave Stephen one as they entered the dark caverns. "The caves are interconnected, but there could be some dangerous spots or cave-ins because of the earthquakes."

"Look," said Stephen. He put his fingers on a cross etched high on the cavern wall.

"It was put there by the early Christians. They hid here to avoid being persecuted by the Romans," said Rebecca. "Some of the caverns were used as tombs or water cisterns, others held grain and food supplies."

The eerie silence in the caverns was broken by the sound of footsteps echoing ahead of them.

"What . . . the?" said Randy.

"I thought the bus driver said he hadn't dropped anyone off here in months," whispered Stephen.

Suddenly they were blinded by a light.

"Who are you?" said a low voice behind the brightness.

Randy put his hand up to shield his eyes from the glare, but he still couldn't make out the figure in front of him.

"We . . . just came up here for a holiday," said Rebecca.

"A holiday?" The man lowered the light. "Search them," he said. As the tall, thin man moved aside, several men behind him came forward, and one began frisking Randy.

"Look, Uriah, he has a gun!"

"Do you always bring a gun when you go on a holiday?" said Uriah as the men brought the gun to him.

"These are unusual times," said Randy.

"Let me see your hands," he said.

Randy turned his hands over, and Uriah ran a small electronic scanner over them, then across Randy's forehead. He did the same thing to Rebecca and Stephen. As he ran the scanner over Faith's left hand, it emitted a loud whine.

"She's one of them. Quickly," he said to the other men, "tell the others to be ready to move."

"What's this all about?" asked Stephen.

"I think you know," said Uriah, who was obviously the leader. "This is not the first time some of Judah's followers have tried to penetrate our ranks. Ever since he arranged for the murder of the prophets, we've become outlaws with a price on our heads. Members of the new world order have been instructed to seek out and kill us."

"I can assure you that we're not Judah's followers," said Randy.

"Members of the new order have an invisible mark that identifies them so, unlike us, they have access to food, transportation, and money." Uriah pointed to Faith. "She has that mark."

"Now wait a minute. I'm a doctor," said Stephen, "and I implanted that chip in her hand when we were in the United States. It was required by her employer as a form of identification."

"What a coincidence," said Uriah. "How do we know you're not lying?"

"I've got a list which I think you'll be interested in," said Randy. "It'll prove that we're telling the truth. Like you—we're running for our lives."

Indecision marked Uriah's face as he studied the four of them for a moment. "It's safer farther back in the caves. Follow me."

They wound their way through the murky caves, finally emerging into one of the largest caverns.

Oil lamps were hanging on the walls, and Faith was amazed to see almost a dozen families present. They'd carved out an existence for themselves; bedding and utensils for cooking were neatly stored in alcoves cut into the cave walls, and there was a separate area where several toddlers played together under the eye of a watchful grandmother.

"This is just one cell," said Uriah. "We have groups hiding all over Israel and throughout the world."

"Then you know about the Rapture?" said Randy.

"I see you've been well briefed," said Uriah.

"No, we figured it out the hard way. Now we're anticipating Jesus' final return. Aren't you?"

Uriah gave him a long look. "Yes, but while we wait, we are still witnessing to other Jews through our underground press and secret meetings. Many have been blinded by the lies of the Antichrist, but a remnant will believe the truth, like us. We must reach those few."

"You're a Jew?" asked Rebecca.

"Yes. And I'm ashamed to admit that at first I threw rocks at the prophets, scoffed at what they said. But they spoke with such authority that I began to listen. As I heard their words, I changed. Now I see that Jesus Christ is the only one who meets all the requirements for the Messiah."

"Just like that, you threw away the traditions of a lifetime?" Rebecca angrily declared.

"I didn't throw them away. I used them as the foundation on which to build my faith in Yeshua. I challenge you to find one prediction of the Messiah in the Tenach that is not revealed in Jesus Christ."

"The Tenach?" said Randy.

"It's like your Bible," said Rebecca with a sigh, "a Jewish Bible." It was too much for her to comprehend. She knew that Israel was yet to play its greatest role, as the earthly home of the Kingdom of Peace . . . but what Uriah was saying . . .

"I'm not ready for any kind of challenge," she said to him.

"But soon you will be. Even now you're questioning yourself. That's the first step."

Am I? Rebecca wondered if her feelings were really that transparent as she made her way with the others to a crudely carved table. It was low to the floor and they sat on pillows around it. Randy placed his briefcase on the table.

"No!" said Uriah as Randy placed his hand on the lock. "We must check it first." Randy slid it across the table, unopened. Uriah gave it to a wispy man with a fringe of white hair hanging over his large ears. He disappeared with it into one of the caverns.

"You understand our precautions—a bomb exploding in this area would kill everyone here."

"I assure you that my briefcase doesn't contain a bomb," said Randy. "I've never relished the thought of suicide."

"Your assurances are not enough," said Uriah. "If your life were at stake, would you trust the word of a man you've never met?"

"I see your point," said Randy as he searched the faces of those who had gathered round the table.

"It's all right," wheezed the frail man as he returned with the briefcase and handed it to Uriah.

Uriah snapped the lock, opened the lid, and withdrew the sheaves of papers. He studied them for a moment. "There's no way you could have this unless you worked for Judah Midian."

"In a matter of days, this list will be posted everywhere and those on it will be exterminated. Yes, I worked for Midian Enterprises, but I infiltrated the organization in order to . . . help people like you."

"Why should I believe you?"

Randy played his last ace. "Did you know Rabbi Solomon Lowenstein?"

"You speak in the past tense, but then many people knew of his death."

"But did they know of his conversion?"

A flicker of recognition passed across Uriah's lined face. "You are the American he spoke of?"

"I was working with him."

"I see." Uriah began to relax. "Solomon had many questions at first, but eventually he became one of us. He helped to organize this group."

"Solomon?" said Rebecca incredulously. "He must have spoken of me also. I'm Rebecca . . . Rabbi Rebecca Greenspan." Her voice grew softer. "We were very close." She paused. "If he had trusted the prophets, he would have told me."

"Solomon knew you were skeptical. What good Jewish rabbi would not be? What I have told you is the truth, ask anyone here." Uriah stood up. "We'll double check your identities; in the meantime I'll assign you a living area. A guard will be with you at all times." He turned to Stephen.

"Several of the children have come down with respiratory problems. Will you help us?"

"Yes."

"Good. Our medical supplies are limited, but we'll try to get whatever you need."

The cave was no bigger than a broom closet, but it was dry. Together Faith and Stephen unrolled the bedding they'd brought with them. The thick stubby candles cast a glow that diminished the shadows and gave the room an almost cozy feeling. The guard tried to be discreet, standing to the right of the entrance where they couldn't see him.

"Welcome home," whispered Stephen. "The accommodations aren't the greatest, but the price is right."

He sank down on the warm coverlet next to Faith. "I wonder if we're going to be able to do any good here. Judah has such a powerful network now, and we're so few."

"If we were doing this in our own strength, Stephen, I'd say you were right."

"But we're not, are we?"

"No. Like millions of Jews and Christians before us, we're looking forward to that day when Good ultimately overpowers Evil."

"That day is almost here," said Stephen.

"We're so close . . . yet so far," said Faith. She placed her hand on her stomach. A flutter as soft as a butterfly's wing pushed against it. What would happen to the small life which even now was growing within her? She wanted to tell Stephen, but not until later—he would only worry.

Stephen put his arms around her. "Now we're outcasts, but so was Jesus in His lifetime. Someday we'll rule and reign with Him. Until then, I hope we can be together."

"For now and all of eternity," said Faith.

"For now and all of eternity," he repeated softly.

The feeble glow of the candles sputtered and grew dim. With their hands and hearts entwined, they knew that together they would find the strength to make it to the Dawn.

ABOUT THE AUTHOR

Gail Black Kopf is a Canadian freelance writer, who lives with her husband in Virginia. A personal commitment to Jesus Christ thirty-six years ago continues to inspire her writing.